MW00967028

A Winters Past

By

Steve Norris
P.O. Box 642
Townsend, TN 37882

norrismtn@bellsouth.net

Website: NorrisMountain.com

2016 Edition

A Winters Past

By

Steve Norris

A Winters Past

All Rights Reserved. Copyright 1997 Steve Norris

No part of this book may be reproduced or transmitted in any form or by any means, graphic, electronic, or mechanical, including photocopying, recording, taping, or by any information storage or retrieval system, without the permission in writing from the author.

Printed in the United States of America

Middle Tennessee

1928

CHAPTER 1

The old preacher turned his eyes skyward and searched the stars for anything that might spark the remembrance of a bit of scripture that could be helpful to this day's mission. The heavens were cloudless, and he could not remember when he had last seen so many stars at one time.

He glanced back to the eastern horizon and found the first glimmer of the sunrise. The dim sliver of blue-gray light stretching across the distant treetops momentarily held his gaze, but the scene could do nothing to revive his wilted spirit. He turned back to the road ahead and began praying again as he had done almost ceaselessly since leaving home long before sunup.

The horse rig turned the corner before the short stretch to the first farmhouse where his old friends, the Kalltons, lived. He could see a tiny yellow light in one of the windows. A sharp snap, like a slamming screen door, sounded from the house. At times he could hear the cows in the pastures on the far side of the farm. A couple of crows were cawing from the woods a hundred yards to the south.

The road turned back westward and a quarter mile later he was slowly rolling along down below the second Kallton family homestead and as before, there was a light on in a window; but he knew that Paul Kallton had milked the cows and was already in town with his nephew starting deliveries. The racket from the horse and buggy alerted Paul's deep-throated tracker dogs and they suddenly began barking from their pen far behind the house. They shut up instantly when a screen door at the house shut with a sharp slap. The preacher watched the house for a moment and, as providence would provide it, he could see another lamp appear on the front porch. The light moved very slowly, almost imperceptibly, as if being carried by someone of advanced age. He guessed it was Paul's kindly mother stepping out to fetch a stick or two of firewood. The preacher thought that he should stop for a predawn visit, and he pondered the idea for several moments before deciding that the morning's mission was too important, and too heavy on his mind, to be so easily sidetracked.

The temperature was comfortable, and a light, rippling breeze breathed across the back of his neck like the draping of a silk scarf. The milking barn was over two hundred yards away but he could, when the breeze was cooperative, still detect the scent of fresh milk in the air. He watched the house as it began to move out of view. In moments it seemed that the whole interior of the house was lit up by a half-dozen lamps. One by one, the family was waking up and stirring.

It was early fall, and the season's comfortable climate invited thoughts of more leisurely pursuits when work and chores allowed. He wished that he could be back home now to hunt some rabbits in the fields before the day warmed up. The idea caused him to think of his son, whom he imagined could come home from the railroad for a few days. The preacher often dreamed that his wife was still with him. He wished to hear her voice once more; it would be enough to refresh his spirit for a time, and perhaps his sleep would be a little less fitful than it had been since her death.

The preacher could remember a winters past when life's existence was little more than endless toiling in grave uncertainties, but his people and his expectations for them were good. He can still close his eyes and remember those days and how it felt to lie in bed with his sweet Mary and listen to that lonely wail of the Southern long after sunset. It was always best after the lights were out, when they would retire together in the quiet afterglow of a hard day's work. The preacher felt his prayers were always the sweetest when they were murmured in the silence after Mary had fallen asleep in his arms. How his heart would ache whenever he thought too long of those days.

The buggy rolled to the top of the next rise, and the preacher turned once more and gazed eastward into the sky. Just at that moment he caught sight of a ray of morning light growing across the sky so quickly that it seemed the Lord Himself was turning up the wick of a celestial lamp. New feathery clouds hung just above the horizon, and several rays of light angled out like the spokes of a wagon wheel. Even the trees nearby faintly glowed with iridescent tints.

Surprisingly for a few seconds, the preacher had forgotten himself and felt a momentary contentment. Like snatching a firefly from the air he managed to recapture a sense of satisfaction with a life lived well. But just as quickly it flew from his heart's grasp. It was a sentiment that he had long ago determined he would not likely experience again. At least not until he was dead and gone on to be in Glory with his Mary and his God. It was selfish to think this way, he knew. He had good feelings often and he tried to meditate on them as he knew he should. So, he worked hard to force his mind to remain in a state of contented resignation. And to appease his spirit, he searched the road ahead for evidence of the growing light. But as the buggy rolled down into the next hollow, the light faded. It seemed that the night had not retreated at all, and he found himself once again dreading the work that he must do this morning.

The road had straightened, so the preacher closed his eyes and listened to the rhythm of the horse's step. He replayed a few carefully scripted phrases in his mind, and he tried to imagine how he would speak them once he reached his destination. Should he begin with a friendly greeting, or should he just jump into it, knowing that his efforts would probably be rebuffed even before he could get started? Should he speak with complete frankness and with no outward emotion, or should he carry an edge of righteous anger in his voice?

He had insisted on carrying out this mission alone. Two able-bodied men, a church deacon and an old friend, had each asked to go along for moral support and, if it should come to it, his physical safety. But the preacher had considered well that such outnumbering firepower would have brought too much intimidation and pressure into the volatile affair. The sheriff had already spent too much time and too many resources on trying to rectify the situation. All that seemed left was reasoning and patience; two things of which the preacher had little remaining.

The preacher looked ahead, and he was grateful to see more light than he had expected. The blue cast of the sunrise had faded and was replaced by a gray haze that penetrated deep into the trees. He leaned up and turned off the already-dim lantern, then for the next half-mile he scanned the woods for deer. The breeze was picking up and the leaves were beginning to scurry.

The surrealism of dawn spread across the miles of forestland and fields before him, and the preacher could see the dimly colored outlines of everything ahead. He was now in the most southwestern corner of the county where little traffic passed. The road began to narrow ahead, where the trees arched and touched overhead. Soon, he could see the run-down house that stood just a few yards from the edge of the road ahead. He gently pulled back on the reins and the buggy stopped. For a moment he gazed at the shack that housed a family of six; and he could feel nothing but dread in his gut. Either he would succeed enough to garner an unstable truce, or more likely he would fail miserably. There was little reason to hope. The man in the house was sure to rail against authority figures of any stripe, and he carried a particular resistance against anyone holding a religious mandate. It had all come down to this. After all this time, the preacher could find no other recourse but to work through the vilest of men; to seek redress through Satan's own.

The preacher sat motionless on the seat trying to verbalize a final prayer. A thought flitted into his mind – he wondered if he might die today. The man's reputation really did not warrant such dire premonitions; but a boiling point had been reached.

He pulled forward and in a moment he had the buggy sitting directly before the house. A couple of dogs barked from the porch. Then a man's voice bellowed from inside the house.

"Goddamnit! Shut yore asses up out t'ere!"

The preacher waited and watched. The windows were covered over with paper and rags. The floor of the porch hung about four feet above the ground, but it was difficult to see from the road because of the high grass and the unpruned blueberry bushes. There was no smoke coming from the kitchen flue; apparently everyone was still in bed.

The front door creaked open, then a naked foot kicked the screen door forcing it to swing out and slap against the wall. A half-dressed, vagrant-looking man stepped out and cursed at the dogs again. The dogs quickly retreated and disappeared beneath the porch. The man gazed around looking for the cause of all the commotion. His eyes met the preacher's and, for a moment, the man seemed taken aback by his presence.

"What yew a-doin' out t'ere, ol' man?" he finally yelled across the yard. His stance turned defensive, then stern. He looked eastward as if to find the sun to determine the time of day; then he turned his gaze back to the preacher. He was clearly offended by being disturbed out of bed so early.

"Roy?" the preacher finally said. Then he realized the meekness in his voice and he spoke up. "I'd like to talk to you for a minute, if you got the time."

"What about, preacher?" the man asked as he loitered down the steps with the gait of a man festered with boils. One of the dogs began barking again. Again the man cursed. The preacher could see a dirty window curtain open and a tiny face peek out. Within seconds, a little girl, about four years old and dressed in her nighties, barreled out the door and ran for the steps. Like grabbing for an escaped chicken from the coop, the man caught her before she could get away and run to the preacher. "Gracie! Git back in th' house. Go on – git now!" the man barked.

The little girl was struck dumb and stock-still. She stared at the preacher with an expression of disbelief on her little face. She loved the preacher and she knew that he would give her a hug and a kiss, but only if she could get to him. Then seeming to realize the futility of her efforts, she turned and ran back into the house. Other curtains opened and shut as the man moved across the yard toward the preacher.

"T'is betta be mighty import'nt, preacher. Gittin' a man outta bed like this."

"It's important, all right," the preacher said.

The man strolled up to the buggy and propped a foot up on a wheel spoke and positioned an elbow to a knee. He stared at the ground, pretending indifference. The preacher decided to waste no time.

"Roy," the preacher said stoutly, hoping to get the man to look up at him and demonstrate a little consideration for his efforts. He paused too long before continuing. The man grabbed the opportunity to put the preacher into a more defensive position.

"Let's git on with it, preacher. A man's got work to do." Then Roy leaned away from the buggy and spit in the gravel.

"I just want to try one more time to settle this problem between you and Tom Buell. This is all getting out of hand; you both got everybody – "

"Now see here, godddamnit – that ain't none of yore affair!" Roy stood back and pointed a waving finger at the preacher. "You done had the sher'ff throw me in jail two times over the last ten years, an' you got no call accusin' me of nuttin' now. You ain't got no proof of nuttin', an' that damn sher'ff of yores ain't got no goddamn proof either." He paused a moment and postured about as if searching the ground for something. "Hell, I'll jist run fetch my gun right now an' I'll shewt yore goddamn ass!" He turned toward the house and yelled, "*Roy Junior, brang me that scatter gun of mine out here – Roy Junior!*"

The preacher felt his face turn pale. He started to reach for the reins and pull away, but he felt his arms lock to his sides. Whether it was out of the sudden gut-punch of terror from Roy or by the providence of God that he couldn't move, he couldn't tell. All he knew was that Roy would likcly fire a shot or two into the buggy roof or into the air near the preacher's face in order to frighten the old man. Over the years Roy had done this a couple of times to other men, though he had never actually hit anyone. He had come very close to causing a deadly scenario in a similar situation once when the gunfire was returned by his own cousin, leaving Roy with a slight but permanent limp. The cousin's action had no effect on improving Roy's disposition. It seemed, to all outward appearances, to only make it worse.

A tall boy, about thirteen and shirtless and with a virility beyond his years, stepped out the door with a double-barreled shotgun swinging loosely from his hand like a pine stick. He walked to the edge of the porch and stopped as if awaiting further commands. His delinquent bearing worsened the anxiety the preacher was feeling. Roy started to yell to him again, but the preacher spoke.

"All right, Roy!" the preacher barked. The preacher felt his chest tightening with panic, but he was surprised by the calm strength in his voice. "Let's just forget the whole thing. I'll turn around right here and go back to Wade's place for a while." He reached for the reins, but Roy's voice held him.

"What yew genu-winely come 'ere to talk about, ol' man?"

The armed boy was still on the porch, now with malevolent eyes aimed at the preacher. He was fingering the gun's mechanisms with the intent of intimidating the old man. Roy had asked the question as if he had forgotten the preacher's previous comments. The preacher determined that the mere mention of Roy's cousin's name was enough to jerk the slacker back to cold reality and cause him to listen, albeit likely for only a few moments.

"We all know you stole that cane press from Tom Buell, Roy. And we all know you ran straight to Columbia and sold it to your black market buyers and then turned around and bought your two new heifers with the money."

The preacher glanced up to find the boy unmoved on the porch. He was now bumping a post with the gun barrel. Clearly he was used to such volatile situations with his father as he exhibited a childlike demeanor of bored distraction. But suddenly a woman stepped out and jerked the boy back into the house. The child cursed, whether at his mother or at the general inaction of the situation at hand, the preacher couldn't tell. The preacher could hear the woman shout the boy down just before the door slammed shut.

"At least go tell Tom you took his press and you'll work out some arrangement to repay him. You don't even have to tell the sheriff. You know you got Tom thinking that Wade and Paul are mixed up in all this, and – "

"Well, that might jist be th' way I want it, preacher. Maybe this here's my way of gittin' back at Wade fer givin' me this here bum leg. If Buell's mad at Wade, then that's jist fine wi' me. I'm glad yew tol't me, ol' man!"

Roy gleefully thrust his arm up in a gesture of mad defiance and turned, walking away. He moved energetically, working hard to show that the limp hardly slowed him down at all. The preacher reined in his growing feeling of exasperation. He determined that there was little hope for redemption in this soulless idler. Roy was too smart for them all. He had practiced many years to discern fail-safe techniques in stealing and concealing, and the whole county had long ago grown weary of it all. If a hog, a tool, or a child's bag of candy disappeared, Roy Kallton and his three boys were automatically suspected.

But Roy and his boys had crossed the line with their daring nighttime theft of the nearly new sorghum press and attachments from the Buell farms. After selling the press to his under-market connections a county-and-a-half away, the high quality Hereford heifers suddenly appeared in Roy's yard the next day. The young cows were of the identical breed that Wade was experimenting with on his farm, so in Tom Buell's mind the connection with Wade Kallton was made. Tom demanded that the sheriff investigate whether or not Wade was involved. The sheriff made a cursory visit to Wade's farm but otherwise refused to investigate such a connection. He knew, as Tom must have known, that Wade would have little to do with his unwashed hillbilly cousin. Thus, a rift was created between the Buells and the Kalltons. It could be the Hatfields and McCoys all over again, and the preacher's church had been split by the idiotic feud. And to compound matters and to add a gothic twist to things, a romantic relationship between two young people, each from an opposing family, had sparked and then blossomed to fever pitch some time before the rift began. Now they were forced apart with no hint of lessened hostilities between their elders.

Roy stepped through the door and slammed it shut behind him. He never looked back to see if the preacher was still there. The preacher turned the rig around and started back home. He should have felt some measure of pride for carrying through with this mission to its completion, fruitful or not. But he felt sick in his gut and he didn't bother to pray to thank God for His safe hand. Nor was the old man thankful that he had come through the ordeal with no buckshot ventilating his buggy.

Shortly he realized how tired he had become in the last few minutes. Home was eight miles away, and he wondered how bad he would feel by the time he returned there. Without looking off into the trees or watching the horizon again, he picked up the pace to a fast trot.

He saw a dozen deer cross the road ahead, but he only cared that they get out of his way. He raised his sleeve up to his nose and sniffed deeply. He was sure that he could smell his dead wife's flesh and hair in the fabric; and he wondered how long he could wear this shirt before it must be washed. He sniffed again and allowed the scent to trance his mind as long as he could hold his breath. Shameless, he allowed his eyes to water up and spill over. Then he prayed a short prayer of thanksgiving that he knew was a betrayal of his true thoughts.

Soon, he rolled past the Kallton farms again and unlike his early morning druthers, he felt no compunction to stop and visit. He continued at a fast clip until the horse began showing signs of fatigue, then he slowed the rig down and began working to get a grip on himself. It wouldn't be so bad, he thought, if his son were still living with him and not working a hundred and fifty miles away. It was a struggle to think that he must return to an empty house. Perhaps a quick hug from little Gracie would have made a difference.

He rolled up to the intersection to turn north toward Braxton. He stopped the rig and looked north and then south. There was no traffic but the preacher lingered. He thought that this would be a good place to rest the horse before wrapping up the journey back into town, then on to his home in the cotton fields on the eastern corners of the county.

"Buck up, ol' man!" a voice barked from somewhere nearby.

The preacher was so startled he flinched as if meeting a hand across the face. He looked around until his eyes landed on a lone dark figure standing near the edge of the road a few yards to his right. It was a stoutly built black man of average height who stood perfectly erect and rigid; military-like. He wore tattered overalls faded to powder blue. Over it was a worn-thin winter coat that was in poorer condition than his overalls. His boots were held onto his feet with lumpy leather laces and fraying ropes. A large, dirty-wrinkled sack sat on the ground behind the migrant. It appeared to be little more than an old bed sheet tied together at the corners to hold any assortment of salvaged belongings, likely the migrant's entire collection of worldly possessions. He was a desperate visage, a vagabond long reduced to scrounging for handouts and piecemeal work wherever he could find it. The only thing that showed any semblance of newness was a large, red handkerchief hanging from a front overalls pocket. Still, his hair was short, neatly cropped; and he appeared to have recently shaved. The preacher imagined that this robustly constructed migrant could probably break a man in half with the large, powerful hands that hung stiffly to his sides.

"Uh, what'd you say?" the preacher finally asked.

"I say, buck up ol' man. Ye look like ye ain't got no hope lef' in 'dis world!"

The preacher could think of nothing to say. He only stared at the young, intrusive migrant.

"It cain't be that bad. Would ye want to be in ma shoes right now?" the migrant continued. His rock-strong face remained unchanged.

The preacher straightened up and gazed a little more intently at the man, and his first inclination was to offer him a ride to town or some pocket change or even a meal. But he sensed that this poor pilgrim likely wished for nothing he had to offer.

"Perchance I was like you, I woulda give up a long time ago, too!"

The preacher glanced down at the leather buggy whip that was stuck beneath the seat springs, but he sloughed off the idea. "You need a ride into town, young man?" he asked.

"No, suh – I needs no help from no man." Then the migrant pulled the crimson handkerchief from his pocket and waved it skyward as if to summon God Himself. "God is ma strength in ma time of need! Him alone will I call upon w'en the night is darkest!"

This man is sadly demented, the preacher thought. He's out here in the middle of nowhere and in need of many things, and he's moiling on me about how I look. A man in his right mind would voice proper thanks for the offer. But all he is inclined to do is evangelize to the occasional passersby on a deserted road.

"All right, suit yourself," the preacher said. Then he snapped the reins and rolled away.

The buggy wheels spun a hundred revolutions before the old man ventured a look back.

He spied through the little rectangular hole in the rear wall of the buggy and searched the road from side to side and as far as the roiling dust would allow. Nothing. Perhaps, the preacher surmised, the man headed down Kallton Farms Road to search for work. Wade and Paul Kallton, like many area farmers hired seasonal workers, mostly transient laborers, to help in the harvest of cotton, tobacco, and other crops. But the Kalltons' harvest of the last feed corn would soon be over and the migrants would be sent home for the winter. The preacher looked through the hole again, but no lone, dark figure inscribed the landscape.

He slowed the rig down and settled back into the seat. As his mind eased from the stress, the pain in his hands stole his attention. He released his clenched grip on the reins, allowing the bloodflow back into his fingers. He played the crazy man's words in his mind and could find no rationale behind the bizarre event. But somehow it was like an icy slap to the face. It would take another mile for the black man's protestations to find their mark. His stern words of admonishment seemed to ricochet throughout the preacher's soul like a spiritual bullet, and cause him to look at things in a less passionate, and more detached viewpoint.

For the rest of the trip home the old man's vigor grew and his disposition mended to the point that he was smiling and sitting fully erect in the seat. For the first time in weeks, the sadness dissipated to the point that any contrary thought that might drift into his mind now would find no anchor-hold. He welcomed that old impulse to entreat the Lord with every breath. He now prayed for Roy and his family as he had done for a generation. Roy's disposition seemed to worsen toward the preacher as the years passed in spite of the prayers. Or perhaps his attitude worsened because of the demons' torments upon his soul by the very virtue of the old man's prayers. The preacher prayed that Roy's boys would not curse and steal as much as their father did, and he prayed especially for little Gracie. There was hope in Gracie. She loved going to church with her cousins who resided two miles up the road. And she could hug the preacher's neck for hours if she weren't restrained.

The preacher prayed for the Buells and he prayed for the Kalltons. He prayed that things would not get out of hand and that the rift between them could be mended. But even if things never improved, there would still be a purpose to it all. He was blind to it now, but he was sure that he would behold its divine workings someday when they would all meet together on the Other Side.

The preacher rolled into town where it would seem every soul was out to greet him. Everyone was drawn to the preacher's happy countenance; it was the way they knew him. And they each waved with a smile as he passed. The morning's mission had been a miserable failure, but no one would know it by the preacher's smile and energetic wave of the hand. What would he be now had it not been for the unnerving encounter with the crazy black man on the road? Why did the man's words shake him out of his depression so quickly and so firmly? The preacher could never know, but he couldn't fight the reality that it was just the elixir that was needed.

CHAPTER 2

The old Model-T, near-like the kickings of an angry bronco, fought Frank Buell at every rut and washout. This was a horse-and-rider road, but it was the only way into the area with a motorcar. At five-thirty this dusky October morning, it was near impossible to make out the worst ruts before banging into them. But time was getting short, and Frank's brother was showing weakness in containing his agitation.

"I ain't got no doubt in my mind, me and you are gonna get into some bad trouble over this, James," big brother said. The anger in his voice was genuine. "You'll make me a promise right now – if she ain't ready at six sharp, you turn right around and git right back here. Understand me?"

James was angry, too. The weeks had worn on him; it had taken that long to coerce Frank into committing to his plot. Coming to blows this morning nearly ended the expedition before it started. Big brother won handily, but it was no vindication for him because it forced not a figment of change in James's mind.

James jumped out of the car and kicked the door shut, then dashed off into the trees. Frank hesitated long enough to see his brother sprinting full-tilt through the trees like a hound-chased deer. Then with a smooth shift of the gearbox he pulled the car away to begin a lonely drive through the back roads south of Braxton. He had thirty minutes to contemplate every regret to come before he must return at the appointed moment. But worse than any misgivings, he hated his brother for his weakness – his violent aversion toward waiting for things to work themselves out; his intolerance toward pondering quiet reason. Frank, like the rest of the family, was sick of living with his brother's innate stubbornness. His younger brother's high-spirited personality endeared him to those outside his home, but it tried the family daily. And Frank, in a perverse twist of vengeance, was ready to give James any opportunity to dig his own wellshaft to fall into. Together they had lied to their father to get the car for a few hours. It was to be a short mission to the next county to pick up a catalogue order for their mother's birthday in a few days, they said. Frank had never lied to his father like this. It now worried him sick.

With the eagerness of a child on Christmas morning, along with the anxiety of an adolescent committing his first act of high delinquency, James raced down the path until, two miles later, he was within a stone's throw of the house. He yanked his watch from his pocket. He was nearly ten minutes early, so he eased back into the trees away from the house and forced himself, against his nature, to wait. In the ashen light a hundred yards away, he could see the tall, vertical slabs of the barn and the stubby silo beside it. The white-boarded fence stood out against the gray pastures like the bands of headlights in a fog. He studied the scene from east to west till his eyes landed on the empty bluetick pens situated just outside the fence. If he had his father's binoculars with him he could be more certain whether his concerns over the absence of the dogs were valid.

The white of the house against the treed backdrop appeared to glow like a sun-reflected cloud. Kelly Jean's mother was working on breakfast for the men as evidenced by the little curling of smoke from the kitchen flue. This quietude of the scene worked against James's nature by compelling his agitation to grow. He broke under the weight of his impulses and quickly worked his way down to a little pine tree near the base of the hill. It was far closer to the house than was safe, and he stared at the window. At a minute till six he could see someone's hands reaching and easing up the window. Then a half-stuffed cotton picker's sack rolled out and plopped to the ground four feet below. The slender girl quickly tucked herself through the opening and landed flat-footed beside the sack. She was outfitted in one of her brother's overalls with the pant legs rolled up her shins. She looked up the hill to the trees searching for James. He moved to dodge out to her but he reversed and stayed put. She grabbed the sack and started sprinting across the yard to the base of the hill, holding her posture low as if dodging bullets.

Again, James moved to run out to her, but reversed himself with a snap of his neck. His peripheral eye had caught a disturbance that snagged his attention like a hooked perch. He squinted his eyes eastward to a spot near the silo. Four mounted horsemen with the blueticks underfoot charged out of a gap in the trees to the far side of the barn. A rope of a half-dozen raccoon pelts was draped over the saddle of the lead horseman; the fruits of a successful night hunt. The distance made the horsemen noiseless and Kelly Jean was unaware of their sudden appearance as she sprinted into full view. James sought to signal Kelly Jean to drop to the ground, but too late. The girl's brother, Jimmy, atop a half-Palomino, spotted the runaway with young, sharp eyes. Jumping nearly out of the stirrups after wasting too many moments in indecision, Jimmy yelled out across the yard to his escaping sister. Kelly Jean was quickly closing the gap on the final yards to the trees. Her father swung off his horse and yanked open the gate, then remounted and slapped his mount hard on the flank. James blazed down the hill toward his beloved. Shaken by the new noises, Kelly Jean tripped and dropped the sack but quickly rebounded. She grabbed and yanked the wrong end of the sack and promptly emptied all the contents out onto the ground. James snagged her arm and dragged her into the trees.

All time was lost and never a word was spoken between them as they began racing crazily through the trees and brush. A furious voice from the yard fired battle orders, which was followed by other voices that ricocheted across the farm like war cries. The blueticks, recharged by all the sudden commotion, began barking and sniffing the ground for new prey trails. One by one they picked up Kelly Jean's scent and worked toward the trees and were only marginally responsive to frantic callback orders from the lead horseman.

The couple had found a straight, northward path and Kelly Jean was working respectably in keeping up with James. But the voice of her mother screaming her name from the porch worked to suppress her motivation. Still, she raced on, determined to disallow the gap between herself and James to widen too much.

The horsemen, two of them day labor migrants, were having difficulty breaking through a barrier of heavy brush along the edge of the trees. But Wade's angry voice frightened James into sprinting through a pine thicket with all his strength. At the far edge of the thicket, James skidded to a stop for only a second to allow Kelly Jean to shorten the gap. He took off again when he saw that she showed no outward inclination to slow down or turn back.

Then the horses broke through the brush, but James and Kelly Jean had nearly a two-hundred yard head start on them in the pines. Still, James knew the riders could be on top of them in a matter of seconds. He motioned for Kelly Jean to follow him into another brushy area forty yards ahead. Shortly after entering the brush, they slid into a ravine that dropped into a narrow canyon-like creek bed. They stumbled another fifty yards down the creek before Kelly Jean dropped to the ground in exhaustion. James stopped with the hope of quieting his heavy breathing so as to discern the distance and direction of the riders. The dogs were still sounding and were now running ahead of the horses.

James stumbled over to Kelly Jean and pulled her up to him. She retched and spit up, falling to the ground. James searched the creek north and south till he spied a small cavern-like washout at the next bend many yards downstream. He took Kelly Jean again and forced her up; and together they hobbled, then crawled into the little cave and pushed up against the dirt wall in the rear. James hoped their location would be secure from the riders long enough for him and Kelly Jean to catch their breaths. But the voices of the two migrants could be heard shouting to each other in the pines. It seemed that the dogs were off in the distance now. It was figured that Wade would keep the dogs near to himself, not allowing them to run loose and possibly attack his own daughter.

Strangely, the woods quieted down. The couple crawled out to get a better sense of the location of the riders. His mind spinning, James was paralyzed into stalling until the riders were likely far ahead up the trail. The only option remaining seemed to be to attempt a backtrack to the thickets and then to maneuver unseen through the Kallton farms and find a new route back to Frank and the getaway car. But just as the couple stood back out onto the creek bed, the two riders blazed over their heads in a successful attempt to jump the creek. Kelly Jean was too startled to catch herself and allowed a yelp to escape her lips. But it was enough. The riders stopped and turned back for the creek. The couple was off and running again.

The riders could see well enough down into the creek to keep the couple in their sights at all times. Then one of the riders pulled his shotgun from the saddle scabbard and promptly fired a shot into the air to alert Wade to their whereabouts. The startled horse bucked and dumped the rider, but he managed to remount quickly. The couple continued racing down the creek until they became blocked by fallen timbers and flood debris. The couple scrambled up a fallen tree trunk. It was still partly rooted in the top of the bank on the west side, opposite the riders. Now the creek was far too wide for the horsemen to attempt another jump-crossing. So one of them turned and headed back to the original crossing point, leaving the other rider to monitor the action from across the creek.

James and Kelly Jean stood up on level ground, turned and looked back toward the remaining horseman. Kelly Jean could never get over her innate fear of these solitary, nomadic-like farm hands; and now to realize that she was being chased by two of them greatly unnerved her. The migrant, with his broad-brimmed hat and heavily grizzled face, sat motionless on his mount and stared at the couple.

James and Kelly Jean turned and ran into a range of heavy brush further northward. Tripping a number of times, the couple plowed their way through the brush and broke out through the other side into a scrubby-treed meadow. James was fearful of the rider coming around the west side. It was no comfort to imagine the kind of treatment he might receive once everyone had caught up with him and Kelly Jean. James's mind was racing to dangerous limits to come up with a new strategy, but the paralysis of panic was gripping him more and more tightly as the seconds passed.

Then the sounds of hoof beats spun them around. The horse and rider bore down on them with startling quickness. Kelly Jean cried out and tore away. James was left trembling. He seized a bat-sized limb dangling nearby and ran to the horse and swung hard at the rider. With four stout swings he beat the man off, and James quickly mounted the startled horse. The rider managed to jump up and give chase. He grabbed a strand of the horse's tail but stumbled back to the ground. Jimmy yelled for Kelly Jean. He swung down and threw her up behind him onto the saddle. He turned the horse around and headed due north for the rendezvous with his brother, still nearly two miles away.

He had to find a fast trail, but with no time to spare he drove the horse through bushes and high grass hoping to find one soon. He could feel Kelly Jean's tight embrace around his waist and her head held firm against the base of his neck. He could hear her whimpering cries that were strangled by the jolting ride.

Running the horse through a long deer run gave James some measure of relief that he would soon be far ahead of Wade Kallton and the other riders. Still, he pushed the horse hard and found sparsely treed meadows ahead as he broke through the brushy barriers separating them. The meadows soon dissipated and the terrain became hilly and wooded with an occasional creek or swampy bog to cross. Finally, they came upon a swift running creek. The trail, he was sure, was just on the other side. The horse was tiring and slowing down. James stopped at the creek and the couple dismounted. Kelly Jean fell to the ground and closed her eyes, exhausted. She crawled to the edge of the water and splashed it to her face. She was enduring the full range of negative emotions, and the heaviness this caused in her chest made her labored breathing even more intense and painful. She could picture herself being chased down like an animal in the heat of the hunt. It was a genuinely fearful imagining and she tried to eject it from her mind. And while she feared for James if they were caught, she sensed a secret hope that her father would catch up with them. She was now pulled between continuing the getaway and giving up, telling James to go back home where it was safe. They could deal with the consequences of their failed elopement attempt with their families in the weeks – and probably years – to come. But James was much too racked with desperation to quit just now. One more hard push and it would all be over, he was sure.

Kelly Jean raised herself enough to crawl to James who was kneeling nearby. The distraught voice of her mother screaming from the back porch still rang in her mind like a bell. She tried to keep herself under control but was quickly overcome and began to cry openly. James embraced her but said nothing. There was nothing to say; it had all been said over recent months. They sat together for several minutes before Kelly Jean began to regain her strength. She worked her mind to find words, but in the distance dogs could be heard.

But these were not the howlings of the blueticks. These were Paul Kallton's bloodhounds; man-trackers trained to hunt anything that left the scent of fear on the trail. They had been contracted at times by law enforcement because of their ability to track anything that left a scent; human or wild. James could remember them on a manhunt for the sheriff a couple of years ago. They were usually kept tethered in a group to long leather lines and could be unpredictable, if not vicious, if they should break free. They were coming on fast, so it seemed sure they were running without restraint.

The couple mounted up and were galloping again. Soon, James found the trail he was searching for. He figured about another half-mile they would be home-free and would vanish from the county by motorcar. It seemed to James that the horse behaved in a manner such that it also sensed they were being tracked by unfriendly forces from the south. The sound of baying bloodhounds seemed as much motivation for the horse to keep moving as other things were to James, so he never had to prod the horse to run from here on.

The trail turned northeasterly, and after a few more hundred yards he knew they were very close to their destination. The road could not be more than a hundred yards through the thickets just ahead, he knew. The howlings of the hounds were only a muffled wail in the distance as he and Kelly Jean stopped and dismounted. The horse turned and trotted away.

Shortly, the couple proceeded to make their way through the thicket toward the road, but they heard voices coming from the area where Frank was to be waiting. They stopped a moment to listen. They had to draw closer, so they worked through a maze of laurel thickets until they were just a few yards from the road. A head-high ridge blocked their view, but they crouched at the base of it and listened. Had some of Wade's men advanced ahead and found Frank on the road? No, that was simply not possible. Perhaps some hunters had found Frank on the road and stopped for a chat; or maybe his brother was giving directions to some land surveyors. But the sounds of the voices seemed too loud and raucous for all that. Kelly Jean thought she could hear some bits of profanity and laughter intermingled with the voices, and this returned her to thoughts of giving up. She looked to the south where the hounds could be heard closing in again, then back toward the road when a profane adjective flew over the ridge. With frightened eyes, she looked back at James.

He motioned for her to stay put while he moved up to investigate. The going was slow as he crawled carefully over the dried autumn leaves. Stopping below the top to listen, he could hear three distinct voices, but none of them belonged to his brother. Kelly Jean watched him intently for any signal to act. She was too afraid now to look back toward the hills, fearful of the thought of finding those migrants and the hounds bearing down on them. She had forgotten that one of the migrants was without a horse now; but knowing that the other one would doubtless be the first to find her rattled her senses badly. She wouldn't know how to react to his commands, or even if she could understand his intentions if he tried to physically take her and return her to her father. She hoped her father would catch up with the rest of the posse if all of this ended without a successful getaway. But even if he did, she was scared for James. She didn't know how she could stand by and watch her fiancé get hit or slapped around, as she feared her father would do to him.

But suddenly James jumped to his feet as if preparing for a frontal attack. He was now on top of the ridge looking down toward the road. Kelly Jean started to run to him but stopped when James yanked a small, blued five-shooter from his pocket that she never knew he had. He immediately crouched to a firing position with both hands on the gun. He was aiming down toward the road. Kelly Jean fell ashen with panic. Something of horrific proportions was happening down on the road to cause James to react so violently. The voices stopped at the boom of his gun. Kelly Jean screamed out and raced up the hill toward him. James cocked the gun for a second shot but was cut short by return gunfire. Kelly Jean got to him just at the moment he was hit by the blast. He fell back against Kelly Jean, and both of them sprawled to the ground and tumbled down the hill to the bottom. Kelly Jean slammed against a tree trunk but managed to pull herself up to her feet. James lay twisted and clearly lifeless a few feet before her. The gun blast had breached his center torso and strewn the viscera up into the trees, and it came down like rain upon her. Kelly Jean stumbled back. For a moment – it seemed minutes – splats of blood and viscous tissue tapped the leaves around her. The dogs were no longer barking in the distance. The voices from the road were silent. She had backed several yards away from James when she looked up the hill, still without taking her first breath since standing up.

Finally, Kelly Jean was jolted by a shrill, wrenching scream that assaulted her ears with knife-like blows, and her throat burned as if hot-branded. She never seemed to recognize her own screaming voice. Visions of foul, demented men glaring down at her and savage hands grabbing at her raked through her mind like a drug-induced nightmare. She felt something, or someone, pulling on her limbs and clothing. Then a sharp slap across the face. Some angry, profane utterances were spit at her in rapid-fire fashion and the world went insane. Then she ran. Like a wounded fawn in mortal terror for its life, she ran.

Her screams were heard, off and on, for hours after the shoot-out on the road. It was not until almost nightfall when she was finally found – huddled, motionless and exhausted – beneath a long-dead and withered willow tree far from the North Road.

CHAPTER 3

"I'll never figure out why you're so cowered by them Kalltons, Gene. Seems we need to get us a sheriff with a little more mettle in his backbone – "

"Tom Buell!" his wife, Annie, barked. "Please don't show yourself today. This is not the place for that – you should know better!" Her eyes were still misty from the funeral. The day had been a gauntlet of grief and she could stand no more.

"If you'd half done your job, we wouldn't be in such a fix right now," Tom continued as if he were deaf to his wife. Annie jerked away and, with their daughter Anne Marie, walked briskly to the car. Tom never removed his eyes from the sheriff as he spoke. The service was over, but Tom seemed oblivious to the discomfort, and pain, of others.

Sheriff Gene Carter endured Tom's angry gaze until his patience was spent. "Now why do you want to go and talk like that, Tom?" Gene asked. "I've done everything – "

"Everything? Everything?" Tom mocked. "Maybe I should just dig up my boy over there and we'll ask him if you done everything!"

The sheriff turned and walked away. The preacher stepped up as if to impede Tom's advance against the retreating sheriff. People were trying to move to their cars and buggies but were interrupted by Tom's outburst.

"Brother Tom, Annie's right," the preacher said. "This is not the right place for this."

"I'm sorry, Brother Silas," Tom said mechanically. His voice lacked any hint of sincerity. "I don't know what got into me. I hope you understand."

As Tom spoke, the preacher watched his eyes follow the sheriff's car as it rolled down to the road and turn toward Braxton. Tom sat himself in his own car and turned to look out the open door. There was still anger in his eyes, and he exhibited no shame that the preacher could see it.

"It just really doesn't seem to matter much, does it, preacher?"

It seemed clear that he was fishing for a response from the preacher. After several seconds of strained silence, the old man bit.

"What do you mean?"

"Well," Tom began, feigning appreciation that the preacher showed an interest, "You work hard, you pray hard, you do right for your family – and what do you get? That's right, you get kicked right in the – "

Annie was still sniffling, but she became alert and reached for her husband across the seat. "Tom, you're such a train wreck sometimes!" she barked. Anne Marie held hard onto his shoulder from the back seat. It was time for Tom to shut up, but there was no possibility.

"You got them Kalltons down there," Tom continued. "You got that Wade Kallton – he don't care about nothing but himself. He just runs that big, fine cow ranch and goes to them fancy livestock auctions, and he don't give no mind to nobody else."

Tom sat still for several moments, eyes now focused far away. Anne Marie began a nervous pat to his shoulder, hoping to quiet her father. Annie turned her face away to hide her shame. The preacher remained unmoved, his body holding the stance of a man leaning into the winds of an approaching tornado.

"How many times you reckon Wade's darkened that church door, preacher? Maybe twice in the last five years? No, that ain't right. There's been a couple of funerals since then. Maybe it's four times he's been to church. Yeah, that's about right – does that sound right, Annie?"

Across the yard a car started up, then pulled up alongside. It was Tom's cousin and business partner, Lucas Buell, and his family. Lucas killed the motor. He started to speak, but he could tell by the preacher's lack of recognition that something was still out of order.

"What do you say, Luke?" Tom said loudly. "You reckon we should even bother to apply for credit this year – seeing we can't even pay off last year's?"

Lucas's wife, Sandra, jerked up and glared at Tom with daggered eyes. He was broadcasting family business again and she was sick of it. A profane silence hung in the air like acrid smoke. No one moved for nearly a minute. The jovial personality that had so endeared Tom to his friends and associates over the years was now lost to the winds. He was a deacon; he was a spiritual pillar of the church. He was expected to uphold the tenets of the faith, but he was spewing blasphemy to all within earshot.

"No one believes Wade hurt your boys, Tom," the preacher finally said. "Nobody knows yet who hurt your boys." There was a restrained quietness in his voice; it seemed that he might expect Tom to attack him if he pushed the issue.

"Papa – no!" Anne Marie wailed as Tom pulled himself out of the car. The preacher stood his ground; he didn't budge. The small crowd remained near their cars and buggies, all eyes directed toward Tom.

"I don't care what you people think!" Tom said loudly for all to hear. "Something ain't right when you do right, you live right, and you pray every day before the sun comes up, and then everything you got is taken away in the blink of an eye. It just ain't right, people!"

Sandra could be heard speaking rudely to Lucas, demanding that he pull away and go home. He pretended deafness as he was transfixed by his cousin's break with reason. Annie was crying, but Tom showed no concern.

"Can't you hear Annie crying, preacher? She's crying because of what I'm doing right now. She wants me to make things better for her, but I'm deaf to her. Now she's going to be upset with me all week because I refused to listen."

The preacher glanced around to those nearby. It seemed that he was looking for someone to help him understand what was going on here.

"Well – I cried to God to help us for a year now," Tom continued, his voice still angry. "But I went broke anyway. My cane press gets stolen from me, then my boy gets shot and killed and my other one's near death right now. I want God to make things better, but He's deaf. Why can't I get upset with God like Annie is with me? Am I a wicked man, Brother Silas?"

Then a vehicle pulled up to the edge of the churchyard. It was the sheriff again; he had returned. He had hoped that most everyone had left for home by now and he could catch the preacher alone. He saw Tom standing before the preacher. He killed the motor. Tom watched him for only a moment, then returned his vitriol to the preacher.

"What's a man to do, Brother Silas? Is he supposed to keep on going as if everything is all right? Can the God you preach about still be trusted after all we've been through?"

Annie finally gave up. Her crying had stopped and she sat stonestill with a faced creased with every negative sentiment toward Tom. Everyone in the yard was silently watching the spectacle with averted eyes. Only Tom, with his mocking gestures, stood out as the only movement in the yard.

"Maybe I should have lived my life as I saw fit. Maybe I should have just stayed on my little farm and said to hell with everybody else like them Kalltons do. Especially that Wade

Kallton. Then maybe I'd be rich, too." Then, with a flinch, it seemed he realized the folly of deleting the fact of his son's death. He added as if it was all meant to be encased in a single sentence, "And maybe my boys would be well, and Wade's family would be suffering terribly like mine is now."

Tom glanced around the yard once more, then he got in the car and started it up. Without a parting gesture of any kind he drove away with Lucas and his family close behind. It seemed the sheriff was eager to catch the preacher. He quickly pulled up near him and stopped. He waited until Tom's car was well out of sight before he stepped out.

"Why you reckon he's still got his mind set on Wade as the guilty party in everything, preacher? He knows Wade's people are innocent, or he should know by now."

The preacher mulled his thoughts. He had answered the question before, including numerous times in the weeks after the cane press was stolen. In his mind it seemed that Tom had completely confirmed his beliefs concerning his motives today. There appeared to be no doubt now that Tom had been envious of Wade's apparently successful enterprises while his own efforts had remained unblessed. Tom's lifelong frustrations with money and credit were now exposed as the true disappointments in his life, and he was taking his rage out on any available target.

"I don't know, Gene. I can't be sure," the preacher answered, clearly spent of all desire to continue on the subject. He was tired of talking and consoling. He needed some time away for himself; he wanted to go home and rest a while. He turned from the sheriff, then loaded up and rode away.

CHAPTER 4

Kelly Jean woke up slowly and looked around her bed as if to search for something lost. Her mother, Esther, as Kelly Jean had become accustomed, was sitting in a chair near her. The preacher was sitting in another chair at the foot of the bed. He simply smiled and said nothing. The window was open, allowing a faint wafting breeze to play with the curtains. Not a sound came from the yard outside, and all was quiet in the house. The caning in the preacher's chair snapped like the sounds of distant firecrackers when he finally moved to reposition his aching legs. The lingering aroma of breakfast was still in the air; but everyone except Kelly Jean had already eaten, and Esther would soon be starting preparations for dinner.

The summer had been long and hot, but there had not been any truly warm days now for several weeks. A light frost had come in late November and a mild winter was hoped for. The farm had pulled through with a small profit this year, and now the hunting season was on. Jimmy had been stalking a healthy eight-point whitetail buck he had seen once down in the south cornfields, and he wanted to take his shotgun today and try to take him. It was a bit of a tradition in the Kallton household to have the first deer taken in the season for dinner on Christmas day. Jimmy was confident he would get the buck with time to spare before Christmas just two weeks away.

The pastor rubbed his face and yawned as if he were in want of a good night's sleep. He looked at Kelly Jean again, smiled, and stood up. Patting Esther's shoulder, he turned and walked out of the room. Esther looked out the window for several minutes as if she were expecting someone to come into the yard. Then she dragged the two chairs back to the kitchen leaving the door open.

"Esther, we miss you and the children at church," the preacher said. "How long's it been since y'all last came to see us?"

Esther was slow to answer as she stood at the washbasin cleaning out a small iron pot. She knew the pastor remembered their last visit and why they no longer attended. So the preacher expected no answer of substance. For several minutes he looked out the kitchen window searching the grounds for Wade and Jimmy, but he turned back when he heard the door to Kelly Jean's room creaked shut.

"Well, Brother Silas, you know – the Buells. We wouldn't be doing the church right if we went back right now," Esther answered.

The preacher nodded slightly as if he only half-heard Esther's response, for to pursue the point any further would have been an unnecessary rehash of a long-ago discussion. The question was meant as no more than a courteous inquiry; his voice tone proving it. He was a bit surprised, though, by the directness of her answer. He looked out the window down toward the springhouse and the flat yard that spread out to a straight tree line many yards beyond. Wade and his son were nowhere to be seen, but he could hear hammering somewhere. His first instinct was to walk out and seek to help some way. But his welcome was spent, and it was time to go home and tend to his own necessities.

The preacher turned to look back toward the closed door to Kelly Jean's bedroom. He could hear nothing coming from the room; it seemed she wished to shrink from his company. It disturbed him deeply that the young girl had turned in to herself and shut him out, or so it would seem to the old man. Her guilt and despair must be unbearable, he often thought to himself.

He had things he needed to discuss with the Kalltons, and he preferred to talk to husband and wife together. He had known Esther since her birth, and he felt free to discuss his thoughts with her one-on-one. As everyone was well aware, Wade would have little else to say on the subject of the North Road incident. Once his opinion had been stated, he stubbornly saw no need to rehash. But the preacher, though duly cautious at times, was thankful that Wade had always seemed to trust him enough to allow his talking to Esther alone concerning any familial subject. Yet he couldn't help but wonder how much longer he would be so privileged. Still, praying that he would not breech any family sensibilities, the preacher bravely pushed the bounds with Esther as he thought of new questions that he felt the family had not been ready for in earlier discussions. As quietly, yet as obligingly as he could, he spoke to Esther.

"Lately Gene's been on me again to talk to you and Wade about letting Kelly Jean talk. He's not ugly about it in the least, Esther – you understand that? I don't tell him anything I know you and Wade wouldn't want anybody to know, but I did say I'd bring his message to you and Wade." The preacher paused. He turned in his chair as if to search the yard for Wade and Jimmy, again to pretend that Esther's response would be acceptable whether she answered or not. He glanced at Esther and noted the posture of deep thinking in the way she gazed out the window. The preacher gamely continued. "He tells me that Frank will never be right again, and he thinks Kelly Jean's the only hope now to get at the bottom of all this."

Now he watched Esther's reaction closely, never checking the yard again. Thankfully, her youngish, expressive face exhibited no negative signals. For several uncomfortable seconds she seemed to play the issue over in her mind. The preacher, along with the sheriff, had broached the subject with Wade after things had settled down, and Wade had made it generously clear that the family alone would decide when Kelly Jean was strong enough and ready to talk. In no unsettled terms, Wade had forced the subject closed. Now if the preacher got no answer, he would quietly drop the subject forever.

"What's really wrong with the Buell boy? Was he hurt that bad?" Esther asked, making it quite evident that any further discussion of Kelly Jean was out of bounds.

"Uh, yeah, I'm afraid so," the preacher said, continuing in the gentle, kindly voice. "The doctors say he's brain damaged, or some such. He must have really taken a beating up on that road. They say he can't even talk yet. Maybe never. They are supposed to bring him home from Nashville next week for Christmas."

The preacher could see that Esther was listening and eager to hear any news concerning Annie Buell. The preacher had long ago determined that, next to her concerns for Kelly Jean, Esther carried great empathy for her old friend's heartbreak. It was a burdensome task for her to recognize her own blessings when someone else so dear to her was being forced to brave the very worst kind of misfortune.

"Esther, they lost one boy on that road," the preacher added. "Pray that they don't lose the other one. May the Good Lord help us if they do."

The room was silent again for several minutes. Then Esther spoke slowly and quietly, as if she were afraid someone might hear.

"Please don't ask about Kelly Jean, Brother Silas. She dreams about the North Road every night, and it would kill her to make her think about it when she's up during the day, much less talk about it."

"Has she said anything at all?" the preacher asked.

"Uh, no. I think I've heard her call James's name once or twice in her sleep. But she just cries mostly. She doesn't really talk that much. Not anything I can make out anyway."

The preacher leaned back hard in the chair causing it to creak and snap. He gazed back out the window and released a long sigh. "Lord knows I love that child. I pray the Lord will let me live long enough to hear her sing again. What a voice that girl has been blessed with."

Unexpectedly, Jimmy entered the back door to announce to his mother about the two headless chickens on the back porch rail. He smiled at the preacher and asked, "You stayin' for dinner, Brother Silas?"

The preacher, nearly as quickly as the crack of a bullwhip, answered, "No, son. I'll be going home now. It's nice of you to ask, though."

Esther was given no chance to respond, but she knew the real reason for Jimmy's hope. The preacher's presence usually meant the added treat of apple or peach pie, but she was sure there was some honor to her son's invitation. She looked at the preacher for a change of mind, perhaps with the intent of repeating her son's entreaty, but his posture was firm and unchangeable. He was pushing himself up from the chair and looking out the window for his rig.

Esther moved quickly and began clearing the table, and the pastor asked if there was anything he could do before he left. Esther said no, that Wade had taken care of everything and that she would, after cleaning the chickens, probably take a short nap. Suddenly the house turned quiet and stifling. It was time to go. The preacher reached and hugged Esther with one arm, then released her at once. He seemed sure that his simple gesture to comfort her was about all she could stand. Jimmy had the pastor's horse and buggy cinched up and ready to go in the back yard, and the pastor quietly left the farm to return to his home.

***

Late that afternoon, Jimmy suited up and headed south to the fields to once again hunt for the wide-racked buck that had become unexplainably elusive in recent days. Not even a hoof print of the deer had been seen in the past week, and Jimmy had started to wonder if it had been taken by another hunter.

Jimmy walked nearly a mile through tall timbers before coming to the northern edge of the hunting grounds upon which he grew up. The land spread out to wide fields of overgrown pastureland to the east where a lone farmhouse could be seen on the most distant hillside. Broad fields of feed corn stretched to the south and the southeast, and the tall timber continued on toward the west over rolling hills of drab autumn shades of brown and gray with patches of evergreens back toward the northwest.

Jimmy stepped across the gravel-and-dirt road that wound westward back to his home. It would have been an easy hike to this point if he had used the road but that would have spoiled the adventure of the frontier. To the east, the road aimed straight for Braxton Road, hidden on the other side of a gentle rise. Burning up barely a half-second glancing each way, he continued his hike southward a quarter mile. He entered a wide stand of trees running along a cornfield where a few hundred stalks were still standing. The cornfield had been left fallow for a year, and he was surprised to see so many stalks still standing strong. With the grit of a hardened pioneer, he marched across the field to another heavy stand of trees on the other side. About thirty yards into the woods he found the low-limbed white oak he had used for a deer stand on a couple successful hunts in years past. A fairly dense growth of winter-dormant honeysuckle covered the ground for several yards around the big oak with open patches here and there.

He easily climbed up and sat himself onto the fourth limb about fourteen feet above the ground and settled back against the trunk. He rested his booted feet atop a handy branch half a shin length below. This stand provided a fine panoramic view of the deer runs that trailed along a year-round creek flowing through the bottom of a meadow-like clearing. He figured he would have less than two hours of good daylight before he had to give up and head back home. A low breeze was just starting to close in from the west, but the cold air was a pleasant relief against his face as he was still perspiring from the long hike.

He sat for nearly an hour doing little but scan the timbered grounds for any sign of wildlife. As a natural cycle, Jimmy expected the woods to begin stirring with early nocturnal activity during that late but short twilight-like period just before sundown. He drew his hunting cloak up tight to his chin and closed the gap around his neck. The sharp breeze bit at his exposed skin like stinging ice flakes. Then he remembered to load his shotgun. He had just started to chamber the rounds when his eye caught a flash of movement to his right about forty yards away. He quickly chambered the ammo and eased back both hammers. A rabbit came scampering out of the tall timbers and ran along the creek at a fast clip and disappeared into brush on the far east side of the meadow to his left. No hunting dogs were heard, so Jimmy imagined a fox might come along at any moment, hot on the trail of the cottontail. He rolled the hammers back forward and waited, but nothing materialized.

The breeze was picking up and getting colder. Jimmy reached up and fastened the top two latches on his cloak and packed his hat down a little tighter to block the wind from his ears. He slipped a mitten onto his left hand to hold the shotgun, but kept his shooting hand free and warmed in his pocket. The light was going down fast, and Jimmy figured a winter storm was moving in and perhaps he should call the hunt off for the day. Then two small deer came bounding out of the timbers at the most distant northwest corner of the clearing. He watched the deer continue across then looked back westward hoping the big buck would appear a short distance behind them.

Soon flecks of snow started swirling in the breeze and the woods came to life with the bustle of rustling leaves and creaking trees. The familiar 'whoosh-whoosh' of an owl in flight drew Jimmy's attention back to the north of the clearing. Jimmy turned quickly to catch a glimpse but the owl seemed to vanish ghost-like amongst the dark grayed timbers. Jimmy looked back to the western edge for one more look before climbing down for the hike back home. But just then, the sharp snap of a twig underfoot sounded from up near the top of the ridge. Then another. And another. This was too much racket for a deer, Jimmy thought. By now the trees were reduced to black columns against a mottled background. Even if the big buck moved into the clearing, Jimmy wondered if he would be able to see well enough to even determine that it was a deer and not some loosed farm animal.

Jimmy had just started his climb down when he heard another twig snap; this one unnaturally weighty and uncomfortably close. He froze to stone, then eased back to his seat as quietly as snow lighting to the ground. Then a spark of light flashed near the top of the ridge, drawing his eyes upward. The light flashed again, then flickered several times as if it might snuff out. When it finally vanished altogether, Jimmy could see nothing but a coal-black void up on the ridge. He locked his eyes onto the spot where the light last twinkled. Shortly, the light appeared again as a steady yellow-orange glowing speck, and this time it started to float slowly down the face of the ridge toward Jimmy. He scrunched down on the limb and hoped the light would angle away and give him a chance to escape. Instead, the light only grew brighter as it continued to move down the hill toward him. It wasn't long before the discordant sounds of footsteps on dried leaves could be heard. Then, a man's voice.

It was well over a mile to the next farmhouse to the east, and Jimmy had no idea why anyone would be walking this deep into the woods this late in the day. The only possible reason being a coon or possum hunt, except these men had no dogs – a requirement for any night hunt. The coal oil lantern continued at a meander down the hill in Jimmy's general direction. Its light illuminated the woodland floor for several feet around, and it wasn't long before Jimmy could make out the shapes of two more men walking behind the one carrying the lantern. Their faces were shadowed and nondescript at this range, and their forms were concealed beneath heavy coats. For the moment, Jimmy felt secure that they could not be aware of his presence up in the branches of the big oak. He remained motionless hoping to hear enough from the voices to determine whether or not they were friendly.

The three men made their way down to the bottom of the ridge and stopped at the edge of the tall trees. The lantern carrier swung the light out into the air to scout the trail ahead. The breeze played with the flame causing the light to flicker as if it might snuff out. The men were regularly talking to one another but their words were unintelligible at this range. Jimmy could see that they were dressed in heavy, unbuttoned hunting cloaks similar his own, and it now appeared that two of them were carrying either tools or long guns.

The men stopped and talked for several minutes before picking up and walking on into the clearing. They had marched due east for nearly half the length of the clearing before Jimmy began to feel relieved that they would pass by unaware of his presence. But he felt his heart accelerate when the men veered leftward to avoid a brush pile and failed to continue eastward after getting around it. Instead, they advanced directly toward the big oak where Jimmy was perched.

A stout, wide-shouldered man was carrying the lantern and he walked with the determined stride of an unquestioned leader. He nodded in the direction of the oak and motioned for the other two to follow. He talked little and didn't seem to pay much attention to what the other two men were saying. As he walked, he exhibited gestures as if he might be looking for something on the ground. Periodically he would stop and hold the lantern high as if to view the surrounding area extending yards from the group. They continued their walk around several trees and stepped into the little creek and started toward the big oak. Jimmy worked to convince himself that he had nothing to worry about yet.

Soon, Jimmy could hear their voices clear enough to understand the occasional word or phrase. The men climbed to the top of the shallow bank of the creek, stopped and looked around as the big man held the lantern high in front of him. Jimmy now feared his presence could be discovered at any moment. He glanced down to his shotgun and saw a glint of light reflecting off the barrel. He pulled it back a bit to conceal most of it with his arm. The men walked on and stopped again just a few yards from the big oak. They were still looking over the ground and now seemed uninterested in anything above ground level. They started to walk again – directly into the hedge of browned honeysuckle and toward the big oak. Jimmy's heart pounded like the piston of a steam engine. He sucked in a long, deep breath, held it, then released it slowly. The big man strode directly toward the trunk of the tree and turned around to the other two men. "Okay, boys," he announced. "This is it!"

Jimmy cursed his luck. There were hundreds of trees in this patch of woods. Why did these men choose the one he was sitting in? The freakish nature of this coincidence caused Jimmy to ask whether he might be in the depths of a bad dream from which he should wake himself. But this was a giant of an oak; its wide reaching branches and the notable circumference of its trunk he figured played into the big man's decision.

The big man reached up to the lowest limb of the tree and broke off a skinny twig and hung the lantern on the remaining stump. Each man was wearing a hat, each of varying brim widths. But they were all broad enough to shield their wearer's faces from above. Thus hampered, Jimmy couldn't recognize any one of them at this point.

The second man leaned a rifle against a tall hedge of honeysuckle and stood back as if awaiting instructions from the big man. The third man was tall and rail-thin and carried what appeared to be a pickax and a shovel. The big man pointed to a spot on the ground about fifteen feet from the tree and said to the tall man, "Start right here."

The tall man studied the ground where the big man pointed. There was a certain perplexed, or perhaps disbelieving, demeanor in his posture. The big man noted this, pointed at the spot again and ordered, "Dig right there where I told you."

His was the voice of someone well accustomed to being in full charge; commanding and strong, demanding immediate compliance. The tall man at once started digging as if he were eager to please his boss. The big man and the other man squatted and sat side-by-side on a lumpy root stretching from the base of the tree. The big man pulled out of his cloak what appeared to be a small fruit jar filled with a clear liquid. He removed the top and took a hefty gulp without offering any to the other men. The lantern still flickered in the breeze, but the light was amply bright for the men to work and for Jimmy to observe every move made on the ground almost directly below him. His curiosity grew stronger than his fear, so he set his mind to settle back and watch the activities below in silence.

The snowflakes danced in the light like summer insects. Outside the pool of light, the woods were black all around. Jimmy knew he should have been nearly home by now, but he had little choice but wait out the men working beneath him. The tall man was making quick work of the hole he was digging. Each time he worked the shovel he tossed the dirt several feet away, so it seemed a sizeable hole was in the making. At first, the men didn't talk much. If there was any conversation at all, it was usually between the two men sitting on the root; and they talked quietly. But as yet, Jimmy had no clue as to the purpose of the digging.

The big man continued to drink from the jar, and the man sitting next to him reached into his cloak and pulled out a small tobacco pouch and a piece of crumpled paper. He rolled a thin rope of tobacco into the paper and quickly lit it in his cupped hands. At times, the only sound, other than the noises of the breeze, was that of earth being worked and tossed up to the ground near the honeysuckle. After a brief interlude, the big man started talking again to the man sitting next to him; but Jimmy could make out only portions of the conversation. The other man said nothing now. He only nodded his head as if to pacify the big man. The big man rattled on about some undefined slights made against him that made no sense to Jimmy. It seemed that the big man was talking louder now than before and was beginning to work his hands in angry gestures as the contents of the jar took hold.

The tall man kept digging without fainting. He had quickly formed a hole about four feet round and two feet deep. The ground was increasingly flinty at this depth, so he alternately worked with the pickax and shovel to break up the hardened earth and toss it away. He refused to exhibit any sign of tiring, and neither sitting man offered to relieve him. He had removed his heavy coat and tossed it aside. Though his breath steamed heavily like engine exhaust in the cold air, perspiration soaked his shirt.

The big man took another swig, wiped his mouth and laughed. He said to the digger in the hole, "How 'bout it, Jackson – see anything yet?"

The man halted his digging and learned on the shovel, hard-eyeing the big man. Jackson had shoved his hat back enough for Jimmy to see most of his face now, and he thought he recognized him as a migrant worker from the local farms. But he couldn't be sure. He had assumed that all the transient farm hands had gone home for the season weeks earlier.

Jackson, finally exhibiting the first signs of fatigue, shot back, "C'mon over here and I'll let you see the back side of this shovel!"

The big man laughed aloud and swigged again. The third man, working nervously on the cigarette, didn't react to any of the bickering between the two. The big man relished the fact that he had irritated the digger, and for several minutes they spit schoolboy insults at each other. The big man's attitude toward the man in the hole grew increasingly vindictive and less humored in tone as if an old grudge was being played out between them.

Jackson dug down another foot before the third man finally stood up and passively offered to relieve him. The tired digger hopped out, picked up his coat and reclined himself on the ground near the hole. The third man tossed off his coat, slipped into the hole and started digging. His movements were slow and lacking in motivation; clearly devoid of the earnestness and energy of the tall man.

Jimmy's first impression of the big man was one of unsettling awe and apprehension, but now this notion was being enforced by the man's overbearing manner and mean-spirited disposition. Jimmy strained to see his face, but it was impossible. The man's voice was unfamiliar and he spoke with a taut, big city accent that only served to increase Jimmy's consternation.

The big man turned up the jar, emptied the last of it and belched like a mud-stuck boot. The exchange of insults had stopped momentarily, but the big man chuckled to himself as if the exchange was still continuing. Then he spoke again. "Hey, Jackson – how 'bout some moonshine?" Then he drew back and flung the empty fruit jar hard at Jackson. Jackson managed to block the flying jar with his arm, but it shattered firecracker-like upon impact.

The big man laughed aloud and clapped his hands twice with the aggression of a delinquent teenager. To Jimmy's mind, the big man's behavior seemed entirely out of balance to his age and size. It could only make some sense when the contents of the glass jar were figured to be at fault. Jackson's face, partly visible for only a second, showed a combination of both fear and anger as he rubbed his arm and made gestures to turn away and ignore the big man. The man in the hole lifted his hat and wiped his face on his sleeve. He slung back a stringy mass of uncombed red hair and slapped the hat back on. He was still unfazed by all the haranguing and continued digging as if he were alone in the woods.

The big man groused something about glass getting splattered around nearby and then said, "What's the matter, boy – cat got your goddamn tongue?"

Jackson stared into the hole. The big man mumbled a couple of semi-coherent profanities at his victim before finally settling down, and all was quiet again as the man in the hole dug down another foot. Finally, he asked Jackson to relieve him. The men swapped positions and the chopping continued.

The red-haired man then slowly walked around the hole as Jackson worked. He rubbed his neck and stretched backward and forward to relieve his weary bones from the workout. He circled the hole eyeing Jackson once again slaving below. The red-haired man seemed nervous and agitated as if expecting something to jump up and attack him at any moment. The big man watched everything intently. He wasn't moving a muscle and seemed alert to catching every movement made at the hole. Certainly something of great comical, or grave, import was about to occur. Jimmy couldn't see his face, but he was sure the big man was near the point of laughing out loud again. Finally, the big man started to laugh but caught himself as the man walked around the hole a third time. Jackson stopped digging, leaned on the shovel and said to the big man, "Okay, Carl, we gone past five foot now, and I ain't seen no box yet."

The big man said, "Keep digging boy – it's down there." Then, dropping his voice to a stage whisper, he said to the man above the hole, "What the hell, Billy boy – what're you waiting for?"

The tall man in the hole didn't seem to hear this question directed to his confederate. He said to Billy walking the hole, "Bring me that light over here. I can't see no more."

Billy walked back to the tree to get the lantern. But instead, Carl reached and grabbed the rifle and tossed it to him. Billy hesitated, cocked the hammer on the rifle and looked at the Carl. Jackson was still chopping in the hole with the pickax and seemed oblivious to the developing situation. Billy stepped backwards toward the hole a couple of steps. Carl laughed quietly, almost to an inaudible grunt. Jackson spoke up again. "I can't see, goddamnit – where's my light?"

Carl said to Billy, "Make it clean, boy."

Jackson stopped digging and looked up. Billy turned to look at him. Then slowly, with much hesitation, walked to the edge of the hole. Jackson said, "What the hell's the matter with you, Billy? You look like you seen a ghost or somethin'. Get me that light like I told you."

Billy said, "Sorry, Earnie – yew been a-talkin' too much. Carl says we cain't let yew keep a-doin' 'at shit."

Billy said more, but Jimmy couldn't make it out as Billy talked down almost to a whisper. Jimmy could never get a handle on the goings-on below him. There was no story to follow, so he could not prepare himself for what was about to happen.

Jackson said, "What'er you a-talkin' about? I ain't done no talkin' to nobody. What's he a-sayin', Carl?"

Carl answered, "Like he said – you talk too goddamn much. Hear-tell you've been bragging about us whipping and shooting those Buell boys up on the North Road. I can't let that continue, son. I told you to shut the hell up, but you keep talking."

The hole was now nearly six feet deep, but Jackson's height provided him a clear view all around. He remained still for several seconds staring at the big man sitting unmoved on the root.

Then suddenly reacting as if he had been sucker-punched, Jackson slung down the pickax and frantically jumped and grabbed the edge of the hole to pull himself out. Carl said calmly but deliberately, "Don't let him out, Billy."

Billy quickly shuffled to the hole and kicked Jackson's hands off the edge, forcing him back into the hole. Jackson tried again. He jumped hard and yanked himself to chest level. But he was summarily kicked in the face and easily forced back down once again. Billy stumbled momentarily as if he might trip into the hole himself. Jackson stepped back in the hole as far from the muzzle of the gun barrel as he could get, but he could move only inches side to side. He held his hand to his cheek where Billy had kicked him.

"What're you a-talkin' about, Carl? I don't talk to nobody!" Jackson blubbered through a constricted voice box. "Who says I was a-talkin' to nobody?"

"Billy here said you talked to Roy again about us working over them boys on the North Road. Is Billy a liar?"

Jackson switched his eyes between Carl, Billy, and the gun barrel. He worked his heels into the rear wall of the hole as if hoping an underground cavern would fall open allowing him to escape. He furiously searched his mind for some utterance to assert his innocence but the truth stayed his tongue. The realization of what was about to happen built up in his mind until the terror spilled over.

"Damnit, Carl Dean! You told me I was a-diggin' for Christmas money for my family, but you just had me dig a grave – my own damn grave! You gonna burn in hell, Carl Dean! You gonna – you gonna burn, Carl Dean!"

Carl stood up as if to stretch tired joints and said with utter coolness, "Kill him, Billy." He then turned toward the tree, worked open his pants and started relieving himself. Billy began to walk around the hole again pointing the rifle down toward Jackson's head. Jackson started to whimper and cry like a child awaiting meted punishment. His voice tightened as he tried to speak, at times constricting his voice to babbling screeches.

"Billy – Billy! Why? You ain't the kind! You don't – "

The big man suddenly and inexplicably exploded with a savage rage borne of suffering a lifetime of fools, real and imagined, and bellowed, *"Goddamnit! Gimme that damn gun – you yellow-belly son-of-a-bitch!"*

Jackson cried out, *"No! No – Carl – no! You'll burn in hell! You gonna burn in hell!"*

Carl stomped over to the hole and snatched the rifle from Billy and immediately, with no aforethought whatsoever, fired a shot down into the hole. Jackson was instantly silenced. He fell back to the rearward wall of the hole and slid out of the light as if his knees were fighting to remain unbent. The shockwave of the gun-blast hit Jimmy full-faced, and its boom seemed to rumble and echo for nearly a minute thereafter. Jimmy recoiled with terror, jerking rearward. He felt his lungs crushed flat, then he lurched forward as his stomach began to discharge its contents, but he swallowed hard. The shock to the eardrums from the blast and the sounds of the breeze masked his movements. It all allowed him to straighten up and exercise some measure of restraint unnoticed. He took a deep, quivering breath and managed to keep himself under control.

Carl stood over the hole until the echoes were spent. Billy stared into the hole, then looked up at Carl and made motions to step backwards. Carl said, "Get back over here. I'd kill you too, but I need somebody to fill the hole. So get your shitty ass to work."

Billy reached down into the hole and pulled up the shovel and started tossing dirt. Carl swung the lantern over the hole and saw the pickax protruding from beneath Jackson's body and said, "Hell with the ax." He kicked in a couple of the larger clods of dirt, then rehung the lantern. He walked back to the root and sat down leaving Billy to finish the job.

All was quiet again for several minutes as Billy worked to fill the grave. Flecks of snow were still happily swirling in the air. Tears wetted Jimmy's face, but he found strength and remained still as he watched the event on the ground come to a close. Billy labored until he filled in the last of the grave, creating a shallow mound. He studied it for a moment before deciding he should continue tossing dirt to fill in low spots around the edges. Carl was chuckling to himself again as he watched Billy. Soon, he was talking again.

"You learn anything tonight, boy?" Billy glanced at Carl as he spoke but continued working with the shovel, pretending to not understand the question. Carl barked, "Who the hell do you think I'm talking to?"

This seemed to shake Billy a bit, and he stood motionless holding the shovel. The rifle was at the big man's side, and Billy seemed to take note of it. "I hear yew," he said. "Yew know I don't talk – I ain't gonna start a-talkin'. I don't wanna go to jail no more than yew do, Carl."

"You're never going to jail, boy," Carl said, his voice nearly breaking into a derisive chuckle. "Your next stop is the graveyard – but you make up your mind how you want to get there."

Billy tossed another shovelful of dirt onto the grave, then looked again at Carl. He said nothing as he tossed down the shovel and started pulling honeysuckle vines and weeds onto the grave to camouflage it. Carl was silent for several moments before speaking again. It was as if he had forgotten the exchange that had just taken place.

"Hey, Billy – how about that big buck I killed last week? Biggest rack I ever seen. Your old lady fix some for you?"

"Yeah, I reckon," Billy grunted. "She can make some fixin's."

The big man laughed and said mockingly, "Yeah, I reckon she can." Then he stood up and took the lantern and turned up the wick, increasing its light all around.

Jimmy watched as the two men made preparations to leave the gravesite. The big man picked up the rifle and raised the lantern to survey the area and examine the grave. He seemed satisfied with the results and said, "Well, Billy, like I said, you learned something tonight – how to dig graves!" Then he laughed so heartily that he almost dropped the lantern. The jar juice was still wearing well.

Billy turned and walked across the honeysuckle and out onto the edge of the big clearing. Carl, in spite of the immoderate juice consumption, followed across the bush with minimal difficulty. Jimmy watched the two men make their way down to the creek before heading back westward into the tall timbers. The big man, swinging the lantern at his side, could be heard talking and laughing as they worked their way though the creek bottom. The voice carried the happy timbre of victory as if a big worry had been lifted off his mind. Billy never uttered a word and walked ahead of the big man to keep out of his way. Try as he might, Jimmy could never get even a cursory glance of the big man's face. The other one, he wasn't sure. His voice seemed vaguely familiar. The shaggy red hair revived the memory of a transient day laborer from a nearby county that had worked only sporadically for his uncle Paul over the years. But otherwise, like the big man, he could never quite see his face.

Even though Jimmy hardly moved a muscle throughout the ordeal, he was debilitated with withering exhaustion. Climbing out of the tree would surely drain any remaining reserve of strength he might have. But he was unable to move until the lantern was far out of sight. His muscles were atrophied to their bones; his nerves not heeding his own commands. He was sure that any move he might make would still alert the men to his presence, even now as the men were making their way through the trees halfway up the ridge. The big man could still be heard – sometimes cursing, sometimes laughing.

Soon, the lantern was back at the top of the ridge where it had first twinkled two hours earlier. The air was black all around the big oak. But a powdering of dull, gray light stretched across the sky. The moon was out there somewhere casting minimal light through cloud breaks. Jimmy was straining to adjust his eyes to the darkness and he, at times, thought he could distinguish tree trunks at some distance away. He debated whether it was enough vision to move through the woods to escape. But he waited until his ears detected nothing but the moving air. He strained his head westward and could find no trace of lantern light. Then he looked at the black ground where the grave should be. Something of unfamiliar origin stirred in his mind and caused him to suppose that the dead man's spirit was haunting the woodland clearing as if this was his home now and Jimmy was an unwelcome intruder. Still, he was regaining some composure; whether it was from physical depletion or that his nerve endings were beginning to take commands, he couldn't know. He had difficulty controlling his trembling body as he stiffly began to unfold for the climb down from the tree. His legs were numb and heavy and a painful throb started to work its way down the moment blood began to flow again. The combination of nerves and the cold air made it difficult for him to grasp onto the limbs as he struggled to ease himself out of the tree and onto firm soil. His shotgun slipped out of his hand and flopped to the ground. He turned his head back westward again. Slowly, he leaned down and felt the ground for his gun. He found it instantly, thankful that he felt no loose grave dirt in the process.

He stood still for several moments. He looked up the ridge to look for the lantern again. The cold air puffing in his face and through his cloak flap worsened his feelings of aloneness and vulnerability. He looked down at the black void on the ground where the grave should be and felt himself become nauseated again. He sucked in deep air, then did it again and again. He pulled the cloak tight, turned north and started home.

***

Wade, Esther and Kelly Jean were sitting before a soft-crackling fire in the front room. For a half hour the discussion had rarely strayed from questioning whether Jimmy had carried a lantern with him when he left the house nearly five hours earlier. It was figured he must have gotten his deer for being late.

Nearly an hour before closing the house for the night, Wade had gone to the smokehouse to check the coals and to retrieve some firewood from the porch. He stopped cold when he heard the distant gunshot coming from the south line. It was past dark, so Jimmy would not have been shooting at deer; but it could well have been a shot fired by nighttime coon hunters. Wade listened closely for the sound of baying hounds, but none could be heard in the brisk air.

***

Jimmy felt as if he were being hovered over by an invisible malevolent presence as he groped through the blackened woods trying to find any familiar trail mark to lead him home. He had turned northward and the cornfield was just ahead, he figured. If somehow he could just get to the edge of the cornfield he would feel home free, even though he would still be well over a mile from home.

The breeze created an abundance of fearful noises in these trees. Noises that Jimmy was sure he had never heard before. Or perhaps his mind was creating new ones. There were footsteps behind him, then he heard twigs breaking as if underfoot. He spun around but could find only blackness. He turned back northward to run. He tripped over a vine but managed to catch himself and move again. Somehow, he was sure the big man was watching and trailing him. Jimmy's eyes watered up again and he felt a constriction move up his chest and tighten around his throat. His legs cramped and he was forced to stop running. He looked back and froze in spite of his strong desire to keep moving. It took a moment for him to begin to realize that the big man would not likely be able to see in this darkness any better than he could. His mind swung back and forth between such logical reasoning and runaway panic. He wondered if he could outrun the big man if it came down to a race for his life. And he determined he must actively accept the idea of protecting himself with his shotgun. He had pictured himself shooting a man in self-defense before, but this was a depth of terror he had never thought could be imagined or dreamed in nightmares.

His legs loosened and began taking commands again. He fought to find his way back to the edge of the trees and, without giving himself time to gauge his thoughts, he rushed out into the southern boundary of the cornfield. He looked to the east to find the distant farmhouse with the yellow sparks of light in the windows. He moved quickly across the field but the ground was covered with dry corn stalks and walking could not be done quietly. Some of the standing stalks were silhouetted against a faint western horizon, and they shook in the breeze like scarecrows trying to come to life. He looked for a man's shape among them. He felt vulnerable in the open space, so he turned his eyes back northward.

Straining to see across the field toward the black timbers, Jimmy imagined the big man waiting in ambush at the edge of the field. His racing mind seemed more certain, as the minutes ticked by, that the two men were trailing him now. The road was on the other side of the field, and he imagined the big man had used it to circle back and cut off his escape. He lowered his shotgun, pointed it ahead and rolled back the hammers.

Soon enough, he reached the north edge of the field. He crouched low trying to peer into the line of trees along the side of the road ahead, watching for any movement or shape that would give away the big man's whereabouts. He turned eastward and walked as many yards as he felt needed to begin to feel some measure of refuge. He kept his ear to the road and he angled toward it as his confidence increased. He found the road, raced across and bounded into the trees on the other side and stopped. He could save time if he used the road to get back home, but that option was lost to the big man's devices. The pounding of his heart competed with the noises of the trees. He now moved as quickly as he felt safe.

***

Wade was suiting up in the front room, readying himself for the hike southward to find his son. Kelly Jean had been sitting at the window, watching for Jimmy's appearance down near the barn southeast of the house. Outside the window, the yard pitched away into a darkness as black as new-mined coal, but the white-washed gate to the pasture was usually visible on cloudless nights when the moon hung high. Esther trimmed and lit a lantern for Wade and admonished him to hurry back with their son as soon as he found him. Wade kept his demeanor straightforward and calm, an effort that was easily accomplished as long as Esther knew nothing of the distant gunshot he had heard minutes earlier.

Wade lifted his rifle from the mantle and slapped on a field hat and walked out the door. Esther, with a stance that suggested she wished to follow, stood in the open doorway watching Wade march swiftly across the yard. The cold breeze swept through the house bringing an instant chill into the front room. The draft of fresh air hit the fireplace and flared up the fire. Esther pushed the door shut and walked over to the window where Kelly Jean was sitting. Mother and daughter loosely embraced one another on the couch as they watched the lantern move down the hill and through the gate. It twinkled from view as it passed into the trees at the far side of the barn.

***

Jimmy had developed a strong rhythm in his step and was moving fast up and down the small rolling hills. He was steadily gaining control of his wits and he felt safer as he put distance between himself and the big oak. He tried to walk in open areas and deer runs and stay clear of a heavy brush and vine undergrowth a short distance to the east. He rarely looked rearward now and he felt safe enough to march as quickly as his tired legs would carry him. Soon, he would be home and safe. He never entertained thoughts as to how he might tell the story to his parents. They would be sure to query him in rapid-fire fashion till the whole story was told. The sheriff would be summoned and the story recited again. The perpetrators would be rounded up and tried and imprisoned. Then he would go on with his life. He would endure nights of bad dreams and periods of doubt over his actions, but he would ultimately get over the horror of this night and grow up to be an upstanding member of the community like his father. And would have a story to tell about how he stayed strong and came out victorious over these criminally malicious men. And above all, his father would be proud of him. This idea was what strengthened him most for the journey ahead, and drove him with a purpose and courage only a father can instill in a son.

He had tramped several hundred yards north of the cornfield when he slid to a stop, his eyes tracking the most distant hill to the north. Perhaps his imagination was working against him again. Maybe, he thought, he had caught a glimpse of a star as the clouds moved across the horizon, momentarily opening up to expose it. But Jimmy had to be sure. He broke and ran to the top of the next hill and stopped. He scanned that distant hill again. He was still too far from home to slow down now. He would be there soon, though, if he could keep moving. But he wouldn't budge until he was sure of the source of the light, whether it be real, imagined, or some perverse combination of both.

Soon, an infinitely tiny pinprick of light could be seen on the top of that distant hill. He watched intently for any movement. Then it flickered and disappeared behind the clouds as he had hoped. He shook his head and took a deep breath, then leaned against a tree while still watching the hill. Steam was rising out of the collar of his cloak, and he suddenly felt very warm standing against the tree. He unbuttoned the cloak to cool off before heading out again. He removed his hat to wipe perspiration from his face with the cuff of a glove, then he pressed his hat back down tight. He looked up again at the hill and searched it top to bottom. He had just begun to walk when he saw the light again; but this time it was far below the top of the hill and floating rapidly down into the hollow.

The feeling of panic and dread returned with a vengeance. Jimmy knew now he would have to take a stand for his life against the big man. His mind spiraled into a cavernous pit of paranoia, and he ran recklessly to the brushy area at the edge of the woods. He tripped twice but managed to throw himself into the thicket. Dragging his shotgun like a stick, he scrambled several yards into the brush and landed in a deer bed that opened toward the woods to the north. He kneeled to one knee and propped his shotgun through the fork of a thick vine. Jimmy thought of making a run to the farmhouse with the lights in the windows. But he figured that if the big man could circle and approach from the north as quickly as he had apparently done, then he would have little chance of outrunning such a strong adversary in a long distance foot race across a mile of open pastureland and fields. It could be just as easy to deduce that Billy was now waiting for him back at the road. Jimmy was being flushed out like a hunted rabbit and forced into a position more advantageous to his enemies. Aggressively taking a stand for his life in these darkened woods was a truly terrifying feeling that threatened to overwhelm his capacity to function. Remaining lucid and clear-eyed when the moment of reckoning came did not seem to be an option that he could neglect. He felt the tears come again. He ignored them and stared into the trees to the north.

He hoped the buckshot would pattern out enough to compensate for bad aim if he could not hold a steady bead on the approaching target. He held two more rounds of ammunition in his left hand so he could reload quickly if so needed. Jimmy recalled the last time that he had the shakes like this was when he shot his first buck three years earlier as a young hunter at twelve years. The excitement had almost overcome him, but he made a clean kill with one shot from the same shotgun he would use this night against what he was sure to be a very dangerous and hostile enemy.

He had lost sight of the light when he took cover in the brush and was wondering now if the big man had abandoned the direct route and was circling around to avoid detection. Perhaps the big man had turned the light off and was waiting in ambush on the next hill. His ears detected noises, real and unreal, that rushed in from every direction. The breeze made the woods a theater of constant movement and noise. Every twitch in the breeze was reason to suspect the big man was very near.

Jimmy's throat expelled an unintentional gasp that he managed to catch before it grew to a dangerous volume. The lantern had suddenly risen so quickly above the crest of the nearest hill he had no spare time to focus his eyes from far to near. It was moving southward at a frighteningly fast clip and Jimmy tightened his finger on the rearward trigger before taking proper time to aim. He lifted the barrel to level and aimed for the center of the light, then upward a bit to strike mid-chest. The lantern was on the most distant hill, it seemed, just a minute before. Now here it was, coming at him like a flaming arrow aimed for his heart. Jimmy tightened his finger on the trigger and held it at three pounds of pressure; one pound shy of sinking a load of buckshot deep into the big man's chest. He started a slow twist leftward to follow the lantern as it moved through a treed plateau forty yards away. Jimmy tested his aim against the lantern and found that the bead was solidly silhouetted against the light. The man's form was growing more distinct and detailed as he approached. He could see the man carrying the lantern through the trees directly across from him now about ten yards closer. The rifle and the broad-brimmed hat made positive identification in Jimmy's mind. The big man's rifle was swinging forward and back like a twig in the wind. Jimmy raised the barrel again to find the broad center of the body. He had to fire at the most advantageous moment. He loosened his finger in order to slide in both fingers to fire two barrels at once with the idea of making a sure kill. He rolled the two reload shells to the center of his left palm making ready to fire again if the big man failed to go down.

He firmed his fingers on the triggers. The lantern was nearly perpendicular in its path to Jimmy. The man's behavior and direction of travel indicated he was unaware of Jimmy's presence. The possibility that the man may be ignorant of Jimmy's close proximity had not registered in his mind. Jimmy assumed that there was a game of strategy and deception being played out here that was above his realm of experience. In spite of the fact that the big man was showing no sign of aggression against him, he was sure that at any moment the man's diabolical plan would be hatched and the war would begin. The big man's sidekick was somewhere out there and would make his part in the plan known soon. But Jimmy could do little more than concern himself with the actions of the singular enemy before him. Exhausted, he was losing his ability to ignore the hallucinogenic thoughts and visions that fought increasingly for his attention. His fingers were numb and stiffened in the cold, and he had to concentrate to remember to keep pressure on the triggers in the event of a sudden attack.

The man detoured westward around a laurel thicket. The lantern flickered as it peeked in and out of vine growths. Perhaps this is where the battle begins as each side sets up forts. Then just as quickly, the lantern reappeared south of the laurels. Jimmy shoved his trigger hand forward to pry out his fingers and release the pressure. He watched the big man leave the thicket and continue due south toward the field.

Jimmy's lungs felt as if they were about to explode. He realized he hadn't taken a breath since he last pressed the triggers. He slowly sucked in a deep breath and let it out just as slowly. The lantern had moved much farther southward at this point and Jimmy could see it heading up the next hill. But he wasn't ready to call an end to hostilities yet. His mind began to concern itself with the problem of the other man. Jimmy imagined himself being set up for an ambush farther north. Perhaps Billy was waiting on the next hill, the second hill, or the fifth hill. He had no way of knowing.

The lantern was out of sight and heading for the cornfield. Jimmy waited several more minutes looking for any telltale signs from the north. Finally, instead of stepping out into the open woods again, Jimmy worked his way eastward through the brush and to the open pasture land. He stepped over a rotted split-rail fence and out into the pasture. He kneeled to one knee and listened, craning his neck every which way scoping for any unnatural sound or movement. It didn't help much; there was nothing natural about this night. He momentarily debated whether he should go for the farmhouse to the east or to make a run home to the north. It was an easy decision. He aimed himself north and started homeward again, zigzagging out into the field to thwart any ambush attempt in the trees.

***

Wade didn't slow down when he reached the cornfield and soon he made it to the stand of trees where he knew Jimmy hunted. He stopped at the edge of the trees and held his lantern high looking up into the branches. He could see the big oak from the field and he spoke aloud. "Jimmy! Jimmy! You in there?"

Wade waited silently for the response, which never came. The breeze was shifting and quickly enough it delivered the first sign of something amiss. There was no mistaking the scent of freshly turned soil – it was too distinct to ignore. He walked into the trees and on toward the big oak. He stepped over the honeysuckle and looked up again into the lower reaches of the oak. The freshly broken twig stump on the first limb was a sign that Jimmy had been there a short time earlier. He circled wide from the tree looking all around, up and down. Then he lowered the lantern and searched along the ground beneath the tree for anything that might help solve this unsettling mystery. The scent at times was very strong. He tried to follow it to its source and soon he found it in the shallow mound of dirt hidden beneath a thin cover of displaced honeysuckle and weeds. He kicked back the cover and stepped on the edge of the mound. It was soft and obviously recently toiled. Footprints were all over and around it. Looking around the mound, he found what appeared to be small shards of glass from a fruit jar. He picked one up and examined it, noticing that it was clean and free of any debris. He sensed a very different odor coming from somewhere, and he lifted the shard to his nose and sniffed. It was unmistakable – the burning stench of distilled corn whiskey, a remembrance that has held with him from his youth.

The seriousness of the situation was ratcheting up moment by moment. Wade cranked a round of 45-75 into the chamber of the Winchester and propped the rifle horizontal, its butt against his thigh, as if to fire in an instant. He listened for any noise and searched for any clue as to what was happening. He held the lantern high and peered as far off into the trees as he could. He called Jimmy again. Silence. He swung the lantern around and headed back home, hoping against his worst intuitions to find Jimmy safe there.

***

Jimmy opened the gate and pushed it shut without bothering with the latch. He slogged up the slope to the house with a wary eye to the black woods behind him. He was still expecting something to happen despite the fact that he was close enough to see the lamps in the windows of his home. He rushed the last few yards to the house and spun around facing the woods. A little gust of wind frightened him enough to stumble him against the porch. He dropped the gun and fought for the steps like a chased blind man. When he landed on the top step, the front door swung open flooding the porch with more light than seemed possible from the little oil lamps in the front room. A figure burst out of the light and grasped him by the shoulder. But Jimmy, unable or unwilling to respond to the commands being given him, jerked away and tripped down the steps. A woman's voice called his name but his mind failed to register. His mother shouted his name again and again until he stopped fighting for his freedom. He looked up at her as if he didn't fully recognize her, then he bent over to retrieve the gun. He slowly hinged open the chambers, unloaded the two unspent shells and let them drop to the ground. He looked to the woods again; still fighting the demons of delirium and paranoia.

Esther was suddenly overcome by a great motherly fear that should have pushed her to immediate action of some sort. But she seemed frozen by a knowing inside her soul telling her that something was far out of bounds with her son – something she was sure she was not fully capable of handling on her own. She stole a glance down toward the gate looking for Wade. She reached for her son again, then, with a voice surprisingly calm, said, "Come on in the house, son. You'll catch cold."

***

Wade, at nearly a run, made the return trip to the house much quicker than the hike south to the big oak. He entered the front door to find Jimmy semiconscious on the floor with Esther and Kelly Jean crouched next to him. Clearly Wade was spent of physical strength himself; breathless and perspiring as no one had seen him before. Esther had tried to prod Jimmy to stay alert and give some explanation for his late appearance and apparent distraught condition. Wade, without a word, grabbed Jimmy by the shoulders and gave him a firm shaking. Jimmy looked up at those above him and tried to sit up. He was helped to the couch as he moaned like he had been punched in the stomach. Wade began the interrogation by coaxing his son to talk, and Jimmy tried to speak but seemed to have difficulty breathing normally. Jimmy spoke several garbled words, took a deep breath and said clearly, "Killed him..."

Kelly Jean broke in and said, "He killed him a deer?" Her voice carried the timbre of someone desperately hoping that things were not as grave as they were sounding. Everyone ignored her. Jimmy spoke again.

"I saw it --"

"You saw what, son?" Wade asked after realizing his son was not going to carry the conversation on his own without some prodding.

"He killed him!" Jimmy said as he broke down and began sobbing.

"All right, son," Wade said. "Sit up – take your time now."

Jimmy managed to ask for water and Kelly Jean hurriedly retrieved it. It aroused him considerably and he became quite alert very quickly. His eyes focused and his neck drew enough strength to hold erect his sagging head. The family listened as Jimmy started relating the story between gulps of water and labored breathing. It was slow, but he was getting along well until he started detailing the event beneath the big oak. As the seriousness of the story unfolded, Jimmy again became too agitated to continue and could only get out one or two words at a time. Jimmy never mentioned a name of any one of the three men throughout his narrative. They seemed to have escaped his stressed memory. Then finally, he recalled the name of the big man as he had heard it screamed by the tall man in the hole.

Instantaneously, as he said the words 'Carl Dean,' Kelly Jean jerked away as if she had been slapped solidly across the face, and immediately clutched her hands to her terror-stricken face. She sucked in a fast, deep breath and screamed a single wail until her lungs were emptied. The family, each of them with a flinch, moved away from one another as if to dodge a hot-fused bomb that had suddenly been dropped amidst them. Kelly Jean backed away toward the kitchen with her hands held tight to her face. Breaking down into labored sobs and shrill breathing, she screamed again, causing the air to stab the eardrums like hickory splinters. Esther ran to her, but Kelly Jean violently pushed her away. She looked back at her brother who was shaken by her reaction. Her face had twisted unnaturally into the contorted visage of abject terror. It was the facial expression of the eternally damned. She started to turn and run for the kitchen, or to some place perhaps unknown even to her. But Esther yanked her back and held tight. Kelly Jean tried to pull away again and almost succeeded before her father jerked her back to him and engulfed her in a tight bear hug, then forced her away from the kitchen doorway. She cried out and fought kicking and punching as a woman would in the midst of brutal rape. Wade held her firm until she expended her strength. She finally fell limp and slumped to the floor. Esther reached down to her, but with the careful movements of someone fearful of being punched. Kelly Jean, her crying not reduced, unexpectedly reached up and pulled her mother to the floor with her. Kelly Jean and her mother sat tightly embracing each other as she continued to wail uncontrollably. Jimmy, not understanding what had just happened before him, could only sit and witness his sister's breakdown. Kelly Jean quickly regressed into a state of catatonic hysteria and started garbling nonsense as her mother rocked her in her arms as she had done most nights when her daughter awoke from her nightmares.

No one in the Kallton house slept on that cold December night. Jimmy sat in the front room until dawn listening to the wind and to Kelly Jean's intermittent cries. Though he never slept, he had nightmares nonetheless; at times fearful that he might fall into spiraling madness as his sister had done. Then, without explanation, his father walked out of the house. When the sun rose above the trees and the light filled the windows, the house fell quiet as the dead.

CHAPTER 5

Wade tethered the horse to an overgrown blueberry bush at the corner of the porch. The dogs under the porch were barking but Wade paid them no mind. He would have shot any one of them that dared to venture out. It was still low light of early dawn and it cast the house as nothing more than a big shack with a rotting wooden porch that was broken up by wide cracks in the floor. Several chickens flapped away as Wade climbed the steps and walked to the door. He reached his hand through a rip in the screen door and banged on the wood door inside. He stepped away to wait for the occupants to answer. Everyone was still asleep.

Two of the dogs finally came out into the yard and carried on loudly and threateningly at Wade. The sour stench of a dishwater outdrain filled the air. In the dim light, he could see a clothesline stretched across a side yard. Several clothing articles were hanging from it; but a number of items were trampled on the ground below. Apparently the clothes had been lying there for several days.

"Goddamn shits, shut yore asses up out t'ere!" someone yelled from inside the house.

"Roy?" Wade answered back.

"Hoo wiz it?"

"It's Wade. Get out here right now." Wade ordered.

The door opened and out stepped Roy Kallton in long underwear britches held up with a half pair of tobacco-stained suspenders. He was shirtless, perennially hair-faced and disheveled. He had a couple more hours of slumber to finish yet. Wade searched the windows for the presence of any one of Roy's derelict sons.

"What th' hell time is it, Wade?" Roy asked with uncharacteristic meekness, scratching a chigger near his crotch. There was something overly stern and unsympathetic in Wade's voice that stood out from their previous encounters. Roy wisely determined that he should rein in his worst impulses to bite back. He turned to the dogs and spat, "I said, shut th' hell up!" Turning back to Wade with squinted eyes, he asked, "Sump'm wrong?"

"You know who killed them Buell boys a couple of months ago?"

Roy reacted as if he'd been slapped: "Th' hell – "

"You heard straight."

Roy stepped back to the front edge of the porch and glanced down at the dogs. He worked his mind fast but could find nothing better than the convenient lie. "I don't know a goddamn thang 'bout t'at, Wade. Yew an' that goddamn sher'ff o' yores – "

Wade hated nothing more than wasting valuable daylight. He pointed a cocked finger, six-shooter style, at Roy's nose and stared him down. Roy chanced a step back, but held his footing.

"All right; just tell me one thing," Wade ordered, the volume rising. "Is Carl Dean back in the area?"

"How in hell would I know – "

"You two was buddies years ago. You'd be the first one he'd contact – don't shit with me."

Roy gingerly stepped around Wade and toward the long end of the porch. Wade made it a point to follow, leaving no more than a step between them.

"Yeah, I see 'im ever' few days. What th' hell yew a-askin' me 'bout them Buell – "

"Just shut up and listen to me, goddamnit. Did you see Carl yesterday? Or last night?"

"Naw, I been here at home fer nar'y a week. But I reckon 'e's at his place. Why th' hell yew a-askin' me all this shit?"

"His place? He's come for the Howard Kallton place?"

"Yeah, 'at's right. Why – "

Wade turned away and jumped down the steps. He cocked back a leg and kicked a dog solidly in the jaw on the way to his horse. Roy sneered, "Just shewt me in my good leg, yew dumb sum'bitch."

***

Wade hadn't anticipated riding the six-plus mile journey toward Braxton and then back up to the end of the North Road to get to the old run-down farmhouse once owned by a distant, deceased relative. Instead, he backtracked to a new clearing he thought he saw earlier in the dim light off the side of the road. It appeared to be the beginnings of a new driveway that might be a shortcut to the old house as the geography would suggest. Sure enough, felled trees lay on each side of a new road cut through the woods leading to the house nearly a half-mile to the north. Stumps still stubbed out of the ground, but the drive was straight.

Wade entered the back yard to find the morning sun now high enough to reveal the true dilapidated condition of the outbuildings, as well as that of the old house itself. The only thing that showed no sign of outward deterioration was a large, fur-based, eight-point set of deer antlers hanging from new nails up on the eave of the porch. Startled, his eyes landed on a still figure working up a loaded bucket at the wellhouse. The man was a perfect fit for the description Jimmy gave of the red-headed man from the killing at the oak tree. Wade quickly recognized him as a transient work migrant from years past. He reached down for his rifle hanging loose in its scabbard but checked his movements. The man at the well turned loose the bucket and made for the house, but Wade ordered him to stop.

"I can kill you before you move another step, Billy."

Billy jerked to a stop as if a leash had been attached to his neck. A few seconds passed as the windlass spun to a blur, then slowed to a stop when the bucket hit bottom. Billy stared back at Wade through loose, nose-length bangs. It required some heavy measure of restraint to resist the impulse to kill Billy on the spot, but it was Carl that Wade had come to see first. Billy would have to wait his turn.

"Where's Carl?" Wade barked.

"In th' house."

"Get him."

Billy stepped easily to the porch steps and started up. The back door opened and a square bulk of a man, muscled like a plow ox, stepped out to the edge of the porch. He strode with the bearing of a man who entertained threats, implied or real, poorly. Wade hadn't seen his distant cousin since they were young teenagers, and he had imagined Carl's appearance as being imposing. But he was unprepared for the visage standing before him.

"Carl Dean Kallton?" Wade asked.

"Is that Wade?" Carl grunt-whispered to Billy. "Yeah, that's him," Billy answered.

"That's right," Carl barked back at Wade. It was clear that he detected antagonism in Wade's voice. Carl began slowly pacing the length of the porch much like a panther would if overtly threatened. The wooden boards were quite flimsy, and it could be imagined any one of them snapping under the weight of this bear of a man. He was about the same height as Wade, but he was quite possibly once-and-a-half Wade's body thickness. Carl had the remnant of a perpetual smile on his lips. But his hot, boring eyes sunk deeply beneath heavy black brows stole any imagined trace of friendliness from his countenance.

"You kill a man on my property last night?" Wade heard himself ask without greeting.

Carl turned full-bodied toward Wade and stopped. His expression didn't change. He raised his hands and placed them on his hips, both legs carrying equal weight. Clearly he was tripped up by the question, but he showed no distinct response. Wade, sure he had hit a nerve, continued.

"You don't worry about how I know. You get the body off my property after dark before tomorrow and nothing will be told to the sheriff, or anybody." Wade checked again for a response which he determined would never come. He added, "And you and your boy there make sure that everything's cleaned up before you're done." Then he jerked the reins and turned to leave.

"Wade?"

Wade turned back to the voice. Carl had not changed his stance. He still seemed to be smiling.

"Like you said – you won't be telling nobody." Carl paused a moment, then added with no change in voice tone, "If you do – I'll come after you myself. I'll kill you then bury your ass where nobody will know."

Wade managed to hold his body rigid and his eyes steady. For a moment, his mind blanked. Then he found the words to return the threat, but with only a nominal measure of vigor. "I don't know what the hell you're figuring on doing in these parts, Carl, but I'll kill your ass if you so much as look at my family – "

Carl laughed aloud with enough antagonism to staunch Wade's comeback in mid-track. "What I'm figuring on doin' in these parts? You reckon?" Carl mocked.

Wade glanced down at his rifle. He was sure Carl could see his eye whites widen. Then Wade said, "After tonight, if I find you or your boy there on my property or near any of my family, I'll shoot to kill on sight."

"Well, goddamn, son – you're on my property right now. What's to keep me from shooting you and throwing your hayseed ass to the buzzards?"

Carl didn't move a muscle when he spoke. He would have held his stance as long as Wade looked at him, so Wade again turned and headed back down the driveway. He heard someone laugh. He was certain it was Billy.

Nothing worked as planned. His own impulses were lost when he found Billy at the well and things worsened when Carl appeared. He had imagined starting the discourse with stifled greetings, then work into the matter at hand. He had questions to battle out with Carl, though he never supposed he would have had the opportunity to ask more than one or two. Nor would the likes of Carl be expected to answer to any higher level of clarity. Because of his son's narrative of the previous night's events, Wade held some of the answers. But there were many he lacked.

Answers to questions like: Who did Carl kill? Why did he kill someone in such a cold, calculating manner? Why did he arrange to kill and bury the body on someone else's property? What part did Carl and Billy play in the North Road incident? How was the murdered man involved in the incident?

Did Carl, in collaboration with Billy and the murdered man, kill James Buell and beat his brother, Frank, to a corpse-like coma? If so – why? Does he know that his daughter may have witnessed the North Road killing? And if so, and most important, why did the mere mention of Carl's name cause Kelly Jean to go into hysterics? That is, what did Carl and his thuggish underlings do to Kelly Jean that would so consume her soul?

The ponderables to the last question ricocheted in Wade's head like a white-hot bullet. He was ready to kill a man over what happened to his son at the big oak. But something in Wade's spirit shriveled when his daughter escaped reason at the mere mention of someone's name. Conscious fear had never been an overt motivating factor in his life until Kelly Jean's screams pierced his soul. Now he was reeling from a new phobia of losing his family and all he had labored and fought for. Yet, while he battled with this fear, he grew more enraged by the moment as he thought through his actions. He determined it was far too early to call an end to this encounter. He pushed his mind hard to determine his next move. He played his options but came up short with any solution that would not require immense amounts of time and resources. The most immediate remedy would cost no more than the expense of two or three well-placed bullets.

He stopped the horse and turned around to return to the porch and kill two men. He traveled ten yards and stopped, then started again. Then stopped again. He gazed up the driveway at the house. It was but a gray smudge in the distance. No movement outside. He jerked his Winchester out of the scabbard and cranked in a round. He kicked to a hard gallop and raced to the house. But a moving window reflected light. Then a glimmer of blued steel. He jerked leftward and hit the trees. He drove hard dodging saplings and tree trunks for a hundred yards before looking back. The house was now hidden far behind a wall of vines and overgrowth. He raced on to a creek and turned southward for the road. Then he crouched down and kicked. In moments, he was back on the road and heading home. He raced past the driveway entrance and looked in. All clear. Soon, still enraged but containing himself mightily, he was back home.

***

Kelly Jean was lying motionless in bed with her mother sitting beside her. She had refused, or had been unable to speak a single coherent word all night. Esther glared at Wade, making it clear they were not to be disturbed. She had nothing to say to her husband after their hushed, but heated, early morning discussion. Jimmy was still in the front room outwardly seeming, for the moment at least, to be unaffected by the night's events. Wade laid his rifle back up on the mantle and walked over to his son. No word had been given to Jimmy as to where his father had gone this morning, but he logically assumed he had gone to fetch the sheriff. He looked at his father with wearied, but expectant, eyes.

"Jimmy," Wade said. He was glancing around at the floor, his gestures more agitated than his son had ever seen before. Wade sneezed, but it was a most unnatural sneeze. Like he was burning up time to think. He cleared his throat and said, "We've got a problem here we're going to have to handle ourselves in order to help Kelly Jean. She's not going to make it if we don't help her. You're going to have to be a man now. We've got to help Kelly Jean." Jimmy's expression showed confusion, but he remained silent. Wade worked his mind hard to keep his words smooth and uninterrupted by unconvincing narrative. "That man you saw killed last night has been dug up and carried away to his family. I just heard that he was the man that killed the Buell boy. That big man you saw that shot him was a distant relative of ours – yours and mine. He killed him because of what he done – "

"But Papa!" Jimmy interrupted, "That ain't what I heard! Carl Dean said – "

"You said he was drinking didn't you, son?" Wade asked. Jimmy nodded. "Well, people say and do crazy things when they're drinking. You don't worry about that. I done talked to Carl all morning about that."

Wade studied his son's reactions to determine whether he was buying the story; but Jimmy's face hadn't changed. Wade was too deep at this point, so he had little choice but to continue.

"This fellow you saw shot and killed last night was one of Carl's field hands. A migrant worker. He done something bad and Carl, I reckon you could say, took the law into his own hands."

Jimmy turned to look off into the yard through a window. His mind reeled with questions that were bouncing off his father's story before he could adequately form them. He seemed to sense that the whole situation was too far beyond his reasoning to aggressively question the grownups in the house. A simple question seemed to be in order, though.

"What's Mr. Carter gonna do about Carl, Papa?"

Wade was quick to answer. Although the conversation had only been a minute long to this point, he felt he had explained enough to his son and his agitation was beginning to spill over. "That's for the sheriff to worry about. I'm sure he'll see to it that Carl gets what's coming to him."

"That's what Mr. Carter said?" Jimmy asked, making the naive assumption that the sheriff was already involved.

"If anybody asks you about any of this, you tell them to come to me," Wade said with an edge of anger. "Even Sheriff Carter or the Buells, or anybody else for that matter. You understand, son?"

Jimmy nodded.

"You know I've been talking to the sheriff since all of this has been going on. We'll just keep it that way for now. We're not going to worry about anything now except Kelly Jean. All right?"

"Uh-huh."

"Did your mother ask you the names of the other two men?"

"Uh – No. She didn't talk no more after you left."

"Don't say anything else about them. Understand?"

For a moment, Jimmy's mind spiraled into confusion so badly that his face dropped into an expression of wide-eyed shock. He recovered quickly and held his facial muscles as tautly as he could. His father appeared to flinch. Wade turned his face away for only a second, but he turned back and nodded once as if to say the problem had been solved. Then Jimmy, from outward appearances, seemed to accept his father's solutions and thereby willing to lay aside any other questions he may have had. The horrors of the night before were now to be stored away into the deep recesses of best-forgotten nightmares, and were never to be spoken of again. Kelly Jean was to be the family's main concern from now on since the North Road murder mystery had now been resolved and laid to rest.

      "Let's do one more thing, son," Wade continued. "Let's not mention Carl's name or the other men's names around Kelly Jean. All these names and such is scaring her. Until we can get all this figured out, let's keep quiet. Okay?"

      Jimmy nodded again. He didn't ask, nor did he think to ask why Carl's name frightened her so. It had something to do with the North Road incident, and Kelly Jean must have seen something. Perhaps, he finally decided, it was not anybody's name in particular that threw her into such a fright. Maybe, for some strange reason his young mind could not comprehend, she broke down because of all the excitement of the night as pertaining to his own horrible experience. He couldn't know. He couldn't put it together. He had other questions concerning motives and events. Particularly the motives of his father. He had nowhere to go to find answers to his questions, so he accepted his father's explanations. He must obey, as a good son should, and keep his secrets to himself as his father had asked. He had no choice but to believe that his father was in full control of things once again.

CHAPTER 6

Braxton merchants were just opening doors for the day's business when Tom pulled up to Jourdan's Feed and Supply on Front Street. It looked to be a busy day, just three days before Christmas. Shortly it would seem nearly every wagon rig and truck in the community would be in town making final supply runs in preparations for the holiday. The sheriff's car was conspicuously parked in front of the new Farmers' Co-op three doors down the street. Several men were standing with Sheriff Carter near the car. The sheriff raised his hand to wave, but Tom kept his gaze purposely short-ranged. Tom tethered the horse and stepped into the store.

The interior of the stout brick-walled building smelled of linseed oil and new lumber, and business was brisk in spite of the new competition down the street. J.C. Jourdan was busy filling a sack at the nail bin when he saw Tom coming in. Tom kept his eyes to the floor as he hurriedly armed up his few items and carried them to the cash register stand in the center of the store. Tom looked around to see farmers, merchants and sawmillers; some had excited, young children with them. It was a cheerfully noisy place with the sounds of laughter and high-spirited conversations echoing about like revival day at church. But Tom was an alien to all of this, as the anxiety of the day ahead overshadowed any positive sentiments he should have felt. J.C. finished an order at the cash register, then started with Tom's.

"How ya doin', Tom? Looks like Christmastime around here, doesn't it?" J.C. asked.

"Yeah, I reckon," Tom deadpanned.

The cash register rang several times before Tom spoke again. "You want to add a couple gallons of coal oil to that, J.C.?"

"All right – two gallons be enough?"

"Yeah, that's fine."

J.C. called his son from the tool racks nearby to take over the cash register. Tom paid his bill and agreed to meet J.C. behind the store to pick up the coal oil. By this time, the group around the sheriff had doubled in number. Now strong words were being thrown about and the sheriff appeared to be taking the brunt, particularly from a new face in the crowd.

Tom pulled the wagon back onto the road and was starting to head around to J.C.'s fuel storage outbuilding. Suddenly, a truck veered around the corner blocking his path. The gelding bolted to the side, pulling the wagon sideways in its tracks. The truck braked and steered around the wagon. A heavy, short-sleeved arm hung out the window. And as the truck rolled by, Tom watched the driver look back at him. The driver was stout and arguably intimidating in appearance. The dark, hardened eyes were shadowed beneath heavy brows that needed trimming. The eyes immediately reminded Tom of those of the malevolent stare he received from a large gray wolf he encountered once in the sorghum fields. There seemed to be the glint of a smile to the man's lips. It had a sadistic quality to it that would discourage anyone from smiling back.

The big man in the truck had done nothing to Tom except look at him, but Tom felt a welling of fear in his gut that he had not experienced since his childhood days when he once tangled with a schoolyard bully. The truck passed on and moved down the street toward Gene's car. The group stopped their discussion to watch the truck pass by. Every new face in town got the same treatment, but these townsfolk lingered too long after the truck passed. There were no smiles, no waves, no gesture of any kind to indicate welcome.

J.C. was waiting alone at the coal oil tank near the outbuilding. When Tom pulled up, J.C. quickly filled his purchase into the gallon jugs on the back of the wagon. Tom waited quietly, thinking of the day ahead, his eyes cast far into the trees at the end of the alley.

"Well, Tom, how's the family?" J.C. asked. Instantly realizing he had moved too fast, he added, "You seen your grandbaby yet? Jessica said Annie talks about him all the time at Sunday meeting."

Tom brightened up and said, "Yeah, they're supposed to be in tomorrow. We'll see him a few days before they go back to Huntsville. Who was that new fellow?"

J.C. failed to recognize the question.

"That fellow I seen in the truck a minute ago."

"Oh. That big fellow in the truck."

"Yeah – who is he? He's new around here."

"I hear that's the new Chicago man that took the old Howard Kallton tobacco farm. That old place a mile or two west of Paul Kallton. I heard he inherited it last year."

"Yeah? What's his name?"

"Kallton. Carl Kallton, I think."

"Kallton, huh?"

"That's the talk around town."

Tom fumbled with the reins a moment, his eyes returned to the trees. Then he looked down at J.C. and asked, "What's all the ruckus down at the Co-op? Carter still trying to scare up a few more votes?"

J.C. stepped up to the wagon, put a foot on a wheel spoke and wiped his brow on his sleeve. "Tom, you remember a fellow down on the south farms by the name of Earnest Jackson? One of Jackson's brothers is here accusing Gene and everybody else of foul play. Gene says his family in Georgia hasn't seen him since Thanksgiving, and he was supposed to be home for Christmas about a week ago. Gene's been – "

"Yeah," Tom said, interrupting; his mind still floating somewhere between here and the afternoon's duties at home. His tone was fatigued and antagonistic; the voice of a beaten man. "I might have seen him once or twice here in town, but ain't no telling what's happened to him down south amongst them Kalltons. They might have strung him up on a liquor run – who knows."

J.C., like everyone else, knew that only Roy Kallton, among the local Kallton families, ever produced and sold illicit beverages. But Tom clearly meant to throw them all into the same corrupted mold.

"Well, that's what the racket's all about." J.C. said. "We have any more trouble around here the state's going to come in for sure. I know Gene won't like it, but it might be the right thing for this county."

"I'll get the state in here if it's the last thing I do," Tom sniffed. "If I have to go to Nashville myself, I'll get the state in here. I'm getting old and tired, but I've got a few good years left in me. The governor's office and the district office knows what's going on down here, and I'll keep on them until they come down here and kick Carter's – "

Tom stopped himself short and shook his head. J.C. could not ignore the exhausted anguish in Tom's face. "Well, I wish you luck, Tom," J.C. said as he stepped away from the wagon. It seemed he felt there would be no gain for anyone if this conversation were to continue, so he made gestures to indicate he needed to return to the store. "We're all praying for you folks."

J.C. was a little shaken, but not surprised, by Tom's overbearing anger. He had known him long enough to appreciate his directness, but he was distressed by how far he had fallen into despair. He returned to the store, trying to believe that his friend was merely working out his grief in the only way he knew how.

Back on the street, most of the crowd around the sheriff had dispersed. Gene saw Tom turn onto the street and he waved to get his attention. Tom pulled up and stopped behind the sheriff's car, then looked down at the sheriff, but said nothing. Gene didn't bother to offer his hand, figuring Tom would be too sullen and slow to accept it. He attempted an affable smile.

"Hey, Tom. How's that grandson I've been hearing about? Doing fine, I hope."

"He's getting along just fine, Gene, just fine. What can I do for you?"

Gene eyed Tom for only a second. Already, Tom was impatient, and it caused Gene to wonder if he should bother. But duty called.

"Tom, word around here is your boy, Frank, is coming home today. I need to talk to him, Tom, if he's able. I've got no good leads on young James's killer and I need your help, if you're willing."

Tom shook his head in disgust and said, "You're still afraid to tangle with Wade Kallton aren't you, Gene? You know he's the one you should've locked up two months ago. Everybody knows he killed my boy, and my other one's near dead now because of him!"

The sheriff was already showing his frustration. He took a small step backwards as if to suddenly give up, but he defiantly returned to his original position.

"Tom, I've already talked to Wade till I'm blue in the face – and you know that!"

Tom popped the reins and the wagon started to move. The sheriff grimaced and grabbed the horse's bridle, halting the wagon. "Now look, Tom – they haven't lost a boy like you have, but they haven't come out of this very well either. Wade's daughter has just about lost her mind over this, and to listen to the preacher talk makes me think the Kallton girl might end up losing her mind completely. I've asked to talk to her again – you know I spoke to her for a few minutes on that day your boys got hurt – but Wade won't let me get near his place when I start talking like that now."

Tom quickly returned his response and spoke deliberately, and his anger was showing by the flush in his face and the strain in his voice. "Well, you won't talk to my boy either, Sheriff. You must not listen too well to the talk around here. My boy can't talk – he can't do nothing. The doctors have given up on him and they sent him home to die. Now git out of my way!"

Again, the sheriff grabbed the bridle. The horse reared up and shoved the wagon backward. Tom yelled him down and glared at Gene. Gene held the horse tight and rubbed its nose. Every pedestrian and merchant on the street, it seemed, stopped moving and turned to watch. Gene became aware of this and spoke loudly. It all worsened Tom's attitude toward the sheriff.

"Tom, I don't know what I have to do to get all you people to listen to me. But I want everyone to know I can't do this job alone. If you're all determined to fight me on every turn, then maybe it's time you all get someone else for your sheriff the next time around. I'm just about fed up!"

Tom popped the reins hard and the wagon jerked away, leaving the sheriff in a swirling cloud of dust and flying pebbles. Tom never ventured a glance back and raced through town like a runaway. The thoughtlessness of the sheriff played hard on Tom's mind, and he drove the horse hard for the first half mile toward home before calming down and bringing himself back under a semblance of control. The sheriff's suggestion that the Kallton's hardship was somehow equal to his own grief grated like a dull saw blade to the head, extinguishing any hope that he might find some small measure of solace in the quiet, uneventful trip back home.

***

As was greatly feared, Frank died on the dusty trip home. He was taken straight to the funeral home and buried the next day in a plain box next to his brother. No tears were shed. No funeral service or memorial of any sort was done. Then Christmas came and departed like an unnoticed breeze. The first snow fell in early January and remained for several days before succumbing to the warming sun. The rest of the winter was mild as expected. Springtime bloomed as colorfully as anyone could remember. Annie's lilacs along the front porch filled the house with their aroma, but it could do nothing to placate the spirit of melancholy that had imprisoned its inhabitants.

For the first time in his life, the preacher felt that something inconceivably malicious was about to happen. The deaths of the two young men were horrible enough, but it was probably not all over yet. Now something stirred in the preacher's soul whenever he looked at Tom Buell. Tom had not abandoned his vindictive persona over the cold days leading up to Frank's death. He said nothing to the preacher concerning his second son's death. And now the preacher could see something in his eyes that held the essence of a lost soul, a vindictive spirit – or a secret plan.

CHAPTER 7

Gene closed the office up early and headed south with his deputy, Harvey Carlson, to investigate yet another far-fetched rumor concerning the murders of the Buell boys. The road south from Braxton made a straight shot to the narrow dirt road dividing the Kallton farms to the south from timber company land, the Buell farms, and the Beulah community on further to the north. Car drivers usually avoided this road, but Gene wanted to drive to the end of it to visit an old plantation house he remembered from many years ago. He had heard that an heir to the property had recently returned from Chicago to take up residence there – whether permanently or temporarily, he didn't know. A recent rumor had it that a vehicle was heard moving, or racing, westward toward the house shortly after the murder incident on the road back in October. The rumor had been traced back to Paul Kallton, but he could only state that he thought he had heard such a vehicle on the day of the incident. There had been so much excitement with the dogs and farm hands, he couldn't be sure. Invariably, Paul had simply forgotten to mention it to anyone until very recently.

The sheriff had grown tired of dealing with the numerous theories and scenarios that had been cranking out of the rumor mill since the incident, but he remained relentless in his investigative pursuit. He had quickly learned that most rumors were, in reality, busybody discussions that had quickly gotten out of hand and taken on a life of their own and soon developed into a 'real probability that required investigation.'

The old road seemed to wind forever through tall pine timbers and through deep draws where the road had washed out through lack of maintenance. The sheriff stopped a couple of times at the washouts to investigate the tracks in the soft soil. The road had been recently and regularly traversed by what the sheriff determined to be made by the same vehicle. Then, as his car approached the last half-mile to the house, the woods began to open up to broad overgrown fields of tall saplings and heavy brush. Very little of the wide-open cotton and tobacco fields that had been cultivated here for generations was evident.

The sheriff and the deputy pulled up to one end of the long front porch of the house. It had been many years since the sheriff had last seen the big two-story house, and he had remembered it then as being a well-maintained, miniaturized version of the giant sugar plantation mansions he had seen in Louisiana. But what he saw before him now was not much more than a gray ghost of the past. The old house still appeared structurally sound, but the white exterior finish had all peeled off, leaving a dark and weather-beaten finish with rotting boards on the porch and all along the lower perimeter of the house. The steps leading up to the porch were over-built with hewed stones and showed almost no deterioration like the rest of the house. The roof structure appeared intact, but many of the green tiles were missing. But the front door was new and the beginnings of repairs were evident where pieces of wood siding had been removed exposing the unweathered framing studs inside the walls.

The sheriff and the deputy walked along the porch beneath the shade of three massive red oaks spaced evenly in a straight line across the front lawn. The yard encircling the house had grown up with scrub brush and grass, but a well-worn dirt driveway passed along the front and meandered down into the woods behind the house. The big smokehouse still stood at the edge of the woods, but its roof was near caving in. The wellhouse, a few steps from the back porch, appeared to be under repair. The men circled on around the house to find three windows boarded up on the inside with new lumber. Gene gazed southward to the new driveway that had been cut through the trees. It shot a straight line to Kallton Farms Road – a convenient passage to the southwestern-most portion of the county.

The back door at the top of a waist-high porch was new like the front. A large, symmetrical rack of deer antlers hung on the eave of the back porch. The eight-point rack still had some fleshy residue and fur on the crown, so Gene figured it was a fairly recent kill. They remained a moment to admire the antlers, then they headed back to the car.

The men had just started to crank up and end the day when Gene stepped back out of the car and turned an ear toward the road. Harvey walked around the car and stood next to him. Shortly, the sound of a motor vehicle could be heard on the road coming toward the house. Then the vehicle, a pickup truck, topped the nearest hill and barreled down toward them. Gene could see a driver and a passenger inside. The truck was coming on fast, throwing up a roiling cloud of dust behind it, and the driver didn't begin to slow down until he entered the yard. He veered the truck around the sheriff's car and slid to a stop in an angry spray of dust and pebbles at the other end of the porch.

Momentarily, the driver stepped out of the truck. The other man got out, threw back an uncombed mass of red hair, then jumped up on the porch and walked briskly to the front door of the house. He opened the unlocked door and walked in without recognizing the sheriff's presence, who had by this time walked up to the steps. The physical stature of the driver immediately impressed the sheriff. He was of average height, but he was built as hefty and solid as any man Gene had ever seen. The broad bulges that displaced his clothing spoke of the firmness of muscular mass rather than any genetic inclination toward flabbiness. The big man stood eyeing the sheriff from the far end of the porch. The sheriff nodded and spoke his greeting. The big man did not respond. He turned and walked to the back of the truck and lifted out a large wooden box laden with hand tools and returned to drop the box up on the porch near the steps. The big man stopped about five yards from the sheriff and his deputy. He shifted his weight to one side and placed his hands on his hips, then looked at the sheriff as if to await an explanation for his presence. Gene stepped forward, extended his hand and introduced himself. "Sheriff Gene Carter," he said.

The big man looked down at Gene's hand and after a moment he took the offer then replaced his hand to his hip. "Carl Kallton," the big man said in a deep barreling voice.

The sheriff studied Carl for a moment before speaking again. Carl carried himself in a manner as though he were confident and fearless; an aspect that Gene would soon determine to be authentic. His lips appeared to carry a subtle, derisive smile. But to the sheriff, Carl's most prominent feature was his eyes. Deep-set under heavy eyebrows, his dark unblinking eyes bore into the sheriff like a spinning drill bit. There was no unsteadiness in his manner, but Gene made a conscious effort to build his own strength of demeanor to match Carl's for every moment he gazed at him. "You must be one of Howard Kallton's kin," Gene said.

"Yep – that I am," Carl answered with no change in his posture or expression. Then he asked in a slightly more brusque tone, "What's your business here, Sheriff?"

"Well, Mr. Kallton, I reckon you heard by now, if you have been around these parts very long, there was a right young Buell boy killed up on the road here back in October," Gene said, motioning toward the road. "Another one got hurt pretty bad too. But he lingered for a while before he died, too. Thought you might help us if you heard any rumors about it." Carl remained solid and motionless while the sheriff spoke, and didn't respond. "You get much traffic on the road here, Mr. Kallton?" Gene continued, after several moments of uneasy silence.

"You're the first one this year."

At that moment, the red-headed man stepped out the door, walked across the porch and picked up the toolbox and turned to walk back into the house. Carl kept his eyes on the sheriff and called to the man. "Billy, you heard any talk about any Buell boys?"

Billy glanced nervously at the sheriff and the deputy and said, "Cain't say I 'ave, Carl." Then he quickly turned and walked back through the door, pushing it shut behind him.

"How about a fellow by the name of Earnest Jackson? Heard of him?" Gene asked. Carl remained unmoved. And unanswering. Gene said, "Well, if you hear anything, let me know. Let's go, deputy."

Gene sternly motioned for Harvey to reboard the car. The sheriff got in and started the motor, shifted into reverse and looked through the windshield at Carl. Carl hadn't moved from his position or changed his stance. His eyes remained full-strength on the sheriff as the car slowly rolled back on the driveway. Gene eased the car around and headed back up the road. He pulled a small square of tobacco from his shirt pocket, jammed it in his side teeth and twisted off a plug. Neither man spoke, both seemingly made mute by the unnerving encounter with the big man.

***

It was a while yet till dark, so the sheriff and his deputy returned to Braxton Road and turned south toward the other Kallton farms instead of heading back north to town. The roads to the south were easily accessible and well maintained, making the ten-minute drive to Kallton Farms Road seem even shorter.

Paul Kallton was rebuilding a wagon bed outside his cow barn when the sheriff pulled up to the gate nearby. Paul saw the sheriff and the deputy, but didn't stop working until they walked up alongside the wagon. "Grab a hammer, boys, there's plenty to do 'round here," he said with a smile. He shoved his cap back, wiped his brow, and leaned back against the wagon seat as if to take a break from the work.

"I've never been too handy with a hammer, Paul," Gene said, returning the smile. He leaned up against the side of the wagon and after a few more greetings, got down to the business at hand.

"Paul, I need to ask you a few more questions, if you can spare a minute?" he asked, looking up at Paul for a response.

"Well, Gene, you've about questioned me out. You got something new?"

"I don't know," the sheriff said, lifting a foot and resting it on a wheel spoke. "You know a fellow by the name of Carl Kallton? He's supposed to be kin to the Howard Kallton klan. And I reckon he's kin to you and Wade too. I just come from the old Howard Kallton place, and he seems to be staying there now."

Paul's weak smile slowly dropped as Gene spoke. He looked away from Gene for a moment, then looked back at him and said, "Yeah, I know of him. I remember him back when we was boys. He was rough then, and I don't reckon he's changed much since. He's a cousin from way back. But I don't claim him."

"You mind telling me what you know about him?"

"Well, I don't know much, Gene," Paul said, glancing down at the sheriff as if he preferred the subject be changed. "I was just a little feller then, but I remember him leaving here back about ninety-eight with his mother, papa, and a little sister for Chicago. Best I recall, his father sold out to his brother Howard and went up north to work in the mills."

"You say he was rough – why do you say that, Paul?"

"I reckon he left here when he was about fourteen or fifteen. Meanest young pecker-wood you ever seen. Every one of us Kallton boys was afraid of him. Wade said he seen him once whip a full-grown man just before he left for Chicago. Liked to skin't him alive. Wade said he was bigger than the man he beat up, even back then. Seemed always looking for a fight, and I don't believe he ever got whipped himself." Then Paul leaned back looking at the sheriff and added with a touch of apprehensiveness in his voice, "Yeah, he was one mean pecker-wood all right. I was glad to hear he was gone. Then I heard somewhere that Carl Dean was back trying to stake a claim on the old Howard Kallton place. Since he was the last of them, I reckon he got it." Then Paul smiled and said, "I hope he sells out and goes back north like his papa!"

"Carl Dean – Carl Dean Kallton? Is that his name?" Gene asked.

Paul nodded and said, "I hear he got in trouble a few times with the law in Chicago and spent a little time in jail. I remember Wade telling me once he heard Carl got picked up for killing a man in a bootleg run out of Chicago about fifteen years ago, but somehow he didn't do time for that one. Any news we ever got about Carl over the years seemed to always be bad news." Then Paul looked back and forth between the sheriff and the deputy and asked, "Did you see him at the big house a while ago?"

"Yeah, we did."

"How'd he treat you?"

"He didn't say much. Guess he was expecting a little trouble."

Gene turned around to a voice that was yelling from the back porch of the house. *"Hi, Gene!"* It was Mrs. Sarah, Wade's and Paul's mother. Paul's fair auburn-haired wife, Ruth, stepped out onto the porch beside her to fetch something from a storage coop.

"How're you, Mrs. Sarah? And you too, pretty Mrs. Ruth?" Gene hollered back with a tip of his hat. The ladies waved and returned to the work at hand.

The sheriff turned back to Paul. He took a moment to pull off his hat, brush back his hair and replace his hat. "Carl had a fellow with him named Billy. I used to see him around town a long time ago. You know him?"

"Billy Wilson? Long, bushy red hair and whiskers?"

"That's right."

"Yeah, he's a transient worker from somewhere west of here. He worked for me and Wade a while a couple of years ago. Didn't feel like I could trust him, though, so I let him go. Think he went down to work with Roy at the sawmills for a while after that. I reckon he just works short jobs for whoever will hire him. Says he's got a wife, but I don't know."

"A n'er-do-well, from my recollection."

"I seem to recall you had a run-in with him a time or two."

Gene nodded but offered nothing to continue the discourse. He looked to the empty dog pen and asked, "Where are your bloodhounds, Paul?"

"I got rid of 'em. They wouldn't track right any more after the North Road killing. Whoever whipped them really messed them up. Blinded one of them."

Gene stepped away from the wagon, placed both hands in his pockets, and casually walked to the barn gate. He looked out across the farmyard toward the rambling one-story farmhouse nestled amid tall, skinny pines that Paul was born in and now lived in with his mother, wife, and two children. The farmstead was well tended and manicured, and the pastoral landscape was pleasing to the eyes. Then, as if snapping out of a trance, the sheriff turned to leave and said, "Well, I appreciate your cooperation, Paul. Wish I could get the same out of Wade, your brother. Give your wife and young'uns my best."

Paul turned back to work on the wagon. Gene and Harvey returned to the car. He started the motor and immediately cut it off, stepped back out and walked back to the wagon. "Paul, when did you last see your cousin Carl?"

"I reckon about thirty years ago."

"Would you know him if you saw him today?"

"Uh, I don't know if I would or not, Gene."

"You ever hear if Carl was around here about the time of the North Road shootout?"

"Well, like everybody else, I heard that somebody was coming back to get the Howard Kallton place. And I seen a new driveway-cut going up toward the house about a mile or so down the road here, like somebody was working on the old place. That could have been Carl, or somebody working for him." Paul quickly realized what the sheriff was asking and added, "How do you figure, Gene?"

"Well, if you recall, we all spent the whole day looking for Kelly Jean. I didn't get around to checking the road near the big house until that Friday, a couple of days later. And I never thought to check the old house itself. That could've given him plenty of time to leave the county until things settled down." Gene paused to unpuzzle his thoughts, then added, "Tire tracks was all over the place, but I knew you, Wade, and the boys hunted your coon and squirrels up that way, so I didn't give it as much thought as I should have."

"I see where you're going, Gene, but why would Carl Dean want to get tangled up in hurting the Buell boys? Wade and his men didn't want to hurt nobody when they was chasing those two young'uns. We was just looking out for Kelly Jean."

"We done covered all that, Paul. No need to rehash it," Gene said, almost defensively.

"No, I mean, what would be his motive? Anyway, I don't think he would know a Buell from a fence post."

"Well, if I could find a reasonable motive, then finding a reasonable suspect would be easy."

Paul thought for a moment and said, "J.C. tells me about somebody seeing a big ugly fellow in a truck in Braxton just before Christmas. Think he says you was in town that same day."

Gene remembered watching the truck roll by the Co-op that Saturday morning. He remembered the big man in the truck as being the same one he saw today. The sheriff nodded and said, "Yeah, I remember." Figuring little was being accomplished here, the sheriff turned to walk back to the car and stopped at the gate when Paul called to him.

"Gene, whatever become of that Earnie Jackson fellow? I don't hear much about that anymore."

The sheriff again nodded and said, "Well, we don't know. His family was making inquiries. You know Jackson's brother was here from Georgia one day looking for him – a real hell-raiser. You sure you and Wade haven't seen him this year?"

"Well, no, Gene," Paul answered, a bit disconcerted. "I think he might have worked with us a while a couple of years ago. But I can't be sure, though. We have worked a lot of transients over the years like everybody else, you know."

"Yeah – sorry to ask again. I just can't seem to find anybody who knows who he was working for this last year. But let me ask you one more thing before I go. I know I've asked you before, and I hope you don't get offended."

"That's all right."

"Can you tell me anything at all about Wade's girl – Kelly Jean? Any new developments?"

"'fraid not, Gene," Paul said with a tone of futility. "Like I've told you – I've only seen her once since the killing. And Esther never tells Ruth much, as always. I wish I could help you."

Gene nodded, sure that he had breached far enough into the subject. "Thanks again, Paul. Give my best to your family."

The deputy was now snoozing soundly in the car but snapped upright in the seat when the sheriff sharply slapped the fender. The sheriff decided one more stop was in order before calling it a day. He pulled the car back onto the road and drove back eastward several hundred yards to the Wade Kallton family farmstead next door.

Shortly, Gene rolled to a stop at the entrance to the driveway and looked up the gently sloping wheelpath to the house located atop a high bald hill. He could see Jimmy Kallton near the woodpile beside the smokehouse looking back down the hill at him. None of the rest of the family could be seen outside the house. The sheriff stuck his arm out the car window and waved. Jimmy hesitated, then waved back and started to walk toward the house. When the sheriff throttled up the motor Jimmy broke and ran to the house. Gene stopped the car at the edge of the yard, turned off the motor, and honked the horn once. In a moment, Esther opened the door and yelled to the sheriff, *"He's out on the east end. He ought to be in about suppertime!"*

The sheriff waved without speaking, started the car and rolled back down the driveway to the road. He looked back up toward the house in time to witness Jimmy racing on foot toward the barn. The boy jumped the gate in a single leap and began running across the upper pasture toward the east end of the farm. It took several minutes for the sheriff to return to Braxton Road; the eastern boundary of the farm. Soon, he entered the lower pasture through a gate in a wire fence that followed the edge of the road for several hundred yards northward. He honked the horn twice and gazed across the pasture looking for Wade. About sixty head of beef cattle were spread out across the pasture and, like curious children, they all stopped grazing at once and looked toward the sheriff's car. Gene turned the car onto a wide path that traveled along the fence and drove to the northern section of the pasture. Another wire fence divided the north line of the pasture from a heavily wooded area just to the north.

Gene stopped at a wide wooden gate at the north fence, cut the motor, stepped out of the car and honked the horn again. A distant voice called from deep in the woods, so he hit the horn once again. He was sure he heard the call again. Harvey pointed into the trees at a movement near the top of the hill. Jimmy soon materialized out of the trees below the nearest ridge, and the sheriff walked to the gate to get a closer look. Jimmy was racing westward through the trees back in the direction of the house. The sheriff could see the boy running harem-scarem as if making a desperate retreat in battle. Jimmy continued on westward, never glancing in the sheriff's direction.

Gene and the deputy stood at the fence quietly looking into the trees in the area where Jimmy had just departed. A wagon path from the gate sloped up the ridge and disappeared over it. Soon, the silhouette of someone carrying a rifle stepped out of the trees and came walking quickly down the path toward the sheriff. Wade Kallton, with his ever-present hunting rifle, walked up to the gate and rested the gun against the gatepost. As usual, he nodded without smiling and spoke his one word greeting, "Gentlemen?" The sheriff reached over the gate and shook Wade's reluctant hand.

"Good to see you again, Wade. You got any strays up in there we can help you with?" Gene asked, motioning up into the trees.

Wade shook his head and said, "I got a big shed up in the woods there I'm cleaning out for some new hay come winter."

"Didn't know you had a barn up in there."

"It's just a shed. We built it back before Papa died so he wouldn't have to tote hay for the bottom pasture. We meant to extend the pasture up to it but Papa died and we never got around to it after that," Wade said. Keeping his ever-serious demeanor, he asked, "What brings you boys down this way? Must be important."

Gene studied Wade's face for any reason to bother. Wade had grown weary of all the endless questions and discussions, and had long ago begun to carry an attitude of indifference toward Gene's efforts to solve the North Road murders.

"Could be, Wade. I just come from the old Howard Kallton place. We met up with a fellow by the name of Carl Dean Kallton. You know him?"

Without hesitation, Wade asked, "You talked to Paul about that?"

"Just left his place."

"Well, he's told you all I know."

Gene felt himself begin to tremble with anger. He drew his eyes away from Wade for a moment in an effort to restrain his impulses. He thought he was ready for this; he already knew Wade was short-fused. He resented the fact that this man kept his family behind a fortress of silence and quarantine because of some vague purpose to protect his daughter. It was understood that she had been injured, emotionally or otherwise, but Gene could see no reason for such secrecy and melodrama. To Gene, Wade was selfish and egotistical. Simply, Wade carried an air of moral superiority and self-sufficiency over the sheriff because Wade was a family man with a wife and children and the accompanying responsibilities; whereas the sheriff wasn't. Gene was regularly asking for help in order to make his job easier, but Wade handled all his problems alone and in silence, never seeking help from anyone. So it would seem, Gene figured, that Wade felt that the Sheriff should perform his duties in like fashion, and stop bothering everyone. But that was not the nature of law enforcement. But Wade seemed oblivious to this fact.

The Sheriff had just seen Jimmy racing on foot from the house and then returning from the shed back to the house. This is a disturbed and twisted family, Gene thought. The family systematically worked against him, as Wade's son had just demonstrated in warning his father of the Sheriff's presence. Didn't Wade want answers like everyone else? What was he hiding? Was he guilty somehow? At first glance, it might seem there was no other conclusion.

Gene pushed his hat back farther on his head and leaned hard against the gate. He looked intently at Wade and said with exasperation, "You're still intent on making my job hard, aren't you, Wade? I feel like everybody's told me all they know, except maybe you. I don't know why you want to hold out on me like this. If you all are innocent like I think you are, then you don't have anything to be afraid of."

"I've told you all I know, Gene. I must have told you three times now. It's all over. If I hear anything else, I'll call for you. Otherwise, I'll handle my own affairs myself. Always have. Always will. There anymore questions, Sheriff?"

Gene, realizing the futility of continuing, pushed away from the gate and said, "Just wish you wouldn't turn your family against me, Wade. They seem to scatter like ants whenever they see me coming. A rumor tells it that your daughter hasn't been seen out of the house since the shootout, way back in October. All this tells me you're a suspect, whether I want to believe it or not."

"You listen to me, goddamnit!" Wade countered. "Kelly Jean's in no frame of mind to do anything, much less talk to you or anybody else about that. I, as her father, will determine the time and place. Any man that tries to go around me to get to her won't live long enough to try again. Besides, you've already had your chance when you talked to her after that Buell boy was killed."

Gene rocked back one step and said, "You know Tom and Annie Buell came out of this a whole hell of a lot worse than you and Esther, Wade. Nearly half their family's dead because of this, and your daughter is the only one that's seen anything that might help."

Wade answered by snatching up his rifle and glaring at the sheriff. Harvey flinched away and quietly ducked into the car. Gene shook his head in futility and turned toward the car to leave, but turned back as Wade began marching away. "I'll probably get back to you every so often, Wade. I'll try to leave you alone, but I have to do my job as the people of this county elected me to do."

The structure of it all was maddening, and Gene's mind never rested from it. Tom Buell was hard to manage because of his anger toward everyone involved, but at least he would talk – vindictively and belligerently – but he would talk. Wade was another matter altogether. Gene felt free to discuss all things with Paul, but he could sense that Wade held secrets and worked from motives that were difficult, if not impossible, to understand. He understood Wade's simple desire to protect his family, especially his fragile daughter. But why would he not at least show some deference for Gene's efforts to find the true perpetrator of the crime? Gene searched his own heart for anything that could cause such caustic behavior in Wade, but he was coming up short with answers.

Gene had no choice but to keep striving by pretending to search for answers. He came to conclude that he was alone in his quest. He was tired and fed up; his efforts as fruitless as peach trees in winter. But he could never entertain thoughts of slowing down or quitting. It was a futile race to nowhere that had to be run as if a worthy goal was in sight. But all he could see ahead was a barren landscape as far as the eye could see.

CHAPTER 8

A quiet and peaceful night was being blessed upon the Wade Kallton family household. Everyone went to bed at nearly the same moment with hardly a word spoken. Hours later, the rest of the family was sleeping soundly when Jimmy woke up suddenly and rolled over in his bed toward the window. The moonlight in his eyes caused him to squint and to turn back away from the window. He pulled a quilt over his head to warm his cold cheeks, but jerked it back down. He lay still a moment and listened. The intermittent popping noise he heard, at first sounding like popcorn in a hot skillet, seemed to be coming from the front room. He listened as the popping continued and he wondered if the embers in the fireplace were still smoldering. Then he remembered that no fire had been made that night, so he leaned up and rubbed his eyes and listened more closely. The tempo of the popping quickly slowed down, and then stopped altogether. Jimmy had not noticed the dogs barking down in the pens near the barn until the popping had stopped. He thought that a fox or a lynx may be trying for the chicken house, but he hoped the dogs would scare it off and leave him to roll back in bed and finish his sleep.

Soon, the popping started again and Jimmy's curiosity ruined his last hope of sleep. He sat up fully, pushed the window open and listened. Then the popping stopped again as if a switch had been turned off, but the dogs continued barking. He pushed the window up higher and stuck his head out into the cold air and turned an ear toward the barn. Over the din of the dogs he could now detect a strange chorus of otherworldly voices, animalistic in nature, which flowed up the hill to the house like a wind blown fog. The cattle were in a fit of some sort and seemed frightfully intent on escaping a commotion in the lower pasture.

Jimmy dragged out of bed and stumbled to the front room. He worked the latch and opened the door to the porch. A lot of barnyard racket emanated from the barn and upper pasture and the dog pens. Several agitated cattle were stomping around aggressively inside the gate, some shoving against it, and he could hear several others stampeding up the hill toward the barn.

He looked around until his eyes caught a strange light lifting from the woods north of the lower pasture in the distance. A pink glow with the likeness of foxfire bulged into the sky above the trees. Jimmy stood half-hypnotized by the light until he spotted the tiny fiery sparks spiraling upwards into the sky like lightening bugs around a light. Four gunshots rang out from the lower pasture forcing him to instinctively duck to dodge any incoming fire.

Jimmy, it seemed with all his strength, slammed the door shut. The house shook to its foundation and Jimmy ran through the house shouting with the babbling incoherence of a terrified child. His father threw himself from bed and into the front room. Esther, in bed with Kelly Jean, screamed out as if being jerked awake from a nightmare. She scrambled to find anything to light the house. Wade grabbed his son, both of them falling against walls in the darkness. Jimmy cried aloud what he had seen and heard. Quickly, father and son jammed on pants and boots and raced out the front door, leaving Esther to calm her now-terrified and crying daughter.

Wade yelled to Jimmy to saddle up two horses as he turned back to the house. He grabbed his rifle off the mantle and ran back out kicking the screen door completely off the hinges. He fired two shots into the air in rapid succession causing the gunshots in the lower pasture to immediately stop. There being only enough time for bridles and reins, it seemed only seconds had passed before Wade and Jimmy were blazing barebacked across the upper pasture to do whatever battle was awaiting them out on the east end.

Immense, swirling masses of sparks were pouring upward into the sky. Some of the larger embers stayed burning long enough to float over and fall into the lower pasture. The cattle were in obvious beastly confusion, as they could be heard making unnerving guttural noises from all over the east end. Wade and Jimmy, both fighting to stay upright on slick-backed mounts, were fast approaching the eastern edge of the upper pasture. A number of cattle were running, some stampeding, against them toward the upper pasture to escape the commotion down on the other end.

As Wade and Jimmy began their descent down the slope to the lower pasture, a car's headlights switched on brightly on Braxton Road and started moving south. Wade yanked back the reins, dismounted, and took careful aim at the car and fired. He rechambered, aimed, and fired again. He cranked in another round and paused to watch the car. It was still moving south, so he fired once again before it disappeared behind a wide stand of trees at the south end of the pasture. Jimmy had stopped to watch his father, but started again as Wade remounted and headed toward the fire.

The outer walls of the hay barn had just started collapsing when Wade and Jimmy stopped and tethered the horses thirty yards away. The roaring fire was still going strong and the heat was still too intense for a close approach. Several cedar trees near the shed had spent most of their fuel and were left smoldering. Streaks of glowing red could be seen in the upper reaches of the scorched trees.

Father and son worked to put out some of the smaller fires around the shed with pine boughs. Shortly, Wade tossed his bough into the fire and called for Jimmy to follow, leaving the fire at the shed to burn itself out. They remounted and headed back to the lower pasture. As they approached, bizarre, haunting cries echoed from across the pasture, some of them not at all like those that should be coming from animals that Jimmy was familiar with. Motionless hulks of dead cattle, scattered across the pasture, were visible in the moonlight. Others appeared to be crawling or sitting on their haunches like giant dogs. Jimmy watched one nearby struggling in the dirt with two strong front legs; its rear portions paralyzed by a heavy gauge shotgun slug to its mid-spine. Wade dismounted, handed the reins to Jimmy, and marched urgently to the suffering steer. Jimmy jerked his eyes away as his father unceremoniously put it out of its agony. He did the same to another with the last round of ammunition.

Back at the house, Kelly Jean sat whimpering in the front room. Esther was terrified to tears that her daughter may break down into a screaming tantrum again, but Kelly Jean managed to stay alert and relatively lucid through it all. Soon, she calmed down enough to allow her mother to light several lamps in the front room and kitchen. Being distracted, Esther failed to notice the escape car racing westward on the road down before the house.

Wade and Jimmy returned to the house, and after several minutes of desperate, nerve-wracked accounting, Jimmy was instructed to ride to his uncle Paul's to get him to fetch the sheriff in Braxton. Jimmy slowly rode the little trail that connected the two farms, and wept quietly all the way.

***

Annie woke up in the stillest hour of the night. She was lying on her side facing the wall, and she remained still, listening. The absence of the sound of her husband's breathing, or his movements through the house caused her heart to beat fast. The moonlight outside reflected enough light through the windows to illuminate the room with a gray haze. She slowly rolled over while watching the shadows on the wall. All of them were still, so she looked next to her to find her husband gone. She softly called to him and listened. She called again, more loudly, and was frightened by the continued silence. She pushed herself up and stepped onto the cold wooden floor. She held her heart and tried to convince herself that there was nothing really unusual about Tom being up in the night. He had done it many times before when he had things on his mind and couldn't sleep. It had even become an expected ritual in recent weeks. But tonight the air was so still and devoid of the essence of life that Annie could feel the coldness in her soul. There seemed no doubt that Tom was somewhere outside the house – but somewhere far away.

She forced herself to move slowly as she stepped into her house shoes and slipped on a robe and walked to the front door. The door was shut and latched, so she lit a small lamp and carried it down the narrow hallway that led to the kitchen. A tiny storage room off the hallway doubled as a clothes closet. It had a curtain hung over the doorway. Annie noticed that the curtain had been pushed aside, revealing the fact that Tom's heavy boots and hunting coat were both missing. She moved to the kitchen and looked out the back door to the car shed at the far edge of the yard. The car was missing. She retreated to the heater stove near the center of the kitchen and set the lamp on it. She looked toward the hallway and said softly, "Tom Buell, you can't do this to us."

She felt herself draw over and she almost tripped into a chair near the stove. She feared the worst as she recalled the angry words spoken shortly after her second son's funeral just two weeks ago. As they were riding home in the car, Tom vented his frustration and grief only once through an angry threat directed at Wade Kallton. Everyone else was quiet, and Annie was stunned to tears by Tom's venomous tone. She had determined, or she had convinced herself, that she was the only one who was able to hear his words in the rumbling car because no one had spoken of the threat since. She had never heard her husband speak with such violently threatening words before, not even after the death of their son, James. But she had not discouraged her husband from talking, hoping that he was just simply working the feelings of frustration out of his system.

She looked down into the coal pail next to the stove. She exhaled a quivering sigh as several unspeakable scenarios stroked through her mind. Quickly, as if to distract herself, she stood up and loaded one side of the stove with several chunks of coal using the little hand shovel from the pail. Soon, the kitchen was warmed from the hissing fire. It was still almost three hours till breaking of dawn, but it seemed that eternity lay before her as she watched and waited for her husband's arrival from the terrible deeds she had imagined for him, but trusting he had not committed on this night. The faith in God they had shared together over the years, she believed, would hold them in His grace and at least keep their actions, if not their words, on the straight and narrow through any trial.

She sat with closed eyes for several minutes next to the stove, praying for her husband's safe return. Then she stood up and walked to the window over the washbasin and continued praying as she looked out to the little dormant vegetable garden illuminated in the moonlight. Her long, gray and white-streaked hair, beguiling her Pentecostal upbringing, hung straight as broom straw down to her elbows. She reached up and worked it into a tight bun on the back of her head and then pulled out several barrette-combs from her robe pocket and placed them in, holding the bun in the familiar daytime style.

The prayers had made her feel a bit comforted, so she lit another lamp in the kitchen and left it on the dinner table to illuminate that side of the room. Shortly, the sound of an approaching vehicle drew her back to the window, and she looked toward the road to see the trees near the road begin to illuminate from the approaching headlights. The car came up the drive and rolled slowly past the kitchen window and down to the shed. The car door opened and shut quickly, and Tom walked briskly, almost trotting, to the back porch outside the kitchen. He kicked off his boots on the porch and tossed them into a large washtub already half-filled with water. He quickly washed the mud off the boots and slammed them against a post, knocking off any remaining mud and water. He had looked once into the kitchen through the back door while cleaning the boots and saw his wife standing inside watching him. He said nothing as he worked with urgent attention on the boots.

He tossed the boots down near the door and walked back to the tub. He tilted it up over the edge of the porch, allowing the muddy water to pour out onto the ground. He walked back toward the door while removing his coat and found his wife standing in the open doorway holding the boots and reaching her hand out to take his coat. They walked in together without speaking and placed the coat and boots back in the little room. Annie returned to the kitchen and blew out the lamps and closed the vents on the stove. She pulled the combs from her hair allowing it to fall back down.

Shortly, they were back in bed, still without a word spoken between them. And soon they were fast asleep once again.

CHAPTER 9

"What are we going to do now?" Esther asked somberly, standing with her arms crossed.

Wade was seated at the kitchen table. Kelly Jean was sitting on the back porch watching Jimmy toss rocks across the yard, occasionally throwing with angry force against the smokehouse. Kelly Jean seemed regressed back into her silent state – none-speaking and humorless – and had sat nearly motionless all morning.

It had been several days since the cattle killings and probably as many as a thousand locals and non-locals had visited the carnage to see for themselves what a field of dead cattle looked like. Wade had grown exasperated by all the gawkers and was ready to ward them off with gunfire. From the first day they had paraded by, sometimes stopping to park along the fence, watching Wade and the sheriff and state investigators ply the field for clues. When some of them began standing along the fence with cameras and binoculars, Wade lost his composure and brusquely ordered Gene to scatter them. A newspaper reporter from Nashville turned pale when Wade aimed his rifle at him from twenty yards away.

Jimmy and Kelly Jean were kept ignorant of, and isolated from, as much of the goings-on as was possible. But Jimmy lacked the proper inclination to refrain from asking obvious questions. "What was Jimmy asking you a while ago, Wade?" Esther asked when she realized she would be getting no answer to her first question.

She was crossing the line with her husband in asking about intimate conversations between father and son. Kelly Jean was her concern and Esther had her hands full with her. But the belligerent sullenness she had noticed growing in her son in recent weeks was beginning to push her into unfriendly territory with Wade. He resented any such imposition that might expose any weakness in his competence as a father. But Esther stood firm.

"Wade?"

"Esther, he just wanted to know who shot up the cows. That's all," Wade answered stoutly.

"What'd you say?"

"I said, we don't know yet."

"That's all?"

Wade nodded.

"I thought I heard him say something about Carl Kallton."

Wade jerked up a bit. "I made it clear to Jimmy he ain't got anything to worry about. I told him again to keep quiet about that. Around Kelly Jean – remember? And I told him what everybody else already knows. It was the Buells. Tom Buell."

"I thought you said we don't know yet."

Wade angrily eyed his wife. It was the only time she had spoken Carl's name since the night of Jimmy's terror at the big oak. Esther turned away to the basin and cinched her mouth. Wade looked out the door and watched his children for several moments. He had categorized the losses and assessed and reassessed the situation a hundred times in his mind. He needed time to himself to mentally step through the situation one foot at a time. Like most farmers at the time, he had no insurance to cover such contingencies; he hadn't even considered it. He wasn't even sure it was available. Money was always tight and every spare cent was needed at home for more immediate priorities. But he had options, and he needed time to think. He needed for everyone to get away and let him breathe. He had slept only a few hours since the cattle massacre, and it was only just now that it was beginning to show in his posture. He stood up and looked out the window at his daughter. Still, she watched Jimmy and his rocks. "Uh, you and Kelly Jean go home to your folks in Parsons for a while. I'll handle things around here," he said. Then he turned for the front porch and walked out.

***

Later that afternoon, the preacher showed up as he had done every day since the massacre. He gave no reason for his arrival. He just showed up to be of service wherever he was needed. But otherwise, he spent most of his time sitting near Kelly Jean without saying much. He was now fearfully concerned for her as never before. He knew she was holding in too much for such a young woman. He knew that the tremendous guilt she was carrying should be reserved only for mature adults who deserved the load. He determined she was feeling greatly responsible for this latest event, and the preacher wished to allay her of those thoughts. But he learned quickly that words had little effect. They only seemed to irritate her. So he just sat quietly in her proximity and smiled whenever she looked his way.

The remaining cattle had been corralled and herded to Paul's place to graze with the dairy cattle while the lower pasture was being cleaned up. Now it was left to the buzzards, and there must have been well over two hundred of them at times. Along with crows and other scavengers fighting for the remaining decaying carcasses, it oft-times sounded like a chorus of screeching demons from hell. More than a few times, Wade had gone near the carnage to fire a gunshot to quiet the bedlam down enough to bring some measure of calmness to the farmhouse. But it usually didn't last long. One day late in the afternoon, a pack of coyotes was seen dragging off chunks of rancid meat and bones as the birds of prey scattered just long enough for them to take their share and move away.

Finally, a stench rose from the pasture and covered the farm with its invisible fog. The scavengers became less numerous and things were beginning to quiet down. Mercifully late one afternoon a shower came, and it rained lightly for several hours. The odorous fog had been defeated, and it made only cursory attempts to revive itself for a few days afterward.

***

"What happened to the car, Tom?" Annie asked in a quivering voice. She hadn't been to the car house in the week after the night of cattle massacre. She knew the sheriff had been to see her husband at least four times since that night, twice the first day; but she was too afraid to ask, or content not to ask, what it was all about. The idea that her husband was the prime suspect in the carnage was becoming too frightening to bear. But when she looked down the hill to see that the car was missing a door, she had to ask. She needed some reassurance that her husband was innocent. And by an unspoken agreement, they had not discussed Tom's late night excursion on that night. As for Annie, she had all but erased it from her mind; not so much willfully, but as a subconscious trick of the mind. Survival became more needful than inborn principals.

Tom sat next to the stove with his elbows resting on his knees. He was looking at the floor and seemed lost in thought for several moments. Then realizing his wife had asked a question, he looked up at her. She was standing next to the window in the full light of day. Her hair was down and bedraggled, framing a countenance of exhaustion and fear. Her skin was chalk-like. Tom told her the same thing he had been telling the sheriff. It had come to sound like a chant, as if he had grown tired of the oft-repeated question.

"It got knocked off when I backed it up across the bridge down here at the barn. I left the door open. When I rolled off the edge, it hit the bank and broke off at the hinges. I threw it in the river. I reckon it got washed away. I just didn't want to bother you with it." Then as a pretext to leave the room, he picked up the coal pail and went for the door and said, "You need some coal for supper."

Annie appeared to readily accept this answer. Tom had answered succinctly and matter-of-factly. So Annie was newly energized, and she pulled a couple of barrette-combs from her pocket and worker her hair up to her head and tightened it into a bun. There was work to do around the house, and she threw herself into it as if she had been delinquent in her duties for too long.

***

Gene had spent a long morning driving the roads looking for any additional clues on the cattle massacre. He had left Harvey on Kallton Farms Road to walk it from one end to the other searching for any trace. Gene once again made the dreaded trip down the North Road to the old Howard Kallton place where it was now known by all that Carl had taken up permanent residence. Carl had returned from town and parked his truck at the familiar spot in front of the house. He had heard a vehicle coming, so he was standing on the front porch waiting. Billy was nowhere to be seen, but it would be assumed that he was in the house since he was almost never seen without Carl.

Gene took a breath and stepped out of the car. He was immediately impressed by the improvements to the exterior of the house. Most of the boards on the sides of the old house had been replaced and the whole structure painted white. The roof was covered with straight runs of new bald cypress shakes. Shiny new glass panes filled the windows. As expected, Carl gave no greeting; only stood and glared his unforgiving gaze. Gene propped a foot up on a porch step and said, "I hear you're raising corn now. Prices have been good lately."

Carl nodded once.

"Is Billy around?"

Carl nodded again. After a moment, he turned and called for his sidekick. Almost instantly, like obeying a blunt military command, Billy stepped out the front door and leaned against a porch column facing Carl. "My boy been giving you trouble, Sheriff?" Carl asked.

Gene ignored the question and said, "About a week ago, we had over a dozen head of cattle shot and killed down southeast of here. You heard about it?"

"Folks shouldn't go around wrecking other people's property, Sheriff. We heard about it."

"I know you don't get around these parts much, Mr. Kallton, but if you heard or saw anything – "

"I sleep like a dead baby. Didn't hear a damn thing."

"Any chance your people happen to find an old Ford car door down on the road here?"

"Not a damn chance."

"You the only ones to use the new road you cut behind your house?"

Carl nodded.

"Mind if I use it to shortcut back to the main road?"

"Only if you ask," Carl answered.

Gene paused for a moment, a bit struck by Carl's quickness to sarcasm, though he was little surprised. Clearly, the man had no regard for anyone in a position of authority other than himself. Gene turned away and loaded up. He drove around to the new driveway taking advantage of the opportunity to visually inspect the back of the house and outbuildings. A high stack of newly dried lumber lay at the eastern edge of the back yard. It appeared that a large barn or similar structure was to be built there. The wellhouse was rebuilt and the smokehouse had been razed. The high grasses were cut down and the yard's radius was now several times wider than before. A couple of migrants were clearing out saplings and brush along the edges.

Soon, Gene pulled out of the driveway and onto the main road, then, after a few yards, rolled up to a small bridge in the road. Harvey was some distance away and walking toward him. Previously, scorched pieces of a car's upholstery were found strewn on the bridge. Every shred of fabric fragment had been picked up by the sheriff and his deputy. It was newly singed as if perhaps some evidence had been burned to cover up criminal activity. It was then compared to the upholstery in Tom's car. A positive match had been made, but the coincidental evidence was only slightly better than useless.

Gene met the deputy at the bridge and stood a moment looking down into the creek, which was running nicely, and several small fish could be seen darting around in the speckled sunlight. Momentarily, a vehicle came rolling down the driveway to the road. Carl's truck drove out onto the road and stopped. Billy was driving, and when he spotted the sheriff and the deputy he promptly wheeled around and headed back up the driveway. Gene just chuckled derisively.

CHAPTER 10

By early summer, Carl's new entrepreneurial venture, well over a mile south of his residence, was beginning to look more and more like an open-air warehouse for an industrial-sized undertaking than a storage lot for the simple moonshining operation that Carl's underlings had envisioned. Now the hollow was filled with high stacks of newly cut lumber, crates of copper sheeting, a hundred wooden barrels and seemingly tons of miscellaneous hardware and building materials. All of the trees in the center of the hollow had been cut down, and the big ones had been sawed to lumber by an impromptu sawmill. It had become a viable town unto itself with its own water supply system, general stock depot, barracks-like living quarters, and a vehicle repair station.

Everyone, including Roy Kallton, his boys, and a dozen trusted migrants, now worked in long shifts, six days a week. A system of site boundary surveillance was in place, which was now required most hours of the day because of the increased traffic in and out of the area. Even though it was in its infancy, a surveillance watch had been set up on the sheriff whereby every move could now be monitored, and relevant information could be quickly relayed back to compound headquarters. Also, the Kallton farms and rural folk to the north and east were passively monitored in case someone became suspicious and decided to look around on his own. But, all in all, the bootleg traffic and activities had been confined to the less populated southwestern corner of the county, thereby not attracting inordinate attention.

All of Carl Kallton's local purchases had been orchestrated to appear innocent enough to the people in town. Even though he was buying mostly with hard cash, he opened up a credit account here and there to create the illusion of honest accounting and cash flow. He was working to earn the respect of the merchants in town with his purchases of lumber and supplies for what was assumed to be the usual farming needs. Locals were suspicious of any newcomer to town, but after learning of his family name and that his money was usually doled out in large increments, these suspicions became less and less consequential as the weeks passed.

Otherwise, no one desired to become too friendly with someone the likes of Carl Dean Kallton. His status as an outsider, along with his malevolent appearance and disposition, motivated most everyone to keep a respectable distance. Little was known of this man except for the fact that he had money. It was supposed that much of it, if not all of it, was ill-gotten.

But all of Carl's major lumber and materials purchases were done far away from Braxton. Any sign of major construction purchases would have attracted too much attention. Most of his large lumber purchases were done directly from the big sawmillers on the Tennessee River. Materials such as copper sheeting were ordered and purchased through out-of-state connections he had developed over the years. It was all shipped in discreetly, and usually under cover of darkness if it could be arranged.

On one nondescript day, Carl called a meeting to his house of his small circle of foremen. The assemblage included Roy Kallton, who had been appointed supervisor over whiskey still operations when sober, and three other men. One of the others was a builder Carl had hired from a county away. He was to be supervisor over the migrants for general construction. Another was an out-of-town ruffian who had been recommended for his farming abilities by Roy himself. He would be supervisor over corn cultivation for distilling needs as well as other more legitimate crops. A fourth man sat at the other end of the table from Carl. He was the only one in the group who wore no overalls. He wasn't fancily attired, but he was dressed top to bottom in northern duds. Carl had told him to get with the program and start wearing clothes in local style so as not to attract attention. Greenhorn was written all over him, but that would have to change. His name was M.C. Colter, and he was a recent arrival from Carl's old haunts in Chicago. He was to be Carl's general manager of operations as well as head of security and surveillance procedures. His one other duty would probably be the most important; sales of the new product to established buyers and to develop new contacts in Chicago and its environs.

Before everyone had settled down, Carl was already speaking.

"All right, boys. Let's size up what we've got here. Roy, how many cookers you got ready now?"

"Six," Roy answered.

"Coleman, what's your status?" Carl asked of the farming supervisor. Coleman didn't understand the question, so Carl clarified. "When do you expect to start planting?"

"In about three days," Coleman said. Instantly, he knew his answer was too optimistic. But Carl demanded quick answers, giving little time to think.

"I expect to have the seed here in a few days, Carl. We'll be ready to go then," M.C. said. Carl nodded approval, and Coleman was relieved to get the extension.

"Is it the Holcomb white corn I asked for?" Carl asked as if this was critical to operations.

"The best of the west," M.C. answered.

Then, Billy came through the front door. Even though there were no lights in the room, it was well lit by the sunlight filtering through the three tall windows along the front. The room was sparsely furnished, as was the rest of the house. A table and chairs and a few other displaced items were scattered along the wall, including a broken spinning wheel in one corner.

Leaned against the wall, behind the spinning wheel, was a dusty, dented and charred door from a common early model Ford Model-T. Carl's men saw it, but kept any questions to themselves. A lone sentry, camping and standing guard in the woods north of the compound, had found it after hearing the car speed by on the night of the cattle massacre. The car had stopped in the vicinity of the bridge and the sentry could hear two frantic-voiced men proceed to cut and beat something away from the frame of the car. The sounds of the work were distinctly metallic, hammer against braced iron. Then the sentry could see a tall flame flare up, then burn out nearly as quickly as it flared. In moments, the car roared away. The sentry found the car door stashed in the bridge understructure early the next morning. It had been hastily burned as if the men had doused it with a fluid and set it afire. The event had all the earmarks of someone attempting to destroy evidence of a crime. Did this have something to do with that late night cattle massacre everyone is talking about? Carl wondered. Of course it did, he concluded even before the sentry had finished his story. The sheriff himself had told him so when he visited. And the whole county was abuzz with the question of Tom Buell's missing car door. Carl examined the door, ripped away a little scorched fabric, found a lodged bullet in its corner bracing, and chuckled. He parked the door against the wall and forgot about it for the time being. The time would come when its usefulness to Carl's devices would be found.

All the wallpaper had long ago been pulled off the walls, leaving strips of glue-hardened paper here and there throughout the house. Other than a few settled spots in doorways and alcoves, the floor was in generally good shape. The ceilings were wood battens with heavy moldings throughout most of the house. But the front room had been decorated with pressed metal ceiling tiles that needed a polishing or a coat of paint to conceal the growing rust. A large stone fireplace with an oak mantle had been built into every major room, including a massive one in the front room, thus resulting in four chimneys of various sizes visible on the outside. Some of the fireplaces still contained ashes from decades ago.

Billy tossed a handful of mail onto the table in front of Carl and left without a word out the back of the house. Carl paused, looking over the pile of envelopes before him. He snatched one up and opened it. "What's this?" he said, shoving a paper toward M.C.

M.C. looked at it for only a second, then shoved it back at Carl and said, "That's the condenser lines we talked about last month."

"I never told you to order any materials for that yet. We don't even know what our capacity is going to be," Carl shot back.

"Condensers? Condensers fer what?" Roy asked, seeming to come awake. "I done built th' damn condensers,"

Carl, snatching up the document, glared at M.C.

"I said, what damn condensers?" Roy demanded, his voice rising.

Carl ignored the questions as he looked over the document. Roy tapped one of the supervisors on the shoulder and asked, "What's this all about? I'm s'posed t'know ever'thang!"

Carl looked up at M.C., motioned to Roy, and snapped, "Tell the son-of-a-bitch."

M.C. leaned up to the table and said, "That's for the big distillery we're going to build in your hollow. It's going to – "

"Why th' hell ain't I been told sump'm 'bout this? What's this here all 'bout, Carl?"

Carl laid the paper down and folded his hands on the table before him, and said in a calm, even tone, "You don't think those little cookers of yours can handle all the corn we're cropping around here do you, Roy? And you think all that new copper laying in the hollow is just for you to build us more of those little cookers? Now come on, Roy – you're not that full of shit."

Roy was lost in confusion, his eyes darting about as if he had been blindsided. His anger boiling, he loudly demanded more explanation. He cared little to be embarrassed by his cracking voice. "Why in hell did yew have me build all 'em cookers if we ain't gonna use 'em? What th' hell's goin' on here, goddamnit?"

"We're going to use your cookers, Roy," M.C. stated smoothly. He glanced at Carl for confirmation. "You'll be turning out some of the best brew Chicago will ever taste."

Roy resented the greenhorn telling him anything he felt he should already know. Still burning with betrayal, he turned to Carl again. "What's th' damn Yankee sayin', Carl?"

For a moment, Carl sat unmoving as granite and stared at Roy with a killer's gaze. The understated smile added a dimension of malignancy to his bearing. With a level voice that sounded forcefully quiet, Carl said, "All right, Roy – maybe you are that full of shit. Here's the story. I want you to plant your stills around a few locations in the county. Most of them will be deep into company timberland where the sheriff doesn't go around too much, or anyone else for that matter. We want to divert the sheriff's attention away from the hollow down here – "

"Damn all that – I'm runnin' my stills down here in th' holler like we said. I ain't gonna move a still after it's done been built!"

Carl had not moved or showed a change in disposition. He seemed willing, for the moment, to let Roy talk himself out if he needed to.

"Hell, we done built th' fireboxes in th' ground an' ever'thang." Roy looked at M.C., then back at Carl as if a light had been switched on in his head. "What do yew mean 'Die-vert th' sheriff from th' holler?' What're yew a-doin' wi' my holler? Yeah, I seen all that shit you been a-stackin' in my goddamn holler! But I thought we wuz gonna make our moonshine d'ere!"

"We are," Carl said with steel in his voice, as if ready to reveal a long-withheld secret of the heaviest import. Or to throw Roy out the window.

Roy shoved his chair back and propped his feet up on the table. He folded his arms and nodded with a smirk as if to say he was ready for a full explanation. Everyone looked at Carl. The big man, with eyes boring into Roy's, said, "All right, boys – here's the big plan – "

Roy sniffed and Carl stared him down. Then Carl proceeded to lay out the details of a grand scheme concerning a new concept in high volume clandestine whiskey processing. He quickly explained that many aspects of the design were to be similar to the processors that he was familiar with in Chicago, but overall he had conceived the new plan himself. It would entail the construction of a giant still that would be capable of turning out several thousand gallons of corn whiskey a day if work continued around the clock.

The cooker itself would have a capacity of between six and seven hundred gallons, dwarfing Roy's home-built twenty-gallon potboilers, and would require a massive and complex copper condenser to process the product from steam to hard liquor. Carl's and M.C.'s calculations had shown that at least 100,000 gallons of fresh running spring water would be needed every 24 hours to keep the operation going. Several creeks and two springs had been located several hundred yards away and this water would be piped in. If these sources dried up or proved too lacking, a well or two would be dug. The cooker would require a more consistent heat source than what a traditional wood-fueled fire could provide. Therefore, a large regulated kerosene burner would be built beneath it. A gas or steam engine pump would be included to handle the product before, during, and after each run.

The thumping process, which was simply the recycling of the half-finished product back into the cooker for the final distilling, would be handled by a circle of ten or twelve fifty-gallon barrels planted in the ground around the cooker. Carl explained this new process as a concept that could theoretically double the alcohol content of the finished product. He explained that when the fermented product heated up in these thump barrels it would rise and fall like a solid mass, thereby creating a loud, continuous thumping sound that, on cool, calm nights, could be heard for hundreds of yards through the woods. By planting each thump barrel into the ground on a set of heavy springs for shock absorption, it was hoped that this noise could be dampened with the intent of reducing chances of discovery by any locals or law enforcement.

Because of the huge amount of corn that would be required, a gristmill would have to be constructed to grind the corn into meal. It also would require a supply of running water to power the grinder. The mill's exact location was yet to be determined. Carl went on to outline the construction scheduling and product transporting methods and how all these operations were to be performed in such a way as to be unnoticed by the surrounding community. A legitimate farming operation was to be run alongside everything else. Other crops besides corn were to be cultivated and sold on the local and regional markets, and chosen workers were to be trained to work the local auctions and farm equipment sales in order to purchase various farming implements that could only be used in everyday farming operations.

In spite of all the best planning one could conceive, suspicions may still arise from the large amount of corn that would be raised on the farm, and the fact that only small amounts would be shipped out as a legitimate food product. Therefore, it was decided that much of the already plowed-up fields would be used for planting of various legitimate crops such as beans, okra, squash and tomatoes, and in a year or two, tobacco. New fields would be cleared and planted with white boiler corn on several plots on the farm located far from the roads and prying eyes. The land would be posted to keep out hunters who may inadvertently stumble upon the clandestine fields. Surveillance and intelligence would be increased as construction of the monster distillery was underway. Carl said that he and M.C. were working on several ideas to keep the local law enforcement in check as construction operations neared start-up. He said it in such a way as if this item was the least of his worries. He appeared confident that Chicago underworld methods were more than adequate for his purposes in this backwoods hillbilly country.

Roy had remained settled just long enough to hear out the entire discourse. He had placed a dip of snuff inside his bottom lip and he was ready to spit as was evidenced by the dribble running down his grizzled chin. Clearly affronted by the apparent closed-door planning without his knowledge, he showed no willingness to hide his displeasure. He looked around for a place to let go of the discharge, then promptly spit toward the nearest closed window, landing short by several feet. "Who's gonna build this here Chee-kah-go still, Carl? Shit, I shore as hell ain't," he sneered.

Carl turned to one of the men and said, "Go tell Billy to bring a spit bucket in here for the wild man." He leaned back, staring with a new coldness at Roy and said, "You'll do what I tell you to do."

Roy spit again, this time with increased defiance and force at the wall nearby. Everyone eased inches from the table and looked at Carl for his next move. Carl took note of this.

"Hell, I'll just take my stills and run 'em myself with my boys, like I done fer years. Damn, Carl – yore ass'll be outta bid'ness t'morrow without me!"

The fact that he was, both at the same moment, sober and tauntingly spiteful toward Carl amazed everyone in the room. Roy often cut it close with Carl, but this time he had kicked out the last board. Carl would allow minor insubordination when the spirits were flowing, but he showed little tolerance for such insolence when minds were not under the influence. Roy's inclination to rebel at the slightest infraction posed some potential to lower team morale if some form of admonition by the leadership was not taken.

Roy grinned enough to bare a gapped line of brown teeth and he spit again. The juice splattered up the wall and streamed down in brown ribbons. He started to pull his feet off the table, but Carl grabbed a foot and yanked hard. Roy's head disappeared below the table as his chair flipped beneath him. He hit the floor, but Carl jerked him up and slammed him hard against the wall. Roy seemed to have been knocked nearly unconscious by the blow, but Carl held him up against the wall with one hand and slapped him solidly across the face with the other. Roy blinked, his face instantly reddened from Carl's clinched hand pressed tight against his throat. He tried to speak, but Carl constricted his airflow by holding him stiffly against the wall, his feet six inches off the floor. The other men twitched in their seats but remained seated. Billy and the migrant house servant, Troy Mays, had come into the room upon hearing the commotion.

Roy was alert but unable to breathe because of Carl's hand. It seemed his head would explode from the pressure, and he grabbed Carl's wrist with both hands but the effort was futile against Carl's steel grip. He made pitiful squealing noises as Carl held him there for what seemed a minute before he spoke. His nose an inch from Roy's, Carl said, "You talk to me like that again and I might get my ass backed up – understood?"

Roy tried to nod, but couldn't. Carl had spoken in an even, unexcited tone. It seemed he was at his most natural when situations were boiling with hostilities.

Roy sat quietly for the next hour as Carl and M.C. wrapped up the session with details of plans for the shipment of the product to northern markets. It was further discussed that most, if not all, of the freight would be handled by entities in Chicago. Also, additional milled corn would be shipped in if and when existing harvests were depleted. Finally, no paper plans of the giant distillery were to be drawn up. All the details were in Carl's head and would be revealed step-by-step as the construction progressed.

The meeting ended abruptly when Carl left the room.

CHAPTER 11

A month later, Roy's wife, Doris, died of undetermined causes at home. The four children were out of the house playing in the yard and a nearby creek when she passed away. Roy was simply loitering around the yard when they returned for dinner at midday. Only Gracie, the youngest at four, ran from the house crying when she found her mother on the kitchen floor. The boys, with stony, expressionless faces, stood silently together at the base of the porch until the undertaker came just before nightfall. He had been notified by the family's cousins after little Gracie ran nearly three miles alone to Paul Kallton's for help.

Two days later, the funeral was held at Beulah Primitive Baptist Church. Everyone remembered Doris, though most had not seen her in years. Only the nearby Kallton families, the sheriff, and a few acquaintances attended. Roy and the boys stayed silent throughout the service until Roy broke down near the end of Pastor Silas's sermon. He could be heard noising garbled phrases about his own sins and wasted life. Whether the racket was genuine or not, no one could tell. As if influenced by an alcohol-based substance, he would occasionally laugh out loud to his own ramblings. It seemed, at times, that two or three personalities, or spirits, were warring for possession of his mind. When the preacher paused to give him audience, Roy shut up and motioned for the preacher to carry on.

Gracie was being cared for by, and sat at the funeral with Paul's mother Mrs. Sarah and his wife, Ruth. She had been cleaned up and dressed in new clothes by the ladies and would seem entirely out of place sitting with her pan-washed, but couthless father and brothers. The little girl was already cried out, and sat tearless through the service.

After the burial as everyone began departing, Gene was seen pulling Roy aside. Rumors had already been voiced about concerning the mysteriousness of the death. The undertaker had found suspicious evidence to show that foul play may have been a factor in her death. A coroner had been called in from Columbia but his work proved inconclusive. Although Doris was an asthmatic, the puffiness of her neck tissues, the markings on her throat, and the blood spots in her eyes revealed the likely possibility of more than just a severe asthma attack.

Gracie stayed with the Kalltons four more days before Roy came for her. As he had been instructed to do, he parked his mule and wagon rig in the driveway at Paul's house and sat there waiting. Only Roy Jr., now fourteen and already sitting taller and filling a wider portion of the seat than his father, was with him. Paul stepped out the door with the gait of a man heavy-minded with a dreaded challenge. "You going to take that little girl away from us so soon, Roy?" he asked.

"Uh – yeah."

Roy's right cheek pouched out an inch from his face; it seemed he had enough tobacco in his jaw to fill a pint jar. His son also imbibed, as evidenced by a similar protrusion of cheekflesh. The sideboards of the wagon below the seat were caked with a decade's worth of tobaccoed saliva stains. Paul looked up at the hang-dog vagrant and like-attired son and cranked his mind for the beginnings of any reasoning that might appeal to any remnant of humanity in the man's soul. Roy and son, even from several yards away, reeked of hygienic decadence. Rationalizing with either one of these derelicts would be like trying to appeal to the empathy of the devil himself, Paul thought.

"Roy, I need to talk to you – "

"Now don't yew start on me," Roy sneered. "I know what ye'r gonna start on me 'bout, so don't even come at me with it."

Paul rocked from hip to hip as if finding his balance for a fistfight. He spoke quickly, letting loose with cold reasoning. "You can't give her a home like we can. Now that Doris is gone – "

"Now yew see here – that ain't none of yore affair! I got a mind to ne'er let any of yew people ever see Gracie ag'in! Yew got yore fam'ly, an' I got mine!"

Paul stepped closer, narrowed his eyes and looked for Roy's eyes beneath the broad brim of the hat he had shoved down to his ears. It was impossible to read his eyes but it wouldn't have mattered. Roy's attitude was always acidic. Paul determined there was no point in straying from the truth of the matter. He eyed Roy Jr. and found that the boy proudly mirrored his father's demeanor.

"You know, if we brought the district authorities in here, you would have to give her up. It might take a long time to get it done, but I believe we can get it done. I'm just trying to make it easy on you and Gracie."

Roy glared down at Paul. He worked his jaw up and down and rolled the wad of tobacco to the front of his mouth. Paul stepped back to dodge the overspray. But Roy leaned over and dropped a stretching sinew of molasses-colored spittle that hit the ground in a staccato splat. He drew in a breath to speak, but the front door of the house opened and Ruth stepped out with Gracie. The little girl already knew her father was coming to get her, so she was dressed and prepared.

"Looky there, Roy," Paul half-whispered. "Just look at how she's all dressed up and clean. Now you know you can't do that for her. Only a woman can make a little girl so pretty."

Roy pretended deafness. "C'mon here, baby doll," he called to Gracie. "C'mon now – Papa's gonna take yew home."

Gracie didn't move, seemingly deaf to her father's directive. Ruth nudged her, but Gracie turned her head upward to Ruth as if asking if she must really go. She remained still, not willing to accept the nudges for what they were intended.

Roy turned his head to the other side of the wagon and let loose with the entire wad. He spit several times to clear his mouth, spraying his son. Paul gestured disgust and turned away. In a moment, Mrs. Sarah stepped out onto the porch. She walked over to Gracie and bent over her to say something. Roy was becoming agitated and impatient as evidenced by his fidgeting and snorting. Gracie seemed to be trying to hug everyone at once, or she was trying to grasp onto something firm and hold tight; it was difficult to tell. Ruth, always concerned about Mrs. Sarah's heart, took over to calm things down. She kneeled and pulled Gracie's arms down and held them to the little girl's sides and spoke to her eye to eye. Gracie affected a fragile smile and began nodding her head as if she were enjoying what she was hearing. Probably promises for near-future reunions and gifts of new clothing. But all this further infuriated Roy. "Let's git along here, Gracie, He said loudly. "Come on to Papa, now! Junior, move your ass over fer yer little sister."

Roy Jr. cursed a single profanity then dragged himself to the far end of the seat. Then he imitated his father's tobacco expulsion procedure and wiped his mouth. Surprisingly, Gracie stepped easily away from the hugs and kisses and made her way down into the sunlight. Roy would have had to be blind to overlook the polished shoes and the new stain-free coat that all fit perfectly. They were girls' clothing – not hand-me-downs from her brothers. Roy had steadfastly refused charity before, but he was not consulted this time and the insult was hardly hidden in his reaction. "Don't yew reckon it's a little warm fer all that getup?" he barked.

Everyone ignored him. Paul walked Gracie to the wagon and hoisted her up, her clean auburn tresses flying wide in the air. She didn't look at her father or her brother. She watched Paul walk slowly back to the porch. Then her eyes shifted to Mrs. Sarah and Ruth. Her cherub-like face was devoid of expression, and her eyes never shifted to her father sitting just inches away on the bench.

Roy popped the reins and the rig turned a tiny circle in the yard and quickly rolled down the driveway to the road. Gracie turned her head back as far as her neck would twist to watch the lovely family that had by now all stood close together in the bright morning light. Everyone forced a smile and waved at Gracie. Gracie only watched with the dull gaze of a child that had been made to mature too far past her four-and-a-half years. She never responded to the waving hands, but no one expected her to. It was always thus whenever Gracie went back home after her short visits.

* * *

Later that afternoon, Carl and Billy rode northward to exercise a little authority reinforcement against his newest reluctant confederate. Annie Buell knew nothing of the recent pact her husband had been blackmailed into making with Satan's ambassador, and Tom was set and determined to keep it that way.

As Tom had beforehand instructed, if Carl could not find him in the fields, he was to park at the car house and wait for him there. Annie, assuming the visitor to be on farm business for Tom, would hopefully not interfere. But today Tom was an easy find. He was driving two draft mules home on the road from the south fields. He was tired and dirty, and in no congenial frame of mind. Tom stopped the mules and stood stone-faced looking at Carl, who had stopped the truck and remained seated in it. Billy's shaggy-headed silhouette was unmistakable next to Carl. A small caliber handgun was strapped to Tom's belt. Carl seemed to be taking note of it.

"Done for the day, Buell?" Carl asked, shutting off the motor. Tom nodded. Getting right to business, Carl asked, "I hear you've been shooting across your field at my people – am I hearing the truth?"

"You heard right," Tom groused. "Your boys are not doing what we agreed to. You keep them out of sight of my house and Luke's house, and we won't be shooting at anybody."

Carl held his gaze tight on Tom. He knew that overbearing pressure and intimidation had not been necessary up to this point. Carl held all the cards and simple leverage should have been all that was needed. But Tom was building his courage beyond his right. Carl got out of the truck and leaned back against the front fender. Tom took a more defensive stance nearer to his mules. He placed his hands on his hips, one near the gun. Carl glared Tom eye to eye without looking down at the gun. The half-grin on his face spoke volumes as to his steel-honed fortitude. Tom's face was starting to take on a more anguished appearance. No doubt he would have desired to use the gun now and remove Carl from his life forever, but any such thoughts vanished when

Billy stepped out and produced gun-cocking noises from behind the open truck door. "You keep your boys up on the north side like we agreed – where I can't see them," Tom added. "And we noticed that your men are cutting a road across our north acreage. We never agreed to that."

Carl nodded and stepped a single step toward Tom threateningly. Tom stepped away and dropped his hands to his side as if ready to draw down on Carl.

"I remember everything we agree to," Carl said. "I agreed to protect you and your cousin from the law by keeping your busted car door hidden away from prying eyes. And you agreed to let us run some operations on your land. I don't recall any talk about no north side or cutting a road or anything such as that. If I need to spread out operations or make a road to facilitate that, I'll do it. It's not your choice to make."

"You got my damn car door, Kallton. Just keep it hidden away and leave me and my family be. And keep your people out of sight. I don't care what kind of business you're running up there – just stay out of our sight."

"My boys tell me they were nearly a half-mile from your house when you took a shot at them. Are you saying my people are lying to me?"

"We have to hunt down a hog or two that get out from time to time. I can't make them run the other way when they have a mind to go north."

Carl chuckled. Tom jerked his hand back as if to pull and fire.

"Billy will kill you before you get off a single shot," Carl said. He paused for effect then added, "You try shooting at my workers again; my men have instructions to return fire ten to one."

Tom looked to find Billy aiming a long gun at his forehead. Tom stood down his aggressive stance, his eyes darting around, no doubt debating within himself whether to still go for the gun. Carl spoke again.

"You shitty hayseeds are a pitiful breed. You and Luke shoot up a man's cows at midnight like brave little boys. Then you take a bullet to your car door and you panic like little girls. Then you break it off and try to burn it up, then hide it under a bridge like playing some goddamn child's game. And then you dare to turn resentful when a man of my standards takes advantage of your stupidity?" Carl glanced down at Tom's gun then turned and stepped slowly to the truck as if daring Tom to carry through with his threat. He turned back and added, "I'll be shipping a lot of materials in at night starting next week. Don't worry your ass about the noise; we'll keep it down."

Then he and Billy loaded up and drove off, leaving Tom, humiliated and seething, standing in a swirling cloud of pebble-tossed dust.

CHAPTER 12

"After four months, this is all I'm going to get. I can't arrest anyone with this. It's all circumstantial and speculative, and I know the grand jury will just kick it right back in my face."

Gene held the state report in his hand like holding a broken and useless tool that needed to be thrown away. If the preacher had tried, he could not ignore the helpless disgust in the sheriff's face.

"Gene, I think we have to figure now that Tom, and Lucas too, genuinely believes Wade Kallton killed his two boys. I can't see how a man could shoot up another man's cattle herd without a lot of motivation like this."

"Well, preacher, I have to admit I've just about come to the same conclusion myself."

"When's the last time you talked to Tom?"

"Last week, I think."

"Still the same?"

"That's right. I have to give the man credit. Keeps his mouth shut. He won't perjure himself with unnecessary talk. Same with Lucas."

"You give up on the door?"

"That car door is probably in Maury County by now. I won't bother myself with looking for it anymore."

"Can I take a look at that?" the preacher asked.

Gene handed the five-page document to the preacher, then took the tobacco pouch from his pocket and rolled a loose cigarette and lit it. He stepped away to gaze across the cotton fields that stretched half a mile from the preacher's front porch. The preacher read every word slowly as if memorizing it. The pages read as a sterile chronology of events with no opinions that could inadvertently steer the reader to make errant conclusions. Only a handful of facts could be firmly established. Investigators were sure that one vehicle carrying two gunmen plied the road the night of the cattle massacre. It was determined that at least thirty shots, perhaps as many as sixty, were fired killing, or mortally wounding, a total of thirteen cattle in Wade Kallton's lower pasture. Others were injured but were ultimately nursed back to good health. By inspection of the bullets and the buckshot retrieved from the carcasses, it was deduced that the gun that fired the most shots was a common .30-30 caliber deer rifle. The other was a twelve-gauge shotgun firing buckshot at very close range. All of the rifle bullets were of the soft-point type, making any inspection difficult as this type of bullet mushroomed or shattered upon impact, thereby deforming it beyond useful examination. However, some of the bullets did have visible striations, or rifle markings, that could be useful in matching them to the perpetrator's rifle, if it could still be found. As it had always been with most rural residents of the area, Tom and Lucas were owners of small collections of hunting rifles and shotguns. Two deer rifles from the collections were taken and examined. Upon testing, it was assessed that none of the bullets had positively been fired from either rifle. It was known that Tom had once owned a third deer rifle. When asked of its whereabouts he stated that he had sold it months ago to a gun dealer whose name had now escaped him.

As concerning the shotgun; a shotgun had no rifling, or grooves, to spin a projectile through the barrel, thereby producing no striations. And buckshot was not traceable to a given firearm, so any investigation concerning this type of firearm would have been a moot effort. No spent shotgun casings were found and only eight .30-30 casings had been found. Upon close inspection, the casings appeared to have been handled by gloved hands. These facts helped lead to speculation that only hired professionals would have had the presence of mind enough to clean up after themselves in this manner. However, this speculation was soon discounted as the Buell bank accounts had been watched carefully for any substantial payoff withdrawals, and none were made in the ensuing weeks or in the weeks before the event.

Several .45-75 caliber casings were found, but these were easily determined to have been ejected from Wade's Winchester repeater when he fired upon the fleeing car and at the suffering cattle. As expected, inquiries of all local suppliers and sellers of hunting ammunition turned up no excessive sales of rifle ammunition in the days or weeks leading up to the massacre, as many of the locals kept caches of such ammo for hunting and target shooting anyway.

Tom's and Lucas's boots were checked for similarities to the soils in Wade's pasture, but both pairs of boots turned up clean the day after. Plenty of telling footprints were found all around the hay barn, throughout the pasture and in the road; but they, as did many of the work boots of the day, had the plain, nondescript leather soles. Both Wade and the sheriff wore similar boots. The car had been left in the road while the gunmen did their work. But the tire tracks were intermingled with all the others already on the road, as well as those made later that night by the sheriff's and Paul's cars and the wheel tracks of the preacher's buggy, further frustrating the sheriff's efforts.

As to the chain of events itself, it was deduced that the gunshots woke up Jimmy immediately after they started. This being so, the torching of the hay barn was no doubt started before the shooting began. This added some additional illumination to the moonlight, enabling the gunmen to kill quickly and accurately, as neither Wade nor Jimmy could remember any flashlights or lanterns being carried by the gunmen. In all, the time from the initial torching of the barn to the moment that Wade fired the first warning shot was estimated to have been only about fifteen minutes. However, many of the cattle had been herded to the most distant northern corner of the lower pasture, thereby adding another eight to ten minutes to the beginning of the episode. Even though the dogs were barking that night, Jimmy said he remembered the gunshots first. Apparently the dogs were only first alerted by the gunshots also, as the fire was long underway before the real noisy action began.

Some of the dead cattle were shot in vital, quick-kill zones of the body, attesting to the skill and accuracy of the gunmen. Some were killed instantly with a well-placed shot to the head. Others tried to run the gauntlet and were shot in the heart area as they ran past, or in the spine from a rearward direction. Those that did not die quickly were left in a crippled or paralyzed condition. Jimmy had described how the gunshots were fired; rather rapidly with short periods of interspersed silence. The gunmen had reloaded their firearms quickly while still trying to keep the scattering and stampeding cattle corralled in the corner.

It was generally accepted that Wade had scored a direct hit when he fired upon the getaway car. Shards of window glass were found on the road where the car was hit, as well as among the shreds of burned fabric found near the creek bridge south of Carl Kallton's place. The shooters, in a panic, had apparently attempted to destroy evidence by fire, but left nothing more than scorched bits of material which could not be positively identified in connection to any particular vehicle. Since Tom's car was missing a door the day after the massacre, Gene had simply deduced that an effort to hastily remove and discard the damaged door was made on that night near the bridge, nearly two miles from the crime scene. But still, without the car door or any other parcel of damning evidence, there could be no indictments; certainly none that could hold firm in a court of law.

The preacher and the sheriff rarely interacted and only saw each other if crossing paths in town. The preacher had given up years ago in his hopes of getting Gene to attend his church once in a while. But otherwise the preacher considered the sheriff a good man. Now the sheriff needed the preacher's help. It was clear that Gene was becoming desperate to find answers and was talking to anyone that would listen, in the hopes of stirring up something, however insignificant, that might finally break things loose.

The preacher turned to the sheriff and watched him for a few minutes. His clothes hung loosely, even disheveled. His hair was shaggy; more lengthy than the preacher could recall from years past. Beyond the sheriff, the cotton fields lay flat, green, and shimmering in the warm summer sun. A little white was beginning to sprout, giving the fields the likeness of a dusting snow. The preacher played his mind for anything that might give the good sheriff reason to hope amidst this carnage of resentful and vindictive souls. Gene never removed his eyes from the solitude of the fields.

The preacher returned to the state report and flipped through as if looking for something to spark the remembrance of things long forgotten. Instead, he allowed his mind to drift to things related to recent events. He thought of the Buells and the Kalltons, with prayers interspersed. He recalled that Tom never drove the car again after the cattle massacre. Tom would not perjure himself among the locals by driving it around with its gaping side for all to see. He had stuck to his story that the door had been demolished by accident and then unceremoniously tossed into a running creek shortly thereafter. When questioned as to the reason for going to all the trouble of disposing of it in this manner, Tom could give no motive. Gene, figuring the effort was futile, made a cursory search of the creek, but found nothing.

Annie had been kept ignorant of all the goings-on concerning events and investigations. She went nowhere. She was content to stay in the house and venture out only to go to the wellhouse or to work in the little vegetable garden a few yards from the house. She no longer encouraged visitors or stop-overs as she lived to make the proverbial axiom 'ignorance is bliss' her daily creed. Tom's and Annie's daughter, Anne Marie, who had already made numerous short visits, was hoping to move back in soon for a more extended stay, as Annie had become withdrawn and more needful of her company.

Tom and Annie had stopped attending Beulah Primitive Baptist Church shortly after the death of James. Gossip and hearsay was kept well outside the range of their circle of friendly acquaintances. But they were well aware of the type of speculation that was spoken throughout the community. The preacher was not ignorant of the tale-bearing and tongue wagging, and finally came to conclude that his pastoral influence over the years had been minimal at best and nonexistent at worst concerning the ethical virtues of many of his parishioners.

The prime bit of hearsay floating about was that James Buell had seduced Kelly Jean Kallton into a sexual tryst that had resulted in her pregnancy. By now, everyone had heard the rumors of the several secret meetings in the woods between the two lovers. After all, what else could have caused the Kallton men to behave in such a terribly vengeful way against the Buell boys? This one was started and gained play throughout the community as it was becoming more evident that Kelly Jean was never seen outside the house by anyone except her nearby relatives and the pastor. And the old preacher was keeping silent about anything concerning the family, thus adding even more fuel to the speculative fire. This rumor was brought to fever pitch when it was learned that Kelly Jean had left the county with her mother in the dead of night for an extended stay in Parsons with family. This sudden plan of action by Esther and Kelly Jean confirmed the truth, as far as many people were concerned. When ultimately it became clear that the rumor was without merit, the preacher smiled at the folly of the tale-bearers and prayed for the righting of their souls.

The preacher, along with two deacons, had visited Tom and Lucas in the sorghum fields and barns several times since the massacre. They were well aware that Tom was delirious with grief and rage over the deaths of his sons. But, they wondered among themselves, where did he get the presence of mind to carry out such a well-executed operation? How could someone with a lifelong reputation for correct living and a God-fearing awareness in his daily walk, fall from grace as this? Perhaps he was naive, but the preacher could not bring himself to believe that his people, much less a deacon, could fall to such depths of depraved behavior. Yet he could not ignore the facts.

During one of these visits the preacher dared to ask point-blank if Tom had had any part, directly or indirectly, in the arson and massacre. It seemed at first that Tom was going to clam up as he had done with the sheriff. But after a moment of feigned introspection, he answered with melodramatic and disturbingly distraught ramblings concerning his own wretchedness in the eyes of God. He carried on about the troubles fate had rained down upon himself, his wife and his family. It was clear that he was working to portray himself, intentionally or not, as a persecuted man pushed beyond his limits of longsuffering. Occasionally, when he stammered for words, Lucas would produce cryptic phrases to goad him along. But through it all, Tom did not confess directly to the preacher's question. When asked, Lucas, himself, would play mute, shake his head as if to feign ignorance then glance his eyes away and defer to Tom.

It was a depraved game the two men were playing on the community, but they had locked themselves inside a rusty cell, and the only escape was to confess. But their anger against the Kalltons gave them, in their minds, enough justification to assuage their guilt by convincing themselves that there was really no way out after all. If, they had reasoned between themselves, Wade could kill with such conscious-free abandon and live peacefully among the locals without legal persecution, then so could they.

The preacher visited Annie often. He would ask questions about family and church, but he would never ask her about Tom's dealings on or off the farm. There was plenty of time for that. It was clear that she had focused her life down to a very small world. What she already knew or suspected about Tom carried more anxiety than she could manage, and she was becoming more proficient every day in keeping her thoughts on the house, the garden, and the purple lilacs and morning glories around the front porch.

Lucas's wife, Sandra, subdued and unobtrusive by nature, was in similar straits as concerning her husband. She was more accepting of a reclusive lifestyle and had easily built a protective hedge around herself and their two children. She now rarely visited the other Buell house; and whenever she did, she never brought the little ones along. Her visits were short and civil, and only involved mutual household needs. She too, had fabricated an artificial world; and it included her husband less and less as he spent more and more time away tending the cane fields with Tom.

The preacher looked back at the sheriff. Gene had not moved. He was still gazing across the scenery, the cigarette smoke floating away in the light breeze.

"Gene, is everything all right?"

The sheriff indicated he heard the question by a slight turn of the head. "Everything's just fine, preacher. Just fine."

CHAPTER 13

When Wade assessed the damages against assets, he found that losing well over ten percent of the herd and several tons of hay in the torched barn in a single incident was simply too much of a financial blow to bear. He was in hock on most of his cattle with no readily liquid assets to cover the losses. Land prices had risen slowly but steadily over recent years; and with over eighteen-hundred acres at his personal disposal, he saw little opportunity to raise the needed funds short of selling off some of his treasured family asset.

When word spread of Wade's offer to sell two-hundred and twenty acres on the south end, he quickly received three offers. One was from M.C. Colter, who found Wade in town two days after the notice in the newspaper. Wade knew who he was, as far as his association with Carl. But figuring he might be able to buy it back pennies-to-the-dollar once Carl was imprisoned or run out of town, if not shot and killed first, he listened, albeit suspiciously, to the offer. M.C. got to the point quickly.

"I'll give you ten percent over the best offer you get."

"Is this you or Carl talking?" Wade asked.

M.C. looked around with a sarcastic gesture of the hands, as if looking for someone else whom Wade might be addressing. "What difference does it make?" he asked. "It's legal tender, the same as everyone else's damn money, isn't it?"

Three days later, the land was sold. Wade never saw Carl during the whole process and the land was deeded to M.C. But Wade figured after things quieted down a bit, Carl's name would mysteriously and conveniently show up on a deed transfer some months down the road. In a perverse sense, he was relieved to be rid of the south acreage. What with the migrant's murder at the oak tree and his son's nightmarish witnessing of it, he was glad to unload the accursed ground for now. If and when he ever had opportunity to purchase the land back, it would be under circumstances where his problems would not be a factor in his family's lifestyle as they were now. This hope might never come to pass, but the family's financial standing, at least for a time, had not skipped a beat.

But a week later, after fully grasping what he'd done, Wade decided to speed up the process to take his land, and his life, back. But in reality, he had become obsessed with avenging the crime that he was more certain, day by day, had been committed against his daughter, and the terror Carl had forced upon his son. He had not been able to sleep a single full night in the long months since the incidents, and the anger was destroying him to the point that he was becoming a recluse even to his own family. He could barely speak in civil tones to his wife anymore, and his children almost never looked him in the eye. Carl had wrecked his life through the terrorizing of his children, and to imagine now that the big man holds the deed to a portion of his heritage caused Wade to curse his decision and to seek some way to bring the world back into focus. He would now cure all the ills in his life. And it was all to be done with a single bullet.

***

Wade clicked the chamber shut and sat back against a tree. A curtain of limbs hung before him. It was still dark and all was dead quiet. The moonlight was weak and the rising morning light would come in less than an hour, and he had no idea when Carl would be getting up. The new barracks were dark too. The white barracks nearest to him had unlit windows all around. The black, or Negro barracks, smaller and set deeper into the woods on the other side, had its open windows exposed, showing no light inside. The back porch to the house was twenty yards from the barracks. And Wade was only twenty-five yards from the porch.

He started for a cigarette but decided against it. He leveled the old rusty .30-30 into a tree fork and checked the hammer. He was ready. If he was afraid, he never exhibited symptoms; and if he thought this behavior was abnormal or extreme, he could not have shown less concern. But, before today, his thoughts had ranged from helpless rage to calm vengeance while studying what to do about the situation that had befallen his family. Now Carl would pay for his sins throughout eternity, beginning at the crack of dawn. Or whenever he stepped out the door.

Wade recalled the first time when he met Carl, then his attempt to return moments later to kill the mad man but being repelled by the glint of the blued steel of a gun out a window. He figured precautions were thereafter taken to guard against any further such attempts on the big man's life. He searched around the darkened yard as best as his eyes would allow. He quickly determined no sentries were on duty. If there were any dogs, they were asleep or inactive somewhere on the other side of the house. Carl's pickup truck was parked on the far side of the barracks alongside an old flatbed truck Wade had not seen on the road before. The front yard was visible from here, and if Carl came out the front door Wade would still have a shot, maybe not as good as the shot he had now, but still he could get him. A light breeze was now starting to pick up and it changed direction, it seemed, every few minutes.

Then after watching several lamplights turn on over a half-hour period, he heard the back door of the house creak open. Someone stepped down into the yard and began walking toward the barracks. He guessed from the figure that it was Billy. In a few minutes, lights were glowing throughout the two barracks, and Billy went back into the house. Other activities seemed to start right away. A dog barked somewhere on the other side. More lights came on in the house, and muffled noises started from within.

Wade eased up to one knee. He checked the rifle sights and could see a relatively unobstructed view to the porch in the growing morning light. In a few more minutes, the back door opened again. Again Billy stepped down to the yard carrying a water bucket and started toward the wellhouse. The door opened again. This time Carl emerged and stepped to the edge of the porch and stopped there. Wade watched as he worked to light a cigarette. A better shot was available down in the yard, but he raised the rifle and rolled back the hammer. It clicked into place and Wade propped his left elbow onto his left knee as he rolled to his right knee and held to a three-point firing position.

Carl leaned against a porch column looking around the yard while puffing on the cigarette. Several branches hung low, but Wade aimed through an easy opening and began to squeeze the trigger. Carl pulled away from the post and flicked the ashes out into the yard. Wade waited for him to lean back against the post. When he did, he turned slightly and looked directly, it seemed, at Wade. When Wade started to squeeze again, Carl leaned away and bent over, looking intently into the trees, again toward Wade. Now a twig hung between Wade's rifle sight and Carl's forehead. Knowing that a blade of grass could deflect a bullet several inches from its target at this range, he released the pressure on the trigger. Carl could see something in the dark woods. Wade stiffened to stone. A deer cannot easily distinguish stationary objects in broad daylight, and Wade figured Carl would be similarly blind in the relative darkness. "C'mon, you son-of-a-bitch," Wade whispered. "Stand up – stand up!"

Carl kept looking into the trees and took another draw on the cigarette, then stepped down into the yard. Wade cursed himself for his indecision. A curtain of twigs and limbs were now between himself and Carl. Billy filled the bucket and started back for the porch. Carl stopped him and pointed into the trees and said something. Wade crouched upward enough to get a sight through the limbs to Carl's midsection. Carl and Billy must have seen this motion as they flinched and started for the porch. Wade was amazed by Carl's obviously well-developed night vision and his luck. It didn't seem possible that Carl could be so aware and alert to his surroundings, but clearly the man was well-practiced in the arts of self-preservation and survival.

Wade followed Carl with the gun sight. Just as they made the bottom step, Carl dodged away and started back for the barracks. He dropped the cigarette and glanced back into the trees. Then, his arms swinging in wide arcs, he raced mightily for the barracks. Wade looked ahead and found an opening just before the corner of the barracks. He aimed and found his spot just as Carl passed across the opening. The rifle boomed and the bullet hit its mark. Carl lurched aside as if swatted by a bear and he slammed to the ground.

Wade stood up enough to see Carl lying prostrate. He wasn't moving. The dogs were barking and Billy jumped back into the yard. A shout came from near the barracks. Wade didn't bother to rechamber the rifle. He had presence of mind enough not to leave any evidence such as a shell casing at the scene. He watched Billy race toward the barracks and disappear into the shadows across the yard. Wade, though concerned that his presence was discovered, was sure Billy could never have seen him well enough to identify him. For a second, Wade imagined chasing Billy down to kill him too, but shortly there would be others from the barracks to witness the deed. He turned and bounded away into the trees. He could hear someone from the barracks shouting again, but no one followed.

***

Back at the house, Wade unloaded the rifle and shoved it underneath the front seat of Paul's car which he had borrowed the day before. Jimmy was still asleep and within minutes he had his groggy son up and dressed. Wade rushed him on to the car and encouraged him to lie down in the back seat and finish his sleep. Then shortly, they were rolling northward for a circuitous route around Braxton to Columbia, over an hour's drive away when driven directly.

It was broad daylight when Wade made the approach to Mount Pleasant. A bridge was ahead, and he made a gradual deceleration and looked back into the back seat. Jimmy still appeared to be asleep, so Wade reached underneath the front seat and retrieved the rifle. No traffic was coming either way. He stopped in the middle of the bridge, quickly stepped out, and with both hands slung the rifle far out into the high running creek. It was a lucky choice, he thought. Lots of fast water, and deep. Rolling once again, he soon found Jimmy sitting up and looking out the window and guessing how far along they had come.

"Should have gone to bed earlier, son," Wade said.

"Where are we?" Jimmy asked.

"Mount Pleasant, just ahead."

When they rolled into Mount Pleasant, Jimmy was finally alert enough to climb to the front seat and ask for the time. "About 7:30," Wade answered.

"Why'd we leave so early?" Jimmy asked.

"Had to make a couple of stops along the way," Wade said matter-of-factly. Made sense to Jimmy – he just slept through them. Probably had to get gas or something, he figured, faintly remembering one stop. Or two stops. Perhaps he was dreaming.

When they got to the train station in Columbia, Esther and Kelly Jean were sitting outside on a bench, their tow sacks and bags next to them. It had been three-and-a-half months since their departure to Parsons. Even still, the welcome was typical for the quiet family. Husband and wife kissed with a noiseless peck while the children loaded the car. Shortly they were heading back toward home.

They had just rolled out of Summertown when coming toward them was the sheriff's car moving at high speed, dust boiling high in its wake. As he shot past, directly behind him was a pickup truck tight on his tail. Looking back, Wade could see several field hands hunched over something in the back of the truck. The tailgate was shut, so Wade couldn't make out the details as it quickly shrunk in the distance.

"Somebody must have got hurt," Esther said softly.

"Yeah," Wade said deadpan. His consternation rose high when he pictured in his mind the shaggy, redheaded driver of the truck. No doubt Billy was the driver, and Carl was not dead. Not yet at least. Maybe the doctors in Columbia were short on miracles today, he thought. He wouldn't get shook up. He had steeled himself from the start. He wouldn't ponder regrets, and he wasn't going to start now by cursing himself for not taking a second shot to ensure the man's demise.

The rest of the drive home was uneventful. The only discussion of any substance was on the subject of Esther's kinfolk, their ailments and daily trials. Kelly Jean seemed the same – quiet, reserved, and unnoticed in the backseat.

CHAPTER 14

Carl Kallton, through inborn determination and the quick action by his confederates, had handily survived the assassination attempt. There were no advanced medical capabilities in Columbia, but he was stabilized there before being rushed on to Nashville.

The bullet had entered the left rib cage and ricocheted around the heart. It skimmed along the breastbone missing the major arteries before lodging near the right shoulder. Bone fragments from the shattered rib had scattered along the bullet path puncturing the left lung causing extensive bleeding into the lung and out the nose and mouth. Luckily for Carl, the heart was untouched, otherwise he would not have made it to Columbia, much less Nashville. The surgeons had debated whether the bullet was worth the effort and danger in removing it. It was removed after assessing that it was not near any vital organs that could be traumatized in the process.

The 200-grain, soft point bullet had failed to 'mushroom' as it was designed to do when traveling through the rib cage of a deer. Usually after hitting bone, this type of bullet will flatten out upon impact, thus ripping through the body a short distance creating a wide, massive, and fatal wound. In Carl's case, as it rarely happens, the bullet held its slender shape as it traveled through flesh and bone. Carl fought unconsciousness throughout the ordeal and even had the presence of mind enough to bark orders to his subordinates at the beginning of the run to Braxton for the sheriff, since neither Carl nor any of his people knew where the nearest medical facilities were.

After the first week, it was certain that Carl would survive. Infections were still a danger and would remain so for a while to come. If the doctors had advice for Carl on matters of healing and rest, they soon learned to keep such counsel to a minimum. Carl took their instructions for medication and therapy to a point. Then he relied on his own instincts. He made it clear that he knew his limitations better than any man, and he coached the doctors sternly when they tried to advise him to rest more when he felt he didn't need to. He had important business to tend to and was determined that the pulse of enterprise would not skip a beat. As a result, he had visitors from the farm at least twice a week, usually M.C. and sometimes the foremen, to discuss business and logistics matters.

After initial visits from law enforcement officials concerning possible motives and suspects, Carl told the sheriff and the state police to not bother themselves anymore. He would find the perpetrator, or perpetrators, himself and handle matters on his own. Visiting hours were all but ignored, and by the end of the fourth week Carl had his own private room strategically located where his personal guards could watch hallways and rooms. To the consternation of hospital personnel, the big man seemed to run his own program. Something was worrisome and fearful about this particular patient and everyone, by unspoken agreement, let him have free reign, as much as hospital policy would allow. Carl had insisted on tight security by ordering Billy to sit guard every night just outside his door. Carl was also keeping a handgun hidden beneath his mattress. He was fairly certain who had tried to kill him, but he would trust no one until he could get back to the farm and work out a strategy.

The big distillery was nearly complete, and to this point M.C. was running the show adequately in Carl's absence. He wasn't the intimidating whip-cracker that Carl was; but since everyone was getting higher wages than the legitimate farmers paid, he had, for the most part, reasonable cooperation, even from Roy. The only holdup in the whole operation was a major design change in the distillery that Carl had made shortly before the assassination attempt against him. His concept for a single, giant cylindrical cooker was abandoned because of structural problems inherent in holding the whole thing together when steam pressures built up to critical and dangerous levels. Instead, several rectangular cookers were to be built in a circular configuration, each with individual thumpers. All this was to be directed toward one giant condenser apparatus constructed in the center of the 'spoke.' The cookers were each nearly half as large in volume output as his original cooker concept; thus, when added together, the whole distillery system was far larger in capacity than his original design. A kerosene-fueled firebox had been constructed beneath each of the cookers. A fuel line ran to each cooker from a central tank on the south end of the compound. Because of the expansive size and complicated design, the workers took to calling the whole operation 'the steamplant.'

A laborious rerouting of a large stream a quarter-mile away had been finished in Carl's absence, and two wells had been dug near the steamplant itself. It was hoped that these three sources, plus a smaller stream nearby, would supply the mammoth daily water requirement for operations during peak production. Several new outbuildings ringed the compound. Over the steamplant itself, a sprawling, low roofed, barn-like structure was being constructed. Two barracks had been built in the compound to accommodate the work crews. Employment opportunities would soon be growing for tested and trusted migrants willing to take the risks.

M.C., with Carl's prompting, had devised ambitious management and staffing strategies for production and shipping of product at the second steamplant now under construction on the remote acreage belonging to Tom Buell. Plans for a lumber mill were being worked on for the recently acquired property purchased from Wade. The mill, like the vegetable fields, would be made to appear legitimate to any locals, such as hunters, that should happen upon it. Then of course, all newly cut lumber would be quietly transported for use in the growing illegitimate enterprises.

Everyone hunted 'free range;' that is, on adjoining properties owned by other people or lumber and pulpwood companies with no concerns about trespassing. But if the larger operations were to begin, then any errant locals, if it came to be necessary, would have to be warned off. While Carl was around, M.C. never felt that he needed to worry about the sheriff. Carl's imposing presence and his knack for keeping everyone under his thumb, so far including Sheriff Gene Carter, had kept security tight. But now, during Carl's absence, M.C. was forced to broaden his scope, maybe even try to think and conduct himself a little more like Carl.

With this in mind, M.C. drove into town one quiet afternoon. He had learned the address of someone he had hoped would become an asset to the operations. He drove down a dusty side street in town and pulled up alongside a broken fence in front of the house. Luckily, he found Deputy Harvey Carlson at home alone. He was renting a room in the back of a large boarding house in town that housed seasonal migrants, and was doing nothing more than leaning against a column on the porch when M.C. arrived. Harvey knew who he was, but gave no indication that he knew.

"Mr. Carlson?" M.C. asked, extending a hand.

"Yeah," Harvey said.

"I'm M.C. Colter. I'm from the big Kallton farm out on the west side of the county. I work with Carl Kallton, helping him run things on the farm, you know."

Harvey nodded. Then after a few minutes of fruitless small talk, M.C. dropped all pretense. "I'd like to talk to you about a profitable proposition," he said. Then he paused for Harvey's reaction. Harvey's face never changed. M.C. backed up to try again. Perhaps Carl was right. These hayseeds needed help in understanding broader concepts of business acumen.

"How long have you lived here, Mr. Carlson?"

"'bout three years," Harvey answered. He was unshaven for the day, this being his day off. He had several missing teeth like the migrants and many of the locals. His attitude was distrustful, even unfriendly; so M.C. had to slow down and, against his style, turn affable.

"Nice place. You own it?" M.C. asked, motioning at the old two-story house.

"No, just rent," Harvey said.

"I had a place like this once a few years ago. Owned it free and clear," M.C. ventured. He now wondered if his building up to a point with his apparent big city condescension would be taken as an insult. It was clear that Harvey was in no position to own anything of this magnitude free and clear. Harvey stepped back to a rickety chair and sat down. He didn't offer M.C. a seat.

"Just what did you come here fer, Mr. Colter? I don't have nothin' to interest you," Harvey said.

"Mr. Carlson, would you like to own this house, or one like it, free and clear?" M.C. asked, again pausing for his response.

"I reckon I would," Harvey said with a nod.

"Work for me and you can."

"I don't reckon I could do that, you workin' fer the likes of Carl Kallton an' all."

"Is that a fact?" M.C. said curtly. "What do you know about Carl Kallton, since you talk of him that way?"

"I un'erstand he has some dealin's with some rough Chicago folks. We all know around here how he made his money a-runnin' licker an' all," Harvey said with unexpected sternness.

"Running liquor? You mean Mr. Kallton?" M.C. asked with feigned surprise.

"'at's right!" Harvey said with a fierce nod.

"No, no, Mr. Carlson. He wouldn't bother with small operations like running bootleg – he hires people to do that for him," M.C. said snidely. Harvey stood up and pulled out a pre-rolled cigarette and lit it. He showed no reaction to M.C.'s sarcasm. "Look, I'm here to offer you something that's not likely to come your way again in your lifetime. I want to offer you a job that's easy and pays big money."

Harvey flared up. "Now see here – I gotta sneakin' suspicion that you're a-offerin' me a bribe of some sort er 'nother. You all done hired 'bout every hand there is around these parts. You all say you're just a-buildin' a big crop farm. But we're watchin' to see if maybe Carl Kallton's just a-workin' a front down here to make liquor – "

"No – I'm not bribing you. A bribe is a one-time payoff. This is for as long as you want to help us," M.C. said.

Harvey took a long draw on his cigarette and stared at M.C. for a moment and said, "Keep talkin'."

"How much are you making right now – in a month?"

Harvey didn't answer.

"About ten, twenty, maybe thirty dollars a month?" M.C. prodded. Harvey shook his head, but M.C. figured he was close enough. "How would you like for me to double that?"

Harvey took another draw. M.C. thought he saw a glimmer of expectation in his eye. He turned and started back to the car. When Harvey stepped down to follow, M.C. knew he had him.

"What is it you're a-wantin' me to do?" Harvey asked.

"Just stay where you are and keep an eye out. And an ear open. If you know of a blockade against us, just let me know when and where. If you hear of the state police or the federals moving in, just find out what you can and pass it along. Nothing more than passing along some information – that's all."

"So you boys are a-runnin' liquor?"

"Look, Mr. Carlson, we're not going to do anything to hurt anybody around here. Nobody's even going to know we're here if everybody cooperates. All we plan to do is service a market up north. We won't even sell to the folks around here, much less in Tennessee. Besides, we don't want to compete with any local operators around here."

Harvey smiled for the first time. Yes, he had heard that Gene had closed down a fairly large clandestine distillery a few years ago. It had taken the sheriff a couple of years to find it, and it was a proud moment in his career. But that operator had no spare change to buy off the law. Lately there had been little motive to watch Carl very closely because of the money he regularly infused into the local economy. Everyone was happy, it seemed, with the little arrangement. And if anyone outside the law suspected anything about Carl, it was kept safely to himself.

"I could get sent up th' river fer a long time fer goin' with somethin' like this," Harvey said.

"Straight cash – nobody knows," M.C. said with an extended hand.

Harvey shook the soft hand so firmly that M.C. winced. "I won't take a dime under thirty bucks a month," Harvey said coolly. Then he released his grip and returned to the house, never glancing back.

CHAPTER 15

"You let me handle the law around here! If there are any payoffs, I'll decide who gets them, and how much," Carl said. M.C. started to say something in his defense, but Carl cut him off. "You know, I could have bought off the sheriff first, then his deputy would fall in behind for half the money – you ever think of that?" He now waited for an answer.

"I don't think you could ever buy this sheriff, Carl. He wants to fashion himself as honest and a standard for this community. I talked with the deputy and – "

"Anybody can be bought – sometimes with a little persuasion – but anybody will sell out for the right price. But I guess we'll never know now, will we?"

"We can still get to the sheriff, Carl – "

"Yes, we can. But when we do, we can never let him know that we have his deputy before we have him. We have to play a lot more cautious now than before."

M.C. didn't see the cause for all the fuss. He felt that the deputy would be an easy target and offered an opportunity for M.C. to show a little initiative outside his regular duties. But it was a relief to have Carl back home. The awareness of his imposing presence seemed to push everyone to a higher level of motivation, and it put a damper on the occasional brawl at the steamplant barracks.

Carl had left the hospital only five weeks after being admitted, which was long before the doctors' projected release. With paranoia working his mind day and night, he refused to lie around until some appointed release date and possibly get ambushed again on the trip home. He left abruptly in the middle of the night and got home in time for an early breakfast and a meeting with the foremen. Carl and M.C. went back to the front room to finish the staff meeting, which had broken for coffee. They had sequestered themselves from the others for a few minutes to discuss upper management issues. The meeting with the foremen was brought back to order.

"All right, boys, I don't have anything else – except one thing. I'm sure there's been a lot of speculation about who tried to take me down a few weeks ago. Carter and the state police are completely in the dark as to the true perpetrators. But I ran the list down and made some deductions. The only serious suspects that ever really came to mind are Tom Buell and Wade Kallton. But I don't think Buell has the balls or the talent to work like this – I heard the son-of-a-bitch missed half the cows he shot at – so that leaves Wade. We're not going to give him opportunity to try again.

"So I want to set up a twenty-four hour guard around this house with men and dogs. If I had a man out there with better eyes than mine, maybe we'd know for sure who tried to do me in. I figure one or two men each shift should do it. I want one posted along the east side toward Wade's place, and the other down on the other side of the barracks about halfway between the house and the road. After I make contact with Wade, maybe we won't need guards anymore. But till then, I won't let it happen again."

"How do you want to approach him next time, Carl?" M.C. asked, "He might want a gunfight as soon as he sees you, even if it's in the middle of Braxton."

"This is not the Wild West. I don't think he will play that hard. You have to figure that he tried to take me under cover of darkness, and leave no evidence. I suspect if he tries again, he'll work the same way, except different, if you understand my meaning.

"If any of you see him on the road, tell him I want to see him. Anytime. Any place. All I want to do is talk to the man." Carl noted the perplexed expressions on his foremen's faces, so he deflected their suspicions. "Obviously he has hard feelings for something he thinks I've done against him. I don't know. Maybe he wants his land back – cheap. I just want to straighten things out and get along.

"Another thing, boys. We were talking about the sheriff a minute ago. Until I can figure something out, I don't want to hear of anyone in this organization talking to him. If he starts asking questions, tell him to come to me. Pass that along to the crews working on the steamplant. If there are no questions, let's get to work. M.C., stay put for a minute."

The three foremen left, leaving Carl and M.C.

"A couple of things, M.C. Traffic's been building up in and out of the steamplant. When things get rolling, we're going to have to do something to distract attention away from the road. I've thought about it, and I think the best thing to do is start a pulpwood mill down south and west of the plant on my property and on Roy's. What with the trucks working in and out, it'll look legit enough. Then we can start moving product out at night when we're full throttle."

"Pulpwood?" M.C. asked.

"Yes," Carl answered. M.C. sat with a questioning look and Carl said, "Damnit, M.C., don't you know what pulpwood is?" M.C. shook his head. "Hell, what'd they teach you in those goddamn Chicago grade schools? Don't worry about it – go tell my construction man, Clint, to go south and see what we've got down there and advise."

Carl shook his head in derision then changed the subject. "I didn't want to talk too much about the sheriff and Wade in front of the boys a while ago. They know too much as it is. Somebody said Gene's been down this way twice in the last month. There's no reason for him to be coming down into this corner of the county. So we need to make a move on the sheriff soon. We'd be in better shape if we could put him on our side before we start up than later. If he can't be bought in a hurry – and I think you're right, he can't be – then we need to work double time on taking him some other way. I have some ideas I think will work."

Changing the subject, M.C. asked, "Carl, what's the story between you and Wade Kallton? You seem convinced it was Wade that shot you. Is there something I don't know? He seemed reasonably cordial when I bought his land for you."

"You listen to me," Carl said, his attitude souring. "You work for me on a need-to-know basis. What's between me and Wade, I'll handle. Your job is to concern yourself with management and security around this farm. You're going to keep security tight because I figure he'll try again in a month or two after things settle down. If he gets through again, it'll be on your ass this time. Understand?"

"All right – fine," M.C. answered. "If you just want me to be your personal house nigger, I'll settle for that, as long as you keep those paychecks coming. But if I hear any talk about problems I should know something about, and I don't, I'm going to look more like your personal asshole among your men here. I can help forestall problems for you if I hear idle talk about things I should know about. I would be a better asset to this organization if I was a little more educated on the games being played in this county. Now – you understand?"

Carl sat with his stony smile. There was no visible reaction to M.C.'s sneering answer. He had tried to keep things uncomplicated, but he could see M.C.'s point. He had mulled it about himself. He needed a confidant within the organization and M.C. was the only logical choice.

After a moment, he raised up and leaned back heavily in his chair. "All right," he said. "If that's what you want." Carl thought a moment to himself, then started.

"Well, we had a little situation up on the old road here back last October. Me, Billy, and a fellow named Earnie Jackson were walking east about 6:30 in the morning. I hired Jackson along about the same time as Billy to work on the house here. We came up on this car sitting over on the right side of the road with the motor running. A boy, about twenty to twenty-five years old, was sitting in it and he hadn't seen or heard us walking. The motor noise, I guess. We stood there behind the car trying to see what it was up in them trees that the boy seemed to be looking for. When after about two or three minutes we couldn't see anything, we walked over to the boy and I said, 'Hey boy, what the hell you think you're doing here on my property?' He was on timberland property, but I figured whatever was going on was probably happening on my land too. Right off, he tried to throw the goddamn car into gear and take off. Well, right off, I grabbed him by the arm and yanked him right out of the car. Must have scared the boy bad because he started shaking like shit. Well, goddamn it, I wanted to know right then what he was doing so close to my property, so I slapped the hell out of him."

"Damn, Carl," M.C. said, "What was your hurry?"

"Well, I figured I didn't have time. Whoever it was that he was looking for up in the trees might come down on us. The boy acted so shook up and scared I figured I could jar him loose and speed things up. I asked him, 'What the hell's going on on my land?' Right then he turned and tried to run. Didn't say a damn thing. Just turned and run. Well, hell, if somebody's running stills on my land, I want to know. So, I slapped the shit out of him again.

"Billy and Jackson started getting a little loud and rambunctious – they'd been drinking all morning and I guess they wanted to join in the fun – so they boxed the boy around a little while I searched the car. He wouldn't say a damn thing the whole time, so I knew then that some kind of illegal enterprise was going on somewhere nearby. That boy, I figured, was waiting for an all-clear signal of some sort to move in and load up with a carload of liquor. Hell, you know how these small-time hillbilly operators haul their product.

"Anyway, I went back to the boy and started knocking him around a little. I was going to make him talk one way or another. I've never seen a boy so scared. I could never figure out why he wouldn't talk. Finally, he said something about a brother and his fiancé. I don't know. Next thing I know, crazy Jackson came down on top of his head with the butt of the shotgun we had with us and knocked him out cold. I yanked the gun out of Jackson's hand and slapped the hell out of him.

"Right then is when it happened. Somebody up on the ridge shot at us. Son-of-a-bitch missed. I swung the gun around and fired. Damnit if Jackson had a slug in the chamber. He always had birdshot in it, but not today. I shot to kill. Naturally I figured it was an operator up on that ridge trying to take us out for working over their runner. He must have been watching us whipping up on that boy."

"So you shot back in self-defense," M.C. said, assuming the only helpful explanation.

Carl nodded and laughed. "That's right. And I killed the boy up on the ridge. I meant to, so that was all right. I figured that would be all of it, so we turned to leave. Then, we heard somebody scream over the ridge. We stopped and waited. We heard the scream again, and then it seemed somebody was running away over the hill. Next thing I knew, a kid went running across the road down a few yards from us, and still screaming. I told the boys to chase her down – yeah, a girl – and bring her ass back. I was still going to find out what this was all about.

"Damnit, Billy got her and brought her straight back. The bitch was fainting on us and acting all crazy and spitting at the mouth. That girl was more scared than any goddamn bitch I'd ever seen. I didn't know how to get her to settle down, so I slapped the hell out of her just like I did that boy. She stopped and looked at me like I was the devil. Hell, I didn't know I was that goddamned ugly. Then the next thing I know, a pack of wild-ass dogs was coming at us. I could hear them first over the ridge where the boy was hit, then I heard them coming our way. Damn, some of the meanest goddamned dogs I've ever seen. I cocked the gun and tried to shoot, but damn old Jackson hadn't bothered to put any more ammo in it. The damn thing was empty. So, I went for some rope I saw in the car. Hell, them hayseeds must've used that car for a freight truck. Had a shitload of gear in the back seat. I worked that rope like a whip on them dogs and managed to force them to back off. I whipped a couple of them pretty hard before they turned and ran off. Hell, I think I knocked an eyeball out of one of them. Kicked another one hard in the throat.

"Then I looked over and old Billy was so goddamn drunk he didn't know what he was doing. Hell, he was messing with that girl over in the ditch down the road a few yards. Hell, by the time I got to him he nearly had half her clothes tore off. She was still spitting at the mouth like a crazy bitch – I never seen anybody so messed up.

"I pulled Billy off and knocked the shit out of him. Hell, he was so goddamn head-drunk he just laughed and yelled out some shit like, 'C'mon, Carl Dean, don't hurt to have a little fun!' I kicked him in the ass because he spoke my name so that girl would know who the hell I am, and I told him to get his ass back up the road. Then I went to the girl and picked her up and tried to put her clothes back on. I don't think the bitch was playing with a full deck because she just stood there and spit at the mouth. I thought her eyes were going to pop out of her head.

"Hell, I guess I messed up. Maybe they were just running off together, but I didn't know. Then I just told the kid to run off. She just stood there, so I told her again to go. She turned and ran back up into the trees. Then she went on screaming again, but she kept right on running.

"Then, in a minute, I could hear someone way over the ridge again. Sounded like two or three men and, from the noise, they were on horses. Anyway, we eased on back up the road. We had left the truck over the next hill toward the house, so we got in and got back to the house in a hurry. But we didn't stop there. I figured that was enough trouble for the day, so I drove on into the woods and we stayed hidden until that night when I took off for Chicago. Figured I needed an alibi. But no one else knew I was here to begin with."

"What's the connection? Who were these people?" M.C. asked.

"The two boys both belonged to Tom Buell. The girl just happened to be Wade's kid. Hell, how was I to know? Damn, why did they have to be on the road when there were three drunk men on the road?" Carl said, shaking his head with a chuckle.

"Doesn't make sense, Carl. Why didn't Wade just turn it all over to the sheriff? If the kid got away, she had to tell somebody," M.C. said.

"Oh, yeah, damn – forgot to tell you. I did have a little talk with the girl. After I picked her up, I told her that she was to tell nobody what she saw. I could tell that she was so messed up that she figured I was the devil, and I said that I would come and get her if she talked. Hell, I told her that! That if she told anybody, I would get her and her family some night when she didn't expect it. Right in the middle of the night I would come right into her house and get her first, then her family one at a time. And to stress the point, I slapped the shit out of her. Well, hell, I still don't think I got her attention, so I slapped her again and yanked her right up to my face, eyeball to eyeball. Then I knew she was hearing every word because her eyes popped out at me like a bug. Yeah, I feel bad about it but, goddamn, what else could I do? Hell, M.C., you know how we always operated."

"How did this work out with Wade? Didn't she tell him?" M.C. asked.

"Hell, I don't know," Carl said with a laugh. "I left for Chicago. When I got back, the sheriff came for a visit and he didn't seem to know anything about what happened. So, I figured I was in the clear."

"Damn, Carl, you had two witnesses against you."

Carl laughed again. "Damn Mother Luck was with me, I guess. I heard the boy in the car died. Damn Jackson must've split his skull. He stayed alive for a while but word was he couldn't talk. Hell, he couldn't talk before we hit him!" Carl looked down at the floor as if in thought for a moment, seeming to chuckle to himself. "I guess the girl took me serious. I never heard a word about her. Of course, I don't know anybody who knows her people other than Roy. But what the hell does he know?"

M.C. asked, "You trust Billy? And how do you know this Jackson fellow won't talk?"

"Aw, Billy's all right. Hell, he knows I'd kill him if he says anything, anyway." Carl said with derisive glee. "And as for Jackson, damn – I did kill him!"

M.C. smiled. If anyone else had said this, he would have reason to doubt. But not with Carl. He would suspect that he was stating the facts of the matter before he would joke around when discussing severe corporate actions.

"Damn son-of-a-bitch couldn't keep his goddamn mouth shut. Billy caught him one day talking to Roy and his boys about what we did on the road – well, I have to be fair, I guess – he didn't really tell him anything, but he was saying things that could have led Roy to think that he knew more than he should have. I warned him once. Then I heard him start to talk about it once myself when Roy was with us, but he shut up when he saw me. Then Billy heard him do it again later that day. Damn, if he talked that way to Roy, Wade's cousin, no telling what he would say to someone else on down the road.

"Anyway, Billy and me, we took him out on a gold hunting expedition one night." Carl chuckled and shook his head in mockery. "Hell, Jackson would believe anything anybody told him. I told him that my old man's father had buried a big trunk of gold bars and coins he had stolen from the Yankees before the war down on some land he once owned. I told Jackson when the law got after him and threw him in jail for the robbery, he said he would die before telling anybody what he had done with the gold. Hell, old Jackson believed the whole goddamn story. I told him I found out where it was supposed to be buried, and I would give him five-percent of the gold if he would dig it up for me. Hell, he was always wanting to make an extra buck. He didn't care how. He'd work, cheat or steal; he didn't give a damn.

"Well, we got together late one evening, and we headed on over to that piece of land we just bought from Wade. Walked right to the middle of it and started digging. Right underneath a big oak tree – biggest one I could find. Told him that it was buried under that tree, and to start digging. Dumb son-of-a-bitch just started digging. Didn't ask any questions. Aw, Billy helped him out here and there, but when he got down about five or six feet, damn, he started getting smart. He wanted to know how far down that trunk was. Then when he asked for the lantern is when we let him have it. Damn, Billy was supposed to shoot the son-of-a-bitch but he didn't have the balls. I shot him while he was still in the hole. I made Billy fill it up real pretty-like; like nothing ever happened."

M.C. was leaning forward, catching every word. This was Carl's style, he seemed to think. Have his adversary dig his own grave; the epitome of effortless problem solving of the most diabolical sort.

"Damn if Wade didn't come and see me that next morning. Told me to dig Jackson up and stay off his property. How in hell he knew, I don't know," Carl said, laughing out loud. But there was a strain of anger in his voice and in his gestures. It was clear he didn't take Wade's knowledge of his clandestine deeds very easily. But he made up for it with a vindictive retort. "But he didn't say a goddamn thing about his girl! So, I guess she still ain't told him what I did to her and them Buell boys." Carl paused for a moment of introspection then added, "But then, maybe she did. That's one reason I think it might have been Wade that tried to do me in a few weeks ago. Billy told me Wade tried to return on horseback that same morning he visited, just a few minutes after he left. But Billy managed to ward him off with a gun pointed out the window here. I don't know what was in his mind. I guess he was going to shoot and kill us both. That's another reason I figure he has the balls to try again."

M.C. asked, "Why in hell didn't he go to the sheriff if he knew about everything that you did?"

"Damn, M.C., how in hell do I know? Maybe he figured he didn't have an alibi. Maybe the sheriff would've fingered him instead of me. I don't know. But I can't figure out how he knew that somebody was killed the night before on his land, and how he figured it was me that did it. Maybe someone saw us walking down the road and told him. How he knows just bugs the shit out of me."

"Did you dig him back up like he told you?" M.C. asked.

"Yeah, we dug his smelly ass up. Right that next night. Threw him in a tow sack and carried him out like a deer on a pole. Well, hell, since Wade knew all about the body, we had to do something. So, me and Billy brought him back here behind the house and burned him to ashes. Soaked him in coal oil, covered him and all his shit with a load of brambles and got rid of the evidence." Carl thought for a minute, then added, "You ever smelled a burning body? Damnedest smell I ever smell't."

CHAPTER 16

"Does he think all men are whoremongers?" someone asked, genuinely angered by the new development.

A couple of men at the other end of the white barracks nodded agreement. The first man looked back out the window at the new tiny, haphazardly constructed square building situated down below them in a shallow meadow a few yards from the cookhouse. At first glance it appeared to be a chapel because of its quaint-square appearance and sharp, steeple-like roof. The sweaty young woman was still there standing in the little building's doorway with her hands on her high, bulging hips. She glanced often toward the barracks as if expecting someone to step out and enter her abode at any moment. And everyone could guess for what purpose.

"Well, go on out there, Joe, an' see what she wants. She might give you more'n you want!" another migrant said with a laugh.

The first man didn't smile, nor did anyone else. He was disgusted by it all. But he, like everyone else in his barracks, was powerless to effect any change in how things were done around the farm. Just a half-hour earlier, Billy Wilson had entered the little building with the woman and returned to the yard fifteen minutes later smiling as if he had found the fountain of youth. He spied a couple of the men peering out the window at him, and with a gesture of wicked triumph he yelled, *"She ain't but four bits! Yeah – just four bits!"*

But after a week, there were no takers at the Christian barracks, black or white. Disgustedly, Carl ordered the woman to evacuate and move to the southern barracks where another prostitute was operating a thriving enterprise. The little building was shut down and, as punishment for the migrants' lack of appreciation for Carl's goodwill, they were not permitted to convert it for Sunday church services or hymn sings in spite of requests.

Then one morning, the activity around the house was pressed to fever pitch. Orders were sent out and all barracks personnel went to their field work early. The house was quarantined and occupied this day with two of the ill-reputed young women and two designated staffers; all, except Billy Wilson, consigned to a square room in the main house where the windows had been boarded up. An atmosphere of malevolent control restrained frivolous conversation and kept everyone to the single-minded purpose of the day.

Carl stepped out of the room and checked his watch. He looked back through the door at the little pink-sheeted bed strategically parked amidst gaudy red drapes and a pair of pink Victorian pole lamps. The women, both wrapped in nothing more than robes made semi-sheer by perspiration, sat mutely on the bed. They looked up at Carl with the expression of children cowered by an over-stern schoolteacher. In the opposite corner of the room, a tall flash pole with a black box camera nearby was readied for action. The photographer, an owlish, rotund Chicagoan from Carl's old haunts, sat on a stool next to the camera. He placed a fat cigar in a tooth gap in the corner of his mouth. He patted his gear vest for matches but his search was cut short by Carl's barking voice. "You forgetting already? I said do nothing to distract from our project this morning. Nothing. No noise. No odors. Nothing from the ordinary that might raise any suspicions. Put it away."

The cameraman dutifully obeyed, then folded his hands before him as if to mock the condescending tone of the big man's orders. Carl clicked the door shut and stood still a moment as if to check the air for distracting sounds. The boarded room had been made light-tight, leaving the cameraman and the harlots in pitch darkness and airless heat. Carl glanced back down the hallway to the kitchen to find Billy standing stiffly against a wall, awaiting orders to act.

Carl moved to the front room and sat to a steaming coffee cup and waited, wordless. M.C., similarly set up at the table, gazed out the windows but never touched the coffee. He wouldn't admit to his apprehension about the morning's efforts going off without a hitch.

About ten minutes till eight, the sheriff's car pulled up out front. Gene lingered for over a minute, eyeing everything about the house as if expecting a trap of some sort to ensnarl him if he were not careful. He moved slowly to enter the house, still checking everything with each step. Carl held the door open for him while holding his cup. Gene nodded and walked in. He removed his hat and wiped the sweat off his forehead and returned the hat. M.C. stood up, introduced himself, shook Gene's hand and offered him a seat. Gene sat down at the table, as close to the door as he could get.

"How about a cup, Sheriff?" Carl asked.

Gene demonstrated by his dour expression that he wasn't happy to be here. He nodded no. Carl figured that was all right – he'll keep him here until he gets thirsty. Gene didn't say a word. He folded his hands on the table before him and looked up at Carl. The big man had asked for a meeting with the good sheriff this morning, and with reluctance, Gene accepted.

"Sheriff – " Carl started saying. He turned to the kitchen and told Billy to bring a fresh cup of coffee anyway. "Sheriff," he started again, "I've been giving some thought to my actions of the past and I think I owe you an apology of sorts. I realize now that I should get along with the local folk if I am to raise a farm amongst these good people. You caught me on a bad day back in March."

Carl paused to study Gene's reaction. It seemed clear that Gene was not going to be patronized. Carl's attempts at friendliness were clearly unnatural and forced. He would have to do better than just talk into dead air to convince the sheriff of his reformed intentions.

"I know you've heard about me, Sheriff. My shadow is darker than most folks'," Carl said with renewed seriousness, then paused. "Where's your deputy?"

"He's just part-time," Gene said. He leaned back in the chair, taking a more relaxed posture. "Mr. Kallton, I'll accept your apology, and if you say you want to settle down and raise crops like everyone else, there won't be any problems."

"You can promise me that, Sheriff?"

"Yes," Gene said, "You haven't done anything that I can see to show me otherwise. Not yet, anyway."

Carl smiled. Or perhaps it was the same cynical grin, just exaggerated. Gene couldn't tell. "Good," Carl said. "Glad you think so."

"You pulling pulpwood out south of the road here?" Gene asked.

Carl didn't miss a beat. "Yeah, got some good mature timber down there. You've seen my trucks?"

"Yeah, I seen one or two. You mind if I drive down and have a look?"

Again, Carl didn't skip a beat. "I wouldn't advise it, Sheriff. The road's too rough right now. We already tore up about a half-dozen good truck tires down there. Why don't you wait till we get it cleaned up, then I'll give you a grand tour?"

Gene nodded, then got up to leave. Surely there was no point in sticking around. Carl was behaving overly casual and cool again. Gene could find no honesty or forthrightness in his persona.

"What's your hurry, Sheriff? We just started here. Thought I'd show you around the farm."

"You seen one farm, reckon you've seen them all," Gene said, his voice tone lacking any interest in Carl's proposal. Billy returned with the unwanted coffee and sat it on the table near Gene. Gene ignored it.

"Please sit down, Sheriff. I want to tell you about the people who tried to take me down," Carl said, sitting down at the table.

Gene stood looking pensively at the door. "Seems to me you ought to let me worry about that," he said.

"Well, you've got enough to worry about. I think I can handle my own affairs. I just wanted to tell you that some Darby boys came down here from Chicago to settle an old score from my rough and rowdy days. I'm sure they got theirs when word got back that I made it. But don't worry about a damn thing, Sheriff. They're not going to send anybody back down to finish the job. They know I'll be on their ass now if they grow the balls to try again."

"Maybe I should deputize someone to stay around here for a while. You never know."

"Not necessary," Carl said, then he turned to the kitchen. "Billy, bring the good sheriff something to eat in here with his coffee."

"Just give me a drink of water, then I'll be on my way," Gene said.

"You hear the man, Billy, fix him a glass of water."

M.C. was now sitting at the end of the table in a darkened corner of the room. Carl was on the other side near the door, a few steps from Gene. A few more words were spoken before Billy brought in a small glass of water. The sheriff turned the bottom up and nearly gulped it whole. He placed the glass on the table and walked to the door, then said, "I'll take a look at your crops on the way out. You boys don't work too hard, now."

The sheriff helped himself out the door. He looked back through the glass at Carl. Carl was gazing at him in that same intense way that he remembered from the first time he met him. It would be hard to trust a face like that, he thought.

***

Gene was jerked awake by the intense sunray that was reflected through the windshield straight into his eyes. The car's steering wheel was directly above his face; a startlingly unnatural picture. He reached up and grasped it and strained to pull himself upright. Something was wrong with his head. It felt tight, as if over-inflated. The simple act of sitting up sent a swelling sensation upward through his body, which quickly culminated in a sudden pounding headache. He felt intense grogginess and fatigue. A touch of nausea played with his body, coming and going like a pendulum. It was a few moments yet before he felt steady enough to sit up without holding onto the steering wheel.

Looking through the windows into the darkened front room of the house, he couldn't find any movement. Carl, M.C., or Billy was nowhere in sight. The front door was shut, just as he had left it. He managed to start the car. He checked the house again. Still nothing. He backed the car across the yard and then stopped to further study his condition.

He looked down to his shirt and pants and found them disheveled. His belt was a couple of notches loose and his shoes felt tight. His hat was on, but was bent and crooked. He checked his pockets but everything seemed to be in place. He fumbled around for his watch and pulled it out. It showed 9:47. He was sweating profusely in the hot car. He stepped out, leaving the car running. He straightened his clothes and loosened his shoelaces and refitted his hat. He returned his gaze to the house and searched it for life. The only sounds being a slow cooing dove a hundred yards eastward and another bird, probably a robin, just on the other side of the house. No trace of dogs was evident.

He still couldn't seem to organize his thoughts very well. As he stood by the car, seconds passed, sometimes minutes, for which Gene could not later account. Soon enough, his mind began to lose its dysfunction and find some measure of traction. The only thing that played strongly in his mind was a feeling of anger and violation. He felt he should return to the house to find the reason for this disturbing turn of events. Somehow, he was sure he would find no answers.

Slowly, he drove the car back across the yard to the driveway that entered the North Road. Still, there was no one visible in the house. Everything was quiet. He drove past the fields that lay spread out to the east and saw several field hands tending to late season crops. They looked up at him as he drove by, but otherwise seemed uninterested by his presence.

In half an hour he was back at the office and was feeling, by this time, as well as he had at early morning.

CHAPTER 17

"How much longer is this going to go on, Wade?"

"As long as it takes."

"You're going to keep quiet about it for the rest of our lives?"

"Esther, I don't expect anything from you other than what you have been doing all along. You keep the house, and take care of Kelly Jean. I'll take care of everything else. The farm. The sheriff. The state. The Buells."

"Jimmy, too?"

Wade flared up. "I can take care of my boy!"

Esther turned mute. The tone in Wade's voice was too savage to push further. She looked down the hallway to the front room. Kelly Jean was there, doing nothing but gazing out the window.

"Go on – just get on out of the house," Esther said with great restraint.

It was yet another fruitless effort to prod Wade to open up on the subject of recent events concerning the Buells and the cattle massacre. Like everyone else, she suspected nothing of her husband's assassination attempt on Carl Kallton's life.

Several times before, she had pushed Wade to explain his motives and reasons for keeping the family in complete quarantine against the authorities and the rest of the world. Secretly she appreciated his willingness to sacrifice his own mental harmony for the sake of Kelly Jean's fragile mind. But she was severely unnerved when Gene took him to jail for forty-eight hours after refusing a cryptic court order to bring their daughter in for questioning. He was released only after Wade threatened severe legal action for Gene's overly aggressive interpretation of the order. Kelly Jean was under-aged and not subject to such orders without parental consent. Esther wanted detailed assurances that things would not get any worse for them because of Wade's determination to defy the sheriff and keep his family hidden from everyone outside the farm.

She had to admit that these tactics seemed to help keep Kelly Jean emotionally leveled. She had to acknowledge, to this point, that Wade was proven right in his efforts to hold the authorities at bay. Esther had known from the day of James Buell's death that her daughter knew nothing of how it all had happened by the simple fact that Kelly Jean had been queried by the sheriff when she was finally found hours after the shooting. Esther remembered how frightened and exhausted her daughter was when she was brought home. Esther still shuddered when she recalled Kelly Jean's unmovable insistence that she knew nothing of the circumstances surrounding James's death, other than the fact that he had been shot by someone who had been hidden from her view by the ridge alongside the road. Kelly Jean was beyond hysterics, and it seemed that any further questioning would have driven her to insanity. Wade cut short the inquisition by the sheriff when it became apparent that he was pushing too hard. The sheriff had talked to her for only a very few short minutes, but it proved too much so soon after the tragedy. The girl had lost the love of her life in the most horrific manner imaginable, and it had come close to destroying her mind.

Ever since, by an unspoken agreement, Kelly Jean had been kept behind an impenetrable wall of protection, and no one ever spoke of the event again. Yet, the strong suspicion that the new man in town must somehow have been involved was eating away at Wade's and Esther's souls. Kelly Jean's disastrous breakdown at the mere mention of his name was a clear reason for Esther's apprehension concerning the big man's involvement in the killings and his likely connection to Kelly Jean's mental distress.

Esther wanted answers, and she had determined that Wade knew something but was withholding it from everyone. It was driving her over the edge at times, but the needs of her daughter kept pulling her back to reality, thus forcing Esther to comply with Wade's leadership in the matter. During quiet moments, she had determined that it was much easier to care for her daughter if she remained comfortably ignorant of all external distractions and concerns. But her inquisitive mind kept her nipping at Wade's heels whenever something happened that shook her sense of well-being and stability.

Wade obeyed his wife and walked out of the house. He was fed up too, but he had long ago convinced himself that he could trust no one with the knowledge he had. Everything, so it seemed, stayed in reasonably acceptable harmony as long as he maintained a firm grip on the reins of control over his family, as well as those of strategy against the outside world. If this meant that others might have to endure a bit of discomfort or hostility against him, so be it. If he could not provide for his family and keep them safe in whatever methods were at hand, then what was the point in earning the titles of husband and father?

He gazed across to the upper pasture and found Jimmy still working with the kaiser blade along the fence. He hadn't slowed down, so Wade didn't interfere. He saddled up his horse with unusual energy, then blazed down the trail toward his brother's house to pick up a couple of hand tools he needed. Paul had returned early from the milk run and, like everyone else, he wasn't in a good mood. He saw Wade coming on horseback and in a minute he had his own horse saddled and he started across the yard away from Wade as if to avoid him.

"Ain't you gonna clean those milk cans first?" Wade asked as he pulled alongside.

"I'll get them later. I got another problem right now, and I'm going to get to the bottom of it right now."

"What's wrong, Paul?"

"Didn't Jimmy tell you what happened while we was milking this morning?"

"No – not a word."

"You even talk to your boy today?"

"I said, what's wrong?" Wade barked, clearly insulted by the inference.

"You remember when I told you about hearing big trucks running late at night down the road here a couple of weeks ago? And you said they was probably running pulpwood out west of here?" Wade nodded. "They ain't hauling timber, Wade. Not at night," Paul said angrily. "They was running nearly all night last night. Every couple of hours a big motor would start running full-throttle, as loud as anything I ever heard in my life. They're big trucks; them big city freight trucks that nobody's ever seen around these parts before."

"So what's this all about? Why're you so upset?"

Paul chuckled derisively. The answer should have been obvious, yet he was sure that Wade understood. "Don't you hear them? Didn't you hear them last night?" he asked aggressively.

Wade nodded. He had heard the truck noise, but it was distant and faint. Surely, he thought, it couldn't be that much worse here.

"The boys woke up about two this morning scared nearly to death. My little one didn't know what was going to happen to us when one of them trucks ground a gear. It sounded like a hundred shotguns fired off all at once! And the cows was so jittery this morning that we almost couldn't get them milked in time to make the run!"

"What're you planning on doing, then?" Wade asked.

"I'm going to go tell them to run their trucks in the daylight hours so we can get some sleep."

"Now come on, Paul – you know better than that. Don't go fooling around with something that's out of your league."

"What do you mean, Wade? What're you talking about?"

"I don't know – it might be some kind of operation you don't need to be messing with."

Paul gazed disgustedly at his brother. He had little patience for such vague, cryptic nonsense. "What does that mean? You know something I don't? Does this have something to do with that Carl Kallton fellow? Tell me what you know, Wade – now."

Wade kept his face straight and poker. "It might be, but I wouldn't know. I think you should just tell Gene and let him investigate."

Paul had endured a sleepless and frustrating night, and he wanted to punish someone for it. He sat in the saddle for a moment to think. Then he decided. "Well, I'm going to run down there and check it out anyway."

He kicked the flank of the horse and off he went. Wade cursed and chased after him. Paul quickly entered the road and turned west. Wade had to work hard to keep up. They dashed down the road for nearly a half-mile before Wade had had enough. "*Hold up, there!*" he yelled. Paul halted the horse and looked at his brother. "What're you getting all excited about? It's just a sawmill operation. Maybe it'll stop in a week or two."

"I done said it ain't no sawmill. I got suspicions it's something big – like a moonshine operation of some kind. One of them big gangster distilleries they bust up all the time in Chicago. And don't play me for a fool. You know as well as I do that ain't no sawmill. You know nobody runs sawmills at night."

"Then go tell Gene. Let him handle it. Why're you bothering yourself? If it really is something like that, you don't want to get involved anyway, do you?"

Paul angrily yanked the reins away and he, again, rode westward. Wade, again, followed. Another half-mile of dirt and gravel passed beneath them. Then Paul stopped again. A hundred yards away he could see a new road cut into the trees heading south. That, he knew, was where the trucks were coming out, and going in.

Now Wade was angry. His brother was going to get into a load of trouble and his ignorance of that fact made Wade want to slap some sense into him. But since he wasn't sure himself of what the trucks were doing, he could say nothing to change Paul's mind. "So what are you gonna do, Johnny Reb – go in and arrest them yourself?" Wade asked sarcastically.

"Bring your rifle," Paul ordered as he tethered his horse to a tree off the side of the road. "I want to be sure where to send Gene."

Wade dismounted and tethered his horse to the same tree and followed his brother into the woods. He started to ask why Paul didn't travel down to the road entrance and go in there, but he kept quiet. He left his rifle in the saddle scabbard. He figured if they encountered any trouble, he would be outgunned anyway. Paul hiked determinedly southward through the woods toward a new and strange noise he had never heard before.

"C'mon, Paul, let's go back," Wade kept saying. A drumbeat of sorts, or the rumbling of some type of heavy machinery, could be heard in the distance and it seemed to grow louder as they traveled deeper into the woods. Paul stopped on top of the first ridge. "Let's go," Wade said. "It's another mile to that thing, whatever it is."

"All right," Paul said hesitantly. For over a minute, he stood motionless listening to the noises coming from the south. Then suddenly, he no longer felt safe or sure of himself. The noise could be felt underfoot and its tone was quite ominous, and it frightened him.

"What're yew men a-lookin' fer?" someone commanded.

Wade and Paul looked down at the base of the ridge to find a seedy looking fellow with a shotgun aimed at them. He was standing between them and the road. Because of the breeze, Wade or Paul hadn't heard anyone walking up behind them.

"Y'er standin' on private propity here. Yew lookin' fer anythang in partic'ler?"

Paul, with fear in his face, looked at Wade. What kind of trouble have I gotten us into, he seemed to ask.

"Just taking a little walk. We'll be on our way now," Wade said with as much conviction as he could muster. Then he started down the side of the ridge toward the road, Paul following. Wade walked an angle toward the road. The seedy fellow kept the gun up and started walking to cut them off. Wade kept moving. "This your land, buddy?" Wade asked, knowing most of it belonged to a pulpwood company, the land to the southeast to Carl's inherited estate. Further southward a few rocky acres belonged to Roy.

"Why're yew really here?" the fellow asked, raising the gun higher as Wade closed the gap. Wade stopped and looked at the fellow, who by now was only ten feet away.

"I said I, uh, we was just taking a walk. We used to hunt down here. Thought we might see a new squirrel nest or two. Why don't you put that gun down – we're not here for trouble. We live just up the road a piece."

"Y'er gonna come wi' me," the man said.

Wade could think of nothing else to say. Paul wasn't saying anything. He figured it best to be quiet and let Wade handle things. But he was shaken. This dirty fellow was completely unkempt and toothless, worse than any migrant he had ever seen. In a moment, the man's unwashed hygiene drifted in the breeze. Wade started walking again. "We have to get our horses," he said.

The man fired a shot into the air. Wade and Paul stopped with a flinch. Wade didn't know if it was a warning to do as he was told, or if it was a signal to someone toward the south woods, or both. The greasy fellow didn't indicate a purpose for the gunshot. But it didn't matter; Wade and Paul were now prisoners to this disturbing stranger's whims.

"All right, what do you want?" Wade asked angrily.

"Like I done said, yew'll come along wi' me."

Wade looked at him with great exasperation. If he could position himself a little closer he could disarm this silly fool, he thought. Paul felt sick for his foolish selfishness and his mind was racing with what to do now. He wondered, too, how easily he could take this clown down.

"Tarn around," the fellow barked. Wade and Paul turned around. They didn't put their hands up; they weren't told to. "Now walk."

"Which way?" Wade asked, figuring it may do some good to keep things confused and complicated.

"Jist git walkin'. I'll tell ye whar t' go."

Wade started slowly with Paul next to him. He didn't know if this fellow would actually shoot anybody. He entertained the thought that if he just started walking toward the road and ignored the man, he wouldn't have the intestinal fortitude to shoot. Wade wondered also that if he didn't react quickly, any reinforcements summoned by the gunshot would soon be on them. Before he could think on his options further, he heard something on the ridge. He looked up. It was the reinforcements; another armed guard.

"What th' hell yew git, Arthur?" the new sentry yelled. He wasn't as ugly as Arthur, but he was every bit as unkempt.

"Two little jackasses, lost in th' woods!" Arthur answered in a strange singsong manner.

"Brang 'em over yonder!" the new sentry yelled, pointing down the ridge toward the west. Shortly he fell in next to Arthur behind Wade and Paul, talking all the way, not all of it making much sense.

"Yew gotta snooper. Boy – yew got us a couple o' snoopers! We're goin' to th' big house, jackasses. The boss is gonna like what we done!" the new guard said. His chin was caked with a week's worth of tobacco juice, and he reeked of backwoods survival. IIc, too, was carrying a pump shotgun. Wade sensed this new one was quite loose in his mental mechanisms.

"Where're you taking us?" Paul asked.

"Big house, where th' boss is," the crazy one said. Arthur then said something to him. His name was Jim. Arthur and Jim talked and laughed all the way like rogue delinquents. They had walked a hundred yards when Jim said, as if the thought had just hit him, "Hey, yew jackasses raise yore hands!"

Wade and Paul complied. Paul was nearly sickened to tears. But he held strong; there would be time for shame and apologies later, he hoped. Wade cursed under his breath, not at Paul or at the guards so much as at the situation in general. They had no idea what to expect to find at the 'big house.' Whatever it was, they hoped to be rid of the two deranged trolls prodding them along.

They turned onto what appeared to be a new logging road. It was the same one they saw connecting with the main road. It led south around a hill to a new square shack where another guard stood outside. A truck was parked on the other side and they were marched to it and told to get up in the bed of the truck. Jim kept the gun on them in the bed and Arthur rode up front with the driver. Shortly they were back on the road and turned westward. Wade looked back east for the horses. They were gone. The driver turned up the driveway to Carl's house. The ride was bumpy and Jim laughed when he was almost tossed out.

At the house, the driver jumped out of the truck and went inside. Wade's and Paul's horses were tethered to a corner porch post. Billy Wilson stepped out for a moment then went back inside. Another armed guard sat on the porch with a large dog next to him. In a few seconds, the driver returned and summoned Wade and Paul to come in, then directed them to the front room. Both Billy and the driver stepped back out of the house leaving Carl, Wade, and Paul alone inside.

"Sit down, boys," Carl said. He was sitting at the table with papers and folders spread out before him. Wade and Paul tentatively complied. Carl stacked a few papers together and pushed them aside. His half-smile was firmly pasted on his face, and he had developed a bit of a potbelly. Probably from keeping Troy, his house help, busy in the kitchen during his recovery.

"Well, seems we've met before," Carl said to Wade.

"If you're holding us prisoner, Carl, you could go to jail," Wade said angrily.

"Who's holding you prisoner, Wade?" Carl asked, pretending to be annoyed by Wade's statement.

"All right, we'll go then," Wade said as he stood up and started for the door. Paul joined him and Carl didn't respond.

Outside, Wade and Paul walked past the guards to their horses without interference. They appeared okay and Wade's rifle was still in its scabbard. They mounted and turned for the driveway.

"Hold up," someone ordered. It was Carl. He had stepped out onto the porch. He then stepped down into the yard and took a moment to light a cigarette. He seemed cockily confident that Wade would wait until it was well lit. "I still want to know what you were looking for on my land," he finally said.

"We was on pulpwood company land, Carl," Wade said. "It's no concern of yours why we was there."

Carl puffed on the cigarette and scratched his head. Wade had had enough of this games-playing nonsense and started heading down the driveway. The farther along he and Paul could get, the better. He figured the guards might be waiting for some command from Carl to stop them or follow them at a distance, for whatever reason.

"Don't you have some questions for me?" Carl said loudly. "Seems everyone is asking questions lately."

A black face peeked out one of the windows from the barracks as they rode past. Light smoke wafted from the cookhouse nearby. It carried the aroma of some over-spicy recipe. Wade let these things play in his mind to displace Carl's taunts behind him.

"You had some questions for me back in December," Carl said much louder, practically yelling. *"I just might know a little more now than I did then."* Wade and Paul kept moving. *"I'll tell you anything you want to know,"* he continued. Wade and Paul were thirty yards past the barracks when Carl hit a nerve. *"Why do you think I killed Earnie Jackson on your land – you got a witness?"*

Paul turned to Wade with a furiously shocked expression. Wade stopped and said something to Paul. Paul shook his head as if refusing something that Wade was saying. Several more things were spoken between them then Wade turned his horse back up the driveway leaving Paul to wait for him outside. Paul's bewildered and frightened expression belied his efforts to remain calm.

Back at the table, Wade said, "All right – start."

Carl feigned ignorance. "What?" he asked.

"All right," Wade said. "I'll start."

Wade figured Carl gained pleasure from playing head games, tripping up his opponent and gaining the upper hand. Carl sat with one arm on the table and leaned back heavily in his chair, readying himself for a verbal sparring match.

"What happened here on the North Road? I know you had something to do with it," Wade said.

"North Road?" Carl pretended to not understand the intent of Wade's question.

"Back in October, here on your road going to Braxton Road – what happened?"

"I'll tell you. Then you'll know why I had to get rid of Earnie Jackson."

Then Carl looked through the door into the kitchen. No one else was in the house. He could see Paul standing next to his horse in the driveway. He turned back toward Wade and sat as motionless as stone for several seconds. As usual, he tried to gauge Wade's response every second along the way. Then he began to speak.

"My boys, Billy and Jackson, were out on the North Road doing a little survey work on the east side of my property. A tree was supposed to be marked with three white stripes showing where my property ended. And they were looking for it. Billy said when they come along a hill, they found one of them Buell boys sitting in a car; it was running. They said it appeared that he was waiting for somebody to come out of the woods. Of course, my boys figured he was running some moonshine operation on my property there, so they started asking questions. The boy wasn't going to talk – he tried to take off. Damn, Billy and Earnie – they both had been swallowing too much goddamn liquor themselves all night – got a little too rough with the boy. They just pulled him out before he could get the goddamn car in gear, and they started, I guess, to beat some information out of him. Billy and Jackson both were new with me at the time. I don't let nobody around here get drunk and carry on like that anymore – "

"Jackson killed James Buell?" Wade asked abruptly.

Carl raised his hand as if to say slow down. "Well, Jackson had my scatter gun with him for popping squirrels there on the road. Goddamn son-of-a-bitch was carrying slugs. I don't know what was in his damn head. Well, about this time I come over the hill in my truck and I see what's going on. The boy was laying there in the road in front of his car. Damn Jackson had lost his goddamn mind and knocked him in the head with the butt of the gun. Knocked the son-of-a-bitch out cold. Well, goddamn, it made me so mad to see what he'd done I just slapped the shit out of him and told them both to get in the truck. But then somebody started shooting at us from a hill upside the road there. And, damn, before I could do anything, ol' goddamn Jackson shot up at him and must have killed him on the spot. Like I said, he was shooting slugs and it blew the boy clean off of that hill." Wade started to say something, but Carl pushed on. "Yeah, Jackson shot and killed that boy off the side of the road and he must've damaged that boy in the car so bad because I hear he died about five months later."

"All right, if all this is true, why the hell didn't you just take Jackson to the sheriff?" Wade asked.

Carl was nodding his head in agreement. "Because Jackson said he would just deny everything. He said it was my gun and nobody would believe my side of the story. Shit, he had a point, don't you see?"

"What difference does it make? Billy saw everything," Wade said.

"Goddamn, Wade," Carl said with a fierce wave of the hand for added emphasis. "Billy used to work for you and your brother. Could you trust him with anything? I couldn't trust that bastard. Hell, he might get on the stand and change his story every time the wind changed. Hell no. I had to play the game right, right from the start – "

"Forget all that. You will answer this one question." Wade leaned up to add emphasis. "What the hell happened to my daughter!"

Carl turned stern. "Didn't she tell you what happened?"

Wade sat for a moment gazing at Carl. Not so quick, he thought. "You'll answer my question."

Carl had an answer, but it was a gamble. He figured Wade had more answers than he was letting on. He said, "I heard someone scream after the boy went down. Then she ran away. I think I saw her running up a hill. I don't know. I figured then that my boys had really messed up."

"Maybe she did tell it. You're not giving me the whole story, you lying bastard!" Wade spat.

Carl was impressed by Wade's courage, his conviction. But he figured Wade was calling his bluff. He said coolly, "I told you what happened, Wade. If you know something, tell me."

"If I find that you did something to my daughter, you're a dead son-of-a-bitch!"

"Next time you'll succeed?"

Gene had not contacted Wade concerning the assassination attempt against Carl, so Wade figured he had not been fingered as a suspect. It seemed Carl was keeping things to himself.

"Why in hell did you kill Jackson on my land?" Wade asked.

"That was a bad move, on my part," Carl said. "It's all right – he ain't there no more. We hauled his ass out, like you told me."

"Why did you kill him?"

"He talked. I caught him bragging about killing that Buell boy. That's all I needed – word to get to Carter. Jackson would just change his story and finger me. I wasn't going up the river for his stupidity. He just kept talking even after I told him to shut his ass up. So I didn't have much choice. You understand."

"Who did he brag to?"

"What the hell difference does it make? He was making too much noise. So, I shut him up."

"What did you tell his family?"

"What difference does it make to you?" Carl asked, obviously irritated by all the messy questions. Undoubtedly he had questions of his own for Wade. Such as how did he learn about Jackson's murder and Carl's part in it? But he would never give Wade the satisfaction of thinking that he had something on him.

Wade thought of the night of terror his son had endured because of Carl's criminally malicious game played out that night. He ran through his mind again his son's flight of terror from the oak tree, believing that Carl was hunting him down like an animal for the kill. And how Jimmy was ready to kill his own father in self-defense, and almost did. That fact alone was enough reason to fill Carl full of hot lead.

"What's going on down south, here?" Wade asked.

"We're starting up a pulpwood operation – "

"Is that why you need men with guns?"

Carl chuckled and looked out into the backyard. "All right," he said, "I'll tell you a little secret. Just betwixt you and me."

This patronizing, flippant attitude of Carl's was expected. Appealing to any compassion or empathy inside of the man would be a wasted effort. Wade would get whatever answers he could, then worry about what to do with the information, and Carl, later.

Carl continued chuckling to himself for a moment, then said, "I don't want to attract any attention. I'm just trying to put together a little quiet enterprise to make a little money, and maybe a little extra to retire on. No one around these parts needs to know what I'm doing. I'm servicing a little market up north, and I'm not about to try to cut into anyone's business around here. I don't want any trouble with anybody."

"Quiet enterprise?" Wade asked. "If it was any louder, I'd have to put earplugs in my cattle. Why didn't you just stay up north and make your liquor up there? Why did you come here to make trouble?"

"Yeah, we're working on that. You won't have to worry about all the noise after we make a few adjustments and cut a new road or two. I got all this land, all eight thousand acres of it, in an inheritance back a year or two ago. You know about all that, don't you? Hell, I figured why not come down here amongst all you smelly-ass hillbillies and make a living where it's nice and quiet? Hell, they were shooting each other to mincemeat up in Chicago. I didn't care to keep getting mixed up in all that shit and get myself killed. Hell, I was shot at a couple of times myself, then I come down here and you give it to me. And you say I'm trouble."

Wade wasn't going to concede anything. And now that Carl was rambling, he figured he'd gotten all he was going to get. He stood up to leave.

"Don't bother going to the law, Wade. I run things around here," Carl said in a threatening tone. He was not so jolly now. "You know, you can have a piece of the action too, for the asking. It's easy money, and that little wife of yours will give you more loving for it." Wade turned to leave. "Wade," Carl said, his voice growing more callous in tone by the second. "You go to the sheriff – I'll plant Jackson's body back under that tree, and I'll tell everybody you killed him and put him there yourself. It's my land now, and I'll just say I found it there when we started cutting off the timber."

Wade glared down at Carl. "Doesn't make sense, Carl. How could you prove that?"

"What kind of rifle have you got?" Carl snapped.

"I've got two or three rifles."

"45-75 caliber?"

Wade didn't answer. No one, except Tom and Lucas Buell knew that Carl had Tom's car door in his possession, with the heavy caliber bullet lodged in it.

"What if Jackson was killed with the same caliber? You're the only one around these parts with a 45-75, from what I hear. Seems to me you had a motive for wasting Jackson on your land."

"You're full of shit!" Wade barked.

"Think so? I understand you and your brother and Roy worked him a couple times over the years. Maybe he was with you instead of me when he, or you, killed that Buell boy."

"You know that story wouldn't hold a drop of water."

"Maybe not in the long run. But think about this: I figure a few migrants might show up and say that Jackson bragged about killing that Buell boy, and he was with you at the time. So, you had to kill him to shut him up. That's why he was killed and buried on your land. Hell, I'll just go ahead and plant his smelly-ass carcass back there right now!"

Wade gestured as if he would use a gun if he had one on him. He seemed to look around the room for one and then said, "Hell, I've worked over a hundred different migrants over the years – "

"Doesn't matter," Carl said. "I'll have people to say you knew him as well as your own brother. They'll say he was working for you, and then it happened and you killed him that night. It doesn't matter if it doesn't hold up in court; you'll go broke just defending your ass. Do you really want that, Wade? Think about your goddamn wife and young'uns."

Wade, in a rage, grabbed a chair and flung it through a front window, then turned to leave. A guard rushed in, but when Wade menaced him with a drawn fist he stopped cold and allowed Wade to pass by and walk out. Carl didn't flinch. He simply sat and smiled.

CHAPTER 18

A month passed and Carl's directive to dampen the traffic and noise around the nighttime steamplant operations was proven trustworthy. A new road had likely been cut through the trees somewhere far away from the main road. Still, a truck would occasionally pull out onto the road. But its lesser racket indicated that it was a smaller freighter, or it was one that was just better muffled. In the end, the road and the woods southwest of Wade and Paul Kallton's farms grew quieter. Enough quieter to allow sleep to return to as normal as could be expected at the disquieted homesteads.

It was early fall and the changing of the seasons was ordinarily a resplendent thing to behold. But the farmers and merchants were simply too busy to take much notice. Each seasonal transition was something to be prepared for, dreaded, or oftimes feared. In Braxton, the cotton gin owner, Ben Townsend, his family, and a couple of seasonal workers were working day and night to process the dozens of wagonloads of cotton that rolled in every day. He still managed to attend church for an hour or two every week, but like the cotton farmers he could spare no more time for anything but cotton. The air was still warm, but some of the trees were signaling the change by the growing dullness of their leaves. It would still be another month before the work routine changed. But then it would be time for woodcutting and food preparations and storage for winter. Gene Carter saw little change in his own routine this time of year. Soon though, the winter fur of the muskrat and mink would begin to grow thick and luxurious, and it would be time to start setting traps. If the season was good he could almost match his civil service salary with the compensation from his two or three months' catch of pelts. It was hard work, but like that of everyone else it was necessary.

Gene had thought that he would drive down to the gin to look for Harvey and tell him to continue working at the gin if Ben still needed him. The state budget was tight this year and he was looking to cut corners, and a good place to start would be to shorten Harvey's hours. He stepped to the door but stopped and looked out the window. The wide alley in front of the jail office was handy for merchants and workers to use as a shortcut from one side of town to the other. He stood before the window and watched several people pass by. All of them looked at Gene and waved.

Then, as he began to open the door, a truck pulled up and dangerously skidded to a stop just a couple of feet short of hitting the wall. Gene waited. Carl Kallton was in the truck with Billy. Carl hurriedly stepped out and walked to the door leaving Billy in the truck. Two passersby in the alley watched Carl with great interest. The town was still abuzz concerning the alleged murder attempt against him. And queries were still steadily directed toward Gene concerning suspects in spite of Carl's public assertion that he had been wounded accidentally. The unforgiving curiosity of the townsfolk pertaining to the investigative progress on the Buell murders and the Kallton cattle massacre seemed to be increasing instead of waning. Outwardly, Gene was enduring the pressure gallantly, but the frustration of it all was working on him like a chronic but worsening itch.

Carl spoke a nondescript greeting. Gene quickly judged that Carl was not on a mission of charity and he held still, not bothering to extend his hand. Carl had stationed himself squarely before the door and glanced backward to check for errant and nosey pedestrians that might enter the office and interrupt this outwardly appearing impromptu meeting whose purpose was yet to be announced. There seemed to be no residual sign of Carl's near-death event three months earlier. Unless an enlarged gut and a heavily grizzled face could be counted as evidence of such change. Gene stepped back to his desk and sat down. "Coffee?" he asked.

Carl, ignoring the offer, sat himself easily into a chair several feet before the desk. Carl glanced back out at Billy. Billy had moved to the driver's seat and made himself obvious to passersby. The truck had been parked too closely to the front wall of the building for pedestrians to walk before the office window easily. They were forced to circle rearward and around the back end of the truck, thus being distracted, or spared, from the goings-on inside.

"Nice weather," Carl said as an opener. "Reminds me of Chicago this time of year. Where's your deputy?"

"Working down at the gin," Gene said while nodding slightly. "He's just part-time."

Carl nodded like Gene. It came across as a mocking of Gene's gesture. But the pasted smile made it impossible to judge motives. The pauses between comments were too long. Gene was already growing anxious to learn the true cause for Carl's visit. He looked out at Billy to find him waving to anyone that might pass by. There were only a few now and Billy spent most of his time trying to gaze through the glare on the window. Carl looked back at Billy then propped a foot up on a knee and cleared his throat.

"Gene. Can I call you Gene? I have a little proposition for you. I have something that might benefit both of us if you agree to work with me on it. You willing to listen?"

Gene nodded. "Reckon there's no harm in that."

"Reckon?" Carl chuckled. "You travel much down in my territory?"

"Well, your people have seen me down there a couple of times. I'm sure they report to you."

"Yeah, they do."

"You're asking questions you already have the answers to. Why don't we get to it?"

"All right. How many years have you been sheriff in this county?"

"You don't know the answer to that one?"

"Not that one."

"Going on fifteen years next month."

"People of this county have a lot of respect for you. Is that right?"

"Respect has to be earned. I hope I've done that."

Carl moved his foot from his knee to the floor and leaned forward a bit. Still, his disposition was unreadable. "Does the state respect you?"

"What do you mean, Mr. Kallton?"

"Call me Carl."

"All right."

"Does the state respect you enough to compensate you for what you've done for all these people?"

"All these people?"

Carl chuckled. "C'mon, Gene. You bust your ass for all these hayseed assholes for all these years for peanuts, and you still have to trap every winter to make enough to live on? Hell, all these people around here even smell alike. Why the hell do you give a damn?"

Gene shuddered internally, but he was reasonably certain he kept his reaction hidden from Carl's eyes. He leaned forward to the desk and fingered a pencil with both hands. "You got a curious way of spreading the charm, Mr. Kallton."

"Carl, please."

"Carl."

"Just speaking my mind, Gene. You want me to speak the truth as I see it, right?"

Gene's patience was spent. "What do you really want?"

Carl reached behind his red-dyed leather jacket to his belt line and drew out two brown paper envelopes; one larger than the other. He leaned forward and tossed the smaller one onto Gene's desk. Gene continued playing with the pencil. He looked at the envelope, then back at Carl.

"Money?" Gene asked.

Carl chuckled. "I'll have one of my men bring one of those to you every two months. Go ahead – open it up. It's yours to keep."

"What are you wanting to do in my county? Liquor? Rum running? Heroin? Interstate graft?"

"Open the goddamn envelope."

Gene flipped open the flap and eyed a small stack of bills, each of them a fifty. Probably equaling several months of his civil service salary. He folded it back shut and slid it back toward Carl. "Not interested," he said.

"How can you know if you are or not. You haven't heard my proposition."

Gene's impatience was showing on his face. He rubbed his eyes then started to stand up to move to the door. He was determined to stop the games if Carl was still set on continuing them. Carl grabbed the envelope but immediately replaced it with the larger one.

"A bigger bribe?" Gene asked.

"Open it up, Gene," Carl ordered. His voice was stern and demanding.

"Why don't you just sell out and move back to where you come from? We really don't need your kind of shit and tomfoolery around here."

"Open it up."

Gene sat back down and ripped open the envelope. His reaction was instant.

"The hell!"

He dropped the envelope's contents as if it all might explode in his hands. He slapped at them causing most of the items to fling to the floor. He stood up. "You goddamn bastard! That's what you sonsabitches done to me!"

Carl leaned hard forward like he might jump and tackle the sheriff. He seemed surprised by, but not unprepared for the sheriff's speed to anger.

"Getting all excited is not going to help you, Sheriff. You might as well just calm down and accept the fact of what you are."

Gene knew what had just happened to him, and he could think of nothing quickly to do. He paced to the door and back with his hands balled up into fists. He turned back to Carl with fire in his eyes. The right psychological moment would soon pass, and he had to decide what to do and do it now. He stepped to the back of the desk and reached for a drawer. Carl slammed his fist on top of it, and Gene flinched as if he had been slapped.

"I don't know what you're about to do, but you better think twice," Carl sneered.

Gene looked for a weapon on Carl, but he could see nothing to indicate that he was armed. Carl kept his fist on the desk and his eye on Gene. Gene backed away.

"A – all right," Gene stammered. "Let's hear what it is you want – then I'll decide."
Then he snatched up the photographs remaining on the desk and tossed them into the trashcan.

"Decide? Did you say decide? I don't think your ass is in any position here to decide – do you?"

Gene moved for the drawer again, but this time Carl quickly reached under his jacket and Gene could hear a distinct metallic double-click. Gene was sure, at this angle, that he could outdraw Carl if he just moved fast enough, but that didn't mean that he would live long enough to get a second shot off to finish the job. Gene looked out the window to find Billy still sitting leisurely in the truck.

"I don't bluff, Sheriff. Not my style. Sit down in that chair and keep your goddamn hands where I can see them."

"You think this is the Old West?" Gene said as he eased into the chair. "People don't behave like this anymore."

"Just keep your hands there up on top of the table. Don't call me on this." Carl eased his hand back out from his jacket. His eyes didn't move from Gene.

Gene remembered the day he was drugged. It was clear now what he had suspected all along. But was it enough to bring him down? Who would believe that the good sheriff could be capable of such immorality? The sheriff looked at the pictures in the trashcan. These photographs were professionally focused, detailed, and hopelessly damaging. Somehow, the sheriff had been posed in various positions; some relaxed, some aggressive, some comedic as if he might be enjoying himself. The pictures flashed through his mind one at a time. They seemed to have been taken in another world. He was there and he was bare, just like the two ladies that appeared to be cavorting with him on the little bed. He was wide-awake, or so it seemed, in a couple of them where he was facing the camera. It was impossible; he remembered nothing.

"All I want is for you to carry on just like you have all along. You'll live your little hayseed life any way you want. Except you'll do as I say," Carl said with utter coolness.

"And if I don't?"

Carl laughed aloud. "If you don't? Think about that goddamn question!"

Gene's face flushed with rage as Carl laughed. Now was the time to move. He jerked up and snatched the drawer open and went for the gun, but the cold steel of Carl's derringer was instantly pressed against his cheek. Carl's humor was gone, and was replaced with a seething glare that defied explanation. It seemed that Carl's eyes could kill with their diabolical strength alone. "You listen to me, goddamnit!" he hissed. "You kill me, those pictures – and more like them – go to every newspaper in the state. You might get lucky and survive your own people, but the state authorities will rain hell down on you so goddamn fast you'll have no choice but leave this hillbilly shithole you call a town. Then where will you go?"

Carl reached for the drawer and removed Gene's gun. Gene's eyes darted around. He looked out the window into the alley hoping someone would witness what was happening to him. Carl seemed to read his mind.

"I'm a lucky man, Sheriff. Ain't nobody going to come through that door, I can almost guarantee it," Carl said as he tossed the sheriff's gun into the trashcan. He then pulled the trashcan away, putting several more feet between Gene and his weapon. "You wouldn't have shot me anyhow, would you? You don't have the goddamn balls."

Gene wondered if he was right. He had hoped to jerk the gun and shoot before allowing himself to think. But Carl was clearly well practiced for such contingencies and stayed far ahead of him all the way. But it would have been all right to kill Carl because Gene determined that his life was effectively over anyway. He could watch his fifteen years of civil service and his hopes for a small nest egg vanish down the drain. Carl sat down slowly, never removing his eyes from Gene. Gene seemed paralyzed.

"Somebody said you went to New Orleans a couple of years ago – that right?" Carl asked. Gene didn't answer. "That's right. They said you went to some fur trappers' convention for a few days. So I guess that was where you met the ladies, right?"

Gene still refused to answer. Or move.

"Nothing's going to change. You just carry on and be the good sheriff that all these people believe you are, and your ass'll be just fine. All I'm asking you to do is to keep quiet about anything you might know about my enterprises. You'll do what you can to keep the state and the feds out of this county. If you know they're coming in, you'll let me know with time to spare. Tell your deputy, I already know he'll cooperate.

"You'll do what you can to keep everyone's attention away from my operations. As long as I keep the money rolling into everybody's pockets, they'll leave me alone. They have so far. But that might not be enough. In the long run, I'm going to need your help, and now I think you will. Understand?"

Gene didn't show any indication that he did, but Carl didn't seem to worry. Both men sat silently for several moments, then Gene spoke.

"When they shot you, I should've let you die."

Carl ignored the comment and said, "You don't have anything to worry about. Keep things going as you are now, and everything will be all right. I'll get Billy to bring this money back to you when you're in a little better frame of mind."

Carl turned quickly and stepped out the door and walked to his truck. Billy slid over to the passenger side. Carl looked back a moment into the sheriff's office through a dirty window. Gene hadn't moved. He was looking out the window at Carl and Billy. A pedestrian waved at Gene, but he never seemed to recognize the gesture.

CHAPTER 19

The sheriff's car slid to a halt behind Carl's house. An armed guard on the porch stepped down and walked to the car. He was standing ready to fire but stood down when he recognized the sheriff's car with the deputy alone at the wheel.

"Tell Mr. Kallton to get out here!" Harvey barked.

"He's not here, deputy. What's the problem?" the guard asked.

"Where is he, then?"

"Down south," the guard answered, meaning the distillery compound.

"Well, let's go get 'im," Harvey commanded as if he were somehow in charge. It seemed that he wished to prove his eagerness to ingratiate himself into the organization, and ensure his monthly stipend.

The guard jumped onto the passenger seat and motioned for another guard on break at the cookhouse to take over his post. Then Harvey wheeled the car around and raced southward as if he had been engaged to deliver an important message to a battle commander. Within minutes the car slid to a stop in front of the guardhouse. The deputy was not allowed to go past the guardhouse that was standing several hundred yards north of the steamplant, so he had to wait for the guard to retrieve Carl from the compound. In a few minutes, Carl pulled his truck up alongside the sheriff's car and stopped. He waited, without greeting, for Harvey to speak.

"State police is gonna be here in two days, Mr. Kallton. Gene told me to come tell you."

"Keep talking," Carl ordered.

"'at's all we know, Mr. Kallton. Gene says it's 'bout some letters sent to the gov'nor some months back."

"What letters?"

"I don't know. Gene won't say. But I know that Buell's been harpin' to the state 'bout his boys a-gettin' kil't."

"What's that got to do with me?" Carl asked with feigned surprise.

"I don't know."

"Gene won't say what the letters are about, huh?"

"No, sir."

"Where is the good sheriff? Why didn't he bring his ass and tell me himself?"

"He said 'e didn't want to see your fat ass if 'e didn't have to."

Carl chuckled and looked over at the guardhouse. Three rough-hewed men were standing on the porch, obviously wondering what all the commotion was about. "Very good, deputy – good work," Carl said. He backed up the truck and pulled over to the guardhouse. Harvey smiled broadly, satisfied that he had done well. Then he quickly turned around and drove away.

"Joe," Carl said to a guard, "Go in and tell Roy to start shutting everything down. And I mean everything, right away." Carl pointed to another guard whose name he couldn't recall at the moment. "You – run up and tell Billy to stay at the house until I get there." The guard broke and began running up the road toward the house, a mile away. To the other man who was a migrant supervisor, he said, "Clint, meet me at the house in two hours." Then Carl spun the truck around and sped up the road passing the running guard and leaving him behind in a fog of churning dust.

Soon, Carl pulled into Braxton and stopped at the post office. He sent an urgent telegram to M.C. in Chicago instructing him to cease all communications and to stand by for further instructions. Later, back at the house, Carl expected everyone to know what to do. He told them to get to it.

Three empty cargo trucks were pulled out of the compound and sent north out of the county. The furnaces in the steamplant had been shut down and the thumpers were starting to settle down. Clint, the migrant supervisor, instructed a half-dozen men to haul up several wagon loads of pine boughs to the compound. They were piled into mounds inside and outside the distillery and set to smoldering. The pungent smoke filled the air with the thick aroma of pine rosin that was intended to dampen the odor of distilled corn in the area. Later, Clint went north to the Buell properties to shut down the work going on there.

A four-mule team was hooked up to the guardhouse and it was pulled down and dragged over the next ridge and left there. It was too close to the main road to be left standing. With its heavy, over-built design and the ever-present scent of corn spirits, it would be a beacon of alarm to any state officer that should happen upon it. Several live saplings and a couple of nine-inch beech trees were dragged up to the road's intersection with the main road and hastily planted there. Other saplings, loads of pine needles, and wild sod were all spread on the road between the main road and the stubbed footings of the guardhouse to create the illusion of disuse. The earth ramp at the intersection was dug up and regraded and hastily sodded, creating the appearance of a continuous ditch alongside the main road.

Back at the main house, all evidence of alcoholic beverages and their related condiments were removed and burned. All business records pertaining to illicit enterprises were packed up and sent out to the foremen's residences for temporary safekeeping. One item of particular attention was Tom Buell's detached and damaged car door that had been stashed in Carl's bedroom for the last seven months. The threat of its discovery by state agents was too great to keep in such close proximity. Billy was instructed to take the door to the steamplant and hide it there until the all-clear is given. Then it would be quietly returned the next day to ensure its safekeeping.

Early the next day, all the wagons and vehicles near the house were fumigated with pine boughs, then were unceremoniously splattered and smeared with various vegetable and animal products such as tomatoes, watermelon, squash and manure. After rotting in the warm sun for a couple of days, everything was figured to appear, and smell, legitimate in a very rural kind of way. All the migrants were instructed to wash their clothes and take a bath. The nearby shack of ill repute was emptied then stacked with dry goods for the cookhouse. The guards were disarmed and put to temporary work elsewhere, out of sight. The two guard dogs were chained and parked beneath the back porch.

That afternoon, Carl sent Billy to Pulaski to purchase a carload of pictures, picture frames, bedsheets, overalls, and Bibles. The rest of the day was spent cleaning up the yards, driveways and barracks of all evidences of anything illicit. Carl did not expect a warranted search of his facilities, but he was taking no chances.

***

Three days later, Tom opened the door to find Gene on the porch with two well-dressed men standing behind him. Gene wasted no time.

"Tom, come on out. We'd like to talk to you," he said. Annie and Anne Marie were in the kitchen. They looked to the front room but didn't move from their places.

Gene introduced the men as officers from the state police. Inspector John Arbor and Sergeant Howard Bruning were traveling from Nashville to Jackson with a request from the governor's office to swing through Braxton. They were asked to make a cursory investigation into the concerns that Tom had reiterated in a couple of long-past handwritten letters he had sent to the governor's office. They concerned his dissatisfaction with the sheriff's efforts to find the killer, or killers, of his two sons. They had not come, Tom was told, to rehash the cattle massacre. It was the first thing Gene said after Tom's face turned ashen. It seemed that he could be thinking that he was now going to be instructed that Wade was ready to press charges as the state had asked him to do. Wade had been strangely reluctant to do so, as if it would have brought great troubles upon himself and his family if he carried through with the state's wishes. The state could do whatever it wanted, but was apparently ready to drop everything if the locals continued to bicker among themselves and refuse full cooperation.

As a secondary mission, the officers were to make a call on Carl Dean Kallton to try to determine whether or not he had truly turned straight and left his old life back in Chicago. It was just paperwork and procedures, Arbor had said. Inspector Arbor was late middle-aged and wore dark shaded glasses. His face, framed by a full head of graying hair, seemed devoid of facial expression. Gene had figured him as intentionally poker-faced, as a good investigator should be. Sergeant Bruning was much younger with a transfixed quizzical expression that belied his newness on the job.

"Mr. Buell, you say in your letters that you feel that you know who it was who murdered your sons. You want to tell us about it?" Inspector Arbor said.

The men were standing in the front yard near the porch. The cool autumn breeze washed the aroma of unharvested sorghum across the yard. Tom lifted a foot up to the bottom porch step and contemplated the issue for a moment.

"I guess the sheriff has told you all that I would say to you gentlemen," he said hesitantly. He was far less forceful than Gene had expected, without even a hint of belligerency. Gene was unsure as to how to welcome this new attitude of compliance. Or it may have been that Tom was simply giving up now. He had gained some measure of revenge against Wade; and in order to keep the law at bay, he seemed to have decided to stop pressing for any conclusion to the unsolved mysteries of his sons' deaths.

"Well, Tom, yes – I have told them, as much as I know, and what you have said. If you have anything to add, now's the time."

"I've had a little time to think things through, Gene. I don't know – maybe I was wrong about the Kalltons. I know somebody killed my boys, but I just don't figure, now, that any of them had any call to do something like that," Tom said. He looked out across the road as he spoke. It was almost as if he had something else on his mind. Gene was more than a little bewildered by his easy compliance.

"Tom, you know I've checked every lead and every angle," Gene said quietly, his eyes searching Tom's demeanor for any clue to help explain his new listless attitude. Then an uncomfortable silence hung in the air for several seconds before Gene added, "Everything leads to a complete dead end. But I won't give up, Tom. Something will turn up one of these days."

Tom continued looking off into the trees. He slightly nodded his head in apparent agreement. What he said next was something that Gene had considered, but he was surprised to hear Tom say it with the high degree of resignation in his voice.

"You remember that tall, skinny migrant that showed up around here about every year or two?" Tom asked. Gene nodded yes. "Well, all I can figure is that he must've done all this to my family."

Inspector Arbor looked at Gene for clarification. Gene said, "Why are you saying that now, Tom?"

"I don't know – he's all that's left. I heard he showed up down south a while, then disappeared right after the shooting." Tom hesitated, then added, "Then I hear from you, I think, Gene, or from Harvey, that he just vanished right soon afterwards."

The inspector still was not making any connection. "What's this migrant's name?" he asked.

"Earnest Jackson," Gene said.

"How does he work into all this?"

"He was a small job migrant who worked short term on these cotton and tobacco farms," Gene said. "I couldn't ever nail down exactly who he was working for on that day. But everyone else involved in this claims their innocence. This Earnie Jackson fellow just disappeared right after this all happened. His family came looking for him, but we never found a trace of him. I figure he probably went off the edge with his liquor and thought he'd have a little fun scaring some kids he found on the road. I know it sounds like a stretch, gentlemen, but I'm still looking under every rock I can find."

"Who was with him?" Arbor asked, clearly affronted by such a flippant and simplistic conclusion.

"Apparently nobody," Gene said.

"Nobody?"

"That's all I can find."

"So you men just concluded on your own that this missing man was somehow responsible?"

Gene nodded slightly with averted eyes. Tom looked off into the distance.

Inspector Arbor didn't like what he was hearing. Pinning a murder, or two murders, on a long-missing man was too easy. It left everybody else off the hook. He looked again at Tom and was disturbed by his easy acquiescence to such a grossly underdeveloped theory.

"Sheriff, are you satisfied that everyone else is innocent of all this?" Arbor asked.

"Yes, I am, Inspector."

The inspector and the sergeant had gone over the whole story with the sheriff upon their arrival and had felt that Gene had covered all the bases. Now they couldn't be sure. They had not been told anything about some stranger named Earnest Jackson. Now it was being dropped on them like a smoking firecracker falling dud, and it brought a swift end to any further questioning on the subject. Naturally they would like to talk to Kelly Jean Kallton, as would the sheriff. But they felt, from Gene's descriptions of her condition and her father's attitude, that their own abrupt appearance in the family's life would only make things more difficult for the sheriff. If Kelly Jean had the answers that were needed to solve the crime, it would seem best, from what the sheriff had said, to leave it to the sheriff and the families to work out as soon as she was able, or willing, to talk.

"Mr. Buell, thank you for your time. We'll keep in touch with the sheriff here and he'll let us know of any new developments," Arbor said abruptly. Everyone shook hands with Tom and the trio left.

***

Gene and the two state officers turned off of Braxton Road onto the North Road and began the trek toward Carl's homestead. No further discussions took place between them. There was clearly no reason to continue with the pretense. Gene could feel the detachment of minds immediately after leaving Tom's place, and he determined that any further discussion would only increase the disillusionment the state officers had gained for the sheriff.

The road had been patched and thinly layered with new gravel and was now maintained to a better condition than the heavier traveled Braxton Road. When they came upon the fields, several workers clearing an old field looked up to watch them pass. On closer to the house, they rounded a corner of trees to find a flatbed truck loaded high with chicken crates parked nearly in the middle of the road. Scattered behind it were a number of crates that had apparently fallen off in transit, and several of them had burst open releasing its startled cargo. Live chickens were scattering everywhere, many of them trying to escape to the trees. Billy and a migrant were working to chase down as many of them as they could and return them to the truck. Carl was picking up and stacking the few crates that had failed to break open. It was unusual, in Gene's mind, to find Carl doing anything remotely menial as this without an acidic attitude accompanying it.

"What's the problem here, Carl?" Gene asked brusquely as he rolled to a stop next to the truck. He was figuring to find Carl quick with a sour rejoinder for these state men to witness. But Gene had only glanced at Carl when he asked the question. He turned his face straight ahead as the big man approached. Carl, imposing as he must have appeared to the officers, walked to the car with an oversized, stiff smile. It was a an unfamiliar countenance that unbalanced the sheriff.

"Gene, how are you?" he asked with an extended hand. Gene seemed to pull, almost jerking his hand away the instant their fingers touched. Carl never skipped a beat, continuing with uncharacteristic cheerfulness. "I just picked up a load early this morning from Jenkins over in Pulaski. I'm glad he takes new credit. I couldn't have got these chickens today without it."

Gene introduced Carl to the officers and stated that they wished to talk to him for a few minutes. "Is something wrong, Inspector?" Carl asked, looking in from the driver's side window.

"No problems that we know of, Mr. Kallton. Just want to talk to you for a minute. That's all," Arbor said.

"Well, let me get my boys set up and I'll ride with you to the house. Maybe show you boys around a little."

Carl cranked up the big truck and pulled it to the side of the road. He said something to Billy then, moving like a teenager jumping into a new car, got in the back seat with the sergeant. The old Buick heaved over a bit but righted quickly. Almost immediately, Carl began speaking appreciatively of the state officers who had interrogated him about the assassination attempt on him back in early July, four months earlier. Arbor and Bruning had not worked on the case, but knew the investigating officers and were familiar with the situation. The case, Carl was now told, had been closed. The whole thing had been written off as an accident, as Carl had insisted. Like Gene, neither of the officers believed him, but they had no evidence to the contrary that would have justified keeping the case open.

Now on the way to the house, in the most amicable voice tone he could muster, Carl spoke proudly of his farming operations and plans for the future. He gave facts freely: the acreage under cultivation, while mentally subtracting the new clandestine cornfields hidden from prying eyes; the number of migrants working for him, minus the ones presently hiding out at the distillery; and his sales and purchases of farming equipment and supplies, of course not mentioning the huge outlays of materiel for illicit enterprises. Carl's braggadocio was masterful; full of pride but sensibly understated. By the time they reached the house, Carl assumed that he had the biggest part of the battle won, as far as winning over the officers. It must have seemed so to Gene too.

The exterior of the house appeared new; a large but tidy country house that would have been the pride of any local homestead. Inside, the house was quiet, being vacant of any workers. Troy had been removed to the cookhouse and instructed to stay there until the officers were gone. Carl offered everyone coffee, but was declined. Carl winked at Gene, and Gene fired an angry glare back at him. Quickly, they settled into the kitchen around the small cook table. Almost immediately, Arbor started hitting Carl with accusatory statements. Carl showed no inclination toward annoyance.

"Mr. Kallton, I appreciate your hospitality and willingness to let us come on to your property without a warning, but I think you know that sooner or later you were going to be talking to someone like us. We know that the heat got too hot for you in Chicago, and that's really why you're here. And we also know you're not building this little empire with honest money. You left quite a trail behind you in Chicago and, I'm sure you will understand, we don't need any more hell-raising trouble makers down our way. That, in a nutshell, is why we're here."

Carl nodded slightly as Arbor spoke, and then said, "Well, Inspector, I mean to turn my ways for the good and pay back what all it is you think I may have done in the past. Just ask the good sheriff here. I've been running my farm here for a few months now and I believe he'll vouch for me."

"We've talked to Sheriff Carter all morning, Mr. Kallton. And he's done just that. However, you won't expect us to just take your word for it in spite of all we know about you. We know that you were never convicted of any major crimes, just petty stuff. It's what we know that you were not indicted for that we're concerned about. In short, you can consider yourself as being on unofficial probation. If we hear of anything from the sheriff here, or anyone else for that matter, we'll be back pretty damn quick."

Carl had by now stood up next to the stove and was filling his cup. He turned toward the window and sipped on the coffee. Clearly he was trying to affect a more sincere appreciation for Arbor's words by the nodding of his head. Gene was mute throughout; he seemed bored, even a bit resentful of the secret game being played here. But the officers were probably assuming that the sheriff had already expressed similar sentiments to Carl before, and was now allowing the officers to bolster his position.

"What do the people of this county think of you coming in and building this little empire so quickly? You know it takes these people several generations to obtain what you have built up here in just a few months," Arbor said coolly.

Gene seemed shocked by this abrupt supposition and, for the first time since entering the house, looked at Carl for his response. There was apparent resentment in Arbor's little inquisition. He seemed to have an unusually hard-biting understanding of the sensitive character of the local populace. Carl's regular infusion of cash into the local economy helped greatly to dampen such resentments among the people. Did Arbor think this might be the case? He might have suspected as much, but he was not given the chance to delve into the subject.

"C'mon outside, everybody – I've got something to show you," Carl said as if the previous accusatory grilling had never taken place. He sat his cup down and motioned for everyone to follow him out the back door. It was clear that Carl was not going to win Arbor's trust. No problem, Carl must have thought; give them a good show while they are here, and maybe their superiors in Nashville will read their reports, then instruct them to find other bad boys to harass.

A healthy stew-like aroma wafted in the air from the cookhouse. Looking across the yard to the ladies' house, a rustic wooden cross hung squarely in the window. This, along with its recently white-painted exterior, gave the little building the appearance of a cozy country chapel. A small black migrant in new overalls walked from the black barracks to the cookhouse. He smiled broadly and waved at his boss and the officers. In a moment, the faint sound of music emanated from the white barracks nearby. Carl directed everyone to the barracks door and opened it. The music continued as they entered. Sitting on the end of one of the fourteen cots inside was a young migrant playing a guitar and singing a religious hymn. He looked up as everyone entered, but he continued singing. Gene stopped cold and stared at him. Was this part of the charade? The singing migrant appeared genuine enough, but Gene seemed to know that somehow Carl was responsible for this conveniently placed musical interlude.

Two small pot-bellied stoves stood back to back in the middle of the barracks. A vase of paper flowers sat on each. There were seven windows along each side of the shotgun building with the head of a narrow iron-framed cot parked beneath each open window. Several cots were covered with the multi-colored, handmade family quilts the remaining seasonal migrants had brought from home, but were turned down to display the new matching bed sheets and pillowcases Billy had purchased. The floor had been scrubbed clean of the daily tracked-in mud. Pine scent wafted in the air. Several framed landscapes and portraits of Christ hung on the walls.

The singing migrant finished the song and immediately started another, now seeming to ignore the men walking through. Sergeant Bruning hesitated a moment as they passed by. He seemed to know the song and appeared, for a moment, ready to sing along. Gene watched the officers closely, looking for any indication that they were catching on to the facade of deception being played upon them. Arbor, particularly, had not changed his expression since the first moment he had introduced himself to Gene much earlier in the day.

Outside, they strolled over to the cookhouse and Carl pushed wide the half-open door. Standing over a swaying twenty-gallon pot of steaming stew was the black migrant and Troy in his old 'cooker' overalls. As if on cue, Troy invited everyone in for a sample. The officers declined. About two dozen pieces of ironware and glistening copper cookware hung from the walls. A wide washbasin and work counter ran along one wall and two square wood-burning cookstoves sat next to each other. Down behind the cookhouse, Carl proudly pointed out the refurbished barn and the new chicken house where the truckload of chickens was presently being unloaded. Across the driveway, Carl started to open the door to the black barracks.

"That won't be necessary, Mr. Kallton. I've seen enough," Arbor said. "You've been plenty hospitable."

Gene cursed under his breath. He wanted to see the whole show. To see how far Carl would carry this incessant game. Naturally he assumed Arbor thought of this as a surprise visit on Carl. Arbor had no reason to suspect that Carl had been forewarned. If he saw something that could lead him to believe Carl was staging the whole thing, he wasn't letting on. By all indications, he seemed reasonably satisfied that Carl had turned his ways and now meant to walk a straight line. Or perhaps that was simply nothing more than the outward impression Arbor intended to portray.

In spite of the probable fact that Carl had built his little kingdom with ill-gotten gains, he calculated he could count on being forgiven by far reaching authorities for his past sins by evidence of his new ambitious enterprise. If not, he would do all he could to plant as many doubts, to his benefit, in as many minds as he could. Experience taught him that this method, when planned and played with precision, worked adequately against more distant and bureaucratically managed authorities. Locally, however, as Gene had the misfortune to discover and now to endure, a more direct and covert method of control works best.

With little more discussion, the officers walked back through the house with Carl. Carl held back in the front room after gentlemanly farewells and then watched the three men step out to the front porch and down the steps. Arbor and Bruning walked to the car with Gene close behind. Halfway to the car, Gene hesitated and looked back at Carl who was now standing in the doorway. Carl gave him another wink and a nod. Gene, feeling that the whole sham had worked, must have been looking for a last hope of something amiss. Carl watched as Gene glanced through all the windows along the front. The windows were covered with new green and white flowery curtains. Everything else around the house was properly organized and swept clean.

Gene alternately felt terrific waves of both rage and resignation. He was enraged at Carl's confidence that he would do his bidding. Then wink in mockery as if the sheriff were a willing co-conspirator. He was resigned to the knowledge that Carl had him in his hip pocket and was smart enough to defeat any attempt to better him at his own game. Since the day of Carl's control over him, Gene stood in awe of the big man's tenacity and resourcefulness. The humiliation and anger he felt were crippling, but he, searching his mind day and night, could discover no viable strategies to break Carl's stranglehold on his life. He could go nowhere. He could do nothing.

Carl looked down at Gene's gun holster. For a moment, it seemed that he would slap leather and bring Carl down to a crumpled heap. Perhaps then, Gene thought, these dim-witted state officers would finally come around and conclude that something was seriously amiss after all. Yet, he knew now after the fiasco of his irresolute observations at Tom Buell's house concerning the vanished Earnest Jackson, the feeling was likely quite mutual.

Then something in Gene's mind snapped. He could almost feel it in his head. As if in slow motion, he turned for the car and walked to it. He entered it with the officers and drove away, never looking back again.

CHAPTER 20

One of Carl's trucks pulled up to the Co-op and Billy stepped out and went inside. He was alone. Seconds later, Gene pulled up and parked nearby. Harvey was not with him. In a few minutes, Billy returned with a cumbersome armload of rolled wire and a half-keg of nails. He dumped the whole load into the bed of the truck, opened the door and jumped in.

"Hey, Billy."

Billy had not yet started the truck when he heard his name called. He looked across to his right to see Gene approaching. The sheriff wasn't smiling, but he didn't appear bothered by anything either. He stepped slowly to the truck window on the passenger side and looked in. "How's work?" he asked.

"Good," Billy said without offering more. He started to crank the truck but looked back at Gene as if he should expect more. Gene had rested both his forearms on the window frame and was looking around the inside of the truck. Billy felt no appreciation for this somewhat aberrant behavior from the sheriff and let it be known with a scowl.

"Where's Carl?" Gene asked.

"Th' farm."

Gene tapped the door, glanced around the inside of the truck again and then looked up at Billy. He smiled slightly and said, "Had your ass kicked lately?"

Billy sat stone-faced for a moment. Gene was looking at him with a happy expression on his face that was highly uncharacteristic of him. Billy reached and started the truck. Gene stepped away and watched as Billy slowly drove away. Shortly Billy was heading back south to the farm. He watched his rear. No one followed. Back at the Co-op, Gene checked his watch. Then he pulled the car away from the curb.

In twenty minutes, Billy turned off of Braxton Road onto the North Road. He didn't like the way the truck had started behaving. He cursed the carburetor, figuring it was dirtied up with all the dust. He traveled down the North Road about a quarter-mile before the truck stalled to a stop. He tried several times to restart it, but each time the engine wore down worse and worse until finally it choked out its last breath. Billy got out and folded back a hood panel and looked in. In a moment, he looked back eastward to see a vehicle throwing up a plume of dust high into the arching trees overhead. The sheriff's car was approaching fast. Something was ominous in the sound of the racing engine and the snapping up-shift of the gearbox. Billy ran for the truck door, but his bad luck multiplied quickly.

Gene braked hard and skidded around the truck, clipping the edge of the truck door and body-slapping Billy to the gravel. Instantly, it seemed, Gene was on top of him and dragging him by the overall straps back to the car. Billy fought to get himself up but felt a stab of pain in his right hip where the door had hit him. Before he could fall back to the ground, Gene brought the butt of his pistol down hard across the side of his head. He was out cold.

It seemed only a moment later that he woke up to find himself in the trunk of a moving car. He pounded on the inside of the trunk lid but stopped when the car slammed to a stop then started up again. He scratched around for any mechanism to unlatch the trunk but could find none. The trunk lid was locked down tight and wouldn't budge.

About a half-hour later, the car slowed nearly to a stop, then turned onto what seemed a very rough and bumpy road. It felt like the car was going to bounce along forever before it abruptly stopped. Billy could hear the sheriff get out of the car and slam the door. He couldn't hear anything or anyone else. He remained as still as he could and tried to listen. His head was still throbbing from the blow to his temple but the crashing pain in his hip screamed for his attention.

He heard nothing but his pounding heart for five minutes. Then footsteps approached the rear of the car. He could hear keys and a rattling chain. The lid raised and the sudden sunlight bore into his eyes causing him to squint. In a flash, he found himself sprawled onto the ground and after a rough dragging across yards of hardwood leaves his hands were roughly handcuffed behind him around a small tree. He fought to kick at Gene but the sheriff was motivated. He slapped Billy hard across the back of the head and shoved him to the ground at the base of the tree to which he was locked. His shoulders and wrists throbbed with pain as he worked to right himself up against the tree.

He could see Gene off over his right shoulder. He was now standing about ten yards away smoking a cigarette atop a small knoll. It appeared that he was looking off into a broad logging clear-cut below. They were atop a ridge and trees were all around, and Billy had no idea where he was. It was likely that the sheriff had driven the car down an old abandoned logging road. He could see that the sheriff had plowed over a few saplings on the way in. He couldn't see any main road from his low vantage point. He looked back to the sheriff but yelled out in pain. It felt as if his hip had been yanked loose from its joint and it hurt worse than his head. He twisted his body a bit and turned back to face the car and the pain seemed to lessen. A black chain with a padlock hung from the car bumper to the ground. Obviously the sheriff had this all planned out well ahead of time. Billy understood now that the sheriff was more resourceful than he had imagined, and he was an easy victim for his devices. Billy looked down at his shirt to see that it was dappled with blood. His pants were ripped; whether from the hit with the car or the rough handling, he didn't know. His head was still buzzing and his arms were beginning to rebel from the unnatural position he was locked into.

Gene slowly sauntered back and stepped around Billy and squatted down about three feet in front of him. Billy tried to look up at his face, but he had allowed himself to slide sideways to relieve the twisting pressure on his arms. He could see the sheriff looking down on him, still smoking a cigarette. "Wha' yew want wi' me, sher'ff!" he asked, spitting each word.

Gene took another draw on the cigarette and looked Billy up and down, head to foot. Billy could feel the sheriff's eyes examining his bedraggled hair and tobacco spittled beard. And he could see Gene's eyes roam down to his unbuttoned shirt exposed behind overall straps that had been stretched down nearly to his waist. Gene glanced down to his boots. They looked brand new, a sharp contrast to the rest of his troll-like attire. The air was cold – too cold to be about without an overwrap of some kind. But Billy seemed immune to the icy breeze that picked up every few minutes. "You ever take a bath?" Gene asked.

Billy jerked himself board-straight, forcing himself against the pain. He looked up at Gene with a new expression of uncertainty and fear. Gene looked at his eyes, not altogether visible through red straggly hair that hung down to his nose. Billy had yanked his head back to see better and had let out an unintended snort. Gene smiled at this comical sound. It seemed clear that Gene was taking pleasure in Billy's helpless position and discomfort. Billy then threw himself forward as if hoping to head-ram the sheriff, his manacles stopping him far short.

"C'mon – Sit up, boy," Gene said. He stood up, then hunched over and grasped Billy by the front of the shirt and, intentionally it seemed, grabbed a fistful of flesh and muscle. Gene yanked him upright and Billy cried out in pain. He swung his face back up at Gene with fire in his eyes. He couldn't keep his hair out of his face and he angrily tried to fling it back. *Son-of-a-bitch! What th' hell yew a-doin'!"* he yelled.

"You're gonna talk, son. I've got a lot of questions and you got a lot of answers."

"Carl's gonna kick yore ass!"

"Why don't you kick my ass?" Gene asked.

"Tarn me a-loose an' I'll whoop yore goddamn ass, an' good!"

To his amazement, the sheriff pulled the keys from his pocket, stepped around the tree and unlocked the cuffs. Billy jerked his aching arms around to his chest and rubbed them together. He looked up at the sheriff who had stepped back around to the car and was removing his gun belt. He dropped it into the trunk and pushed the lid down. Gene turned around and stepped to a narrow clearing twenty feet from the car. Billy was still sitting against the tree trying to work the numbness out of his hands. Gene was standing with his hands to his side, facing Billy about eight feet in front of him. "C'mon, boy, whoop my ass," Gene said in mockery.

Billy eased up on his feet, favoring his good leg. Again he looked around. He still couldn't determine where he was. Just scrubby trees everywhere. The logging road meandered over a rise and disappeared beyond. A whiff of cotton scent was in the air. Billy surmised from that that he must be somewhere in the eastern part of the county. He looked at Gene. He had that strange smile on his lips again – a signal that the sheriff was confident of his game. Billy looked down at Gene's belt and boots. He could find no firearms or knives. Billy figured he could turn and easily outrun the portly sheriff. But then Gene could grab the gun out of the trunk and shoot him in the back before he could make ten yards.

Billy looked at the car. The trunk appeared to be open about an inch. While calculating whether he could yank the gun belt out before the sheriff could stop him, he looked again at the sheriff. No change. Still the eerie smile and dead gaze. Billy bent over slowly as if stretching his back, moving stiffly as if mindful of his pained hip. At the same time, he stanced himself for a lunge at the trunk. When the sheriff displayed the first sign of growing annoyed with Billy's gestures, Billy charged for the car. Out of the corner of his eye he could see Gene coming at him. Billy flung the lid up and yanked at the gun belt. He danced back out of the way with the gun in hand. Gene skidded to a stop short of the car. Billy snapped back the hammer and shoved the gun at Gene's face. The smile was gone.

"I jist as soon shoot yore ass as kick it!" Billy said with vindictive pride. Gene's face held nothing more than a blank stare. "Jist what the hell yew a-tryin' to do, asshole?"

Gene looked at Billy for a moment before answering. "I just had a few questions, Billy. That's all."

Billy felt newly powerful and confident. He wanted to pistol whip the sheriff or put a bullet in his leg, then watch him writhe in pain just as he had done. But first, he was curious. "Questions? What th' hell!"

"What happened to me last day of September? What did Carl put in my water?"

Billy smiled an ugly brown-toothed smile. "What makes yew think I'm a-gonna tell yew nothin'?" He laughed and added, "Hell, I don't 'ave to do nothin' but shoot yore shitty ass."

"Tell me, Billy. I want to know. Kill me if you want to. But tell me first."

Billy was taken aback by this quiet request at first. But he was still seething over his treatment to this point. He smiled his grimy smile again, then looked around the car. He asked, "How come yew knowed my truck was a-gonna quit? D'yew do sump'm to it?"

"Yeah, I sabotaged it."

Billy eased the gun's hammer back to safety, then twirled the gun in his hand. He'd defeated the sheriff, so he wanted to draw a little vengeful satisfaction from the situation too, and ask a few of his own questions first.

"I funneled a handful of sugar in the gas tank," Gene said matter-of-factly. "Figured it'd go a few miles before it petered out."

"Damn, that'll bust the motor. Carl'll kick yore ass."

"C'mon, Billy, answer my question," Gene said in a quiet, effective voice.

"Yeah, we put sump'm in yer water," Billy said with obvious pride. "Think Carl called it coral hydrake."

"Chloral hydrate?" Gene asked, surprised by Billy's quickness to answer.

"Yeah, that's what I said."

"How'd you get me to look like I was awake and enjoying myself with the ladies?"

"Aw, I don't know much 'bout that. Some kinda trick pi'chers is all I know. We kept a-proppin' yew up, an' yew kept a-fallin' on us like a rag doll!"

"Doctored pictures, huh? Well, you all made some good ones," Gene said. "Where'd the girls come from?"

"Hell, I don't know. Same place the pi'cher taker come from. Chicago, I reckon. Hell, Carl gits people from all over." Then Billy straightened up, finally realizing he'd talked too much. "Git in the goddamn trunk!"

Gene looked at him with apparent surprise. He pointed to the car and said, "In there?" Then he smiled. This gesture infuriated Billy. "Move now, goddamnit!"

Gene reached up slowly to the open lid. He grabbed the handle, then slammed it shut. Billy cocked the gun again and aimed it at Gene's face. "Yew gonna ride in that trunk – I don't give a shit – dead'r alive."

"You won't answer any more questions first?" Gene asked. Billy was getting angrier by the second. He fumbled with the trigger, then it seemed he started to squeeze it. "All right, I'll get in," Gene said. He took the handle and eased the lid back up. Unhurriedly he placed his hand down behind the spare tire rack as if he were going to pull himself in. Instead, he fumbled with something for a moment that was hidden from Billy's eyes and then he lifted out a handgun hidden deep inside the rack. He looked slowly up at Billy. He was holding the gun away from Billy, pointing it toward the car.

Billy's eyes seemed to pop out of his head. He was startled so badly that he nearly dropped the gun. "Drop it!" he commanded.

"Shoot me," Gene said calmly.

"Drop the goddamn gun!"

"Thought you was going to kick my ass," Gene said tauntingly. Then he slowly turned the gun toward Billy with the seeming intent of observing Billy's alarm grow by degrees. But Billy yanked the trigger. It clicked. Again he yanked. Another click. He pulled the trigger four more times. Four more clicks. Gene smiled. Billy flew into a panic. He drew back to throw the useless gun at Gene. Quickly, Gene pointed downward and fired a round into Billy's new boot.

Billy dropped to the ground screaming. Then he flipped himself over twice in the dirt with the searing pain. The hole was perfectly placed dead-center through the top of the boot. Gene could see a nasty bulge on the bottom of the sole. He figured the bullet didn't go completely through, probably because it hit a bone. It was obviously causing a great deal of pain, as Billy wouldn't stop screaming and cursing.

Gene bent over and picked up the empty gun and the gun belt nearby. He tossed them back into the trunk and closed the lid. He shoved his new gun into the back of his belt. He walked over to Billy, who by now sat hunched over and holding his shot foot in his hands. Again, without regard for his pain, Gene grabbed Billy's right arm and proceeded to drag him back to the tree. "Holler all you want; nobody's going to hear you out here," Gene said. He shoved Billy back against the base of the tree trunk, then he walked back to the spot where he was before. He repositioned the gun to the front of his beltline, where Billy could see it.

"Yew tricked me, yew son-of-a-bitch!" Billy blubbered. He held his foot away from him, as if it would help ease the pain. He had tried to remove the boot, but the pain was too much to bear.

"How's it feel?" Gene asked.

"Hurts like hell!" Billy yelled.

"No – being tricked."

Billy was still in too much pain to bother with questions and answers, so Gene waited for him to come back to what remained of his senses. In a few minutes, Billy reclined himself next to the tree and held his head as if he still had a headache. He had quieted down a bit and lay rocking slowly back and forth.

"I hadn't shot you in the head – at least not yet," Gene said. "You ready to answer a few questions?"

Billy acted deaf. The first realization to flash into his mind was that Gene intended to kill him. At this thought, his foot ceased hurting for the moment. The notion that he was going to die grabbed hold of every nerve in his body. He lay still on the ground. He had to force himself to stay alert to his surroundings, and not panic. He fought to force his mind to work up an escape strategy, but the pain returned vengefully and was soon compounded by the growing realization of his new predicament.

"You're going to answer a few questions," Gene said.

"Yew gonna kill me?" Billy asked.

"You answer my questions, boy, and you'll live forever."

"I need a doctor – my foot's a-hurtin' real bad. Yew don't get me to a doctor, I'll get gangrene!"

"You answer my questions; you'll get healed up real quick," Gene said. Billy slowly raised himself up and leaned back against the tree. Gene was frightening him more that ever with his smile. "Now, what happened on the North Road back in October a year ago?"

The sheriff sat squatted in front of him again, fully intent on getting answers. Billy appeared to genuinely not understand the question. Gene clarified, "You know, a Buell boy was killed on the road back middle of October last year. Tell me about it."

"Wh – w – why yew reckon I know anythang 'bout that?" Billy asked with feigned surprise.

"C'mon, Billy, don't shit with me. I know you know who did it. You drag this out long enough, you'll lose that foot."

Billy's mind was spinning like an unbalanced flax wheel. How could the sheriff suspect him? He continued to feign ignorance. Gene said, "Carl had something to do with it – I have no doubt about it. I knew right after the first time I met him that he did it, or at least had a part in it. Wade and Paul never lied to me. They didn't have anything to do with hurting those boys. But I know that Carl knows something. And if he knows something, then I figure you know something too. And you're going to tell me everything – right now."

Billy looked at the sheriff with a new expression of apprehension. If he was going to die anyway, he didn't figure on telling anything on his boss that shouldn't be told. But Gene was quick to change his mind for him. He pulled the gun from his belt and cocked it. He aimed it at Billy's other foot. Billy recoiled in horror. He started breathing rapidly, a thin rope of mucus expelling out his nasals.

"If you don't know anything – fine. Make something up," Gene ordered.

Billy pulled his foot away from the trajectory of the gun and raised his hand to Gene. "Okay – okay – I'll tell yew ever'thang!" he cried, now starting to sob.

Gene uncocked the gun and returned it to his belt. He sat down on the ground and turned his ear to the unfortunate vagabond before him. Billy turned his head down as if he were trying to concentrate. His foot was fighting for his attention. He looked toward Gene with as best a serious expression he could muster. He could feel a heavy quiver in his throat; he figured it could help him to sound sincere.

"I d – d – didn't want to hurt nobody, sher'ff! I – I – I di… I – I was – "

"Just slow it down – just the facts. What happened?" Gene demanded.

"There was this feller – Earnie Jackson. He kil't that boy, sher'ff! Yeah, shot 'im deader'n a tree stump!"

Gene's expression changed from a look of ambivalence to anger. Even if Billy was telling the truth, Gene was intent on keeping this pot boiling. "You telling me the truth, Billy?"

Billy stared at Gene. He was trying to control his shaking. He could see that Gene held no empathy for his pain, nor faith in his accounting. Billy had become so filled with fear that he was babbling. He knew he would have to sound more believable. The only way to do that with Gene would be to tell the truth.

"Okay – okay – I – I won't hold back on yew, sher'ff. I – I'll tell yew ever'thang – no holdin' back! No holdin' back!"

"That's all I asked for."

Billy pulled his swollen foot up to him and held it. "Leave the boot on. It'll keep the bleeding down," Gene said. Billy didn't intend to remove the boot. He just wanted to control the pain. He looked off into the distance as if recounting a past event.

"I don't rightly remember how it all started, sher'ff. Me an' Jackson started a-drankin' late that night before the North Road killin'. We started gettin' drunk with Carl 'bout three or four that mornin'. Yeah, Carl got drunk hisself, too. He brung some of that whiskey with him from Chicargo 'bout a week before. Roy was with us fer awhile but he had to git back to his wife an' young'uns. He don't know nuthin' 'bout what happened there on the road. We was livin' there in Carl's house ever since he come down from Chicargo. An' we got drunk a lot. He don't let us git that way now. Jist Friday nights.

"W – we was really drunk. W – we'd been a-shootin' with Carl's scatter gun. Blowin' birds and squirrels outta the trees off the front porch. Musta kil't a dozen squirrels and birds outta them trees right after sunup. We didn't have no call to be messin' with no guns bein' as messed up as we all was. Carl had shot out some windows in his house that mornin'; used up all his bullets in his twenty-two. Me and ol' Jackson thought he was gonna shoot one of us 'cause he was a-shootin' all over without aimin'!

"Well, we run outta squirrel shot, so Carl sent Earnie back in the house to fetch some more ammo, and we set out fer some shootin' up the road. Hell, Carl was wantin' to shoot sump'm. He was lookin' at me an' Jackson like he was a-gonna shoot one of us. Then he blowed a slug at Jackson when he was a-standin' next to a tree. Damn – blowed a hole the size of yore fist in the tree just a half-inch behind Jackson's head. Scared the hell outta both of us. We all got in the truck and rolled up the road a piece. We found some deer tracks in the road so we jist started walkin'. We was makin' too much racket, though. Prob'ly scared every critter outta the county."

"Get to it, Billy," Gene ordered in perhaps his angriest tone yet. It seemed clear to Gene that Billy was stalling for time with his frantic and incessant discourse. He talked as fast as the thoughts would pop into his head as if to spout them out before he had opportunity to forget them. He was glancing around through the trees and back up the road, apparently hoping someone might happen upon them and rescue him. Gene didn't seem concerned with being discovered by anyone.

"W – we come up over the next hill there an' Carl told us to shut up. They was a car sittin' down in the road there. A boy was in it. He hadn't heard us 'cause the motor was a-runnin'. Like he was a-waitin' on somebody. Carl told us to lay back, an' he eased on up to the car. He – he got right up on the boy b'fore he knowed we was on him. Hell, I don't know if Carl said nuthin' to him or if the boy said nuthin'. I seen Carl grab a-holt of the boy and yanked him plumb out o' the car. J – j – just like throwin' a rag doll, he throwed that boy down on the road. Me and Jackson run down to Carl. He told us to hold the boy whilst he went over and looked in the car. He come back and grabbed a-holt of the boy and wanted to know why he was on his propity."

"That wasn't Carl's land. It didn't come that far east," Gene said. Billy continued.

"We was all still so drunk – hell, we jist messed with him. Hell, I musta hit him once't myself. That's when Carl done it," Billy said with a resigned slowness. He looked at Gene as if the big secret was about to be revealed. Gene hadn't changed his expression.

"For no reason, he dragged that boy over to the car and throwed him over the front of it. The motor was still a-runnin' so the hoodtop was scaldin' hot. Me and Jackson had knocked a lotta blood out of him, and when Carl throwed him on that hot hoodtop he let out a holler and that made Carl mad. Uh, Carl slapped him a couple of times b'fore he figured out the car was hot. Then he just knocked him clean up and over the car. M – me and Jackson, we was drunker'n skunks, we figured we'd have us a little fun. W – we didn't mean to hurt nobody sher'ff. We – we got the boy and dragged him back up on the car. I think Carl musta broke his neck or sump'm, 'cause he wud'n actin' right. His eyes was rolled back in his head, and the hot car didn't bother him no more.

"Carl picked the scatter gun up and poked it in the boy's mouth like he was gonna blow his head plumb off. But that boy was right near dead, so I reckon it didn't matter much. I reckon Carl seen that the boy was messed up and he let him fall on the ground. He did – didn't know.

We – we, uh, we was all a-makin' a ruckus, and I reckon we never took no time to figure it out. Hell, Carl said we messed the boy up, so he slapped the hell outta Jackson. I just run up the road to git away from him.

"Then somebody shot a gun from the woods. Hell – I – I – I don't know – somebody was a-shootin' at us from the woods! Damn, ever'thang was a-happ'nin' fast. Carl whooped his scatter gun around and shot up in the trees. Says he kil't somebody – that other Buell boy. Hell, we jist all stood there. Carl was just a-walkin' along there a-lookin' way up in them trees, reckon tryin' to see someone else a-comin' at him."

Billy's foot was starting to distract him from his story again. He grimaced heavily and a tear squeezed out of his eye. He worked to ignore the pain and continue.

"Then we heard somebody a-screamin' up in them trees there. Right up over the ridge. Then right outta them trees, there come this girl. Hell, she wudn't right in her mind. N'er seen nobody put on like that. Like a crazy dawg, just a-foamin' at the mouth and a-screamin' like some bobcat. She jist come a-runnin' out down the road there like she didn't know we was there. Like she was a-runnin' from sump'm er other up'm 'em woods.

"Carl told me to run fetch the kid. Hell, I run fetched 'er all right. Hell, how's I supposed to know it was Wade's kid? She had on overalls and dirt and mud all over, and hair all over her face. Figured it was some migrant's kid that got mixed up in a moonshine run or sump'm. I was so damn messed up myself, hell, reckon I started messin' with the kid. I sh – sh – shouldn't have – damn wouldn't have if'n I knowed it was Wade's young'un!"

"What do you mean, Billy – what do you mean 'messed with her'?" Gene asked. Billy didn't want to volunteer anymore, but figured it was in his immediate best interest to continue.

"L – like I said – I was drunk. You don't think much when yo're drunk – hell, I sure don't. I was gonna have a little fun with that girl, I reckon, sher'ff. I even got some of her clothes plumb off. Then them damn dogs come. It was all a-happ'nin' too fast. But Carl – I don't rightly know how – run them dogs off right quick, with a rope. Got the rope out of Buell's car, Carl said. Hit a couple of them dogs and ran them off scared. Next thang, he's slappin' me around and a-throwin' me back on th' road. That girl was just sittin' there in the ditch like she'd been kil't – whiter'n a ghost. Reckon she figured we aimed to kill her too. But Carl yanked her up by the arm and dragged her on up in the trees. I don't know what he done. Me and ol' Jackson jist stayed there in the road. I don't recall much – seems like Earnie was a-cussin' and a-carryin' on. Reckon it was all too much fer him. Killin' that Buell boy up on the ridge, and now the girl was gettin' raped by Carl. We could hear the boy by the car makin' a racket, too. Like he was a-cryin' and a-carryin' on.

"Then d'rekly, we could hear somebody callin' from way on up the other side of the ridge there. They was still a long ways off, but if we stayed real quiet, we could hear them. I run over there to tell Carl but he comes a-runnin' back. He heerd them voices too. Tells us to run back to the truck right quick."

"Carl raped Kelly Jean?" Gene asked.

"I – I – I d – don't rightly know. He wouldn't ne'er say. I didn't see him a-pullin' up his britches er nuthin'. I reckon he just told her a thang or two. I don't reckon he had the time to mess with her like I did. We jist jumped back in the truck and eased on back up to the house. Me and Jackson laid out in the woods fer a couple of days, but Carl run back up to Chicargo. Says he needed a' alibi. Reckon so he could say he was in Chicargo that day if anybody as't."

Gene removed a handkerchief and wiped his face, and shook his head in disgust. He looked at Billy with an intensely angry glare. He should have done this many months ago, he thought. Yet something was wrong with Billy's story. There was clearly a conflict between Billy's account and what Gene had determined to be the truth concerning the chronology of events on the North Road. He had thought all along that Wade and Paul had arrived shortly after the dogs, which would not have given Carl enough time to mess with Kelly Jean after the dogs arrived, as Billy had detailed it.

"You say them dogs came while you all was hurting Kelly Jean – or afterwards?" Gene asked.

"Huh? Uh – after, I reckon."

"After?"

"Uh, I don't know – ain't that what I said?"

Gene determined that it was probable that Billy was confusing himself in his fumbling efforts to pass some of the blame to Carl and away from himself. He concluded that the exact timeline of events really didn't matter, though. Billy's memory had been wilted by alcohol and Wade's and Paul's memories of events were not exactly flawless either. Even still, Gene figured there was enough truth here to pin the crime on Carl and his drunken duo.

"Where did Jackson go after all this?" Gene asked.

"M – my foot's a-hurtin' real bad, sher'ff. I need a – a – a doctor real bad!"

Gene ignored him and waited for an answer.

"Carl kil't him. Jackson was a-talkin' to Roy 'bout the whole thang. Reckon he didn't feel so bad about it all if he figured that it was all fer fun, and killin' them boys was just a' accident. He didn't tell Roy we done it, but Roy might figure we did. Least that's what Carl said. I don't know why he was a-talkin' to Roy 'bout it. Reckon, like I said, it helped settle his mind. But Carl told him to stop. But he jist kept right on. Reckon it was workin' on his mind too much. So, Carl figured it wouldn't do no good to send him back home er nuthin'. He jist figured Earnie would jist talk to somebody else, like the law, and it would come back to him. So, Carl shot and kil't him."

"What'd he do with the body?" Gene asked.

"He fin'lly burnt him up. Burnt him to ashes. Right out there in front of the house. Underneath them oak trees. Put kindlin' and brambles and gasoline on his ass and all his shit and lit him afire."

"Did you see it?"

"What?"

"What did you see, Billy?"

"I seen him shoot him and burn him both!"

"He just shot him right there and then burned him?"

"Uh, naw – he shot him on Wade's place, south end, then burnt him up the next day."

"Wade's place? What do you mean, Billy?"

Billy then proceeded to tell the story of all the events of the night, admitting that it had been planned that he, Billy, was to shoot Earnie Jackson, but that he couldn't bring himself to do it, thus requiring Carl to finish his dirty work. He detailed how Carl had convinced Earnie of a treasure trove buried on another farm beneath a big oak tree, and that it could only be recovered under cover of darkness, so as not to be discovered by the landowner. Jackson, needing ready cash to get back home to Georgia and defend himself and his family from creditors, was ripe for such a fraud.

Billy recounted how Wade had shown up the morning after Jackson's execution and demanded that Carl remove the body from his land. Billy described exactly where the event had happened, how the body was grotesquely misshapened from rigor mortis and the compression of a half-ton of earth. He recalled how Carl's disposition had turned as mean and malicious as he could ever remember after Wade's visit. How Carl had not easily recovered from Wade's having knowledge of Carl's murderous behavior on his land, and that Carl couldn't figure out how he knew what he knew. Gene determined that Carl could not easily handle others having any kind of an advantage over him.

"Did Carl ever figure out how Wade knew?" Gene asked.

"Ne'er did. And it's been a burr in his saddle ever since. Reckon that's why Carl figured it was Wade that tried to kill him. Or fer what Carl done to Kelly Jean. I don't know. Wade come up and talked to Carl once't after he got back from the hospital. I don't rightly know what 'appened. I recollect I had to fix a busted window w'en Wade left."

"Fix a window?"

"Yeah, Carl and Wade was a-talkin' in the front room and Carl said Wade got mad an' throwed a chair through a front window. Then he saddled up and left. Paul was with him, but he waited fer him outside."

"Paul – outside? Did he hear any of the goings-on in the house between Carl and Wade?"

"Naw – I – I know he didn't. I was down at the chicken house and I seen him out in the yard waitin' fer Wade. My foot's hurtin' real bad, sher'ff. I – I – I done told yew ever'thang!"

"How much liquor is Carl putting out a day?"

"Goddamnit, sher'ff – gangrene's a-settin' in! I can feel it – my leg's gone numb plumb up to my knee bone. I ain't answerin' no more questions till you git me a doctor!" Billy spat with new tears in his eyes. He punched the ground with his fist, then slung his hair back out of his eyes glaring up at Gene; for the first time losing control over his anger since deciding that Gene intended to kill him. *Damn it, git me a goddamn doctor!"*

Gene figured he had bled this rotted turnip dry. He stood up, then stretched his arms out and yawned. This uncaring gesture infuriated Billy and he beat the ground again, then attempted to get up on his good foot. "Sit down, boy. You ain't getting up," Gene said with utter coolness. Billy sat back down and watched Gene as he slowly sauntered around him and the tree. Billy rolled himself over halfway, still trying to relieve the pain. Gene was looking back off into the trees and the clear-cut, seeming to be thinking about his next move. "Does Carl have anything on Tom Buell?" he asked from behind the tree.

Billy cursed and yanked himself back up against the tree. He looked around as if looking for a weapon and yelled, *"Go ahead, you sons-a-bitch! Blow my goddamn head off! I ain't answerin' yew nothin', no more!"*

Gene, still cool and unconcerned, walked easily back to Billy and asked, "You through answering my questions?" Billy had fallen beyond exasperation. He started pulling himself up on his good foot. "You going some place?" Gene asked. Billy tried to hop away. He fell to the ground on his first attempt. "You're going the wrong way – town's back toward the west," Gene said.

Billy tried again and again, each time with the same results. Then he tried crawling. Gene pulled out a rolled cigarette and lit it. He watched Billy as he painfully worked to traverse the ground on all fours. He could see a thin trickle of blood coming out of a crack in the bulge in the bottom of his boot. Billy tried to balance his weight on his right leg as he crawled along, but he needed all four members to move, so he cursed with pain each time he tried to pull up his left leg.

"It'll take you four days to make Braxton at this rate, Billy," Gene said, slowly moving forward behind Billy as he struggled along the ground. He looked as pitiful as the poorest transient crawling along with his pants soiled in the crotch from fear. He was wearing a brown shirt, which would be white when clean, and with close inspection Gene could see a half-bloated tick on the back of his neck. Gene noticed though that the hair looked cleaner than he would have expected. Probably because Carl required his closest confederates to take an occasional bath. Too bad he didn't require the same for their clothes.

Billy stopped for a moment to restretch his bum leg, then he proceeded. He could hear Gene behind him. By now he was about ten yards beyond the car. Gene saw a pile of leaves about six feet ahead of Billy. Figuring the pile would make an adequate blood blotter, Gene pulled his gun and aimed it at the back of Billy's head. The gun was the double-action type, which did not require it to be cocked before being fired. So Billy never heard the click of a hammer. The bullet slammed through Billy's head, throwing him over the leaf pile.

Gene stood with the gun still aimed at Billy's prostrate body. A wisp of smoke drifted out of the neat round hole in the back of the head. Gene didn't see any blood expelling out of the hole or from the front of Billy's head. Most of his face was buried in the leaves. Huh, Gene thought, people with no heart must have no blood.

CHAPTER 21

"But winter's coming, Wade. What're we going to do?"

Esther watched as Wade, once again, allowed another bucketful of well water to slowly pour from the bucket into the drain basin in the kitchen. This time he held it up high enough to allow the morning light from the window to filter through it.

"What's wrong, Mama?" Kelly Jean asked.

"I don't know. I reckon the water's gone bad."

"Why? What made it do that?"

No one answered Kelly Jean's second question. It was as if she had not asked it at all. She stepped back from the activity at the basin and sat down at the table. For two hours she had been instructed to stay inside the house as everyone else behaved so strangely that it made her want to hide away or go to bed and wake up again in hopes that things will have returned to normal. She had watched most of the activity through the rear kitchen window, and she felt a growing desperation to learn why Paul had been making unexplained trips back and forth between the two homes with a bucket of his own. Her father had drawn up perhaps a dozen buckets of water out of the well and examined the contents each time. He seemed to hope that eventually the awful truth was really only a temporary fluke that could be rectified by drawing out the bad water, leaving the good. Now they were in the kitchen with more water samplings, and treating it all as if it had been judged an omen for the end of the world.

Kelly Jean had earlier watched her father angrily fling a full bucket of water against the side of the wellhouse, and she saw Esther run out of the house to stop his tantrum. Kelly Jean was watching and Esther had to let him know. Then all at once, Wade, Esther, Paul and Jimmy turned and looked from the wellhouse through the kitchen window at Kelly Jean. Kelly Jean's eyes were clearly visible to them even though they were many yards apart, and they found an inexplicable expression of confusion on her face that caused them to stiffen up and affect a crippled smile.

In a moment, Jimmy returned to the kitchen with yet another bucket, this time it was only one-third full. "I reckon it's starting to dry up," he said.

Angrily, Wade said, "Take it back out."

Jimmy returned to the porch and flung the water out into the yard. Even from here the water looked like used dishwater as it rained to the ground. For no discernible reason, the house quieted to near-total silence when Jimmy returned. Shortly, Paul returned with Ruth, both without a word or a bucket. They were somber, almost distressed to tears. All the grownups looked at one another more helplessly than had ever been witnessed before. It was time to give up and let fate deal with them as it wished. It seemed that Esther was ready to cry and strike out at someone. She had worked gallantly for months to control her rage over knowing that Carl Kallton had terrorized her son and forced the family into a netherworld of covert memories and self-deceptive mind plays. The guilt she bore because of Jimmy's secret burden had caused her to search her son's eyes each day for signs of his own rage against everyone involved in his forced quarantine. And the idea of Carl's probable connection to Kelly Jean's distress had long ago begun to push Esther beyond her bounds of grace and longsuffering.

Esther had never seen Carl, nor had she been apprised of Wade's second encounter with him when he and Paul were taken prisoners. But she had recently, through one of her quiet discussions with the preacher, learned of his malevolent appearance, his personality, and his growing power, economic and political, among the leaders and merchants in town. It wasn't right, she reasoned, for someone of his persuasion to gain such favor so quickly among the good people she knew. So he had turned from his corrupt ways in Chicago to come and live the life of a virtuous dirt farmer among the common agrarian locals? It was a disturbing thought, and it was compounded by the fact of living with a husband who behaved increasingly covertly every day and aggressively brushed aside her concerns. Wade had given her only cursory tidbits of his encounter with Carl the morning after Jimmy's nighttime terror at the big oak. In the end, any of her knowledge concerning Carl was all third hand. And Ruth was careful to never volunteer anything new that she may have learned from Paul.

The Buells – Esther had quickly forgiven them. They had lost sons. She understood their grief, and she joined her husband in not pushing for a conclusion in the investigations against Tom. Tom's actions, along with those of Lucas, were the deeds of depraved men, but she wondered that she may have been equally vengeful if her daughter had similarly died in the incident and the circumstantial evidence had initially pointed to Tom as it had done to Wade. The tragedy of it all had so overwhelmed her sense of reason and justice that she couldn't imagine herself seeking retribution against Tom and Annie.

So when Wade suggested that they sell some property to compensate for their losses, she readily agreed, believing that any further actions against Tom and Annie would only serve to destroy their spirits and forever ruin any future possibility of finding their way back to living any semblance of normalcy again. Through it all, Wade had kept Esther in the dark concerning who the real purchaser of the land was. Gene was stumped, yet relieved, by Wade's decision to sell the land along with his apparent refusal to bring suit. But Gene's job was nonetheless toughened a little more each day by too many citizens in town, related and otherwise, continuing to dog him with presumptuous questions concerning the situation that he felt they had no business asking.

Such as Esther's thoughts were, her motives for releasing the Buells from retribution were fairly opposed to Wade's. His were self-preservation; fear of loss of control. Fear of the unknown. But the results for the family, she had to admit to herself, were the same: unwavering, unbounded protection for Kelly Jean's mental well-being; ensured unity of the family that legal entanglements could threaten; and refuge from an intrusive and frightening outside world that the ensuing publicity a civil trial against the Buells would destroy.

Esther believed she could feel Annie's grief, and she seemed to know, through some unfathomable spiritual connection, when Annie couldn't sleep or pray. Even while overwhelmed at home, she felt Annie's longing and the famine in her soul. Esther often thought of her and wished that she could hold her tight in her arms and console her forever, if that's what it took. Every day that the feud had kept them apart had, even before the North Road incident, torn Esther up inside a little more, and she was ready to take matters into her own hands before the tragedy destroyed everything.

She remembered the night when she was sure she had heard Annie crying. It was in a house somewhere unfamiliar, but she could hear Annie crying and praying in such depths of heartbrokenness and despair that she simply couldn't stand it any longer. She struggled to find Annie and console her if it were possible, but everywhere she turned it seemed that Annie was still a room or two away. It seemed to matter little how gallantly she fought the darkness searching for her old friend. But she could distinctly hear her calling her younger son's name. It was James, before Frank died. Finally, after an exhausting search, Esther found Annie and clasped her arms around her, not wanting to let go. Then a faint ebbing of light began to fill the room as her cries softened to a whimper. It was working, she thought. I've found my old friend again and it's going to be all right.

With the slow realization of someone waking from a deep, dream-laden sleep, Esther began to see the details in the room around her. She could still hear the cries, but soon she realized that the room was very familiar after all. Feeling as if she had been played for the epitome of fools, she rolled back on the bed and laid Kelly Jean back onto her side and began patting her on the back to help calm her down. With her other hand she pulled up a quilt corner and wiped her eyes, soaking it through like a dry cotton boll sopping up raindrops in a storm.

"Esther?" a man's voice said from the doorway. "Everything okay?" It was Wade. She could see his face in the light of the small oil lamp left burning on the dresser. He had heard Kelly Jean's cries and was concerned that Esther was taking too long to settle her down.

"Yeah – it's okay now. It's okay," Esther said, glad that the shadows shielded her watery eyes from Wade. "She just had another bad dream. We're okay now."

Wade stood at the door for a long time saying nothing. He had heard Kelly Jean crying out for James, and it seemed that it was going to go on all night. But soon Kelly Jean was asleep again, and Esther lay awake the rest of the night trying to figure out what it all meant. Now, to add to all her fears, the water had turned to rancid tea, and she had no frame of reference for understanding what was causing it. For all she knew, these things happened naturally, and there was nothing to do but wait for it to clear up on its own somehow.

***

"Did he put something in it?" Kelly Jean asked, still sitting at the table.

"What?" Esther asked.

"Did somebody put some poison in it, or something?" she clarified.

"What are you talking about?" Esther asked fearfully. Then she looked at Wade, who had stopped messing with the water when Kelly Jean asked about someone being culpable in spoiling the well water. He froze like a statue with his back to his daughter. It seemed that everyone froze so swiftly that the temperature dropped.

"What do you mean, Kelly Jean?" Esther asked again.

Kelly Jean reacted as if she suddenly realized that she had unwittingly uttered some terrible family secret that ripped the fragile veil of tenuous peace over the house, and she wished now that she had kept her mouth shut. Of course, she had assumed that she had asked a question of little significance. She had expected someone to merely answer the question with a mild rebuke or to simply brush her off, but she was looking as if she had been slapped across the face. Esther began to make things worse by walking slowly toward Kelly Jean as if she were about to mete out some sort of punishment for misbehavior.

"Huh?" Kelly Jean asked.

"Who are you talking about, Kelly Jean?" her mother asked.

Now Kelly Jean felt that peculiar buzzing sensation in her head that made her wonder if she was only dreaming. At first, she was certain that she had said something that everyone was determined not to hear. They knew something, she was sure, but it was beyond her comprehension to understand why it was so important that it deserved this kind of treatment. Paul and Ruth had stepped back as if they were trying to remove themselves from everyone else's consciousness. She could see outside that the sunlight was still bright, but somehow the shadows were oppressively heavy and covered the house as though a thick storm cloud drifted over the farm.

Something had changed. Somehow, someone had turned off the forward march of time and froze the whole world at the same moment. Kelly Jean could see her mother's eyes – they were direct and penetrating. Then, like a spirit lifting away from its body, she felt herself splitting into two forms; one was her body, the other was her mind – which had moved to a couple of inches in front of her forehead. She had experienced this sensation numerous times before, but not to this degree. Somehow, though, she could still feel the heaviness of her body. But she was so detached that it didn't feel in the least bit burdensome or restrictive. She ordered herself to lean back in the chair, but she only had to think it. Without any effort, she felt the chair touch her back as if it had moved on its own to meet her. She could tell that her heart was beating fast, and her chest was heavy with that feeling of dreadful anticipation, but her mind was free now of any such fear. Mentally, she felt none of the painful reactions that her body was experiencing.

It had seemed like several minutes had passed since her mother had queried her, but then she realized it had only been a few seconds. Unexplainably her mouth opened and she spoke. "Those old migrant men, Mama – you know," she heard herself saying with words plain and free of consternation. "You know I never liked to see them up so close to the house."

Esther looked back at Wade. She was still wracked by something, and now Wade was acting as if he had heard nothing. Paul and Ruth were still silent, standing near the door to the porch. The farm hands had been sent home weeks earlier and it would make no sense to accuse them of anything this long after their departure. Kelly Jean had initially spoken of some particular man spoiling the water, not of two men. Had she seen something? Did she know something that everyone else was ignorant of? Kelly Jean could not decipher her mother's motives or intentions. She was lost.

Then the everyday sounds of activity began to fill the room again, and Kelly Jean began to regain her senses, and it was painful. She felt the pain in her chest as if she had been punched. But if she kept her breathing steady and quiet, she was confident that no one would notice her trembling shoulders. She watched her mother return to the basin with Wade, and she behaved as though nothing had happened. With only a cursory glance back toward Kelly Jean, Esther could see that she seemed normal again; still fearful, but otherwise normal. Then, as was the case minutes before, no one paid any more mind to her.

It would be several hours later deep into the night that Kelly Jean would awake with a jerk, her mother fast asleep next to her. The little incident at the kitchen table flew back into her mind. Now she knew she had lied about the migrants. She didn't mean to say what she had said, but she remembered that she had no control over herself. It seemed that the words had exploded out of her mouth without the permission of her mind. But she remembered her statement concerning the bad water that had caused her mother to react so strongly. Then her heart began to hurt again, and the constriction reached up her throat when the picture of a particular man's face, a big man's face, flashed into her mind. It was, to her, an ugly face; one she could never gaze upon for more than a second. Instantly her hands flew across her body, then to her face, as if to protect herself from incoming blows. It didn't make sense and she was not in control. It only made sense to her that a bad person, perhaps like one of the migrants, could have somehow been responsible for the bad things that happen to them. But the logic of this conclusion was lost on everyone else, but it was the only deduction that made sense to her, and she couldn't remember why it seemed so logical at the time. But she knew that her father, like the other farmers throughout the county, needed the workers to help with the planting and the harvesting and the feeding. So, why did she see the man's face everywhere, then work hard to forget it, then only to see it again when she needed to rest?

Without conscious effort, her mind seemed to have found a way to conveniently bury the memories of certain past events that would devour her soul if they were allowed to live within her head without restraint. But like spoiled children, the memories would manifest themselves at inconvenient times without regard for Kelly Jean's emotional harmony. They could return and haunt her with blurred perceptions and unwelcomed sensory distractions that would steal the remaining shreds of her sense of security and innocence. It was not difficult to hold these flitting thoughts at arm's length during the day, but her mind was more easily manipulated by the demons of the night.

Then, just as quickly, it was over. She was able to forget the big man's face, or why she impulsively reached to protect herself. It all seemed familiar, then completely alien. It was all a joke. Something from a bad dream. It was confusing to her that she was beginning to remember details of the worst dream – the one with the big man's face and the dark blue eyes. But lately she was getting much better at controlling, or hiding, her fears. Her heart often beat fast, and she still felt the painful heaviness in her chest. But as she practiced to forget her nightmares and to cast aside her feelings of anxiety and dread, she could control her emotions better and better as the days, and the months, passed by. Or so she thought.

CHAPTER 22

"I don't know, boss. He just said, 'Tell the chief asshole to get down here.'"

Carl rapped the top of the table with his fingers. M.C. was back from Chicago and sitting across from him. One of his foremen had brought the message from Wade who was waiting down on the road.

"Very good, Coleman," Carl said. The foreman left, leaving Carl and M.C. in the front room alone. "How did he know I was here?" Carl asked.

"He probably just guessed that you were here," M.C. said.

Carl nodded and looked off through a window. Then he yelled into the kitchen, *"Troy, run fetch Jesse."* Carl stood up and walked through the house to the kitchen and out the back door. One of the guards was standing near the wellhouse and looking off down the driveway. When he heard Carl step out onto the porch he turned around to him. Troy was already out of sight down the North Road on horseback to fetch Jesse Bridger, Carl's new right-hand lieutenant, from somewhere out in the fields.

Carl stood against a porch post, apparently trying to guess at what Wade was up to. But figuring it would be ten minutes before Jesse returned, Carl instructed the guard to go down the driveway and tell Wade to come up to the house, where he would be on Carl's turf. In several minutes, the guard returned without Wade.

"He said he ain't a-comin'. He told me to tell you to get yore ass down there. That's what he told me to tell you."

Carl looked back toward the end of the North Road. M.C. had come out and stood beside him. "What do you think he's up to?" Carl asked.

"I don't know. Maybe it concerns Billy."

Carl looked over at the truck, which was standing near the middle of the yard with half its crippled engine dismantled and spread out on the ground nearby. Billy had vanished with hardly a trace; the stalled truck being the only evidence of foul play. Carl instructed the guard to get another man and arm him. They were both to head down to the road to Wade and wait there. They were to say nothing to him. Shortly, Troy returned with Jesse. Carl and Jesse walked out to the black barracks and boarded the big flatbed truck parked there. M.C., still on the porch, did not fail to notice the handle of a six-shooter sticking out above Carl's rear waistband.

***

"You looking for the chief asshole?" Carl asked after slowing the truck to a stop at the end of the driveway. The two guards had placed themselves well, one twenty yards to the east, the other to the west. They were both standing in the middle of the road with shotguns held ready to their sides. Wade was on horseback near the driveway entrance. His rifle scabbard was empty. Clearly he wanted to talk, and nothing more.

"Is that you?" Wade answered.

Carl didn't crack anymore of a smile than he already had. Jesse was trying to get a clear view of Wade past Carl through the driver's window. His head bobbed around a little like he was looking for something to happen. In a moment, Wade dismounted and began walking over to the truck. Both guards moved in slowly but warily to get a better watch on things. They eyed Wade up and down. They could see no weapons. Carl sat silently without answering obvious questions, as usual. Wade stopped a few feet from the truck and kept his hands stiffly to his sides. It was a good place to give Jesse a good look at him.

"We're having water problems up the road here. I think you know it, and you know why," Wade said forcefully.

Carl didn't react at first. Jesse leaned forward and rested his arm on the dashboard. Wade figured him to be nearly as mean as Carl, and probably faster tempered. Jesse's black eyes fired from their whites at Wade like bullets. His chocolate face was stern with tight muscles and sinew, carrying the countenance of a man rarely bested by his enemies.

"Why do you figure I know anything about your affairs?" Carl asked.

"We have to have our water back like it was, Carl," Wade stated without acknowledging the question. "I figure you're sucking all the water out of the ground down south here. You're going to have to shut down your operations."

Carl laughed out loud. Jesse hadn't figured out what was going on, but he laughed too. Wade remained stonefaced. Then Carl looked off down the road toward the east, behind Wade. A car was coming toward them. It slowed down as it approached. Wade could see that is was Paul's dented Oldsmobile. Paul had a passenger, and Wade thought it was Ruth until it was close enough that Wade could see his wife, Esther, sitting on the passenger side. It passed on by – the guards standing firm, forcing Paul to veer to the edge of the road to pass. Wade's temples reddened and their veins bulged. Esther turned her head and looked intently at Carl. Then they picked up speed and drove on.

"Your brother and his wife?" Carl asked. Wade didn't answer. Carl seemed to chuckle. "I can take care of your water situation, Wade. I don't need to shut down, but I can fix your water."

"I don't need nothing fixed. I just need it back like it was."

"Okay, you'll get all the water you need. Now, I got a question."

Then Paul's car quickly turned around and returned. Again, he drove past slowly. Again, Esther was trying to eye Carl. Wade moved to approach the car, but it picked up speed, passed him by, and then shrunk into the distance. Clearly Wade was infuriated by this unexpected event.

"Some shit going on here I need to know about?" Carl asked.

"Don't worry about them. You got a question, or was that it?"

"Where's Billy?"

"Billy Wilson?"

"Yeah."

"Why are you asking me? He's your boy."

Carl checked Wade's reaction to the question and quickly deduced that he was sincere. He answered, "All right, about your water. Until your wells start running again, I'll run a water line up to your place." Carl could see that Wade was not showing any negative response to this idea, so he added, "How's your cow ponds?"

"What?"

"Cow ponds. Don't you have them for your cattle?"

"We might."

"How are they doing?"

"They're low and dirty. We keep them up with ground water and pumps. But now, thanks to you, we can't even do that."

Carl pretended to think by furrowing his brow and looking down at the road. Then he had more ideas. "If I run a one-inch line up to your place and one to Paul's and keep them running, say, eight hours a day – that'll keep you going until your wells are up?"

"Till my wells are up? You shut down today and I figure it'll take six months before I get good water again. What do you say I should do till then?"

"You not hear so good? I said I'll run you a line and give you good water till your wells are up."

"You ought to know there's not enough water in the ground around here for what you're doing. If you don't shut down all the way, my water's not ever going to be right."

Wade didn't like to hear himself talking so much with the likes of Carl. The more words that were spoken, the more things seemed to gravitate toward Carl's advantage. Against his better judgment, he tried to pull Carl into a discussion of his intentions. But it was like trying to talk a hole through a stone wall. Carl was now gazing intently at Wade. Jesse seemed to fidget for some kind of action.

"Your water will get back like it was. It'll be as clean as moonshine in no time." Carl looked around at the two guards, then added, "You want those goddamn water lines or not?"

"You'll run your lines up to the north side of the road, and I'll connect and run my lines from there on up. And I'll send you the bill when it's done," Wade answered. Then he walked back to his horse and mounted up. "You'll bury the lines all the way up and across the road. I'll be ready to connect in two days. And I expect plenty of pressure to run it uphill to the ponds."

"That's a tall order," Carl said.

"Fill it."

***

"But why did you go alone, Wade?" Esther asked tearfully, trying to control her quivering voice.

The whole morning had been a trauma to her, and her life had changed within a matter of hours. At first, Wade ignored her as he glared angrily at his brother. Paul glared back, but he felt sheepish again, and out of control. Ruth was holding Esther and she slowly worked the porch swing back and forth hoping to calm Esther, and herself, down. She could see Wade glaring at her husband, and she didn't like it.

"Why did you do that, Wade? You could have gotten yourself killed," Esther continued. "I have never seen anybody so mean-looking in all my life – never!"

"You always let a woman tell you what to do?" Wade groused loudly to Paul.

"Now you listen to me!" Ruth barked at Wade. "I'm a woman and I'm telling you to stop it – now!"

Wade stepped away from Paul and turned his gaze toward Ruth and Esther. Now it was

Ruth's turn to do a little glaring. He reached down to grasp Esther's arm, but she yanked it away and joined Ruth in glaring at him.

"What have you not been telling me?" Esther asked. "Is it true that he's running a big moonshine still down there and nobody's doing anything about it?" Again, Wade looked at Paul, but he refrained from glaring. Wade then glanced through the windows making sure no one in the house could hear the discussion. "That man's got the devil in him, Ruth," Esther said. "I just know it. I don't know how, but I know it!"

She had quickly changed the subject; too frightened to learn the truth about Carl's enterprises, as she had already been too weakened over the months by her knowledge of Carl's probable involvement in whatever happened on the North Road and to Kelly Jean. Now she felt as afraid as she had on the day of the North Road, but it was different now because she had the terrible feeling that she may have to deal with the reality of Carl's presence in her neighborhood for the rest of her life. It was bad enough to pretend that the big man didn't matter that much in their lives after Jimmy's experience at the big oak. She had convinced herself that the family's self-imposed quarantine was all done, as Wade had insisted, to protect Kelly Jean and to shield her from the inevitable legal entanglements that would be required of the whole family. Suddenly, Esther felt every bit as weak as her daughter. Lately, the guilt that she bore for acquiescing to Wade's efforts to dismantle Jimmy's reasoning after his witnessing the execution at the big oak was becoming more than she could bear. Carl would leave soon and return to the big city, she reasoned to herself. Or the sheriff would ultimately run him out of the county. She couldn't imagine the man remaining to live amongst common farmers while pretending he was one of them.

Early in the morning, Wade had left secretly before anyone had noticed his absence. He had been quieter and even more sullen than usual, and angry the night before, after the wells had dried up. But Esther had glimpsed him leave down the road on horseback toward the west. She knew he had no reason to do that, even though the rest of his family lived in that direction. He always took the wagon path connecting the two farms, not the road. So she knew something was out of bounds, and she was going to find out for herself what her husband was up to this time.

She had found Paul and Ruth in the house when she arrived on foot. With an edge of desperation in her voice, she had dredged the truth out of Paul concerning Carl's activities and their connection to their water problems. She pleaded with Paul to take her to the place where he thought Wade might have gone. With a combination of great reluctance and anxiety, he agreed to help, but he insisted that Esther stay in the car and, otherwise, do as he instructed. It would be her first encounter with Carl, and he knew that Wade would take offense at his efforts to place his wife in the line of danger. But Esther was going to walk to wherever Wade was, and she was going to find him, even if it took all day. She had no reason to anticipate that her first encounter with Carl would inspire within her such profound feelings of malevolence and of losing control.

On the first drive-by, Carl gazed back at her with such heretofore-unknown intensity that she felt she was somehow being violated. This was a man, she thought, that had something more to him than she ever thought could be gathered from just a mutual gaze. He followed her more with his eyes than with the turn of his head. It could be, it seemed to her, that he was planning something for her. Something, she felt, more personal, or intimate, than she could bear to imagine.

On the return drive-by, Carl was looking in Wade's direction. But just as Paul's car entered Carl's visual periphery, his eyes – not his head – swung instantly back to her own eyes, again communicating something beyond her understanding of things. As before, she alternately drew her eyes to his gaze, then away before a well of fear could build up within her. For the first time in her life, she felt that it would have been all right to kill someone. It seemed that no conscience would have to be consulted before committing the deed. Without logical reasoning or criminal evidence, something within her had passed judgment upon Carl. He was evil incarnated, compassionless, and diabolical.

Neither Wade nor Paul had prepared her for what to expect if she should ever cross Carl's path. Perhaps they were not affected as she was. Perhaps she was overreacting because she had never known anyone like Carl, whereas Wade and Paul, being men and more widely traveled and associated, probably had grown accustomed to meeting a broader variety of people in the world than she had ever had opportunity to.

"Wade – tell me – what did he do to Kelly Jean?" Esther finally blurted out. "What did he do? Tell me!"

All eyes were on Wade, and his discomfort was instantly visible. He knew something, perhaps not about Kelly Jean, but it was clear enough that he was withholding something very important. "I don't know that, Esther," he said. "I don't know any more than you do. I just figured that he would have been gone by now, and we wouldn't have to worry about all this anymore."

Ruth could feel the anger build up within her as she watched Esther begin to behave as if she was being reassured by Wade's comments. But Ruth had no reason to dispute Wade. She wanted to challenge him further, but it would have been inappropriate, if not futile, to do so.

Esther stood up. She suddenly remembered that she had left Kelly Jean and Jimmy alone at home. But she didn't rush because she realized that things were different now. She knew all along that she had little choice but to allow Wade to handle things as he saw fit – she wasn't up to the task. She had no more strength to worry about such things, and what reserves she had left would be used up tending to home and family. It was all too worrisome and tedious, and she didn't want to think about it, or even allow it all to work on her conscience anymore.

Strangely, she had new insights about her life and the needs of her family. It would be all right if she went home and stayed there. Things would be different from now on, and she was going to make sure of it. She had seen the devil in Carl's eyes, and the experience taught her that she could keep the unseen malevolent forces at bay if she did the right things at home and let the Lord handle those things that were beyond her control.

As if she had suddenly forgotten all the events of the day, Esther turned for the steps and in a clear, soft voice, she said, "Wade, I'm going home now."

Wade took his wife's hand and led her to his horse. He took the horse's leader and began the earnest march homeward, neither of them stealing a glance backward again. Paul and Ruth could hear Wade's voice. His tone was urgent and convincing. He was working again to bring his wife back down to the familiar and the safe. He kept Esther's attention tight to his argument. Her anger was a vanishing vapor now and she clung to every word. Paul and Ruth watched from the porch, helplessness being their only companion.

CHAPTER 23

A week later Tom found himself working an old patch of ground nearly a half-mile south of the house. It was newly leased acreage and it hadn't been turned in years. It was a mess and Tom hoped to have it cleared by spring in time for cultivating. A young transient farm worker Tom had hired for the project was busy cutting and piling saplings and brambles at the east end of the field. Tom worked his way toward the opposite end with his mule team and drag chain.

The morning had started cool and breezy, a typical autumn day, but turned warm and balmy by midday. It was a sharp contrast to the cold days of the week before. Tom looked up toward the western tree line in the distance and saw a cloud developing. In time it grew dark and ominous, and swept low in the sky. The air was deathly still, but the clouds were churning a little along the bottom edges. Tom whistled to his worker and motioned for him to run back to the house. Tom could see him looking fearfully at the dark cloud as he proceeded to cross the field. "Run tell Luke to open up the storm house!" Tom yelled.

Tom yanked the drag chains away from a fallen tree he had wanted to remove from the field. In a moment he had the mules turned and facing toward the house. All he had to do was give them a prodding and soon they would be back at the barn. He looked around at the dark-shadowed trees along the south side of the field. There was not the slightest hint of movement in the air. Not a bird chirped nor a leaf fluttered. It seemed that in just a few minutes the sky had changed from a simple midday overcast to dusk. In a flash of paranoia, Tom imagined Carl hiding in the trees, ready to pounce out and harass him anew about some imagined offense Tom had committed against Carl's workers. Tom angrily expelled the thought and gazed back up at the clouds. Fearfully he gazed toward home and hoped he could make it before the clouds gave way.

Then unexplainably the mules bolted and charged away as if they had been shot in the flanks. The mules made a beeline for the barn with the clanging chains skipping along behind. "What the devil's got into them jackasses!" Tom spat.

Then he fell to the ground; rather he was thrown to the ground by a violent blast of wind that seemed to swing down from the sky like a mile-high pendulum. Immediately, behind the western tree line, a giant black finger with expanding dimensions and mass stretched from the sky down to the ground exploding everything it touched. Tom was near the center of the ragged field that was fifty yards from the nearest edge. He had never before experienced such head-crushing noise. All he could do was crouch in terror on the ground and slap his hands to his ears. He couldn't hear his own screams.

The tornado began snapping trees and throwing them high across the field like matchsticks. He looked upward to see the mammoth black column of uprushing air sucking up tons of foliage, mud, and debris and slinging it up and away with such terrific anger and ferocity that it all seemed somehow intelligent and as malevolent as hell's worst. For the moment it appeared to stand still, contented on drilling a hole to the core of the earth.

Tom was lifted upward and thrown high against a tree. He felt his shirt rip away. He managed to bear hug the tree trunk and hold on. At this elevation he was stung with dirt and debris that hit him like bullets. He was still screaming for his life. His eardrums imploded, muffling the roar of the tornado. His body was taking a severe pounding, and the windblast had already scraped his near-naked body raw and bloody. Tom tried to keep his eyes tightly closed.

The super-negative air pressure was attacking every soft point in his head, seeming to extract his eyeballs from their sockets. Through his eyelids, he could see the intense flashes of lightning that bolted nonstop all around.

The pounding wind wasn't letting up. It was increasing. The cyclone was now moving and coming closer. Tall trees were pulling themselves from the ground and shooting upward toward the boiling firmament like rockets. The debris was increasing and growing from fist-sized chunks to tree trunks and root clumps. Tom was sheared off the tree by something huge and fierce. He flew through the torrential whirlpool and was slammed against an unyielding clay bank along a shallow creek. The creek bottom had been vacuumed dry by the winds, and was alive with whipping vines, pelting clods and rocks; all mingled with a stinging water spray.

Tom was in great bodily pain and was exhausted to the edge of death. The terrible wind was reaching down into the creek and tossing him along like tumbleweed. His ears were tightly plugged with substances unknown and his bloody eyes could now only see flashes of blinding light and flying masses of earth and trees. He labored to grab something to hold onto, but his hands would not obey his mind. Whether he had lost the strength to grasp or nothing would stay still long enough for him to snatch, he couldn't tell. Every attempt to help himself was an utterly useless gesture. Nothing was stationary. Everything was moving.

The tornado was a distinct, solidly defined column of coal-black compressed air that arched up many hundreds of feet. It was capped off with a mile-wide angry cloud that appeared as solid as granite. Swirling masses of cloud vapors, earth, and trees formed shapes of demonic faces, wings and claws that poured out of the top of the tornado and were devoured then tossed away by the dense mass above.

Tom, now semi-conscious, was slammed once again against the clay bank giving him a front row view of the otherworldly event taking place before him. With what was left of his strength, he sank into the mud and waited. He couldn't have moved if he wanted to. He was still alive, but death was stalking nearby. His heart had stopped pounding and was now beating more slowly with a heavy rolling motion that worked painfully against a broken rib. His entire left side felt as if the skin had been ripped off with a dull knife. But the physical pain was not enough to distract his attention from the event that was still destroying the world before his eyes.

The tornado had moved off farther toward the northeast. The landscape was not recognizable. Everything was sharp and jagged and turned inside out. A stinging rain raked horizontally a hundred miles per hour. The tree line toward the north looked like a comb with its tines broken or missing. Lightning was still blitzing the sky and finding purchase with the ground all around. Several bolts exploded near the creek, but Tom didn't seem to recognize the concussions. He lay dazed and beaten against the bank, and his eyes, bulging and bleeding, panned the distance; sometimes watching the tornado, sometimes gazing at nothing in particular.

The tornado moved on to distant hills and its worst effects began to lessen, but the wind was still wreaking havoc. The storm had been raining hell for only a few minutes, but it seemed that it would never end. At times, it appeared to continue to lighten up, then a maverick blast of wind would toss an uprooted tree across the field. From the west, a smaller tornado entered the field and skipped quickly across, touching ground only once as it chased after its mother toward the east. It, too, was gracefully arched and shaped similarly to the first one, but was petite in comparison. It lifted its tail up into the clouds as it crossed the northern tree line, and whipped back and forth below the cloud like the tail of a snake. As it disappeared over the horizon, the storm began to lessen once again, and the sky soon started to grow lighter.

Finally, the thunder and lightning moved on over the horizon, leaving an everyday rainstorm that soon washed a stream of slush and mud down the creek and bathed Tom's wounds in a gentle salve. He felt no pain now as he drifted into shock. Then, he rolled over onto an exposed root and appeared to fall asleep.

CHAPTER 24

Jimmy and his two young cousins stepped away from the barn behind his uncle Paul's house. They were told to finish cleaning up tornado debris from around the barn before leaving for other duties, but Jimmy and the boys had heard voices outside. It had been two days since the tornado, but the farm was still littered with the shattered skeletons and splinters of a dozen large trees. It was still a mess in spite of long hours used up in brush piling and burning. Looking down the hill, they spied several men standing in the trees beside the road. The men were well over a hundred yards away, but the breeze was carrying the voices right up the hill to the barnyard. Jimmy told the boys to stay put, then he walked down the hill for a better look. Halfway down, he stopped and gazed through an opening in the trees. He could see his father and his uncle Paul standing together with some other men huddled nearby. He couldn't understand a word at this distance, so he worked his way a little further down the hill. In spite of Jimmy's order, William and Robert had sidled up behind him and were following.

His view obstructed, Jimmy climbed up to a low limb in a wild pear tree. Both his father and his uncle were standing together and appeared to be watching four other men working on something at the side of the road. As had been the routine for everyone since the tornado, Jimmy figured they were cleaning up more debris from the road. Among the four men stood a big man – bigger than his father – that Jimmy pegged as the supervisor. A black man was with him. The big man was talking. The words were still unintelligible, but it all suddenly sounded vaguely familiar to Jimmy, like a bad dream long discarded. It even felt familiar hiding here in tree limbs listening to something that perhaps was not intended for his ears.

He tried to hear any tidbits of conversation, but could pick up only enough to know he had met this man somewhere once before. A trench had been dug up to the road and, as far as Jimmy could see, some pipe was being fitted and laid in the trench that ran deep into the trees toward the south. In a moment, one of the workers took a pickax and began to chop through the compacted gravel. Memories of another digging expedition instantly flooded Jimmy's mind; again something was frighteningly familiar with all of this. He fought to retain order and calmness in his head and keep his eyes focused on the happenings taking place before him.

The big man stepped over to Wade and Paul and said something. Jimmy began to think that something was not honorable with this event. Something imponderable churned in Jimmy's mind, giving him the impression that his father was engaging himself in something secretive, and likely questionable. But soon, Jimmy decided that he was not going to figure out the business on the road and he climbed down to return to the barn. He was feeling upset and fought to settle himself down from some growing discomfort inside his mind.

"That's our second cousin," young William said.

"What?" Jimmy asked.

"That big fellow is our cousin. I think his name's Kallton, like ours."

Little Robert asked his brother, "I thought his name was Carl Dean?"

"Yeah, Carl Dean Kallton," William said.

Jimmy felt his face turn pale. He jumped back to the tree and gazed at Carl who was now standing next to his father. "How'd you know?" he asked, his voice urgent.

"I heard Mama and Papa talking. They said he was big and mean!"

"How do you figure that's him down there?"

William looked quizzically at Jimmy as if he didn't understand the question. He didn't answer. Jimmy stared again at Carl. It all became instantly clear. He could remember the wide bulky shoulders and the bulldog stance. The way Carl walked around as if his arms and legs worked on heavily pistoned joints. His gestures overbearing, even threatening. Even from here, Jimmy could see the heavy black eyebrows, but the beard was new. Jimmy became quickly agitated and anxious. His two cousins watched him make angry gestures, and wondered what had been said wrong. Jimmy watched Carl spit orders to his subordinates, using unnecessarily profane language. Wade and Paul were still standing by watching, unaware of the spies on the hill above them.

He killed a man! Jimmy's mind screamed. *I saw the big man do it! He killed a migrant worker in cold blood!*

Again he felt that wrenching pang of terror that he had endured for hours on that dreadful night. He couldn't figure out how to decipher the picture before him. Carl Dean, the murderer and devil, standing just a few feet from his father. Jimmy looked at his father. Wade wasn't saying much. He appeared neither happy nor upset. He appeared as he always does while working on the farm – just that strict, determined look on his face.

It had all been complicated enough without this new development. Something had happened between his father and his uncle Paul. Sometimes it seemed that his uncle wished to have as little as possible to do with his father lately. It had something to do with the water problems. Somehow his uncle was rebelling against something that Wade wished to do. Perhaps the event unfolding on the road had something to do with it.

A powerful sense of betrayal fell over Jimmy. Carl Dean was supposed to be in jail, or in some distant prison somewhere. Isn't that what his father had told him – that the sheriff was going to get Carl? But Jimmy could see the big man on the road, free, and standing alongside his father.

Jimmy, being young and unlearned in the ways of the world, knew nothing of all the legal wranglings that would be required for the conviction of a killer. As far as he knew, the sheriff had been informed and Carl was dispatched and taken care of. But clearly something was desperately askew. Now he must calculate everything anew, and try to understand the confusing contradiction taking place on the road far below. I'll ask Papa when he comes home, Jimmy thought. The questions in Jimmy's mind lined up like the cars of a stinking, sun-baked cattle train: Why isn't Carl Dean in jail? Why, Papa, are you talking to the man who you know murdered a man? I told you he did – maybe you didn't believe me? Why are you talking to the man who Kelly Jean is so afraid of? Don't you remember, Papa, when Kelly Jean cried and tried to run away when I said 'Carl Dean' that night?

Jimmy turned to his two little cousins, who were now distracted by other things. They knew nothing of the secrets Jimmy knew. Suddenly, Jimmy felt desperately alone and un-innocent. He was no longer of the simplistic and unsullied mind like his cousins. He knew something they didn't. Something unclear, shameful, and sad. It would take time to figure out. It would be a while yet before he could put everything together. The reasons why his father never allowed him to go to town any more, or to make the milk deliveries with his uncle. Why his father had pulled him out of school. He had stopped wondering about church. No, I won't ask Papa, he thought. Something's wrong. So wrong that it felt it was the essence of nightmares. I'll wait. I'll have to work on this on my own for a while.

A hard lump grew in his throat that soon hurt. He felt his face frown so heavily that he thought he should hide away until he could regain some composure. He suddenly felt a strong compulsion to run, to race away and hide from his father until an answer to this new quandary was found. Somehow, he couldn't quite hold tight to the reasoning aspect of his mind. His search for firm grounding with his father had been deteriorating for many months. Now it seemed hopelessly lost.

He turned for the barn and motioned for the boys to follow, and they complied.

*＊＊

It was on a day nearly three weeks later that the skies remained overcast all day long with a horizon-to-horizon quilting of billowy clouds. A slow, cool breeze moved across the yard at an unchanging clip. The dry fallen leaves of early winter could be heard from inside the house fluttering across the yard. Tom lay quietly in bed listening to every sound around the house. He had never purposely listened to such things before, but with what was left of his hearing he was soaking it all in as if it were all meant for him alone.

Peacefully, the last two days had passed with comforting temperatures and cloud-filtered sunlight. Tom had been left alone in bed since arriving home from the hospital. Annie was there, but she was sad since Anne Marie and baby Tommy had left for home soon after the tornado. Tom moved about very little today, as he had done every day since returning home. He was still trying to figure out the new-found and unexplainable spiritual elation he had felt since that day when it all came rushing back into his mind like a runaway train. For the first time that he could ever remember, he felt life as he knew it should be felt. During some contemplative moments, he was filled with a previously unknown satisfaction in his simple existence, and it took some time for him to begin to realize that this sentiment may be abnormal. Even the jarring flashbacks and the sleep-robbing nightmares he had experienced in the hospital had not dampened his new spiritual highs. He had played everything back through his mind a hundred times since the amnesia had lifted, and he could find no conclusion for his new mental state other than that he was thankful beyond measure to be alive. He should have been dead. It was a lightning bolt, not the tornado, the surgeons had said, that had torn his body like a rag doll. He was lucky, by the providence of God, that he had not been sawed in half by the direct strike.

Tom reached again to his left ear, hoping to detect a sound. It still hurt to snap his fingers with the missing nail on his middle finger. Both ears had been tightly impacted with dirt and debris, but his left eardrum had been destroyed by the lightning bolt. He was lucky to have hearing restored in his right ear. He was told that, during the torrent, the fact he was covered with a profusion of perspiration and rainwater probably saved his life. Instead of traveling through his body and exploding his heart, the lightning traveled along his outer body using the layer of moisture as a conduit. But he still suffered life-threatening spots of burned flesh, especially on his left side that continued to be of concern because of the possibility of recurring infection. He had lost some mobility in his leg, and he would be bedridden for another month. He would have lots of time to sort his thoughts once his mental mechanisms were brought back on track.

Tom gazed once again across the room at the foot-powered sewing machine Annie had used over the years to keep the family clothed. A stack of colorful cotton squares lay on top waiting to be sewed together for another quilt top. Up above, the quilting frame hung a foot from the ceiling. On it was a near-finished quilt. From Tom's position, he could see the blue and white striping on the underside. And on one end, where one side of the quilt had been rolled up, he could see a particularly handsome red, brown, and yellow log cabin design that Annie was famous for. Then a new idea entered his mind. Tom imagined asking Annie to lower the frame and finish the quilt. He wanted to watch her. For the first time ever, he wanted to watch Annie make a quilt. He had never entertained the idea of that before. But he wanted it now. How precious was Annie, Tom thought. What a mountain of gold she was. Tom had valued her always, but had he ever said that he loved her? Yes, he could remember a few times. But it was a shame that he could count the times on his fingers.

Looking out the window, Tom watched the trees yield to the breeze. The tornado damage to the house didn't bother him as it normally would have under different circumstances. There was plenty of time before planting to worry about repairs. They were blessed that the house had escaped major damage, but he had to watch the trees through the undamaged windowpanes. Boards had been applied over the broken ones. A couple of golden maple leaves drifted to the ground. In a moment, a fox squirrel climbed up a tree and sat on a limb directly in Tom's view. If he had his .22 rifle he could dispatch that fat squirrel and get Annie to put together a fine stew. Tom chuckled at the thought of it.

It was quite saddening at times to recall that just yesterday he could sense the presence of his two lost sons around the house. Tom had drifted to a pleasant afternoon nap in the quiet house, and later awoke to a twilight awareness. For a while, the house was like it used to be, two years before. He saw Frank and James outside tending chores. They were waiting for their father to get up and come out to help them. He could see them standing together with long hand tools working on something in Annie's garden. They were laughing and talking, and Tom could almost understand their words.

He wanted to draw closer to hear a little better. The boys were happy, and Tom wanted to be a part of it. With his good hand he grasped the side of the mattress and began to pull himself to the edge. The effort woke up the wounds on his side. The sharp pain brought Tom back to reality with such suddenness that he shook his head. The beautiful dream was gone, and Tom plopped back into the middle of the bed. The vision was so real-to-life that he consciously tried to trick his mind back into that priceless moment with his sons. He thought that he could lie in bed forever if he could somehow be allowed to continue the dream undisturbed.

As he ran this dream through his mind once again, he reached up and wiped a tear off his cheek. He looked back out the window and found the squirrel was gone. Annie was back in the house working quietly in the kitchen. She moved through the house as quietly as a ghost. She was thinking of Tom and his sleep. Tom closed his eyes, hoping to see his boys again. He wanted, too, to be rested up for the preacher's visit soon, when he was up to it. After that, he was going to ask Annie to finish that quilt.

CHAPTER 25

Sunday morning had become, in too many ways, a work day like every other day of the week. Jimmy stood alone at the woodpile with a sledgehammer, wedge, and an ax. He was angry and confused; a state of mind that dominated his feelings all the time now. It was already several weeks into deer hunting season. It had always been the most exciting time of the year for him. By now, the aroma of gun cleaning solvent and decaying fall leaves would draw his attention to all the secret happenings occurring deep in the woods all around the farm. One night the week before, the screams of a bobcat were heard several times pealing from the woods north of the house. And rabbits were seen scampering along the edges of the fields almost every day. Prey critters, such as rabbits and squirrels, were on an upswing cycle this year and deer were plentiful too. Too plentiful to be sure, since many farmers were complaining of extensive forage damage in their fields. The herd needed to be culled, and Jimmy would ordinarily be ambling to get the first chance.

Frustratingly for Jimmy, his father had made no efforts this year to begin preparations for the new season. It had been a yearly ritual ever since Jimmy could remember to preface the hunting season with a few weeks of gun cleaning, carbide lamp repairs and deer scouting. But for many months, it seemed, his father drifted about in another world. He had become self-involved in things that Jimmy could not fully grasp. Wade had grown strangely distant and preoccupied and, at times, almost sulking. Jimmy had been kept ignorant of the true nature of the water problems on the farms, and there were many things he had wanted to ask someone about. But feeling that he wouldn't be given the full story, he kept his curiosity to himself. Even if he pushed for answers, he wasn't sure how to go about forming the questions.

Jimmy had heard his parents talk about selling off some of their land to recoup some of the losses of the cattle massacre. But which land? Where? How many acres? Who was it sold to? They wouldn't say. What is the truth behind the massacre? Do Wade and Esther know something that he doesn't? Jimmy remembered that terrible night all too well. He remembered the terror, the wrenching sounds, and the many tossing and sleepless nights thereafter. He was as much a part of things as anyone, yet he felt he was kept in a quarantine-like lockdown. Additionally, what was the situation with Carl Dean Kallton? Was his father cutting some kind of under-the-table deals with this fearsome villain? The devil who cold-bloodedly executed a defenseless man? And the mere mention of whose name somehow throws terror into Kelly Jean's heart? And how is he connected to all the water works now occurring across the farm?

Jimmy, to a certain extent, understood the importance of keeping everything quiet for Kelly Jean's sake. That much, at least, had been partly explained to him. But even at that, his father could at least cue him in on some things when they were alone, away from Kelly Jean. But no; all things were secretive and deceptive, even when it came to the sheriff. Even Gene Carter was kept in the dark on everything. That was for Kelly Jean's sake too, he was told. But exactly how and why, it didn't make a lot of sense. It had something to do with keeping all interrogating authorities away from Kelly Jean for her own emotional well-being, or some such. But Jimmy quickly figured out that the sheriff was not pleased with his father for shutting him out. For a long time he lived in fear that his father would be hauled off to jail again. Yet everyone was expected to treat the sheriff respectfully, but to work together to keep him at arm's length.

Jimmy slammed the ax down, sinking it deep into an oak block. He yanked out a handkerchief to wipe his face. At that moment he heard the peal of the church bell. Beulah Primitive Baptist Church was three miles away, and yet the bell could still be heard. Jimmy stood and listened until it stopped. The bell was always rung just before Sunday School at ten o'clock. That meant that he had three more hours to finish the cord he was working on before dinner.

Somewhere out there, Wade was knocking himself out again trying to rectify the water situation to the point that things would eventually return to some semblance of normalcy. He had built a big wooden reservoir up on a knoll behind the springhouse and had rigged a water line between it and the springhouse. If the water lines running from the road connection could be kept pumping at all hours, then perhaps the springhouse could be returned to its original purpose. Then, on warmer days, Esther wouldn't have to keep running to Paul's everyday for fresh milk. It could be kept fresh from day to day as it had been done for many years. Wade had figured the springhouse ran on about ten thousand gallons of fresh water daily from the little spring beneath it when the water was normal. It had decreased to a fraction of that, which was no longer enough to refrigerate everything that Esther kept in it.

Then, like a magnet attracted to rusty metal, Jimmy's mind returned to the thought of his father and his apparent dual standards. To distract himself he looked up at the house. It stood white on a hill and in heavy contrast to the gray barn, smokehouse and springhouse around it. He never realized before how vulnerable it looked up on this bare hill. He wondered if it would burn to the ground as quickly and easily as the hay barn did back in the spring. He remembered how he and his father had fought the blaze at the barn and how it seemed that the inferno mocked their feeble attempt at bringing it under submission. Instead of lessening, the fire only seemed to increase with their every effort to stop it. From any point in the lower pasture he could still see six or seven tall black-charred tree trunks standing in the area where the hay barn had once stood. They were still nearly as tall and stout as they were before the fire. Jimmy figured they could stand strong for several years before they rotted down. He had wished his father would cut them down. They were ugly reminders of the second blackest night he would ever know. Every time he looked at them he could still hear the unnatural wrenching cries of the dying cattle in the pasture all around him.

Jimmy looked far across the farm to the grazing cattle. Some of them were near the fence that ran along the road. They would still be easy targets for whoever had a mind to shoot at them again. He remembered the talk about Tom and Lucas Buell being the only real suspects. This idea Jimmy never understood. It was so foreign to him to think that good friends could turn and betray them as they had. Jimmy never completely got a grasp on their motives, so he never asked.

Jimmy turned a full circle and gazed at all the placidness around him. It was all easy on the eyes and settling to the mind. But somewhere, somehow, an unfathomable evil was lurking just outside his field of view. He felt that at any moment it could all end. He imagined Carl Dean killing someone again. It could even be himself, he thought. He remembered the night when he found himself running for his life from the big man, and nearly shooting his own father in the process. His life had come to feel so terribly temporary; like it could all change in an instant. A shot fired or a match struck or, as in Kelly Jean's case, an errant word spoken. Or even a freak autumn tornado, like the one that almost killed Tom Buell over a month ago.

They had almost lost the farm he had heard his father say. Just because a few cattle were lost they could have lost the farm. Jimmy didn't know to question whether or not his father, out of frustration, was exaggerating. He just took everything his father had ever said at face value. Thus

Jimmy learned to ignore his own feelings for the good of family and security. He had trained himself to forget his own nightmares and conduct himself like everyone else, but he wondered how long he would be required to live in this manner.

He gazed up at the house again. He found a face gazing back at him through a window. It was Kelly Jean. A new idea entered his mind that refused to leave. He stepped from the woodpile and motioned to her. Shortly she stepped out alone. He motioned again. In a moment, she was bundled up and walking across the yard toward him.

"What're you doing?" she asked. Immediately she saw that something was out of order in her brother's eyes. She turned her body half away from him as if she might decide to go back to the house.

"Can you keep a secret?" he asked.

"Uh – yeah. What?"

"You remember that big man I saw shoot and kill a man last year?"

Kelly Jean stepped back. "Why do you want to talk about that?" she asked.

"I saw him!"

"Huh?"

"Yeah – last Tuesday, just down from Uncle Paul's house. He was with Papa and Uncle Paul!" Jimmy sensed his sister wouldn't understand. Soon, he would come to realize how correct his instincts were. "I saw him Tuesday," he continued. "He was down on the road with Papa and Uncle Paul!"

Kelly Jean went mute. She stared at Jimmy as if looking through him.

"He helped Papa and Uncle Paul with the water troubles."

Again, Kelly Jean stared.

"He's our cousin. Carl Dean. Remem – "

"No – o – o! That's not him!" she commanded, her voice suddenly constricted.

"Huh?"

Kelly Jean eased a step away from her brother. She clearly couldn't stand to hear any more.

"What do you mean? I know it was him. I'd know him a mile away!" Jimmy said. Kelly Jean looked away from Jimmy for a moment as if trying to figure something out. Her face was a mess and getting worse, and it frightened Jimmy. "What's wrong?" he asked.

"How do you know what's in my dreams?" she asked, her voice constricted.

The question made no sense at all. Jimmy needed to talk to someone that he could trust, and he turned to his sister. He had not really had the opportunity to talk to her one-on-one in many months. Now he was beginning to wonder if he had breached the line of the family's unspoken sacred bond, and the family would pay dearly as a result.

"What're you talkin' about?" he asked. His voice was low, as if he were afraid someone else would hear him.

"Where'd you hear that name?" she asked. "I never told it to nobody!"

Her voice was unstable enough to cause Jimmy to feel he might panic if she were to break down and scream as she had done the last time he had mentioned Carl's name. He could turn and run into the trees until it was all over, he thought. But then how could he explain things? He could not hide from his deed. Then he thought that he would have to restrain his sister if she went berserk again. He wasn't sure that he could do that alone. He should not have asked Kelly Jean to come out and talk to him.

"What're you talkin' about?" Jimmy asked, now with a constricted voice himself.

Kelly Jean opened her mouth, perhaps to cry out, but someone's voice yelled from the house. She turned to look. It was Esther. "Kelly Jean?" her mother called. "I need you."

It was thirty yards between themselves and the house, and Esther stayed on the porch peering down the slope of the yard at her children. She was waiting for a response.

"She'll be up in a minute!" Jimmy yelled. Kelly Jean seemed oblivious to the fact that her upset expression could be visible to her mother. Thinking fast, Jimmy called her back. "Kelly Jean!" She spun back to her brother. Her face hadn't changed. Esther returned to the house. "Sister – why are you sayin' stuff like that?"

Kelly Jean seemed to search the trees behind her brother as if expecting something to jump out and frighten them. Jimmy turned to look, but found nothing that would warrant his sister's interest. "Uh – what's wrong?" he asked.

Kelly Jean had lowered her gaze to Jimmy's chest area, again looking as if she were looking through him somehow. The mere mention of the name of Carl Dean, an entity from another world – the world of her nightmares – drove her into that netherworld of confused perceptions again. It did not seem possible that she could have forgotten Jimmy's mention of Carl's name the night he witnessed the murder beneath the oak tree. But it seemed she had.

Jimmy didn't know what to say next. He had seen Carl with his father and the experience had tossed his world upside down, almost as badly as that night of the murder. He had hoped that Kelly Jean would know something that could help him to understand things, but he had made a serious mistake in asking her.

"Go back up to the house," he said. He checked her eyes, and he worried that her countenance would not have time to correct itself before she returned. Everyone would see it, and he would have to explain.

Jimmy could see their father returning from the pasture to the barn. Jimmy was expected to have a half-cord of wood split by now, and it was only half finished. Now he was sure that any possible punishment would be doubled because of the twisted deed he had perpetrated upon his sister.

"He's not real!" she suddenly demanded. "He's not real, you hear me? *He's not real!*"

Then why was Papa working on the water problems with a man that doesn't exist? he wanted to ask. Jimmy was unable to understand the full depth of what was happening here, but he knew that things were desperately deceitful and hurtful. Again, he was alone with his fears, and his anger. He could never trust anyone because he could find no one to listen or understand. It was clear that everyone was willing to live a lie in order to have some semblance of outward peace. Everyone was expected to shove the truth as far away to the back of their minds as possible in order to 'protect' the weakest among them. But the truth was that as long as the lie was perpetrated, the weakest one would fall deeper and deeper into self-deceptive fantasy.

"He ain't real, I know," Jimmy heard himself say. He looked up at the house. Everyone was still inside. Then Mrs. Sarah stepped up to the door from the inside. He could see her clearly through the narrow vertical glass in the door. She looked down and the door quickly opened. Gracie ran out and onto the porch. She was not used to Kelly Jean being so far from her.

"Ke'wy Jean!" Gracie yelled, *"Catch me!"*

Kelly Jean spun around and watched Gracie hop down the steps, then begin running down the slope toward her. Even from this distance, Jimmy could see the nasty, red cut-mark that ran vertically from Gracie's hairline down to her right brow; the apparent result of one of her father's drunken rages. But now Gracie cried out with unblemished joy. Suddenly, Kelly Jean perked up and she bent down to scoop Gracie up into her arms.

"Why are you crying?" Gracie asked excitedly. She proceeded to wipe a tear from Kelly Jean's cheek. The smile on the little girl's face dropped to a frown. Curiously, the frown drew a smile to Kelly Jean's face. Never before had little Gracie shown such empathy for someone else's sadness. She had become so accustomed to watching others cry and fight that she had seemingly lost the innate ability to show proper empathy for others until now.

Jimmy watched his sister and Gracie swing together in broad circles of sheer delight. It was happening as if the previous event had never taken place. This was Kelly Jean's joy – Gracie – and she could turn Kelly Jean's emotions on a pinhead with little effort. Gracie's long, freshly washed hair and new winter coat flew high in the air as Kelly Jean spun her around in her arms, and they laughed together. By the time they reached the porch they were dizzy and delirious with play and laughter.

Kelly Jean glanced back at Jimmy with an expression that was blissfully devoid of any discontent, then she giggled when Gracie tugged her hand. Together they bounded up the steps hand in hand, and entered back into the house. Jimmy returned to the woodpile. Shortly, he exhausted himself with the hammer and wedge. And the unfortunate event was, like so many other things, pushed to the back of the mind.

CHAPTER 26

As the preacher had hoped, everyone was already in the house. The morning's cold rain had conveniently put them there. New events occurring at the Buell homesteads required his immediate action. He detailed the high points quickly and solemnly before Esther asked the first question. "Do you know what Lucas says about all this?" she asked.

Sadly, the preacher nodded no. He had not been able to get Lucas to talk. Tom had confessed everything to the preacher and to Annie. Everything except Lucas's part in the whole affair, leaving that part for Lucas to confess himself. Even in Tom's most repentant and newly self-deprecating manner, he still couldn't bring himself to implicating Lucas. He told everything that he could short of hammering even the first nail into Lucas's coffin of culpability. He had insisted that if Lucas had anything to say, he would simply have to do it himself. But Tom confessed as to how he, excluding any mention of his cousin, had driven down to Wade's farm on the night of the cattle massacre. Then how he had toted two firearms and a fruit jar of gasoline onto Wade's property and carried out his revenge against him. Though the story was short and simple, many details were described including how he was surprised that most of the cattle had already conveniently corralled themselves in the corner of the lower pasture near the road, making his deed much easier to execute. He detailed how he had stuffed most of the shell casings into his pockets after each shot in order to leave as little evidence behind as possible. He described the details of Carl Kallton's ultimatum and that he now worked under the subjugation of Carl's every whim. Carl now possessed the damaged car door and was using it to blackmail Tom. Like a growing cancer, Carl's illicit empire had expanded into Tom's rearward acreage where the construction of a new clandestine distillery was well underway. It was all exactly as the sheriff had guessed it. Tom said the door had a bullet hole in it. It had been beaten off the car frame and dumped at the bridge near Carl's house after a failed attempt to burn it up. Tom described how the car shook like being hit by a lightning bolt when Wade's bullet struck.

"We don't know what Luke is going to do, Esther," the preacher answered. "He won't talk to any of us right now. Tom said he was in a rage. I think we're just going to have to wait till things settle down a bit before anyone bothers Luke about this."

"Does Gene know about all this?" Wade asked.

"Yeah, he pulled up just as I was leaving."

"What'll happen now?" Esther asked.

The preacher thought a moment and said, "I reckon Gene will turn it back over to the district people. Let the grand jury have it again." The preacher looked at Wade eye to eye and said, "Tom told me to tell you that he'll work out any arrangement you want to get you back in stead financially. He'll sign over some of his property or sell it and give you the money. Think about it a few days."

Kelly Jean and Jimmy were sitting within earshot in the kitchen. Wade and Esther had met the preacher at the front door and, discovering the seriousness of the preacher's visit, had held him there figuring the children would be out of range. The preacher was considerate; he kept his voice down, almost to a whisper in spite of the fact that the rain drumming on the roof muted every other noise in the house.

"Will Tom go to jail?" Esther asked.

"I don't know. Gene has said a simple confession might not be enough to get him in trouble. He's still looking for some hard evidence – like that car door. And we know Carl has it now." The preacher looked through the kitchen door. He could see Kelly Jean and Jimmy's feet parked under the table. They were quiet and still. Apparently Gracie was back to her home.

"How about the rifle he killed my cows with?" Wade asked.

"Well, he said he threw it into the trees somewhere out on the west county line. It was dark and he's not sure where along the road he threw it – "

"Look," Wade said, interrupting with uncharacteristic earnestness, "I'm not looking to get even. If he'll pull through and make right on his promise – we'll just forget everything. I've been hurt, but I'll let bygones be bygones if he'll make good."

Again, the preacher looked into the kitchen. Kelly Jean and Jimmy hadn't moved. Ordinarily they would have enthusiastically come out to greet the preacher. Perhaps it was the preacher's initial greeting, or lack thereof, that tipped them off that this was a very important, and perhaps urgent, visit. He felt a bit regretful that he had ignored them like this, and he figured that they would forgive him if he didn't wait too long to say something.

"What caused him to change his mind and confess, preacher?" Wade asked.

"Well, I think the Lord had a little talk with him through that cyclone. After getting thrown around in them trees by the hand of God – that would get anyone's attention," the preacher answered. He spoke with a voice so quiet and soft that Wade and Esther had to step closer to hear. It was the preacher's way of demonstrating the spiritual drama of the whole situation. "And I guess he finally got fed up with Carl's blackmailing him and decided it was time to bring a stop to that too."

Then the preacher bounded off into the kitchen and immediately things got noisy as he leaned over the table and bear-hugged Kelly Jean and Jimmy. Standing back up, the good preacher burst out in song with the chorus of his favorite hymn.

"Oh, who will come and go with me? I am bound for the Promised Land!"

***

Earlier, Gene had arrived at the Buell house and parked the car in the middle of the front yard just before the day turned rainy. He didn't want to block the preacher's horse and buggy in the driveway. The sheriff's visits, always official in recent months, had been kept very short, only a few minutes at a time. But it was figured that he had now intended to stay a while. The preacher was already walking out to the buggy when Gene pulled up. He didn't tell the sheriff anything as to the content of Tom's confessional. The preacher determined that anything he might say could muddy the situation and reduce the import of Tom's statement. The preacher had come to accept the sheriff's increasing attitude of general indifference, so he just waved and left as he had come.

Gene paused at the door and looked in. He didn't knock and continued standing there while he lit a cigarette. Tom sat in a rocker in the kitchen and could see Gene at the other end of the house. It was clear to see from nearly thirty feet away that the sheriff didn't wish to be here. No doubt Gene had an idea what was coming and was taking his time about arriving. He smoked the entire cigarette on the porch and flicked the butt out into the yard. He turned and opened the door and walked right in without knocking. Tom had moved the big rocker from the front room to the kitchen near the cookstove. He was spending a lot of time there now recuperating.

Gene stepped slowly through the front room and made a circle around the quilting frame that hung from the ceiling down to about twenty-eight inches above the floor. On it was a nearly finished quilt that was rolled out on the frame about seven feet square; probably the largest quilt Annie had ever made.

"C'mon in the house, Gene," Tom said as the sheriff entered the kitchen.

"Where's Annie?" Gene asked.

"Oh, she's out and about somewhere. She'll be back directly."

Gene looked out the windows around the kitchen as if looking for Annie. In years past, he had always enjoyed just sitting and listening as Annie told humorous stories that would have been tedious and uneventful if told by anyone else. Tom figured that the good sheriff could use a little humor now from the looks of him.

Gene sat down and pulled out his tobacco pouch and started another cigarette. Tom sat silently for a moment and watched the sheriff. It seemed that Gene was all alone with himself and had the world's burdens on his mind. It took him too long to get the cigarette rolled and lit. Annie could be heard climbing the back steps to the porch and then setting something down with a thud. Gene straightened up and looked through the door glass like he was hoping to see Annie as she used to be, and ready with a new story to tell. She opened the door and walked in as quietly as a mouse and looked first at Gene, then at Tom as if asking what had been discussed up to this point.

"Annie, how 'bout some coffee?" Tom asked.

Annie removed her overcoat and dropped it over a chair near the stove. It was cold out, but the house was kept warm by the stove in the kitchen and the fireplace in the front room. The sheriff continued watching Annie and still seemed uninterested in anything Tom had to say. Gene gave the cigarette continuous treatment and it wasn't long before it was down to the butt.

It was soon evident to both Tom and Annie that the sheriff was keeping mute as he had not spoken a word since asking Tom about Annie's whereabouts when he first walked in. Tom slowly worked the rocker back and forth and stared at the sheriff, wishing he could get some confirmation from the sheriff that showed he was ready to listen and discuss the issue at hand. Suddenly, Tom felt that the sheriff might no longer be fully capable of finding his way through the harrowing tunnels of deception that he had been forced to crawl through for the past many months. Tom knew that he was greatly responsible for all that the sheriff had been put through. He had planned to detail his confession fully and then he would spend as much time begging forgiveness from Gene as he figured necessary to ensure the good sheriff of his sincerity. But the sheriff's apparent indifference and solitude was throwing him off.

"Where's Harvey?" Annie finally asked.

"Ah, taking the week off. Says he wanted to go hunting a while," Gene answered.

Again, except for the fire in the stove, the room was quiet. Gene leaned back in the chair and stared at the floor. The cigarette had burned down precariously close to his fingers and he seemed unaware of it. In a moment, he felt the fire between his fingers and he flinched, dropping the butt to the floor. It fell and rolled into a crack between two boards. He leaned up and ground the butt down deeper into the crack with his boot. Impulsively, it seemed, he reached for the tobacco pouch again, but then decided not to bother as he pushed it back into his coat pocket.

"You had anything to eat this morning, Gene?" Annie asked.

"I'm all right, Annie. Thanks," Gene said so softly that he could scarcely be heard.

The silence continued a few more minutes before raindrops could be heard dropping on the roof. Thankfully, to break the stalemate, the staccato of rain and sleet against tin quickly increased, filling the house with the soft, gentle sound of a waterfall. Tom could see that Gene was gazing out the window watching the rain come down. The room was filled with the blue-tinted light coming through the windows and Gene's face was clearly illuminated down to every detail. Tom studied the deep lines in Gene's face, some of them, he remembered, not being there just a few months ago.

"I hope Brother Silas gets his top up on his buggy before he gets wet," Annie said. Gene looked up at her and seemed to smile. It seemed that he wanted Annie to talk because he perked up a bit every time she spoke.

"Annie, tell Gene what you're going to do with that quilt when you get done with it," Tom said finally. Annie looked at Tom with a betrayed expression as if a secret had been exposed. She hesitated too long, so Tom decided to help her. "Brother Silas said your quilts are getting a little threadbare, Gene," Tom said, all the time looking at Annie for some sort of confirmation. Gene was still gazing out the window at the rain. He didn't make any sign of affirmation about what Tom was saying. But it didn't seem to Annie that Tom was, in the least, uneasy or apprehensive about his brazen attempt at reconciliation with Gene. She would have preferred to have finished the quilt and quietly given it to the sheriff without any fanfare whatsoever. But Tom, like James, she thought, never had the patience to wait for the right moment.

"Annie said she would like you to have that quilt on the frame there in the front room. I thought she was going to give it to me or Anne Marie, or sell it to them city folk. But Annie – "

Tom stopped himself in mid-sentence and stared at Gene. The sheriff was still watching the rain with an unchanged expression.

"What'd you call me here for, Tom?" Gene asked; his voice devoid of any degree of empathy. The edgy tone in his voice suggested that he was indeed put off by the patronizing foolishness Tom had so carelessly foisted upon him. Tom had a straightforward speech ready for the sheriff. Now he was struck dumb by Gene's abrupt question. He tried to form words with his lips but nothing came out. Annie quickly poured up two fresh cups of coffee and delivered them to the two men. As she handed the cup to Tom, she said quietly, "Tell him, Tom."

CHAPTER 27

Gene returned home and then holed himself up for two days inside his house, hardly venturing even a look out into the street. He had plenty to eat and adequate wood fuel for the stove, so these conveniences helped to quell any compunction he might have felt to stir amongst the townsfolk in spite of recent events. He opened the little door to the stove and shoved in a big stick of hickory and slapped it back shut. The cold evening was still young but the western horizon was darkening fast, erasing what remained of the red-orange clouds hanging low in the sky. Gene took one last look at it all before closing the door for the night. He had brought in a couple sticks of firewood and unceremoniously dropped them at the base of the stove. One stick rolled and hit the back leg of the stove and nearly knocked it off. It had been loose for years, but three bricks stacked underneath kept the stove from tipping over.

He shoved an old towel along the base of the door to keep out the draft. He took off his coat and tossed it across the end of the table. Somewhere a draft was still getting in, but from where he couldn't tell. The stove fire was hissing along nicely and Gene sat a skillet on top and poured a jar of bean soup into it. He stepped to the back porch and retrieved the water bucket for the coffeepot. A thin crust of ice that was in the bucket slid out and fell onto the side of the hot stove. It caused a noisy cloud of vapor to explode upward to the ceiling. A coal oil lamp sitting on a pedestal near the table had been lit but the room was still too dark, so Gene lit a couple of well-used candles on the other side of the room and sat them in opposite corners.

Before entering the house, he had detected the pungent scent of a polecat in the breeze, but he figured he could get away from it in the house. But now he could smell it as strongly as ever. The skunk must be moving closer to the house, he thought. In years past some wild critters had moved in and set up housekeeping underneath his house, but he had taken care of that by nailing chicken wire all around the perimeter. Finding no refuge here, Gene figured, the skunk would move on to someone else's house on down the street.

Gene sat for an hour at the stove and finished off the entire can of beans. With it he had eaten some stale biscuits and washed it down with the coffee. Soon, he couldn't smell the skunk anymore and figured that since the wind was from the west, the skunk had probably moved on toward the east end of the street. Just when he thought his critter problems were over for the night, an object hit the roof with a sharp thump. Then it sounded as if a full-grown man might be running down the ridge of the roof from one end of the house to the other. It was only a squirrel, but the tin roof could amplify the smallest disturbance and shake the tiny house nearly like thunder.

The fire in the stove had quieted down to a sizzle, so Gene shoved in two more sticks. Then he worked the grates back and forth causing the ashes to drop to the catch basin in the bottom. Quickly enough, the fire was back up and cooking and he closed down the vents halfway to keep the fire from burning too hot. He placed the lamp on the table and sat down. For a moment, he sat and pondered the night before him, and it seemed by his posture that he might have begun to pray or meditate. But then, as if to snap out of a trance, he sat upright. Nearby, a large stationary pad and several sharpened pencils lay neatly together and Gene reached over and pulled it all toward him. He fumbled around with his shirt pocket and found his reading glasses and placed them on. Then, with an expression of determination for the task before him, he looked down at the paper pad and slowly rubbed it from top to bottom to flatten it out. Again, he sat quietly as if deep in thought or meditation. Then he reached over and turned the lamp wick up a little. The light brightened across the table and without further thought he picked up a pencil and began to write.

**

Annie went to the front door and opened it. Tom watched her immediately turn and walk back to the kitchen without a word spoken. Then Lucas stepped in. It was cold, dark, and gusty outside, and the air blew in and woke up the inside of the house with sudden bluster and noise. What had Lucas done to frighten Annie so? Lucas didn't seem concerned about Annie's reaction. Tom eased up to a sitting position on the bed and quickly determined that it would be wise to hold his words until Lucas spoke. But, true to his nature, his mouth paid little attention to his mind. "Cold outside, ain't it, Luke?"

Lucas's countenance held a bearing far beyond any justifiable fury that Tom could fathom. It was enough to frighten Annie away before any words were spoken. Tom wished to get up and attire himself for this impromptu meeting, but Lucas was instantly standing over him as if to dare him to attempt anything other than Lucas's wishes.

"Cold outside? Is that what you said, Tom?" Lucas asked smoothly.

"Yeah, Luke."

Tom leaned back slightly and worked to gain a little more control over his tongue. Lucas's eyes were angry, but his lips were carrying the hard smirk of an embittered loser bent on revenge. Tom could see something similar to Carl's persona melded into Lucas's speech and appearance.

"I've taken a little time to think about what you've done to me and my family," Lucas began without even the beginnings of a greeting. "And all I can think to do is ask you a few questions to help me understand your actions these last few days. First, you think the hand of God was in that damn cyclone? You think God Almighty himself was trying to set you aright?" Lucas seemed to pause a moment to allow his words to find their mark. "It that what you told the preacher, Tom?"

Tom shook his head in answer to Lucas's question, but it was a lie. He did determine that something was divine in nature in the experience, and he had said so openly to several people. But like a reprimanded child, he hoped to answer Lucas in whatever manner was required to calm him down. But Lucas discerned the lie. He pulled a chair up and placed it squarely perpendicular to the side of the bed blocking any escape route. He sat down and leaned toward Tom as if expecting him to listen patiently and answer any query Lucas may decide to ask, and for any duration of time required. Then Lucas asked, "So – you're the only man alive that can talk to God and get an audience with Him? Like Job? Is that your story?"

Lucas determined to expose Tom's soul and find the flaw in his character that had caused him to decide that he had suddenly found the answers to life's questions. And that everyone else should quietly accept any decision he made, mattering not whether it produced negative consequences for others. Lucas sat leaning forward with his gaze fixed coldly onto Tom's eyes.

He waited for Tom's answer. He never fully blinked.

"Well, Luke – " Tom said, stopping abruptly. He knew he could never give an adequate answer to satisfy his enraged cousin. Lucas hadn't moved; he didn't seem to be breathing. Tom had to find words in spite of the obvious futility. "I don't know. I reckon I thought you'd understand." After pausing, he added, "That's the best I can do." Then he lay back on the bed and fixed his eyes to the ceiling. Still, Lucas hadn't moved. Other than the breeze whipping around outside, the house remained deathly quiet for several minutes as Tom stared at the brown water-stained boards in the ceiling. Then, as perfectly as a well-written script, which he had likely been practicing in his mind, Lucas spoke.

"I stood by you and listened patiently to all your grievances ever since your boys died. Then I helped you shoot up Wade Kallton's cows because of the retribution you demanded from him for killing your boys. I lied to Gene Carter for you. I risked my life sneaking back south, in the dead of night, trying to get your car door back for you. I lied to Sandra for you. I gave my life for you. I would do anything for you. But when I needed you most, you wouldn't listen and you played me for a *goddamn fool!*"

Tom rolled his head over to look out the door to the front porch when Lucas raised his voice. Nearly a minute passed before Lucas continued.

"I know how bad you was hurt when your boys was killed. I loved them every bit as much as you did. And I gave my life to help you get through it, even if it meant breaking the law to settle the score. Now you take it upon yourself to be high and holy and confess because you got scared of God, or some such foolishness. Nothing I could do could change your mind. You said you'd protect me as best you could, but you don't think people are so stupid as to think you acted alone do you? They know two men killed Wade's cows. Who do you reckon folks think that second shooter might be?"

Finally, Lucas leaned back in the chair. He ran the old thoughts through his raging mind again while allowing Tom to reflect on his comments. With regrets, the only conclusion that he could seem to come to was that if he and Tom had just managed to continue the conspiracy of silence, then eventually things would settle down and the past would, if not be forgotten, at least be forgiven by most. He knew that his conscience would always condemn him, but he would always rely on Tom to remain strong and stand as the justification for his deeds, even if they were completely lawless and filled with debauchery.

Lucas had mentally placed himself in Tom's situation. He had imagined how he would have reacted if he had found himself in such a terrifying situation and had also concluded that God had shown him a small taste of judgment with a tornado. Battling for one's own life at the portals of eternity must be an unfathomable experience that can change one's perspective on things. It was hard, however, to think that he would have betrayed a friend and favorite cousin as Tom had done. Lucas imagined he would have waited for weeks, if not months – or even years – for Tom to understand and to stand in agreement first. Tom had jumped to a confession quickly after telling Lucas of his intentions. He didn't wait for Lucas to develop a better argument, nor did he give Lucas time to fully prepare Sandra and the children for the inevitable results of a confession. He told Lucas of his intentions, then he did it.

"You back-stabbing bastard!" Lucas hissed. "I'm going to see Gene in the next few days and make my own little confession, after I take a little time with Sandra – as if I have a choice now." Then he stood up, half-kicking the chair away. He yanked open the front door and was gone.

Tom looked around the far side of the room at the boards in the windows where the tornado had thrown limbs and rocks through. Again, he imagined Annie's terror as she crouched and screamed in the hallway as the storm shook the house like it had been built of twigs and straw. Part of the roof had been blown away and the rains poured in like waterfalls. There was no one to help Annie when the doors and windows were blown out and she was left to fend for herself as the elements tried to kill her. It was easy enough to imagine what she experienced; Tom was in the midst of the torrent himself. But Annie had real reasons to live freely and to be protected, whereas he knew he deserved nothing more than the permanence of death. What had happened to the spiritual realizations that he had experienced when he realized he had survived and everyone was well? Surely, he thought, everyone would have felt as he did. Why was everyone not thankful, as he had been? Why did no one else reason that God had spoken, and that it was time to come together and seek forgiveness and peace among themselves? It was, to Tom, the only logical conclusion after staring death in the face. But instead, everyone seemed to show pity and derision toward him when he had demonstrated his newfound sincerity concerning redemption and forgiveness. But then, what could a man expect from the community after what he had done in retaliation against another?

Tom needed someone to be near him now. But in spite of his need, he wished to be alone. He needed to hear the preacher pray a simple prayer. A spiritual hymn would be nice, but he couldn't ask Annie. She hadn't been able to sing in over a year. It would be nice to hear Gene laugh again, or to hear Lucas or Sandra read a Psalm. But he fell back and closed his eyes. He listened for Annie, but there was only silence in the house.

***

The good sheriff had written down every thought that had yearned for many months to be released. With sad resignation he tossed down the pencil and surveyed the finished work before him. He hadn't counted, but he figured he had filled at least twenty-five pages with small, longhand text. If he had discovered anything new about himself in the last four hours, it would be that he had little patience for nuance and understatement when expressing himself in written form. He had started with a short vignette about his own early intentions, in his youth, to find a place of service where he could serve and protect anyone who needed his help, and to live blameless and harmless among his fellow man. Naively he had assumed that all his good works and intentions would be reciprocated in some fashion, and in the end he could find comfort and rest in a pure conscience. Admittedly, he had few options growing up in nominal poverty, but he grew to feel blessed with his chosen profession. Now he realized how laughable it all was and how futile his efforts truly were. All it had gotten him is the ridicule by certain of his peers and a heart disappointed and broken by the derision of those who callously played him for the village fool.

Gene shuffled back over to the stove and shut off the fire. He looked out the front window into the dirty, furrowed street. For a moment, he failed to notice the old bluetick hound on the porch that had showed up a couple of months ago and began to live off the food scraps tossed out by the residents. No one knew who the dog had once belonged to, but everyone, including Gene, had benevolently and regularly ensured that the old dog had what he needed to get by. Somehow, he had felt a kinship with that dog. He, too, had come to like living with the local folk and earning his keep through their good will. He trusted them and he believed they trusted and believed in him. Sometime, somewhere, somebody had taken care of and fed the dog or else he would not have made it to this advanced age. Now he was on his own – cast aside and forgotten. Gene once thought the dog must be stupid to continue to trust in people after being betrayed by his master. Perhaps the old dog had arthritis or some other ailment that prevented him from hunting any more. Notwithstanding, the old dog still had trusting eyes and believed someone would still be around to meet his needs.

Gene tossed out an old gravy-soaked biscuit from the table for the dog and shoved the door back shut without bothering to replace the towel at its base. He reached and snapped the latch shut, locking the door. He turned back to the letter and played the highlights back through his mind. The most important parts he felt were well detailed so as to not leave any confusion or doubt. No punches were pulled on detailed events, names, spoken statements and opinions. He had written down all he remembered from Billy's coerced confession as well as the fact of Billy's demise, the sheriff's own responsibility in it, and where the body was buried. He detailed all that Billy had said about the North Road incident with all the names involved, including Billy's alcohol-induced aggression against Kelly Jean. He fingered Carl, Billy, and Earnest Jackson for the murder of James Buell and the savage beating and subsequent death of his brother, Frank.

The fact of Earnest Jackson's death and Wade's knowledge of his death and the events surrounding it were fully described so as to remove all doubt. The next paragraph explained Billy's statement concerning Carl's suspicion of Wade's attempt on his life.

Gene finished with a long lament concerning his own sorrow and regret for not being as thorough and attentive as he could have been, and for not bringing more order to the investigations and not providing stronger leadership earlier when events warranted it. He admitted to cowardice under Carl's thumb and he detailed his own, as well as Harvey's, complicity with Carl's little empire, and how they had helped keep cover for his illicit enterprises. He had already detailed as much of Carl's business activities as he could, including the probable location of fermenting operations down southwest of the Kalltons and what he suspected was happening on Tom Buell's land, much of which had been confirmed by Tom himself just two days before. A long, single, sarcastic sentence, as a parting shot, charged everyone to not feel any pity for him if and when the illicit photos of himself with the ladies were ever to be distributed about. He would hope that some would enjoy the photos and remember the smile he seemed to have in one of them. It was to have been the only 'pleasure' that he had been allowed to enjoy in the last fourteen months.

Because of Tom's confession, there would be demanding calls from the community to shut Carl down and put him under arrest and to start prosecutions against all those involved in helping to build the empire. It would be necessary to call in legal enforcement assistance from neighboring counties and to deputize as many as would volunteer from the local populace. In order to get things done in an orderly fashion, he would have to do things with proper procedures and protocol. The days would be long and the nights would pass sleepless and anxious. This, again, would make him appear slow and waffling; but if he were to allow emotions and passions to escalate to the point of hysteria, and perhaps a lynch mob to form because of it, someone would surely get hurt or killed. And he would carry the bulk of the blame.

Then Gene forced his mind to go blank again. Almost as if in slow motion, he stepped over to a chair where his gun holster hung and retrieved his revolver. He walked back to his bed in the far corner and sat down on it; whether to pray, to clear his mind, or to hold back tears, Gene himself didn't seem to know. He sat motionless with the gun held on his lap for several minutes, then he lay back on the bed and made himself as comfortable as he could, as if he might sleep until morning.

Two houses down the street, an older widow woman was throwing out a large pan of dishwater. She threw the water far and long. It hit the ground with a whump, as if the water had held its shape like a heavy folded quilt and hit the ground square on its face. Must have hit the top of the chicken coop, she thought. In the darkness it was hard to tell. Immediately thereafter, she heard a muffled pop a short distance up toward the west end of the street. She couldn't see anyone outside in the moonlight. She stood only a moment listening closely. No movement, that she could see, occurred in the yards next to hers. Must be that old dog hunting for scraps again, she thought. Or someone slamming a door.

She turned and stepped back into her kitchen and closed the door behind her. She shoved an old towel along the bottom to keep out the draft. The old house was still drafty. But where it was coming from, she couldn't tell.

CHAPTER 28

It was a scream that should have broken window glass. Immediately, Esther was on the floor scrambling for footing on the smooth foot-worn pine boards. Unfortunately, the lamp had gone out and the room was as dark as a cave. Again, a scream pierced the darkness so savagely that Esther found herself screaming too. It seemed to take a brief eternity for Wade to get to the room. All he could find were two females screaming so piercingly that his eardrums felt as if they were being hammered with spikes. He could see nothing, but he ran into the room and was immediately smashed across the side of the head with someone's open hand. Jimmy had bounced out of bed and was somewhere in the kitchen nearby. Nearly paralyzed, he groped the darkness, too terrified to think what to do.

Fearful of hitting Esther or Kelly Jean, Wade wildly swung his arms hoping to snag a human body. A glass object, perhaps the oil lamp, was hit or thrown across the room and smashed against the wall nearby. The room was a mad theatre of hand-to-hand combat and noise and Wade could not determine how many people were in the room besides Esther and Kelly Jean.

Again, he could hear glass breaking. It sounded like a windowpane. The two women never broke breath and kept the volume to earsplitting levels unceasingly. Things kept breaking and moving. Wade was on top of the bed. He had managed to grab someone next to it and yank them down, but was knocked off balance by a flying body. Jimmy was still in the kitchen, and Wade could hear something fall or crash in there.

Wade had jumped back upright and then tackled someone near the dresser and tried to wedge her between the wall and the dresser. The lamp had been smashed and the smell of coal oil was in the air and glass shards were scattered across the floor. The wet substance splattering the walls and floor was either oil or blood; Wade couldn't tell. He had started to pull someone, whom he determined to be Esther, from off the floor and drag her into the kitchen.

He yelled at Esther, fiercely trying to get her to recognize him. Kelly Jean was still in some sort of maniacal rage and was tearing at curtains and beating at walls, apparently trying to escape from whatever or whoever was attacking her. Wade shoved Esther through the door and into the kitchen. She fell across the table pushing it hard enough to crash against the basin counter on the opposite wall. The windows in Kelly Jean's room were covered with heavy curtains that Kelly Jean had not yet managed to rip down. Wade tried to determine where she was in the room. From all the racket it still sounded as if someone else was in there with her; it was impossible to tell.

With a headlong run, Wade threw himself back into the room raking his hands back and forth in the air trying to grab his daughter. He found her, but was met with a punch across the forehead that was followed up with another one across the side of the neck. Wade swept his arms around and gripped her in a bear hug that locked her arms into his chest but left her legs unhindered to kick and flail about like a mad mule.

"Somebody get a light on!" Wade yelled above Kelly Jean's screams.

Someone had been pounding on a wall in the kitchen, for what reason Wade couldn't determine. It seemed that someone was trying to get somebody's attention, or was trying to find their way in the darkness. Then Esther could be heard crying loudly in the kitchen and making noises among the shelves and counters trying frantically to find a candle and matches. Jimmy had found a lamp on the table but had dropped it near the back door when Esther hit the table. The spilled coal oil had filled the kitchen with its odor and the danger of fire multiplied the fear in the house.

Wade had managed to keep his footing and hold onto Kelly Jean in spite of the oil on the floor. He was shaken badly by the severity of Kelly Jean's screaming and thrashing about and by the fact that she didn't seem to be wearing down. He started to work her away from the corner of the room toward the doorway while fighting to keep his footing and bearing in the darkness. He stepped on something large and furry-like near the foot of the bed. It didn't move, but gave way like an animal's body when he put pressure on it. Finally, he found the doorframe and with all his strength he shoved Kelly Jean against the door causing it to slam back against the wall. *"Where's that goddamn light?"* he yelled.

All at once, Kelly Jean stopped screaming and seemed to go limp. It gave Wade enough time to pull her into the kitchen and force her to the floor. Esther was in another room, still clamoring loudly for a lamp or candle. Jimmy was gone, somewhere out the door. Wade began calling Kelly Jean by her name. With what was left of his breath, he tried to keep his voice calm and subdued in hopes of finding an unfrayed nerve in the house. He could now hear Esther making angry noises under her exhausted breath, still trying to find a workable, unbroken lamp. Several were in the house, but all the excitement seemed to blank out her mind as to their whereabouts. Wade determined that she was in Jimmy's bedroom. He commanded, "Over the mantle – over the fireplace! Get a match from the fireplace!"

Esther stumbled out of the room and to the fireplace. She had forgotten about the matches in the metal box hanging next to the mantle. Kelly Jean had begun to cry with a low voice that quivered with fear; clearly still oblivious to the fact that all was now safe. No one else was in the bedroom; at least Wade didn't hear anything or encounter anything that would have confirmed that there was a real intruder. He had Kelly Jean's hands held to the floor beside her. She was no longer kicking or fighting him.

"Esther?" Wade barked. Just then, a flicker of light flashed in the front room. In a second, Esther entered the hallway with a lit match. She still had not found a lamp. "Don't come in here – there's coal oil all over the place! Fetch that lamp in the bedroom there!" Wade ordered. Shortly, she returned with a lamp glowing brightly. Esther, seeming to be having difficulty holding herself erect while fighting to catch her breath, stood at the doorway looking around the kitchen floor for the coal oil. Finding none nearby, she sat the lamp on a chair and gently pulled it toward Wade and Kelly Jean. She was only wearing a thin slip for bed and Wade was in long full-body underwear with the top unbuttoned and hanging to his waist. Kelly Jean had a slip similar to Esther's, but it was badly soiled with blood, coal oil and urine.

"Is he gone?" Esther asked, her voice hoarse from screaming. She was still doubtful that an intruder may still not be hiding in the house.

"Who?" Wade asked; his lungs spent of their last breath.

Esther seemed confused by her own question. She leaned over and cautiously glanced into the bedroom.

"Who?" Wade asked again.

"The window fell in, like somebody broke it and came in. Didn't you hear it?" Esther said fearfully.

"I don't think anybody's in the house. I would have found him if there was," Wade said.

Even still, like Esther, he kept eyeing the room suspiciously as if expecting to confirm his worst imagining. "Where's Jimmy?" he asked. He was crouching over his daughter, still holding her arms to the floor.

"I don't know," Esther answered. She leaned heavily against anything that would hold her up. She pushed her hair back continuously as it fought to remain hanging over her eyes. Kelly Jean was alert and gazing up at her parents. She had no fight left in her and Wade released his grip on her arms allowing her to begin catching her breath.

"Where's Jimmy?" Wade asked again, his voice laden with worry for his missing son. He looked back down at Kelly Jean and found that she could recognize him, but she still seemed afraid because of her shifting gaze. Wade slowly stood up allowing Esther to kneel to the floor next to Kelly Jean and tend to her. Wade lit another lamp and used it to enter the bedroom where the war had taken place. He found the floor severely splattered and smeared with coal oil, bodily fluids and blood, and lamp glass was broken into small glittery shards here and there. Kelly Jean's bloody handprints were found high and low on the walls.

He quickly made his way to both windows and examined them by pulling the curtains wide open. He found a single pane broken in each window, but the window nearest to the bed was splattered with blood and large bird feathers and down. Part of the curtain had been torn away. The light from the lamp glistened against the bloody window and it reflected a dull crimson tint across the room. He was still barefooted and had to keep looking down to the floor to step around safely. He could begin to take his time now and let loose his tightened muscles and relax a bit.

No one else had been in the room as first feared. He called for Jimmy but got no response. He stepped back around to the foot of the bed and found the big predator bird at the base. Wade lowered the lamp to the floor being careful to avoid the coal oil. He saw a very large, and very dead, owl flattened out as if it had been stomped a dozen times by large human feet. Wade determined that it was killed upon impact with the window. Then its momentum carried it across the bed with its full weight of several pounds slamming with enough impact against the iron footboard to splatter viscera against the opposite wall. He couldn't remember hearing the impact – he was awakened by the screams – but it would be easy enough to imagine being jerked awake by something akin to a cannonball being fired through the window.

Kelly Jean had completely quieted down and Esther was talking to her in soothing tones. Wade could see Kelly Jean's bloody feet in the doorway and it appeared that some blood was still flowing from glass cuts as evidenced by the growing crimson pool nearby. Esther was cut also, but seemed oblivious to the pain. Before Wade could begin to move back to the kitchen, a car's headlights flashed through the front bedroom window and the car's engine could be heard revving up to the back porch. It seemed that in a matter of seconds, Jimmy entered with Paul and Ruth close behind. Paul was carrying a shotgun and a flashlight. Both of them, like Jimmy, were only half-dressed. Ruth was wearing a long, heavy coat and a pair of Paul's oversized boots. They stopped cold in the doorway between the porch and the kitchen. They were breathing heavily as if they had just run a marathon.

"Jimmy, run out and fetch me a bucket of water," Esther ordered. She had begun to tend to Kelly Jean's wounds. Her feet were cut, but Kelly Jean seemed to be in a mild state of shock and appeared as oblivious to the pain as Esther. Wade stepped back into the kitchen before fully realizing he had a small cut on his right foot. Nonetheless, he picked Kelly Jean up like a rolled quilt and carried her to the front room and gently laid her on the couch. He dashed to his bedroom to get properly dressed. He quickly returned.

"Was somebody in the house? Jimmy said he thought somebody broke into the house!" Ruth finally said, still breathless.

"No, nobody broke in. An old half-blind owl flew through the window. I reckon Kelly Jean and Esther thought somebody was trying to get in through the window," Wade said.

Esther had gone to slip on a robe and to retrieve towels and clean bed sheets for bandages. She heard what Wade said and added, "I don't know what was going on. All I know is something come through that window and shook our bed like somebody was breaking in. When Kelly Jean started screaming, I thought someone was trying to get us, so I started yelling too. I have never been so scared in all my life!"

Esther's hair and clothes were nearly in as bad a shape as Kelly Jean's. Wade had found fistfuls of dark hair lying on the floor in the bedroom and surmised that Esther had lost a few locks when Kelly Jean was fighting the 'intruder.' Wade leaned over Esther with the lamp as she began clean-up work on Kelly Jean's feet. Several plugs of hair and skin appeared to be missing from Esther's scalp as evidenced by the little crimson bald spots on her head. Ruth had stepped over to look and was clearly shaken by all that she was witnessing. She retrieved a pillow and placed it beneath Kelly Jean's head. As she did so, she got a better look and saw that the damage was worse than she had first thought, and was fearful that just simple first aid measures may not be enough.

"Where's Paul?" Wade asked. He looked back through the kitchen and saw the beam of a flashlight shine through the damaged window into the bedroom. He could hear Paul and Jimmy talking outside the window, so he returned to Esther and held the light over Esther's head. Ruth had begun to wash the wounds on Esther's scalp while Esther worked on Kelly Jean's feet and a couple of cuts she found on her knees. Thankfully, the house was quiet and calm. Kelly Jean lay still as the women worked. A quilt had been brought to her and she covered herself against the cold air. Her face was a mess but she wasn't crying or making a noise. Esther gently swabbed her feet with water-soaked towels and watched Kelly Jean's face to monitor her reactions to the pain.

"Kelly Jean?" Esther asked.

"Uh-huh?" Kelly Jean answered.

Esther had rinsed her daughter's feet to remove broken glass then applied some medicals. Finally she wrapped a piece of bed sheet around her left foot to slow bleeding from a cut. They were both beginning to feel greater pain from their wounds. Shortly, Kelly Jean began to wince and cry out with pain.

"What did you think was in there?" Esther asked her daughter.

"Huh?"

"Did you think somebody was trying to get you?"

"Yeah, Mama."

Then Esther extracted a piece of glass from Kelly Jean's foot causing her to cry out. With a flashlight she examined her daughter's injuries as carefully as a surgeon. Ruth was still trying to work on Esther's scalp but was ready to give up; she was making Esther's job difficult.

Like trying to query a young child, Esther asked in a soft, calm voice, "Well, who did you think it was, child?"

Kelly Jean looked up at all those looking down at her. Paul had returned with another lamp and was holding it above everyone, and Kelly Jean was showing confusion by the new expression on her face. The question, in spite of being asked in a light, noncommittal manner, seemed to be of great interest to everyone above her. Still reeling from the terror of the night and the pain in her body, Kelly Jean needed time to think the question through.

"Who did you think was trying to get you, Kelly Jean?" Ruth asked with a bit more conviction.

"Well," she started apprehensively, "I thought the big man was coming for me."

"What big man?" Ruth asked.

"Carl," Kelly Jean answered as if it should have been obvious to all.

The house fell silent. It seemed that the breeze outside stopped as if a switch had been flipped off. Then Kelly Jean began to feel crazy again. In her daytime world Carl was not real; he was just a discarded product of her nightmares. So why did she mention him in front of everyone, as if they should have known all along? The contradiction was clear, but she had nowhere to go; her nightmares were too powerful and they could no longer be ignored.

"Carl? Carl who?" Ruth asked, appearing to be the only one not struck speechless by the answer.

"Carl Dean," Kelly Jean answered slowly and fearfully as if supposing she was giving the wrong answer. Esther again tried to continue working on Kelly Jean's injuries and to refrain from showing any reaction. It was the right answer, but the one most feared.

Hoping to keep the momentum going, Ruth asked, "Why do you say that, honey?"

Kelly Jean searched the eyes of all those above her, still with the bewildered expression. It was like a bad dream. Everyone was staring and waiting for an answer that she seemed to think should have been clear to them all. Was it a trick of some sort? Why were they trying to learn something that they should have understood long ago? No one appeared angry but their faces seemed surprised, or aghast, as if she had knowledge of something that could push them to anger. But would it be anger at her, or someone else? Would they be angry that she had misunderstood something, or that perhaps they were thinking she was playing some strange game with them? No, that couldn't be. The night had been too terrifying for games. There was no place for games here.

"He said he was going to come and get me some night when I was sleeping," Kelly Jean answered with a question in her voice.

"Carl Kallton?" Ruth asked.

"Uh – no – Carl Dean!"

"When did he say that to you?"

Again Kelly Jean searched the eyes above her. "Don't you know?" she asked. She was drawing up her right foot as if trying to alleviate the pain that was fighting for her attention. Both feet were now wrapped tightly with strips of bed sheets. Esther stroked her ankle to help lessen the pain.

"Kelly Jean, baby, when did he say these things to you?"

Again, Kelly Jean worked her mind to think of an answer. Esther's eyes were tearing up, but she used a towel to keep her face dry. Kelly Jean said, "I don't know, Aunt Ruth. I think it's all just a dream. An awful dream. A really awful dream."

"Now don't you do that. You just tell me everything so we can help you, honey. Don't be holding back on us, okay?" Ruth said as if afraid of losing momentum.

"I don't know – I just don't know!"

"Is it something that happened on the North Road over a year ago? Is that where you saw

Carl Dean?"

"Yeah – yeah!" Kelly Jean exclaimed with wide eyes. She again looked at each one above her. She saw her father standing behind everyone, in the darkest corner of the room. He appeared intensely anguished, or angry. To Ruth it seemed that a light of sorts was flickering on in Kelly Jean's memory. In spite of the pain in her body, she suddenly seemed more receptive now to the inquisitiveness of others.

"But it was just a nightmare – he's not a real man, is he? Is he?" Kelly Jean asked. She was gazing into Ruth's eyes hoping for affirmation of her own understanding of the situation. She had voluntarily, and impulsively, mentioned Carl by name as if assuming that he was known by all. He couldn't be real; he was too frightening, too terrifying. Kelly Jean came alive with fear. For a moment, it was thought that she might fall into panic again. "But nobody ever says anything about him!" Kelly Jean continued.

Then braving into long-forbidden territory, Esther asked, "Don't you remember when Jimmy came back from hunting last year, and he said he saw Carl Dean – remember?"

"No. Uh, yeah, Mama! But I don't remember anything about – but you made me go to bed right after that, so I thought I had done something wrong and nobody said anything about him since! After James was killed, I thought everything was because of me. It was all my fault!"

"You mean you thought that since James was killed, you thought everything was because of your doing?" Ruth asked.

"Yeah, I know – I know I was bad and I was wrong in what I did. So, I thought I wasn't supposed to talk about what happened on the North Road – because it would make everybody upset with me again."

"Baby, tell me!" Esther pleaded, letting the tears flow. "What exactly happened up on the North Road?" She had pulled herself up close to her daughter and waited for her to speak freely, without fear for the first time, of the occurrences on that fateful day.

CHAPTER 29

The old clock on the corner table tick-tocked too loudly for such a small room, but the house wouldn't have been the same without it. The clock face glistened with a silver reflection in the lamplight. It was three o'clock sharp, about an hour since the owl crashed through the window. The house still smelled of coal oil; its scent intermingled with that of medical iodine in the front room. Paul had stacked four hickory sticks in the fireplace and heated the room to a cozy warmth. Jimmy stood away behind everyone else, never making a sound. He watched his father stand back at the doorway and he listened to his mother's gentle interrogation of his sister for answers to long-ignored questions.

"You don't know, Mama?" Kelly Jean asked.

"I know that James was killed, and somebody hurt Frank real bad and he died too. Everybody knows that."

"Yeah."

"What else happened, honey?"

Kelly Jean didn't answer.

"Kelly Jean?" Ruth asked. "Do you think that we all already know what happened on the North Road? Is that what's bothering you?"

"Yeah, Aunt Ruth. I thought you all knew everything. Why are you asking me now?"

"Baby," Esther said, "We don't know anything. We thought you were hurt so bad by seeing James die. We figured it wouldn't be right to make you talk about something that you seemed too afraid to talk about."

"What do you mean, Mama?"

"Well, you ran away, remember? Papa and Uncle Paul and Mr. Carter had to hunt you down. They found you under that tree and you looked like you saw a ghost. Papa had to bring you back holding you in the seat of the car because you were crying so bad, remember?"

"Yeah, Mama. It was a terrible day. It was a terrible, terrible day!" Kelly Jean said in a frightened voice.

"Do you remember – don't you remember that first night? Don't you remember how every time you fell asleep you would wake up screaming every hour or so?"

Kelly Jean nodded.

"Well, we didn't want to cause you no more harm by having you talk about it," Esther said. "The only one who knows what happened on the North Road is you. We don't know what happened. Nobody knows but you!"

"Nobody?"

"Kelly Jean, your papa and your mama – and the rest of us – none of us know," Ruth said. "We'll never know – not unless you tell us!"

"You don't know, Mama?" Kelly Jean cried.

"It's all right," Esther said, "It's not your fault – it's not your fault!"

A blizzard seemed to be brewing outside. The wind was up and was wreaking havoc with a couple of loose windowpanes in the kitchen. Occasionally a gust would hit the house making it seem as if it might shift on its foundation. It was a fearful sensation that reminded everyone of the day of the tornado. The weather was calm just an hour ago, but now the cold air blowing through the damaged windows in Kelly Jean's bedroom was fighting the fireplace for control of the temperature inside. Wade went to close the door to the room, then returned and resumed his quiet but tormented posture.

"Now you just take your time and tell us everything, if you can," Esther said.

"Well, where do you want me to start?"

"What happened when you and James got up to the North Road?"

"Oh – well," Kelly Jean began while working to clean her face with a wash rag. "We got off the horse and we ran him off, you know. And first thing we heard over the ridge was some talking – bad talking. It was like they were cussing and swearing and saying things like they were drunk or something. I got real scared, but we were hiding under the ridge trying to figure out who it was without looking. But since Frank was over there we had to see who it was, so James got up on the ridge to look. And I could hear the dogs coming, so I started up that ridge behind him. I could hear them dogs getting close, so I figured that we weren't going to make it. I was going to tell James that I was going to go back home.

"But – but before I could, I saw him pull out a gun! I didn't know he even had a gun! But he pulled out the gun and he shot at something. But when I got up to him, someone must have shot back at him. There was no doubt in my mind he was killed. And all I remember after that was I screamed and screamed. I ran up over that ridge because I thought somebody was coming over it to get me, so I ran the other way to get away. But I think I ran the wrong way. I went down the ridge, then back up to the road, I think. I knew I was going to be killed too!"

"Did you just run away?" Esther asked.

"Yeah, just as fast as I could. But I remember, too, that I saw somebody come after me and he threw me down. I think it was that old Wilson man that used to work for Papa and Uncle Paul a long time ago."

"Billy Wilson?" Ruth asked.

"Yeah, you know, with the red hair and whiskers. But his hair didn't look the same. It was a lot longer than I remembered, and it covered up his face. But I was so scared I really couldn't tell that much. But he threw me down and I tried to get up and he pushed me down again."

"What else did he do, honey?" Ruth asked when Kelly Jean paused too long.

"I don't know. I couldn't understand what he wanted. I just tried to run and I ended up running down the ditch there along the road and I tried to get away. I thought that he was just trying to stop me and take me back to Papa, but he pushed me back to the ground and tried to hold me still. He was breathing real heavy; he wasn't acting right. He was poking me and pulling at my clothes. It was like he was trying to take my overalls off. And he was taking his pants off too!"

Esther rose up in her seat but restrained herself mightily. Wade was stone-faced and kept his eyes on his daughter. Ruth kept the momentum going. "What did he do next?"

Kelly Jean shook her head sternly. It seemed that she might be trying to shake loose foggy memories more than display any attempt to withhold information. She rose up on the couch a bit and propped herself against the pillow.

"I don't know – I was crying so hard. I think I kicked him once. I can't remember. But then somebody hit him and knocked him away. I thought it was Papa. But it wasn't Papa – it wasn't Papa! It was all like a dream, like it wasn't really happening. That's why it all just seems like a dream, because it was so terrible – so terrible! And nobody's ever said anything about those men on the road. So, after I woke up the next day – I knew James was killed – but I couldn't think about those men anymore. I figured those men were all just part of a bad dream that night! I just couldn't get all those things right in my head anymore!"

Like lapsing into a fit of self-exorcism, Kelly Jean seemed to be taxing her mind to its limit by the pained expression on her face. She was earnest in her efforts to place the memories in the context of reality and describe the events in as best a concise narrative as she could. She had little frame of reference for describing Billy Wilson's true intentions, so her mind failed to place the event in the realm of reality.

"It wasn't Wade? Who was it?" Esther asked.

"No, Mama – I don't know who it was. He was a big man and I never saw him before! He just pulled me up to his face and made me look at him. I couldn't scream or nothing. I just knew he was going to kill me too! I know he killed James, so I figured he was going to kill me! Every time I tried to get away he would just shake me and make me look at him. But I could hear the dogs coming over the hill and I think he got scared, so – "

Again, trying to divide nightmare fantasies from reality, she thought long and hard about what she wanted to say. Her mother waited, restraining herself from saying anything. Jimmy looked at his father and he followed Wade's gaze up to the fireplace mantle where his rifle lay. It was always loaded and ready to fire with a crank of the lever. His father had the gaze of determined anger, and Jimmy figured he had a good guess as to what was on his mind.

Kelly Jean had displayed no outward displeasure or anger at those around her for their apparent reluctance, or refusal, to engage her in discussions on the subject throughout the months since the incident at the North Road. It could very well be interpreted as callousness or indifference on her parents' part for placing her under an umbrella of protection so broad, with the intent of protecting her, that her own need to grow past the tragedy was ignored. Simplistically, she had been kept in an environment of forced serenity and quarantine for the duration of months. Then it would be years, or longer if necessary, in hopes of bringing her to a more controlled temperament with the belief that she would someday simply 'get over it.' The barometer of her improvement was figured to be in her sleep, her dreams and nightmares, where her true spirit manifested itself. Soon enough, however, reality and dreams became one until, finally, all fearful memories were categorized as manifestations of dreams. Kelly Jean had learned to disbelieve her own perceptions and leave all judgments to the adults around her who, until now, had seemed relatively rational and benevolent.

"What did he do then, Kelly Jean?" Esther finally asked.

"Mama – he hit me! He hit me so hard! Right across my face! He said he'd kill me! That's what he said, Mama! And then he said, 'You tell your old man anything – I'll come into your house and I'll kill your whole family!' Then he cursed me and called me a dirty name!"

"He hit you?" Wade asked in an unusually hoarse voice. He quickly coughed to clear his throat.

"Uh – huh," she said, now sobbing but still managing to speak.

"Is that all he said?"

"Yeah, he – he said he would come into our house some night and get us all!"

"You thought that meant he was going to kill us all?"

"Yeah."

"So, that's who you thought was breaking through the window tonight?" Esther asked.

"Uh-huh!"

"What happened after he said those things?" Ruth asked.

"Well," Kelly Jean said hesitantly, "He pushed me down and I got up and ran away!"

"Did he tell you his name? How'd you know it was Carl Dean?" Paul asked.

"Oh, that – that Wilson man hollered, 'Carl Dean!' Then the big man cussed back at Wilson real bad!" After a moment of reflection, she added, "Didn't he go to jail?"

Esther looked up at Wade with shame. "No, baby," Esther said, returning to her daughter. "We didn't have any way of proving he was a part of all this. Nobody else even knew that he was around here back then. Do you think that if Papa had any idea that Carl was involved in any of this that he would be running around free right now?" Esther said incredulously, looking back up at Wade. Then realizing the hypocrisy of her argument, she drew her eyes away.

Kelly Jean looked up at her father with a questioning expression and asked, "Didn't you see him on the North Road, Papa?"

Wade shook his head and said, "All we found was James Buell dead and Frank hurt bad. We got there too late. Carl and Billy and Jackson must've run off before we got there. We just got there too late."

"Jackson?" Esther asked. "Who's Jackson?"

***

The clock tick-tocked louder than ever. Otherwise, there was silence in the room for several seconds. It seemed like minutes.

The fire in the fireplace had quieted down. Esther had initially turned her head toward Wade. But as his answer was slow in coming, she shifted her chair around and gazed up at him eye to eye with such surprise and curiosity that Wade was taken off guard more by her gaze than by her question. He was hopelessly knocked off track by his own blunder of mentioning an unmentionable, but he could think of no snappy retort to help begin repairing the damage. Paul and Ruth hadn't moved, neither had they bothered to look at Wade or Esther. It was as if they already knew something and didn't want to be a part of the new developing debate.

"Who is Jackson, Wade? What are you talking about?" Esther asked when Wade failed to respond.

Kelly Jean squinted her eyes at her father trying to see his face hidden in the shadows. Jimmy had initially shown no reaction, but his curiosity as to how his father would answer was as fired up as his mother's. He knew who Jackson was – he had witnessed the man's execution – but he remembered that his father had instructed him to keep quiet about names. With his young mind he had assumed that the situation had been handled by the grownups. He was never asked about it again. But his confusion over all this was as bad as his father's efforts to mend his gaffe. The room seemed to shrink a bit each second that Wade withheld his response.

"Esther, let me tell you something," Wade said sternly. "Some things are going on out there that I'm trying to protect you all from. I've been asking a few questions around town, and I've just about figured out who done what, and when, and where. It's just best that you keep out of it till I get it all straightened out."

Like a slap to the face, Esther recoiled and looked back at Kelly Jean. With renewed fear in her voice, she turned back to her husband and asked, "Wade, what are you talking about?

What's going on here? Who is this Jackson?"

"He was with Carl and Billy that day on the North Road. He was from Georgia. He was working with Carl at that time."

"How do you know these things?" Esther asked.

She looked back at her daughter. Kelly Jean seemed to shake her head no. She could vaguely remember the third man. She didn't know his name. Of course Esther could never forget Jimmy's terrible night at the big oak over a year ago. She knew he had witnessed the murder of some transient worker and Wade had taken charge and turned it over to the sheriff. That is what Wade had told her. She, like Jimmy, trusted him. So, the problem as she understood it, at least from a legal standpoint, had been handled. But since Jimmy had not mentioned the victim's name, she never made the connection. Jimmy held silent – he knew nothing to do but watch and listen to the stumbling debate before him.

"Like I said, I've been asking a few questions. You let me handle this," Wade answered, now with an added edge of anger. He pulled his foot off the couch and stomped the floor, causing the house to shake. He had stood firm in the shadows, but he stepped toward the fireplace and, with a very visible tremble in his hands, reached for his rifle and pulled it down to him. Savagely he cranked the lever and slammed it shut, loading the chamber with a heavy 45-75 bear cartridge. Defiantly he gazed across to those in the room and exposed his full countenance in the light.

"Wade!" Esther shrieked. *"Wade – what are you doing?"*

His face was flushed red and his eyes were those of the possessed bent on vengeance. The corners of his lips quivered like he was on the edge of exploding. It was unnatural. He slapped the rifle from his right hand to his left, and then he reached up and grabbed a handful of rifle ammo and jammed them into his pocket.

"Wade!"

"You all just stay put. I tried to kill this son-of-a-bitch once, and failed. I won't fail again!"

"Wade – stop it!" Esther screamed.

Paul had stood up and moved toward the door as if to block Wade's exit, or to open it for him, he didn't seem to know which. Ruth hadn't moved, other than to place her hand assuredly on Kelly Jean's arm. Jimmy jumped up and looked around wide-eyed and anxious.

"Paul – Run fetch Gene!" Esther yelled.

In an instant, Wade had retrieved his coat and boots and left out the back door with the rifle ammo clanging in his pocket. Helplessly Esther stood in the middle of the room and spun around twice as if searching for a solution in the air. Ruth could hear Paul starting the car and she saw the headlights turn on and illuminate the yard. Her heart had begun to beat hard and fast and, against her own wishes, she began to cry.

"Come here, Esther!" Ruth cried with an outstretched arm. "C'mere, Jimmy!"

Together they huddled and held onto one another like they were fighting for their lives in a storm-tossed, sinking boat. Kelly Jean had sat up and was grasping onto everyone as hard as they were grasping her. Esther, between sobs, had begun to pray to the Almighty like the demented and her words poured out in barely coherent torrents, clearly desperate for an immediate remedy.

"Mama – is he going to get Carl Dean?" Kelly Jean asked too meekly for all the racket, her own eyes wide and darting. But her mother didn't hear her in spite of being held tight in her arms.

In a moment, Jimmy managed to wrench himself away from their grasps and run to the kitchen, through the back door and out into the freezing and buffeting breeze. It was a strange sight. Paul was working desperately to block Wade's path with the car much like a cutting horse at a rodeo. The growl of the engine was loud, but Jimmy could still hear Paul yelling out of the car at Wade. As the headlights swerved around at each attempt, he could see his father making a zigzag dance away from the car. Easily Wade stepped back and forth around the car as Paul kept driving in erratic circles trying to block him off. More than once, Paul swung in tight and bumped Wade with a fender. Finally, Jimmy could see his father break and run for the tree line, fifty yards northward. He headed for a low-lying swampy pond that he knew Paul could not navigate with the car. Paul cursed loudly when the car sunk its front wheels nearly to the axle, forcing him to stop. In seconds, Wade disappeared into the darkness leaving Paul behind with the stalled car.

Esther was still making a lot of noise in the front room. Surprisingly, Kelly Jean was the quietest of the trio. From the back porch, Jimmy could hear Ruth making spiritual petitions nearly as loudly as Esther. He hopped down to the yard and began running toward Paul and the car. The sky was black with only a handful of stars exposed between the clouds. The only light available was that of Paul's car which had now aimed down into the swamp. It reflected precious little light back up into the trees. Jimmy aimed himself for the car and poured on the coals. Paul was revving the engine, desperately trying to free the car from the muck.

Jimmy hit a rock and tripped to the ground and slid on his face for what seemed several feet. He bounced back up and started again. Paul was still spinning the wheels and Jimmy could see mud being slung out across the swamp in the lights. Jimmy was closing the gap in good time but Paul beat him to action. With a sudden surge, the car yanked itself out of the mire and raced in reverse for many yards before Paul gained control, and then he spun the car around so quickly that he was unable to see Jimmy in the headlights. For only a flash, Jimmy was in the light. He was still too far away to yell at Paul to get his attention.

With a shift of the gearbox, Paul made the car bounce back across the field all the while working hard dodging trees and saplings. In an instant, he had blown past Jimmy and aimed the car for the driveway and the road. It seemed that if he didn't slow down, he would overshoot the turnoff at the driveway and careen headlong into the trees across the front yard. Jimmy had reversed himself and was trying to get Paul's attention. But Paul was long gone. Jimmy could see the headlights down the road swinging back and forth, obviously the symptom of a car barely under proper control.

Jimmy ran back to the back porch and bounced into the kitchen. The women were still crying and praying. The crying was incessant and loud, shaking Jimmy to his core. He raced to his room and grabbed his double-barrel shotgun and yanked open a chifforobe drawer and pulled out a box of shotgun shells. He yanked on a coat and switched his shoes to boots. He was making so much noise that he was sure that the women could hear him, but they were so driven to lamentations that they seemed to show no awareness of his presence just a few feet away in the next room. He grabbed a carbide headlamp off the shelf over the bed. The room was practically pitch-dark, but he found everything he needed quite easily. He marched out of the room and into the kitchen back toward the back door. With one last backward glance, he caught a glimpse of his mother's eye around the doorframe. He wasn't sure she could see him through the tears, but he lost no time to good-byes. As he kicked open the door he was sure he heard his name screamed above all the noise. He sped up and made for the tree line a hundred yards away.

CHAPTER 30

It seemed that she couldn't stop herself. Esther had stopped her praying and for ten minutes she had wailed. It was the voice of a wife and mother driven to madness with hysteria and grief.

But Ruth had had enough. She had done her part in praying; it was time to act. She was ready to allow Esther to carry on and cry herself out. But upon observing Kelly Jean, Ruth determined that even though she was still crying with her mother that she, nonetheless, seemed lucid enough to listen to reason. Ruth took Kelly Jean's hand and squeezed. Kelly Jean responded by gazing up at her aunt. Ruth turned and entered Esther's and Wade's bedroom and got herself dressed as quickly as she could. She found a work dress and slipped it on and promptly found a pair of Esther's boots and socks and in a minute she was ready for battle.

Back in the front room, she grabbed Esther by the arms from the rear and yanked, forcing her to stand up. Esther stumbled and jerked around toward Ruth. It surprised Ruth how this simple action so suddenly brought Esther back to her senses, but only for a moment.

"Now – we gotta settle down and get our minds together on this!" Ruth said, almost shouting. "It's not going to do us any good to stand around here wailing and carrying on like a bunch of dogs howling at the moon. Now let's all just settle down and figure out what we're going to do!"

"Where's Jimmy?" Esther asked with a new wail.

"I don't know – maybe he went with Paul to get Gene," Ruth guessed. "Look, everybody's upset. Kelly Jean's upset – don't you see, Esther? We're going to have to settle down. Now you go find some good clothes and I'll help Kelly Jean, okay?"

Obediently, and sniffling noisily, Esther hobbled away to the bedroom. Ruth had carried a lamp in and sat it on a chest of drawers. She lit a small lamp sitting on the mantle and turned to Kelly Jean. "Kelly Jean, let's you and me go to your room and find you something to wear," she said.

Within a matter of minutes, soiled and bloody bed clothes were changed to day wear, injured feet were re-medicated and re-wrapped and the three women were dressed for winter, Ruth still using the heavy coat she had arrived in. It was better than anything Esther had to offer. Esther had managed to dress herself with a pair of new thick leather boots her family had given her for Christmas and had slid herself; dress, boots and all, into a bulky pair of Wade's overalls. With gloves and two scarves wrapped around her head and being engulfed in Wade's hunting coat, she looked like she was too bulked up to move. Kelly Jean was similarly dressed in a pair of Jimmy's overalls with the hem of the legs pulled up to underneath her long dress, still leaving enough to extend to her ankles. Together the trio looked quite comical in their diversity of color and dress. Except for the scarves, they might have passed as outlaw migrants on the run from the law. When they had gathered together in the kitchen, Ruth began to laugh at the sight of Esther and Kelly Jean standing together in the doorway.

"What?" Esther asked.

"Just look at you two – you both look like you're going to hunt possum!"

It was all that was needed. Kelly Jean laughed first and Esther followed with a giggle. Smiles were on all three faces and for the moment spirits were lifted. It helped greatly to settle nerves and get all of them to cooperate and think as one. Three lamps were filled and lit. Two of them were metal lanterns, the hand-held type made for such occasions. Ruth ordered everyone, including herself, to drink heartily from the water pail on the counter.

"Where are we going?" Esther asked.

"We're going up north. We're going to get all the help we can get."

"Paul's gone to get Gene, isn't he?"

"Yeah, but we're going to run fetch the Buells!"

Esther gasped and looked at Kelly Jean. She failed to find words to express her surprise.

"Look, after we tell them everything we know, I think they'll be on our side right away," Ruth said. "Maybe Tom and Luke can run help Wade right quick if we get there soon enough. At least it's worth a try – what else can we do?"

"Yeah, okay – we can hitch up a horse and wagon. But – ," Esther said, stopping herself short. Then realizing the futility of time, Esther stammered for a solution. But they needed a faster way – like a car or a shortcut. It would take them too long to hitch everything up and get moving. An instant remedy was required. They stood silently a moment mulling options; then Kelly Jean spoke up.

"I know a shortcut!" she said excitedly. The two women looked at her, bewildered. "It's nearly eight miles going around the road to Braxton. But we can go through the woods and get there in an hour if we don't stop."

"Walking?" Ruth asked.

"Yeah."

"We can't walk that far with these feet," Esther said.

"But mine don't hurt no more – I can make it!" Kelly Jean said proudly. Esther worked her feet in her boots and realized that she was relatively pain free.

"We don't know the way – we'd get lost, Kelly Jean," Ruth said.

"No – I know where the trail is, remember? Me and James used it going to the North Road a few times. And he said the trail going north from the road is clear all the way."

"Are you sure?" Esther said.

"Yeah, we'll have to get across some creeks but I know we can do it. I did it a few times myself!" Then, embarrassed, Kelly Jean clamped her mouth shut. She had never admitted to traversing the trails at night with James, but it was clear now. Her secret knowledge of the land to the north was now necessary for a new desperate journey.

"Are you sure, Kelly Jean?" Esther asked. "Are you sure we can get there that fast?"

"Yeah, I'm sure – if we don't stop."

"But Ruth," Esther said as if realizing something worrisome. "You're pregnant – you can't do that!"

"I ain't that pregnant!" she retorted. "I can still run with the best of 'em!"

"What about your boys?"

"Oh, Mrs. Sarah got up. I know she's worried, but she'll take care of things."

"Hey – reckon we ought to carry a gun?" Esther asked.

"For what?" Ruth asked.

"We might need it in the woods. Some critter might get us!"

Back in the bedroom, Esther scrambled around in the closet and pulled out an old lever action .22 that Wade and Jimmy rarely used. But it appeared to be in fine shape. "What kind is it?" Ruth asked.

"I don't know."

"Let me see." Ruth grabbed the gun and cranked the lever open like a man. She peered inside the chamber and saw that it was empty. "Where do you keep the bullets?"

From the same closet, Esther pulled out a box of ammunition and handed it to Ruth. Ruth spilled the contents out onto the bed and hurriedly checked the caliber. "Perfect!" she said excitedly. Then she rammed six rounds into the magazine and dropped the rest into her pocket. "Let's go!" she ordered.

"You know how to use that?" Esther asked fearfully.

"Just call me Annie Oakley!"

Ruth was working hard to keep emotions up, but she had her limits. As they proceeded out the back door into the darkness, Esther could be heard in the fast moving breeze sniffling and weeping with the same nervousness as before. The glass lamp that she was carrying promptly blew itself out in the wind. The two metal lanterns were doing well and flickered brightly in the blustery night air. Esther tried to set the darkened lamp onto the porch but promptly dropped it as they descended the steps. Ruth turned and looked down at the lamp on the ground and saw that it had not broken. Esther stood it up and ensured that the flame was completely out. Feeling safe that it could not start a fire, they turned for the tree line directly north of the house and trooped on with Kelly Jean taking the lead.

***

Jimmy had circled the swamp and run through the woods until he fell exhausted. In spite of the freezing air, he could feel perspiration running down his back. He was already thirsty; he hadn't thought throughout all the excitement to get some water for himself. Leaning against a tree, he tried to slow his heavy breathing long enough to listen for his father's movements in the woods. The woods seemed alive because of the winds. If he could hear Wade tromping through the trees he would have to be very close to him. But everything was building to a torrent and flecks of snow were stinging his face. He didn't know what he should do, whether to call out for his father to wait up for him or to remain silent and wait for daylight, then try to catch up and help his father. No, Wade would demand that his son return to the house and stay put. If his father was truly going to gun Carl down, he knew that his father would not want him to be anywhere nearby.

Sometimes he thought he could hear someone moving through the woods. His heart was still beating double-time, and the arteries in his ears drummed steadily, making the noises around him all the more confusing. He remembered the headlamp in his pocket but he didn't reach for it. He had enough presence of mind to realize his father could see the lit lamp a quarter-mile away and he may inadvertently become a target if gunplay ensued in the darkness.

He, once again, felt that intense stab of aloneness and loneliness down in the pit of his stomach. He should have been used to it by now, but it was there to stay no matter what he did to try to alleviate it. If he could have remembered to grab something off the table on his way out, like a biscuit or a piece of jerky, he was sure he would have felt better by now with something in his belly.

Jimmy broke open the chamber of his shotgun and slid in a couple of rounds. He didn't know if he had loaded birdshot or buckshot or something in between. Maybe, he hoped, he would not have to fire a shot until daybreak, then he would know what he had loaded. He snapped the gun shut and began his trek to the west. The woods were so noisy that he didn't feel he should bother to step lightly. As quickly as he could, he picked up the pace, after pulling his flip-down fur-rim cap down over his ears.

***

Wade had grabbed a thin coat on the way out of the house, but he wasn't cold. Like Jimmy he was perspiring, but even if he weren't, the rage boiling inside him would have kept him warm. It was like a furnace that had been fueled and stoked to its hottest temperature. When he had mentally snapped back at the house, he gave himself permission to wage total war against his enemy, and at that moment he wanted to kill. But he would have to wait until he could close the gap between himself and his intended target. Instantly he had unleashed the demons of rage that had been living within him for the last year, and he was now in complete unison with them.

The woods were black, but Wade marched at a steady cadence as if he could see every obstacle in his path. He guessed that it would be two hours before the first sunrays broke the horizon. If he got himself into the house at the first flash of lamplight, he could dispatch Carl quickly and return to the woods before anyone realized what had happened – if the sentries 'cooperated.' Like everyone else, he had heard of the disappearance of Billy Wilson. But if he is found in the house with Carl, Wade would ensure that two birds would be dispatched with one stone. He had no war plan; but he intended to work by the seat of his pants, figuring that taking the time to calculate each move as he worked would give the enemy time to think and counterattack.

It was still about two miles as the crow flies to Carl's house. Wade remembered the guards and the dogs around the place, and he was determined to kill them all if he had to in order to eliminate Carl. The ammo was jingling in his pocket. As quietly as he could, he redistributed them to as many pockets as he could find. In a few moments they didn't make a sound. But the woods were loud in the fast breeze, so he probably didn't need to worry.

He found an old wagon path and walked it as far as he could. Sometimes a dim ray of moonlight would open up between the rushing clouds and he could see far enough ahead to set his itinerary for some distance. He figured those guards would be stationed on the outer boundaries if they were still up and awake. Or they might only come out shortly before Carl roused for the morning; he had no way of knowing. Another mile, he estimated, and Carl would be dispatched to hell.

Soon, he entered an area of thick underbrush and vines. He did not remember this problem the first time he had come this way to kill Carl. He knew that the new fields lay just ahead, and if he could find them he would be at his destination very soon. The North Road was just a short distance to his right, he knew, but he didn't want to go that way. It would be the first area to be guarded. But he turned toward the road to get around the bushes and quickly found another broad area of widely spaced trees and saplings. The woodland floor was covered with the dried leaves of cottonwoods and poplars, the types that make a lot of noise when walked upon. But as a gesture of defiance, Wade allowed himself to walk with naturally heavy steps across the leaves, not caring if it made him easier to detect by any possible sentries ahead.

Soon, to his right, he could see the North Road. It was a dark gray stripe that ran east to west through the woods. To the far side he could see an open field with dried corn stalks swaying in the breeze. He was happy to think that the fields would not be planted again. After Carl was made dead, perhaps the land would be bought by a timber company and planted with tree shoots or left to overgrow with weeds and critters. Wade was anxious to speed up the process and find out. He stumbled into a narrow creek, broke through a thin sheet of ice and slogged through the shallow freezing water. He stepped up into a line of trees along the other side, then he bounded out onto the edge of the first field that seemed to have been planted with small vegetable plants months earlier. With long, high strides he could step onto the top of each row and cover a lot of ground very quickly. He felt a little pinch under one of his toes; the apparent symptom of the broken glass. His heart was beating at a fast drumbeat but he wasn't tired. He continued the fast march across the field, and the sound of his heavy footsteps atop the crumbling rows sounded akin to the chugging of a locomotive. His rifle was held at the ready across his chest and its safety was off, ready to kill.

Another two-hundred yards and he would be entering Carl's front yard. The noise of the wind and the woods was still sounding aggressively all around. The noise was his friend. It would ensure that he could get very close to his target before being found out. As he closed the gap to one hundred yards, he slowed his pace until he stopped near the edge of the field and stood there like a statue. For several minutes he waited for a lull in the breeze. But the wind had not let up since he left the house. Gazing all around, all he could see were the gray-black mottled ground and the black tree trunks before him. He was much closer to the North Road, just a few yards. He reached up with one hand at a time to massage his ears. They felt nearly frozen and it hurt to touch them, so he alternated his hands over each of them for a minute to get the blood re-circulating. He gambled that he was not close enough for any sentries to know, yet, that he was there. He turned the gun down and aimed it forward from his waist and he entered the trees.

***

"Where are we, Kelly Jean?" Esther asked.

"The trail goes over the creek just up ahead, Mama," she answered.

The woods were alive with the sounds of swaying trees and snapping limbs and the wind was picking up. Down a long gracefully sloping incline, the women marched. The meadow just ahead was clear of vines and underbrush and Kelly Jean remembered it well. She knew that just on the other side there would be a deep creek with a footbridge, if it was still there. About twenty yards away, a large tree limb broke and hit the ground with a solid thump, and they could feel the vibration underfoot.

"What was that?" Esther asked, her voice barely audible in the noise of the blizzard.

"It ain't nothin'," Ruth barked. "C'mon!"

Ruth had passed her lantern to Esther as she had the rifle to carry. Being the most anxious to make the trip as quickly as possible, Ruth moved ahead of Kelly Jean and cajoled them to pick up the pace. Everyone was breathing heavily with exertion.

Before the meadow turned to incline upwards, the creek could be seen as a thick black line running from one end of the meadow to the other. Stepping to the edge, they held out the lanterns and peered down into the creek. Above the wind, they could hear water running deep below them. Kelly Jean swung her lantern high and low searching for the footbridge.

"Where can we cross, Kelly Jean?" Ruth asked.

"There was a footbridge here – two big boards. It's gotta be here somewhere."

Kelly Jean turned to the right and walked along the edge holding the light high. The woods were familiar, yet they were not. Feeling as if she had made a tragic mistake, Kelly Jean began to get angry with herself and to talk as if she had led everyone astray. "Aunt Ruth, I'm afraid the bridge has fallen in. I'm scared we're not gonna make it."

"Down here! Over here!" Esther screamed from many yards downstream.

Ruth and Kelly Jean turned and raced toward her. They had not realized that Esther had left them. She had found the footbridge.

"Is it safe?" Ruth asked breathlessly as she and Kelly Jean met up with her.

Peering down at the boards, they appeared the same to Kelly Jean as they did over a year earlier. The boards were several inches thick and showed little sign of deterioration. "James said they were cedar – they're not supposed to rot," she answered.

Without any further discussion, Kelly Jean moved past Ruth and Esther and stepped quickly, but lightly, upon the boards. Esther had reached up to stop her but Kelly Jean jerked away. The boards were springy, but to Kelly Jean they still seemed as strong as ever. With what appeared to be a well-practiced dance, she moved gracefully toward the middle and on to the other end without slowing down, all the time with the lantern held high. *"C'mon in – the water's fine!"* she yelled from the other side.

Ruth eased to the bridge and worked to balance herself on the first step. She used the rifle to balance herself and, moving much slower than Kelly Jean, she eased out to the middle and tried to build up a little speed for the upward approach to the other side. Kelly Jean and Esther held the lanterns high on either end, illuminating the whole scene. She reached up and Kelly Jean handily pulled her up to solid ground.

Esther didn't wait. She bravely marched onto the bridge nearly as quickly as her daughter, not giving herself time to think or to lose balance. The lantern swung wildly in her hand a couple of times but she bounced up to Ruth and her daughter with the energy of a teenager. The timing was good because the wind suddenly whipped up a nasty gust that seemed to last several minutes.

"The Lord must've heard your prayers, Esther," Ruth said as they took a moment to catch their breaths. It was a serious statement and everyone seemed to realize the truth in it as they gazed at one another with a new feeling of determination and purpose.

For another mile they marched, crossing a running creek while balancing on rocks barely exposed above the water's surface, and slogging across a marshy field and through a couple of brier patches. When they found the North Road they sat on the edge-bank along the ditch and rested. It was another mile yet to Beulah Church Road where the Buells lived, but the worst had been conquered. Amazingly, Esther and Kelly Jean were experiencing only minor foot discomfort from their injuries to this point and were eager to continue.

Silently, they sat and gazed into the trees on the other side searching among the black woods for an opening. It was supposed to be the door to a yellow dirt path zigzagging through the trees. But it was still as dark as it had been an hour earlier when they were still in the house. Kelly Jean had followed the path from the south very well, but she was only vaguely familiar with the area to the north. They would have to search for the 'clean' trail that James was once familiar with and hunters and deer had used for generations. Somewhere nearby, James had met his end. Kelly Jean didn't try to search for any familiar landmarks such as the little nondescript ridge along the road. It was an uncomfortable feeling sitting here knowing that her mother and aunt were probably imagining similar thoughts.

Halfway to the North Road, Kelly Jean had found the spot where she and James used to meet. Esther and Ruth had assumed that the rickety bench at the base of the tree was nothing more than a makeshift deer stand that had been used by hunters over the years. Kelly Jean paused at the little bench and nearly lost her composure at the sight of it, but she forced herself to stand tall and move on. She kept the secret to herself and couldn't imagine what her mother would have said had she told her of the several late night rendezvous that had occurred there. Esther, like everyone else, had learned about the secret meetings but knew little of the extent or the duration or the number of them.

"We need to go," Ruth said. Together they jumped the ditch and stood in the road. A flurry of snow swirled around the lanterns and was forming fancy patterns of circles and arcs in the twisting breeze. With the lanterns held high, they crossed the road and gazed into the dense woods looking for the path.

"We're gonna have to get in the trees to find it," Kelly Jean said.

They jumped the other ditch and plowed into the trees and found a clearing about ten yards from the ditch. No path was visible yet and again they held their lanterns high. For several moments they searched the woods and found several old paths meandering about, but no distinct trail that fit James's description. Fearfully, they jumped back to the road and searched from there. About twenty yards to the east, an open spot in the trees was visible in the lamplight. The women made a beeline for it and entered the newfound pathway and started the final leg of the journey. Ruth and Kelly Jean had quickly moved ahead up the trail. It was a yard wide, clear of debris and flat; perfect for a fast hike. They had walked several yards ahead before realizing that one of their group was missing. The light had dimmed. One of the lanterns was lagging behind.

"Esther?" Ruth yelled.

"Back here!" Esther called from near the start of the trail.

"What's wrong?" Ruth asked as she and Kelly Jean rushed up to her side.

Esther stood in the middle of the trail with the lantern hanging down by her side. Confusion was etched on her face and Ruth was afraid that she was not going to endure until the end. If she was going to break down now, Ruth couldn't imagine a worse place for it to happen.

"Esther, honey, c'mon – are you all right?" Ruth asked.

"Oh, I'm okay. I'm just fine."

But the confused expression was still on her face and she wasn't moving. Tentatively, Ruth took her arm and asked, "Well, what's wrong?"

"Well," Esther said, "I gotta pee. And I don't know how to do it with all these clothes on." At first, Ruth was a bit stunned, but looking at Esther dressed up like an Eskimo she couldn't help but start giggling. "I'm not playing, Ruth – I need to go real bad!"

Kelly Jean began to laugh out loud with Ruth. Physically, Esther was the smallest of the trio and, with the scarves wrapped tightly around her face and the long coat hanging to her ankles, she looked like a child with a perplexing problem. "I need to go too!" Kelly Jean announced, still laughing.

Ruth decided that too much time had been wasted. She took Esther's lantern and sat it on the ground and lay the rifle down near it. As quickly as she could, she worked Esther's coat buttons loose and helped her with the dress and overalls. Kelly Jean had an easier time of it and was already relieving herself at the base of a tree behind a bush. "Hurry up!" Ruth ordered.

Esther did the same to an unsuspecting tree nearby and, just as quickly, she redressed and retrieved the lantern and handed the rifle back to Ruth. "What about you? I remember when I was pregnant I needed to go every five minutes!" Esther joked.

"I'm fine – let's go," Ruth commanded, destroying the humor of the moment.

To make up for lost time, they picked up the pace and marched almost double-time. And, other than a lot of huffing and puffing, showing little sign of fatigue from the journey. James was right; the trail was wide and clean and, for most of the way, straight. Most of the time the women were silent. Esther prayed for strength and Kelly Jean listened when she did. Ruth watched the trail as the leader and found marks of deer hooves and raccoon feet in the frozen soil the whole length of the trail. Occasionally, the footprint of a dog, or a coyote, crossed the path. She entered a broad spot in the path and was startled by a large splattering of blood and fur on the ground. She guessed that the rabbit had been young as evidenced by the tiny cottony down interspersed with the smooth light brown fur. No dog or wolf tracks were nearby, so she figured that a predatory bird of some sort had attacked and eaten most of its prey before taking off with the remains.

Ruth waited for Esther and Kelly Jean to catch up and together they stepped over the carnage and moved on. Nothing was said of the mess in the trail. Ruth, with a tinge of irony, had wondered if it could have been the same dim-witted bird that had crashed through Kelly Jean's window a couple of hours earlier.

Ruth was amazed at the speed of their trek. With the lanterns she could see far enough ahead to verify the type of terrain they were to encounter. Mostly, though, they filed through heavy woods of cedar, tall pines, and mature oaks; some of them with trunks bigger than anything she could remember. Here and there, the trail branched off into smaller paths, but the main trail kept a northward direction and Ruth was hoping that very soon they would find Beulah Church Road and then onward to the Buell homes.

The wind was still whipping up a torrent of movement in the trees. Everyone was wearing gloves, but Ruth still needed to protect her hands from the biting cold by switching the rifle from one hand to the other in order to warm them up in the coat pockets. Finally, she figured out that if she wedged the rifle under her arm she could jam both hands into pockets, but after a while she found that she could move faster if she had one arm to swing free. She looked back at Esther and Kelly Jean, and they were doing well in keeping up. Kelly Jean's lantern was lighting the way, so Ruth couldn't get too far ahead. Blessedly, the cold ground helped numb hurting feet.

Then they came upon a large tree that had fallen across the path. It almost appeared as if it had been tossed there by the hand of a giant. Carefully, the women crawled underneath the tree trunk to the other side and started again. The woods had changed at this point and they held up the lanterns and looked all around. Tree trunks and limbs were lying broken and tossed all around them. Turning to the left with the light, Esther let out a scream but caught herself before frightening the others too badly. At first glance, she saw large, dirty arms reaching out and groping wildly in the wind. She instinctively pulled away and looked back at the thing that had frightened her. A giant red oak tree had been uprooted by some huge mysterious force and tossed onto its side exposing its massive roots, which extended outward toward the path. Many of the heavier roots stretched out as far as ten feet with many smaller dangling roots branching out and whipping in the wind. It all gave the impression of dozens of monstrous snakes biting the air for prey. Below the mass of roots was a black pit, yards deep, where the tree had uprooted.

"This must be where that tornado hit," Ruth said. Then realizing the need to move on, she ordered, "C'mon – we're almost there."

Soon, the path connected to the corner of an old sorghum field and skirted along the edge to the other side. The path was still passable but tougher to traverse because of fallen trees and storm debris. The light of the lanterns shone across a few yards of the field and illuminated some of the damage from the tornado. Everywhere they could see, dozens of trees, large and small, lay in jumbled and broken heaps. Some of the trees were still anchored in the ground but had been pushed or knocked over at crazy angles. It was a chilling sight and Ruth could imagine how much more chilling it would all appear in the daylight. The field, Ruth knew, had to be close to a road or a wagon path. Beulah Church Road, she was sure, lay just ahead.

CHAPTER 31

Wade saw an open space past the trees about forty yards ahead. He wasn't sure, but he thought he could see one of the chimneys standing high among the trees. The wind was blowing from the west and seemed to be holding this course most of the time. He knew that as soon as it shifted, his scent could be carried straight to the guard dogs and his cover would be blown. Hoping the wind would hold, he steadily strode through the trees with his finger on the trigger. Most of the way he was able to walk in relative silence through a stand of pine trees where enough pine needles lay to form a bed of soft, springy padding underfoot.

Moving quickly, he managed to get within thirty yards of the house. He crouched down and worked on his ears again. He could see the straight-edged outlines of the house and the barracks behind it. To his right was a heavy line of bushes that obscured his view and his path to the front door. He didn't know where the dogs were hiding. He remembered seeing two large, gray dogs at the back porch in September. He suspected that one might now be chained at each entrance.

To the left, the path was clearer and much more accessible to the house. He could run to the back porch and get inside the house within seconds but would probably be greatly hindered, and his enemies alerted, by any dog under the porch. The odds were, he calculated, the front door was guarded to a lesser degree, but it would be tougher to traverse to the edge of the yard, then cross the yard, then climb the steps, then cross the wide porch to the door or a window. All the side windows were high off the ground and difficult to see, much less find in the dark.

It was time to act. Soon, the sheriff and his company of deputized men would be rushing in to intervene. Wade backed up and circled the line of bushes toward the front yard. The driveway connection to the North Road was just a few yards away. He stepped onto open ground along the edge of the yard and paced as quietly and carefully as he could to the corner of the front porch. He eased over to the steps and looked around. The wind was still blowing from the west, but his luck nonetheless ran out.

Just as he began to move up the steps, a dog, with the heavy bellow of a bear-sized canine, barked aggressively from the far end of the porch. Again it barked, this time with the savage tone of an animal in attack. Slowly Wade stepped back to the ground and squinted his eyes in the direction of the dog. Then a second dog rounded the porch at the same end as the first. It also sounded very large and savage. Wade was trapped. He moved up the steps, the dogs following and intent on ripping flesh. He swung around near the top when one of them lunged at his ankle. He aimed the gun down toward the growling. He determined their locations and pointed toward the one he felt was the nearest. He hesitated only a second until he was sure of the dog's exact proximity, then he pulled the trigger. In the flash of the blast he could clearly see the other dog with its white fangs glistening. He slammed another round into the chamber and put a bullet down its throat. The shots quieted the dogs instantly. The second dog had collapsed on the steps and Wade kicked it off on his way back down to the yard. The blasts of the rifle, he was sure, woke up everyone within a half-mile of the house. He chambered another round.

At the corner of the house he hesitated a moment. A light shone out from a window at the end of the white barracks. It appeared to be a flashlight and Wade crouched down as close to the ground as he could and began moving toward the back of the house. He wasn't sure where Carl was in the house but soon, he hoped, Carl would try to find him.

He heard footsteps, or some manner of fumbling about, inside the house. Now one of the dogs began howling in pain at the front porch. Otherwise, he couldn't hear anyone moving around outside. Wade had gambled that no guards were watching from the outside; so far the odds were in his favor. At the rear corner of the house, he looked around to the back porch. He heard another thump inside and he tried to guess where it came from. Hoping to see a light turn on in a window, he aimed the rifle up at the nearest one. But after nothing happened he turned back to the barracks and it appeared that other lights, likely oil lamps, were being lit.

Again crouching, he quickly sprinted to the door of the white barracks and turned the handle. It was locked, so he lightly tapped on it. He looked back at the house. He knew someone was in there and he was gambling that, for the moment, the occupants were too afraid to come out to investigate. To Wade's relief, someone opened the door and a crack of light filtered out into Wade's face. Someone was standing behind it and holding it firm, obviously fearful of the gunshots. Wade threw himself at the door and pushed it open enough to wedge himself through. On the other side, several workers, some barely awake, were staring at him. The one at the door was nearly as big as Wade and stood with an angry glare and said nothing.

"I'm not here to hurt you," Wade said. Then he reached for the coal oil lamp that the man was holding. When he resisted Wade swung the barrel of the rifle right up to his face. He had no time to waste. The man relinquished the lamp. Back outside, he ran back to the house. The light illuminated the house brightly at first but the breeze was trying to snuff it out. As quickly as he could, he ran to the windows along the east side and selected one and promptly, with a powerful thrust, launched the lamp through the window. The room inside ignited with a thump and a flash. He tried to peer inside, but could see nothing but unfocused pulses of yellow light.

He had long determined that no sentries were stationed near the house, so he took his time about trotting to the other side. There he found a darkened side yard, but the illumination of the fire inside the house could already be seen by a dull, throbbing glow of light across the front yard. He listened closely as he stood inches from the wall of the house. He thought he could hear movement inside but he couldn't be sure. He looked back around at the back porch and the door was still shut.

Wade bounded around to the front porch and looked up at the door. Someone was moving inside, he was sure, and from the movements of the lights through the windows, he determined that a battle was happening inside to kill the fire. Then he heard someone shout. It sounded like Carl. Worried that the occupants would be successful at snuffing out the fire, Wade ran to the black barracks and turned the handle. It opened and he entered. Wade strode to the nearest lit lamp and took it. For a second, he looked around the room. Except for two black faces staring at him from cots, the room appeared identical to the other barracks. He examined the two faces for the man named Jesse Bridger he saw with Carl in the truck. He wasn't there. Back outside, he used the light to search for anything that might help speed up the torching process and extract the enemy from within the house. He saw a small, dismantled truck – the one that Billy was driving the day he vanished – near the corner of the barracks. He swept the light over an area littered with engine parts and mechanic's tools until he spied a glass gallon jug half-filled with a yellow liquid. He wedged the rifle beneath his armpit and lifted the jug by the little loop on its neck and held it up to the light. He jerked the cap off and sniffed. He was lucky. It was gasoline; probably used for cleaning the truck's internal motor components.

Like he did the first time, he found a window on the west side and slammed the lamp through. He ran to the front yard and threw the gasoline jug with all his might through a front window. A gunshot boomed from inside. Wade crouched to the ground. Another shot rang out. Then another. Wade determined that the shots were fired from near the rear center of the house. Someone was firing shots to ward him off. He circled to the east side and saw that the occupants had been only moderately successful in crippling the fire. Back at the rear he could see that the bomb he had thrown through the west side had taken on a life of its own. Still, no one had tried to escape the house. The gasoline had not yet ignited.

Wade began marching around the house, making a lap every minute. Carl couldn't stand the heat for long, he figured. Soon, every window in the house was glowing brightly. Both chimneys were exhausting billows of black smoke. Wade had just started another lap around the west side when the gasoline ignited. It caused a concussion that blew out several windows and long red flames curled out of the windows and reached up to the roof. Quite suddenly, a half-dozen migrants ran out of both barracks and a strong voice started yelling orders. *"Run fetch some buckets! Get that bucket up outta the well!"*

A fire brigade was being organized among the migrants, and in less than a minute the migrants were racing around the yard with water buckets for the fire. Wade had returned to the back porch and saw what was going on. He decided to get their attention. He stepped to the area near the well where the men were filling water buckets. He swung the rifle around where all the men could see and he dramatically aimed the rifle at the house, albeit high in the eaves, and fired. The 45-75's blast shook the barracks and halted the men's efforts to retrieve water. Wade stepped over to the well and grabbed the bucket out of a man's hands and threw it down into the well. He chambered another round. *"All you people get the hell out of here! Go on – git!"* he yelled.

Everyone obediently backed away. Wade didn't have time to waste. The house was beginning to cook through the exterior walls. Glass was breaking out all around the house and another dog was barking somewhere south of the barracks. Someone yelled, *"People is gonna die in that house!"*

Wade circled the house one more time. He wasn't worried about the migrants but he should have been. Someone, attired only in long underwear, met him near the rear east corner of the house and demanded to know what was going on. It was a short, but commanding, black migrant. *"What the hell are you a-doin', man?"* he yelled. It was a horror too great for him to imagine. People were burning to death inside the house, and a madman with a gun and with rage in his eyes was waiting to shoot anyone trying to escape the inferno.

Wade pushed him back with the butt of the rifle and ordered him away. *"I told you people to move away!"*

Just then, a gunshot tore through the wall of the house and slammed into a tree several yards from Wade and the migrant. Both men ducked and sprinted back to the wellhouse. The other migrants had hidden themselves somewhere behind the barracks and trees. In the growing light of the fire, Wade could see the migrant's face. His expression was intense and angry.

"The people in that house hurt my children!" Wade yelled. *"And I'm gonna bring them to justice here and now! If you want to help me, find yourself a gun! Otherwise – get the hell outta my way!"*

The migrant turned mute. At least two people were in the house, Wade determined, as evidenced by all the shouting going on inside. The migrant clearly couldn't stand watching a house burn down with people in it. But he couldn't ignore the anger in Wade's voice and the determination in his eyes, and the rifle in his hands. It was a standoff of sorts, but not for long.

Something exploded out the back door of the house. Wade swung around and aimed the rifle toward the porch. A man had crashed through the door and threw himself off the porch and to the ground. He didn't appear to be on fire, but his clothes were singed and puffs of smoke were coming out of his shirt. He seemed disoriented but was clearly relieved to be out of the inferno. He was much smaller than Carl. He stood up and looked at Wade, then the rifle. It was Troy Mays, Carl's house servant.

"Is Carl in there?" Wade yelled.

"Yeah – 'e's on fire!" Troy answered, clearly terrified by the rifle muzzle aimed at his nose.

"Anybody else in there?"

"No!"

"Where's Billy Wilson?"

It was clear by the reaction on Troy's face that he knew nothing of Billy's whereabouts. Wade motioned for him to go away and leave the scene. Troy ran for his life down to the south driveway where other migrants were holing up. Wade turned back to a new black migrant and asked, "What's your name?"

The man was fully dressed with a heavy winter coat buttoned only once at the bottom. Curiously the corner of a clean silk handkerchief, crimson in color, poked out of his top overalls pocket. It stood out against his dull, dark attire like a red flag. "Walta, suh," he answered.

"You stay here, Walter – I'll be right back," Wade ordered, adding extra emphasis by pointing sternly at Walter.

Wade wasn't allowing himself more than a few seconds on each end of the house. He was going to work to give Carl the impression that he was being attacked from all sides by more than one attacker. The house was grumbling with the sounds of the roaring fire and popping glass. The fire had broken through the roof and was leaping out all the windows. It was starting to heat up the woods and barracks. Wade was beginning to feel confident that he would not have to shoot Carl, but that he would die a coward's death inside the blaze rather than come out and face him.

At the front porch, Wade peered to the inside through the holes where the windows used to be. He could see a cool spot in the rearward portion of the front room, as if the fire had not yet attacked the floor or the ceiling inside the blazing perimeter. It was possible, he thought, that Carl could still be alive and well and was working out his escape plan at that very moment. The fire had just begun to attack the front porch at the roofline. Below the porch floor, all was still dark and untouched. The two dead dogs were lying at the base of the steps. Wade pulled several rounds of ammunition out of his pockets and replenished the spent cartridges. He wanted a full magazine to unload into Carl's dying body if he should come crashing out.

Again, shouts could be heard around the back of the house where the migrants were. It was obvious to all that the fire was hopelessly out of control now. Wade began walking back around to see what all the commotion was about. He peered into all the windows. He determined that no one had tried to escape into the back yard.

"You gonna let that man die like that?" someone yelled at Wade.

"He's no man – he's a goddamn animal!" Wade replied.

At that moment, a hard thump could be heard at the front of the house. Wade raced back around to the west side and to the front. The fire was hot and things were beginning to fall off the house and sparks were flying high into the sky. Wade ran into the trees to get away from the heat and sparks. He ran into several thickets on his way around and it slowed him down considerably. He entered the front yard and stopped. Everything was lit up nearly as bright as daylight. Debris and sparks were beginning to fall like rain and the wind was carrying it off for hundreds of yards into the trees. The danger of the barracks catching fire was becoming increasingly possible.

Wade stood at the edge of the yard and looked all around, particularly at the front door. The doorway was wide open. Wade peered inside and saw flames everywhere. The floors and ceilings were ablaze. Irregular holes as large as doorways were opened through the walls by the fire.

Then Wade found the door itself. It was lying at the base of the steps near the dead dogs. At first, Wade determined that it had been blown off its hinges. He looked down at the ground. There, in the wide patches of bare earth, he saw a trail of splattered water leading from the porch all the way across the yard to the north edge. Large, wet boot prints had left indented impressions in the bare dirt. No, the door had been knocked off its hinges. Carl had escaped, soaked to the skin with waterlogged clothes as protection against the fire.

Wade spun around as if he had been shot at. He expected Carl to be getting a bead on him at that very moment. He ducked down low to the ground and gazed into the trees along the north. Out his peripheral vision he saw someone standing motionless near the center of the north road. Wade swung his rifle around with his finger tightening on the trigger. Snapping the rifle to his shoulder to fire, he froze with one knee on the ground and his target in his sights. With another half-ounce of pressure from his finger he would blow a hole large enough to put his fist through.

Wade yanked the rifle up and away from the target. He stared at his intended victim with a shudder. Instantly, a wave of nausea fell over him. The young man that he was about to destroy had stiffened with terror and dropped a long firearm to the ground. Wade glanced back to the north side of the yard. The woods were brightly illuminated from the fire and Wade looked all around for Carl. He had vanished.

The young man was crying. Wade could see his face clearly. Wade remained on his knee for a moment to catch his breath. He dropped the butt of the rifle to the ground and propped himself against the barrel. It was as if the wind had been solidly knocked out of him.

Walter walked around the house to Wade. He stood between Wade and the house with the heat of the fire to his back. He turned to look at the young man at the edge of the yard. Walter watched the two men; they were both in great anguish. Any passing observer would quickly determine that they were father and son.

***

At first, Esther had thought that someone else had answered the door. Then she saw the long, straight, gray hair that fell to one side when Annie leaned around to open the door. She had no look of surprise on her face as expected. She had no smile, but nonetheless she moved eagerly to open the door when she finally recognized who was knocking.

The night was so blustery that it seemed to take too long to get anyone's attention inside. Esther and Ruth looked through the storm-damaged windowpanes in the door and found Tom and

Annie both lying on their backs sound asleep in the front room. Ruth had knocked until her knuckles were raw, but when Annie woke up, she quickly climbed over Tom to get off the bed.

Annie swung the door wide and, with a flick of the hand, motioned for the three women to enter quickly. With both lanterns shining brightly, the room lit up like daylight and all together they looked at Tom, still in the bed, to see that he was just beginning to stir. The house smelled of yesterday's stew and old biscuits and for a moment the women looked around the room taking in old memories that had been lost until now. Strangely, without a word, Annie motioned for everyone to follow. She entered the kitchen and popped open the door to the heater stove and promptly stuffed in enough paper and dry kindling to start a fast, noisy fire. Esther and Kelly Jean sat the lanterns down nearby; the rifle had been left on the porch.

"Why don't y'all get yourselves a chair there and pull up to the stove. You all look like you could use some warming up," Annie said in a considerate tone as if she had talked to them just the day before.

There were no hugs or kisses to welcome her guests. But it seemed that Annie refused to recognize the distance of time between them or the rift that had parted their families for the last fourteen months. She worked heartily in the kitchen to please her early morning visitors. She opened the cook stove and slid out a small pan piled high with day-old biscuits. With a meek smile, she placed them atop the heater stove then turned for the front room. "Tom, you getting up?" she said loudly.

Kelly Jean had promptly sat herself down near the stove and began working to remove her boots, and with a yelp of pain she worked the sock off her most painful foot. Tears returned to her eyes when she found that the sock was soaked crimson from her earlier injuries. She watched her mother do the same with her own feet, but thankfully her own injuries were much less painful and bloody. Quickly, without asking how such harm had occurred, Annie retrieved her nurse's case and moved to Kelly Jean and began working to clean the re-opened wounds. Silently, Ruth took a lantern for the outhouse and opened the back door. "You need some help?" Esther asked with a chuckle.

In a moment, Annie paused from her work and leaned up to Kelly Jean and kissed her cheek in hopes of slowing the tears. "Mrs. Annie," Kelly Jean said, "My feet are okay. I'm just worried about Papa."

Esther had joined her after quickly redressing her own wounds and embraced Annie as she gently washed Kelly Jean's feet with soap and water. The blood had nearly stopped flowing out of the wounds, and they didn't appear to be deep enough to dissect any muscles beneath the skin. But she suffered blisters from the long hike. In only minutes, Annie had tenderly wound both sanitized feet with fresh cotton bandages and found clean socks to cover them.

Still, through it all, Annie had asked no questions. She knew there had to be a good reason for these events and she trusted Esther to fill in the gaps when it became appropriate to do so. She actually seemed eager and happy, as if nothing unusual was happening and good friends had returned for a friendly visit.

When Ruth returned, the room was filled with a toasty warmth and Tom had just entered the room with a lamp of his own. "What're you girls doing out his time of night? How'd you get here?" he asked.

He was sorely disheveled and his nightclothes were almost loose enough to fall off. But acting unaware of his appearance he affected an uncomfortable smile as he examined each face.

He was taken aback by this abrupt, early morning visit from members of a family that he had once considered his foes. To the ladies he appeared strong and healthy; there being no outward evidence of the tornado injuries everyone had heard about.

The room woke up with the chattering of overwrought women. Esther, Ruth, and Kelly Jean seemed to break into a chant of desperate voices as if they had been forced to stay mum until Tom entered the room.

"We're in trouble!" Ruth said, raising her voice to quiet the others. "Wade's gone to kill Carl Kallton, Tom! He learned the truth about everything and he's going to kill him tonight!"

"What truth? What are you talking about?"

"Tom, we know that Carl Kallton killed your boys. Right there on the North, uh, that road you all call the South Road; Carl shot James, then he hurt Frank. We know all about it. Wade took off with his gun to kill Carl because he hurt Kelly Jean too. But he didn't know about that until tonight. He – "

"How do you know all this?" he asked, interrupting. He slipped on an old tattered robe. Graciously, he patted Kelly Jean on her shoulder and seemed genuinely interested in their well-being and in what they had to say. Ruth looked over at Kelly Jean. She was glad to see that she seemed alert and energetic and even relieved to be where they were in spite of her father's dangerous endeavor at that very moment.

"Well, Tom – it's a long, long story. We can tell you all about it later. We can – "

"Where's Paul?" Tom asked, again interrupting.

"He's gone to get Gene. He left the house over an hour ago. They should be back at the North Road by now."

"How'd y'all get here?" Annie asked.

"Oh – we walked," Kelly Jean answered.

"You walked here? With those feet!"

"Well, yeah. We came through the woods!"

"How'd you keep from getting lost?"

"Annie!" Tom barked. "We have to help these people; we can talk about all that later!" Turning back to Esther and Ruth, Tom asked, "Wade's gone to kill Carl? How long ago was that?"

"Just before Paul left to get Gene – over an hour ago," Esther said.

"You think they've really had time to get back and stop Wade? Carl would kill anybody – I have no doubt about that!"

"Where's Jimmy?" Annie asked.

"He's with Paul," Esther answered.

Ruth looked at Esther with surprise. It was clear that Esther believed Ruth's earlier guess that Jimmy had hitched a ride with his uncle. But Ruth didn't correct her because she couldn't be sure herself.

Tom settled down into his old rocker and looked at the women one at a time. "Did Carl say that he killed my boys?" Tom asked with an angry edge, though it was clear that his anger was directed at Carl, not at the ladies.

"No, Tom," Esther said. She looked at Kelly Jean, then back at Tom. "Kelly Jean did; this morning, a couple of hours ago. She was there and saw Carl at the road when it all happened!"

"Kelly Jean?" Tom asked. "You saw Carl do this?"

Kelly Jean nodded, but Esther continued.

"Y'all know we didn't know about this, don't you? You know we would've told you if we had known earlier, don't you? Well, something happened at the house a couple of hours ago and Kelly Jean told us everything. Kelly Jean saw enough to know who did it. But Tom, Kelly Jean didn't actually see Carl pull the trigger or see him hurt Frank, but she was there. And he did something terrible to Kelly Jean and told her not to tell anybody what happened. So we figure he's guilty in what happened to your boys."

"He did something terrible?" Annie asked. "He didn't hurt you, did he, honey?" She looked at Kelly Jean with sincere empathy in her eyes. It was as if she expected that Kelly Jean might still be enduring some form of physical pain from the incident with Carl over a year ago.

"No," Esther said, looking at her daughter. "It wasn't like that. He hit her and scared her real bad, and told her to keep quiet about who she saw there and what happened there."

"Did Wade go after Carl by himself? Are you sure?" Tom asked.

"Yeah – I've never seen him so upset, Tom. And I'm afraid that he's going to be killed now, just like Frank and James," Esther said with a sniffle. "He lit out of the house with his gun, and as upset as I have ever seen him."

"He didn't know the truth until tonight?"

"He didn't know anything – just like me. None of us knew a thing until Kelly Jean told us a while ago."

With a start, Tom stood up and turned for the front room. Tom aggressively fished around in the storage closet in the hallway and pulled out his boots and some heavy hunting clothes. He was full of strength and vigor, clearly recovered from any lingering limitations from his injuries. Annie had turned around and was watching him and she looked as if witnessing someone in the process of getting himself into trouble. "Tom – what are you doing?" she asked with a bit too much emotion in her voice.

"I'm going to help Wade, Annie. He's going to do what I should have had the courage to do months ago."

"Tom, we didn't come here for your help. We came here to tell you the truth," Esther said, half-lying. She had tears in her eyes and she was beginning to talk in the same pleading tones that she did when Wade first took off on his homicidal mission. "We came here, Tom, because we needed your wisdom and comfort. Your family has suffered enough. You lost two good boys, and now we need you."

Ruth disagreed with Esther, but she didn't say so. She had expected Tom and Lucas to move like gangbusters and get to Wade's side before Paul did. She thought that Esther would be just as anxious about getting help for Wade as she was for Paul. She was surprised at Esther's comments, but what she was saying was proper and considerate.

Tom looked at Annie and Esther from the hallway. They were now practically sitting on top of one another. Annie had sat herself on the arm rail of Esther's chair and had engulfed Esther in her arms. Then the women heard the unmistakable metallic sounds of a shotgun being opened and loaded with ammunition. In a moment, Tom returned and stepped to the stove and gazed down at Annie. She gazed back, eyes never wavering. Tom searched for words. He felt terrible pangs of guilt that he had put her through hell for over a year and he was now about to crush her spirit once again. "Annie – are you with me on this?" he asked.

It was the most presumptuous question he could ask. No longer could he hold his gaze on his wife. But he waited for an answer. He had done everything else without her blessing. He felt strongly that if he worked this mission against her wishes, he would fail – or at least make things worse. The answer she gave was more than he had asked for, and far more than he deserved.

"Tom," she said, "I love you. And I want you to come back home."

CHAPTER 32

The preacher woke up with a pounding inside his chest and it hurt. He sat up in bed instantly and the pounding was so severe that he was sure he could hear it. It took only a second or two for him to arouse himself enough to listen more attentively. He could hear someone yelling far away. Someone was pounding on the front door and yelling his name.

"Brother Silas! Brother Silas!"

The excited voice echoed throughout the house and across the fields. The preacher yanked the bedroom door open. It sounded as if his name was being yelled from the front room. Quickly, he stumbled toward the front door and groped around until he saw the car lights shining across the front porch. He found the door and unlatched it. The fierce winter breeze shoved the door back in his face. Instantly, Paul was in the room and his booming voice felt like bombshells exploding in the preacher's ears.

"Brother Silas – Wade's gone to shoot Carl Kallton and I can't find Gene! Do you know where he's trapping?"

"Paul – settle down!" the preacher ordered. He felt as if he had just been jerked out of bed and slapped. Paul shut up momentarily and the preacher searched around for a lamp. He raked a match on the wall, lit the lamp, then looked at Paul.

"Brother Silas," Paul said with greatly forced restraint, "We know what happened with the Buell boys and Kelly Jean on the North Road over a year ago. We know it was Carl Dean Kallton and Billy Wilson that killed them boys. And, Brother Silas, they nearly – they threatened to kill Kelly Jean!"

It was too much, too fast. The preacher's nerves were badly frayed by all the sudden commotion and his heart was beginning to hurt. "Where's Wade now, Paul?" he asked.

Paul could see that the old preacher was having difficulties, so he lowered his voice and spoke much slower. He filled short sentences with as many details as he could jam into them. "He's gone to kill Carl Kallton, Brother Silas! An old owl crashed through Kelly Jean's bedroom window and she thought Carl was coming in to get her. She told us all about what happened on the North Road. And when she got done, Wade wanted to kill Carl right then and there. He got his gun and he tore out of the house and left on foot to get Carl!"

"Why didn't you go get Gene, Paul?"

"I tried to find him, remember? He wasn't home. So, I figured he was out trapping. Don't you know where he's been trapping lately?"

"No – he quit trapping last year. That's what he told me before the season started. You didn't see his car at the house?"

"Uh – I don't know. I reckon I didn't take time to look." After an uncomfortably long pause, he added, "I'm sorry for doing this to you, Brother Silas. Are you all right?"

"I'm fine. I haven't seen Gene in over a week; right after Christmas. He just seemed to me that he wanted to be left alone, so I haven't bothered him for a while."

Paul nodded and turned back to the door. He was on a desperate mission, but he felt bad for his treatment of the preacher.

"Go on, Paul," the preacher said. "Find your brother. I'll round up some help and get out there as soon as I can."

***

The preacher loaded up fast and raced to Braxton. It was four-thirty in the morning, but since the sheriff was an early riser the preacher figured that Gene wouldn't be too put out by someone knocking on his door so early. He didn't want to give Gene a heart attack like the one he just received from Paul, so he knocked softly when he arrived. It was still pitch dark and the whole house was black inside and out. Even the light from both carriage lanterns could barely pierce the darkness beyond the porch.

The preacher knocked again, this time a little harder. He heard something behind him walking in the leaves. He looked around to find the old bluetick coming toward him from near the horse and carriage. The dog bounded up the steps to the porch and promptly lay down under the porch swing nearby. The preacher listened as closely as he could for any movement inside the house. It was a futile effort; the wind was making too much racket. After knocking once again, he turned and stepped back down to the ground to retrieve one of the lanterns off the carriage. He swung the lantern high in the air and aimed it toward Gene's car. It was parked at the rear of the house as usual, with just the back end visible from the front of the house. The preacher considered walking around to the back and checking the back door, but the sheriff's bed was in the front room.

He stepped back up on the porch and knocked on the door again. Still, there was no response. With a strong tug, he found the door latched tight. Lifting the lantern up, he tried to gaze in through the glare of the glass. In a moment, he had the lantern turned in such a way that the entire front room was brightly illuminated and he could see through the glass without the interference of the reflected light. "This is not right," the preacher whispered to himself. Still, everything was quiet in the house. He could see the heater stove and the table across the room from it with one corner of the foot of the bed partly visible around the doorframe. Back at the carriage, the horse let out a sneeze and began to back up, pushing the carriage backward toward the street. "Hold up, there!" the preacher ordered.

Almost instantly, the horse stopped. The preacher looked around for anything that might have spooked the horse. Must have been something in the air, he thought; the scent of some unfamiliar critter or whatnot. But the air was blustery and shifting; it didn't make sense. The preacher repositioned the lantern in the door to get a better look toward the bed. He thought he could, for a moment, see the outline of a boot lying cradled in the top quilt. From this position, though, he couldn't tell if Gene's foot was in it. Without further thought, the preacher stepped off the porch and walked quickly around the house to the back porch. Before going up the steps, he looked around the car and back yard. He could find nothing out of place. He stepped up to the back door with the lantern held high. Again looking inside, he saw nothing that could warrant any kind of overly negative suspicions. He tapped lightly on the door and without waiting for a response he pulled on the handle of the screen door and swung it open. The wooden door inside was not latched, so he pushed it open several inches. Loudly he called Gene's name and listened. Still nothing. He stepped one foot in and stopped. Immediately, he could feel the hair on the back of his neck stand up like quills, and he froze.

It took him several moments to begin figuring out what was happening to him. Whether it was an odor in the air or a strong discernment within his spirit that had stopped him cold, he couldn't quite decide. His first instinct was to sniff the air for a clue. Something was there, no doubt. He looked around with the lantern in the tiny kitchen and pantry. The only thing that immediately came to mind was the distinct impression of a dead animal lying for days in the hot sun. The faint scent of death wafted so lightly in the air that it took several moments for the preacher to put it all together.

Taking another moment to collect his wits, he tried to determine if he could hold his breath long enough to make it to the other end of the house. He backed up onto the porch and gulped in a lung full of fresh air. He lunged himself inside, then he stampeded through the house to the front room. He stopped in the middle of the room and quickly panned the light around in a circle visually memorizing everything his eyes could find. The stove was out and cold to the touch. The windows were covered with curtains and only the glass in the door was left partly uncovered. The table in the corner was holding a large bowl layered inside with the crust of dried soup, apparently several days old. A coffee cup and a spoon were next to it. On the other end of the table a well-used pile of writing paper and several pencils lay together. Everything else was in place. Then he swung around to the bed and paused, but only long enough to get a glance. His heart was already pounding; but now with his body and mind being besieged with panic, his heart began hurting again. He needed to breathe, as he had held his breath the whole time. Inhaling, he found the stench unbearable.

Hands shaking, he unlatched the front door and barreled out, almost tripping over the threshold. He sat the lantern down on the porch and stepped out into the yard, trying to relieve the discomfort in his oxygen-starved lungs. Resting his hands on his knees, he panted heavily for several minutes. He gagged and spit up. The horse snorted again, and again attempted to back up with the carriage. Still short of breath, the preacher yelled, *"Whoa!"* Now I understand what has been spooking old George, he thought. Then he looked up at the dog on the porch, still barely visible in the darkness. Then he thought, with sad empathy, reckon the old dog's gotten used to the smell.

Looking around, he saw no neighbors nor heard any movement down the street. The street was deathly quiet. For whatever reason, the bluetick barked a couple of times causing the preacher to nearly jump out of his shoes, then all was quiet again. The preacher forced himself to shuffle over to the porch to retrieve his lantern. Got to get to a neighbor, he began thinking. He grabbed the horse's bridle and gently nudged him backward. The carriage was nearly in the street when he stopped him. "There – that shouldn't be so bad," he said to the horse.

Then the preacher could hear a horse and wagon coming down the road from the north. Then he could see a dim lantern dangling. He stumbled toward the road and began swinging his own lantern like a drunken man. The driver clearly suspected something amiss and made the steed pick up speed to a trot. Shortly, he slowed the rig down to a stop in front of the preacher. "Who's that?" the preacher asked.

"Brother Silas?" the driver responded. The man was bundled up with layers of coats and quilts, apparently suited up for a long, cold ride. The preacher stepped up nearer to the wagon. The driver turned the lantern up and the preacher recognized him as the foremost blacksmith in town, evidently setting out early to make a delivery run out in the county somewhere.

"Go fetch Harvey Carlson," the preacher ordered. "I've got a serious problem here. You know where Harvey lives don't you?" The blacksmith didn't answer for a moment. He was hoping to learn what the problem was and the preacher, anticipating this, said, "Gene's been shot – I'm afraid he might be dead. Can you get Harvey for me?"

With a nod, the man snapped the reins and rolled down the street at a gallop. Soon enough, he was gone around the corner at the end of the street, leaving everything in silence once again.

***

By daybreak, Deputy Harvey Carlson still had not arrived. Several of the neighbors had already gathered in the yard near the preacher's wagon. He had fought off several efforts by a couple of them to enter the house and examine the situation. One of them, a man the preacher had seen in town only a few times over the years, began to question the preacher's assessment of whether or not the sheriff was actually dead. After intense accusatory questioning of the preacher, he again began to demand entrance into the house in order to see for himself.

"Well, go ahead – but you won't stay long," the preacher said. He was, as evidenced by his tone and gestures, dog tired and fed up.

"Who do you think done it?" someone asked from the growing crowd.

"I don't know," the preacher answered. "After being dead for several days like that, we may never know."

"Did he shoot himself?" a new voice asked.

The preacher shook his head and said, "I just don't know."

"Harvey's not going to know what to do," someone said angrily. "We better get someone from the district over here."

Everyone seemed to be directing their comments to the preacher despite the fact, from the start, of his statements concerning his own ignorance of the situation. The man that had gone into the house to investigate returned to the group and verified the worst. "Yep, he's been dead for days – I'm sure," he said.

The crowd had grown to number at least seventy-five people by the time Harvey showed up. He was on foot and it had taken him twenty minutes to make the trip from the boarding house. "Haven't you talked to Gene in the last few days?" someone asked as he walked up.

Harvey shook his head. "No – he told me to take off a week or two." He was as nervous and as rattled by the news as anyone, and it was visible to all. A number of people appeared to be weeping. The sheriff had no family, but it seemed that some considered him as such by their displays of emotion.

"Before we go in that house, Harvey, we better open up the doors and air it out – it's pretty rough," the preacher said.

"Ben, why don't you run fetch Mallory," Harvey said to Ben Townsend, the cotton gin proprietor who had arrived shortly before he did. Everyone knew Harold Mallory as the local representative for the only funeral home in a three county area.

One by one, the crowd worked its way toward the house. Everyone except Harvey and the preacher stopped at the base of the porch. The preacher asked one of the men to go around and prop open the back door. Harvey shoved open the front door and looked in. He seemed genuinely horrified by the contents of the front room, both by what he saw and by the odor. He pulled a handkerchief out of his pocket and covered his nose and mouth. He stepped into the room as cautiously as someone entering a trap. The preacher eased in behind him holding his sleeve up to his face.

With difficulty, while holding the handkerchief, Harvey lit the two candles and the lantern on the table. He was looking around the darkened room as best as he could in as short a time as possible. He could see someone on the bed that resembled Gene's general height and physique. A massive splattering of brown-darkened blood defaced the papered wall next to the bed. Dozens of finger-size lines were smeared in frantic crisscrossed patterns across the blood, leaving evidence of a terrific struggle after the gunshot. A bloody and death-stiffened hand grasped the corner of a pillow in a tight fist. It seemed that Gene had been trying to shove the pillow to a more comfortable position beneath his head during his dying hours, or days. Excrement and urine stained his clothing and it appeared that some bed sheets had been used to wipe fluids from his body, and they lay wadded up on top of him like hardened mounds of clay. It pained the preacher to wonder how long Gene had remained alive and suffered all alone. Obviously, the self-inflicted gunshot was poorly aimed, shortening his life to a few days of hellish self-awareness of his condition, alongside relentless physical misery of the worst imaginable kind. Gene's face was turned toward those in the room and, with what was left of his eyes, seemed to be staring up toward Harvey and the preacher, who had by now stationed themselves about five feet from the bed. The revolver lay on the floor near the foot of the bed.

There was a tiny table, used for a nightstand, standing at the head of the bed. Lying near the edge of it was the little New Testament Bible the preacher remembered giving to the sheriff years ago. It had been laid squarely atop a folded red handkerchief as if a valuable gem had been carefully placed there.

Harvey was so shaken by the whole scene that he was cursing quietly to himself, seemingly oblivious to the preacher's presence. The preacher had already grieved himself past tears and all he could do was stare at the poor sheriff's lifeless body. The activity in the front yard had, for the most part, become quiet and orderly. Everyone seemed to be waiting for answers and all eyes were on the front door. More town residents were arriving by the minute and by the time the sun was completely up, numerous horse and carriages, wagons, and cars blocked the street. As many as two hundred people were standing in huddles in the yard and street. Several men had stepped up onto the porch and were trying to gaze in through the windows and the door. Enough light was entering the windows to illuminate the front room clearly. Harold Mallory from the funeral home arrived and solemnly worked his way through the crowd, climbed the steps and entered the door. By now, the odor had all but ceased to repel even the most squeamish, and breathing was easy and relatively natural in the house.

Harold deftly removed the soiled sheets and pillow. Here and there he brushed away dried mouse waste then examined the damage to the body the mice had done. The rodents had chewed and dined on the weak points of flesh, especially around the eyes, nose and fingers. Originally, the preacher had thought that the sheriff's badly damaged appearance was the result of atrophy and decay, but this new revelation was nearly more than he could bear.

"Looks like he didn't die right away, preacher," Harold said. "Must've been many hours, or maybe days, after the gunshot. He suffered bad."

There was no crowd control outside and it would soon begin to show. The preacher started out the door to do what he could to calm emotions and get the people to disperse. He turned to look back one last time. He had thought that Harvey was behind him, but he found him standing at the table looking down at something on it. The preacher froze and watched. He remembered the stack of papers on the table. He had figured on returning to help examine the house after everyone had vacated the property. He had hoped that no one would take it upon himself to gratify his own curiosity without the benefit and consideration of an organized team effort by a few respected townsfolk and the required legal authorities.

But Harvey was helping himself to everything on the table; and when he began flipping through the papers, the preacher wondered if the deputy was looking for anything in particular. As if being stung by a bee, Harvey slapped the papers together and glanced around wide-eyed. Harold looked up at him but quickly returned to his duties. Harvey looked at the preacher with an expression much like that of a child caught stealing. They gazed at one another long enough for the preacher to know that something was outside the bounds of propriety.

Obviously trying to control his gestures and movements as nonchalantly as possible, Harvey turned back around and began to roll the papers up into a tight roll and it appeared to the preacher that he was trying to stuff it down behind his belt. Looking around the top of the table as if starting a professional examination, Harvey worked to ensure that the paper roll was well hidden in his britches. The preacher was standing at the threshold of the door watching. Harvey was aware of being watched and was calculating his next move.

"He's probably been dead nearly a week," Harold said. "Seems as if someone would've checked in on him if he hadn't have been seen around town in that time."

The preacher didn't respond, as he, like Harvey, was calculating what to do next. I can't let him leave the house with that suicide letter, he thought. Then, before allowing himself to think too much, the preacher asked loudly, "What'd you find there, Harvey?"

Harvey feigned an expression of surprise with only a glance toward the preacher. Without answering the question, he said, "I reckon we ought to start a fire. It's mighty cold in here."

Quickly, the preacher motioned for two men, including Ben, to come to the door. His motion was expressed urgently, so both men quickly bounded up the steps and looked in. Without explaining anything to them, he again asked Harvey the same question. "Harvey, what'd you find over there?"

Clumsily, Harvey pulled the papers from his belt and started to stuff them into the stove. He retrieved the matchbox from the top of a nearby pedestal and, as quickly as he could and with a tremor in his hands, he opened the matchbox and proceeded to light the papers. Instantly, the preacher was on him, slapping at the matches. The other two men had no notion of what was going on but, putting full trust in the preacher, they helped to separate Harvey from the paper roll in his hands.

Viciously, Harvey punched at everyone and anyone. The papers fell to the floor and were kicked apart in the ensuing fight. He cursed and shouted at the men and demanded that they respect his legal authority. His shouts grew loud and shrieking, to the point that other men from the yard came to the door. Bewildered, they only stood and watched, not knowing who was fighting whom.

Harvey landed a nasty punch across Ben's face, throwing him toward a very stunned Harold. Together, they fell across the bed onto Gene's body. Graham was doing all he could to bear hug Harvey to stop his thrashing about. The preacher had alternately tried to deflect Harvey's punches and grab at the papers on the floor. Twice he had fallen to the floor, but the papers were getting a real beating from all the kicking, stamping feet.

Realizing that something of very serious import was happening, three of the men on the porch entered and reached Harvey immediately after the preacher slugged him with his best Sunday punch. Heavily restrained, Harvey looked more like a madman having convulsions than a lawman exercising his authority. He was so heavily dosed up with anger and contempt for his situation that he could do no more than babble illogical nonsense to those in the room.

"Drop 'em damn papers – 'at's a' order! Keep away from 'em damn papers, I say!"

"Quiet down, there!" Ben ordered.

Like someone possessed, Harvey glared at Ben and shortly began speaking to him in a less aggressive tone, but his voice was still marked with malice. "You think you c'tell a damn lawman what to do? Who done gone an' give you author'ty?"

Three men were holding Harvey in vise grips while the preacher worked hastily grabbing up the papers. He had raked it all together into a pile, then stacked it into a disorganized mess. Ben had placed himself between Harvey and the preacher, who was still breathing so heavily from the boxing match that everyone was concerned for his well-being. Even Harold had stopped his examination of the body and was looking at the preacher, perhaps wondering if he would soon have another unwanted corpse to deal with.

The preacher rolled up the papers and fell back into a chair against the wall so heavily that it was thought it would go through the wall. Everyone had become so concerned with the preacher's condition that they had forgotten about asking what the battle was all about. Harvey had shut up and his three restrainers had loosened their grips to the point that Harvey was standing freely between them. Harold quickly covered Gene's body with an old quilt and stepped back out onto the porch, away from the situation inside. The preacher allowed the papers to fall to the floor in a single pile and looked up to ensure that Harvey was not able to get to them again. All eyes were on the preacher.

"What's going on here?" one of the men next to Harvey asked. He didn't know who should answer the question, so he had asked it for anyone who would know the answer.

The preacher wiped the heavy perspiration off his face and rested his elbows on his knees with his face in his hands, obviously too exhausted to worry with questions just now. Except for heavy breathing, the room was silent for several tense moments. Harvey was still as red-faced as ever and he began planning his escape. Nearly a minute passed before he bolted away from the men holding him. He slapped open the door, banging it against the wall. *"Let him go – just let him go!"* the preacher shouted when one of the men started out after him.

Harvey jumped off the porch and ran to the street. He stopped there and looked back at the bewildered bystanders in the yard. He flung an obscene gesture to them all, then angrily turned and walked quickly away.

"I am so tired," the preacher could be heard saying. He had spoken it so quietly and with such conviction that Ben at first thought that he might be praying. Hardly anyone had taken the time to look over at the bed at the body during the whole episode. Everyone stood around the preacher waiting for him to speak or to move. Outside, it seemed everyone was trying to find a window or a door to peer through, still wondering what all the new fuss was about.

It wasn't long thereafter that everyone came out of the house single-file and left for homes and businesses. Harold returned to finish his work. Several volunteers, including Ben, stood guard around the house, but Harvey never returned. Later it was learned that he had left town so quickly that most of his belongings were left behind. He was never seen or heard from again in Braxton.

***

The story of the sheriff's death had taken precedence over announcements of the plume of black smoke that had been spotted in the brightening sky out to the west. The blustery breeze had carried the smoke all the way to town, and its haze, along with a flurry of blackened ash, was just beginning to draw enough attention to warrant an investigation. The preacher had failed to tell anyone of the events playing out at Carl's place. He didn't have much to tell. All he knew was the little bit that Paul had told him a couple of hours earlier. He was back out in the yard near his buggy. He carefully folded the papers and stuffed them into the little toolbox under the seat. Abruptly, he turned around and yelled back to the house – *"Ben! Ben – can you come out here?"* In an instant, Ben was there beside him. "We've got a serious problem out at the Kallton farms this morning," the preacher explained. "It's probably too late now, but we really ought to get out there and see what we can do. I think Harold can finish up around here without us."

"What's wrong, preacher?"

"Well, somehow, Wade discovered that Carl Kallton was the one who killed the Buell boys. He – "

Ben reacted as if he had been punched in the chest. "How did he find that out?" he asked.

"I'm not sure. But he took off two or three hours ago to kill him. That's what Paul said. I need to get down there right away and see what I can do."

"Are you okay, preacher?" Ben asked, obviously still alarmed by the old man's apparent fatigue.

"I'm okay," the preacher said, waving his hand as if to brush away the notion. "And you might help me out if you're willing, Ben, if you would round up a few good men with guns and come down and help me."

As a gesture of concern, Ben quickly turned for his car and asked, "Where do you want us to meet?"

"I'm not sure – just come on down to the Kalltons' and we'll figure it all out down there."

The preacher repeated the story to a couple of other men in the yard. He then mounted his buggy rig and turned it around in the yard, forcing the remaining crowd to move out of the way.

"Where's all that dust coming from?" someone yelled across the yard.

The preacher stopped and looked all around. The rain of ashes was heavy enough to cover everything with a thin sheen of gray-black powder, and the breeze was still out of the west. He had sat down heavily on the padded seat causing a puff of dust to rise in the air around his head. The people in the yard were examining the dust on their clothes and on the porch.

"Something's on fire out to the west!" someone said.

"Oh, somebody's burning some brambles," someone else said.

Knowing that burning anything outdoors in this breezy weather wasn't very smart, the preacher feared the worst. He pulled onto the road and turned for Braxton Road and tore away like the wind. Those still standing in the yard and near the street could not ignore the alarm on his face. Gradually, everyone's attention drew away from the deceased in the house and toward whatever was happening in the west.

CHAPTER 33

Earlier, long before daylight, Wade had found himself standing just yards from his son. If it weren't for the light of the fire to make the identity of his target unmistakable, he would have killed his boy. For a moment he stood looking at his son, and then he remembered Carl in the woods. He ran and grabbed Jimmy by the arm and pulled him behind a tree on the far east side of the house. Walter seemed to have decided to stand guard in the front yard beside one of the oak trees. Everything was moving in the breeze, but Carl was long past gone.

"What are you doing here, son?" Wade yelled above the roar of the flames.

"I'm gonna help you, Papa!"

"Do you know what I'm doing, boy?"

"Yeah – you're gonna get Carl!"

Then gunshots rang out. Like firecrackers, they continued, sometimes like tommygun fire. The flames had found Carl's cache of ammunition and it was reacting, it seemed, all at once. Wade, Jimmy and Walter instinctively ducked behind trees farther away from the house.

"Go back home, Jimmy – I'll handle this!" Wade yelled.

"I ain't goin' nowhere – I'm stayin' right behind you all the way!"

Carl could be circling the house setting up for an ambush. There was no time to waste. *"Walter!"* Wade yelled. Walter was easy to find in the trees with the red handkerchief reflecting the fire light brightly. *"Come here – I need you!"* Walter quickly found his way to Wade and looked at him, waiting for him to speak. *"I want you to stay with my boy – keep him out of trouble. Don't let him get too close to anything!"* Then Wade looked at Jimmy and said, *"You stay with this man right here!"* He pointed at Walter with stern emphasis to stress the point. *"You two don't let one another get out of your sight – understand?"*

Walter seemed to take no offense by this stranger's dogged intentions to give him orders. He appeared content enough to follow Wade's directives, and Jimmy appeared to take no offense to having a babysitter along; he showed no noticeable reaction at all. Wade gazed at his son for a moment, then he turned to leave, but just as quickly he turned back to Walter and yelled, *"Do you know where Carl might have gone to?"*

Walter pointed toward the south and said, "I reckon he might head down to his operations down across the road."

Wade spun around and walked quickly southward. All the migrants were milling about at the south end of the back yard. Wade marched directly down the middle of them toward the south driveway. *"Any of you see Carl come through?"* he yelled at them all.

They seemed too shocked and bewildered to answer. Troy was standing among them. Their main concern was the danger of their own barracks catching fire. The fire had grown so hot and intense that it would seem that the buildings could burst ablaze at any moment. Wade noticed some of the men casting furtive glances southward. Then one of them pointed down the driveway as if he was fearful that this mad gunman might shoot someone for refusing to answer the question.

Carl was moving fast; he was already out of sight. Wade moved quickly southward and soon he vanished into the darkness. A migrant, referring to Carl, yelled out, *"You set th' son-of-a-bitch on fire!"* Momentarily, Jimmy, toting the shotgun he had dropped, and Walter came through and marched on hurriedly, keeping a respectable distance between themselves and Wade.

***

The first faint signs of daylight were breaking across the sky, and by the time Wade would find the road, he had hoped he would be able to see well enough to find any sentries blocking his way to the compound. He cursed the wind. It made the woods so noisy that he could imagine Carl behind every tree. The light of the fire could not reach more than a hundred yards down the driveway, so he hoped that Carl would be as blind as he was. Wade was making a lot of noise as he moved. He could feel a thin layer of gravel underfoot and the little stones ground loudly against the cold-hardened earth underneath.

Far ahead, he could hear something moving. He could also hear someone behind him. It sounded like the footsteps of two people and he determined them to be Walter and Jimmy. Wade bent over and scraped up three medium sized rocks and proceeded to throw them at the noise ahead. He stopped momentarily to listen after he threw the last one. Still, the sounds hadn't changed. The sound had mixed with the wind and it was impossible to determine anything. Knowing that Carl might be carrying a gun, Wade was content for the moment that it was dark. By daybreak he figured to get himself into a full defensive position near the compound, then take offensive measures from atop the nearest ridge or from behind a stand of trees.

The driveway seemed shorter than he had remembered from the first time he used it over a year ago. He found the road and stopped. He patted his near-frozen ears and warmed his raw hands. Roy lived nearly a mile to the west. Wade entertained the thought of waking him up and taking him at gunpoint to the compound in order to find the fastest and safest entry to the center of the compound. The narrow road leading to the compound was a hundred yards to the east. He listened, but determined that no one was walking in the gravel of the road.

Shortly, Walter and Jimmy marched up behind Wade and stopped. They stood silently a few yards away. Wade turned and looked. In the faint morning light, he could see them standing only a foot apart from one another. Jimmy was on the right, tall and slim. Walter was built similarly to Wade and stood an inch or two shorter than Jimmy. He had buttoned his coat to his chin concealing the red handkerchief. Wade knew they could see him. They were all sitting ducks for anyone with a straight shooting gun and good night eyes. The sound of a twig being snapped underfoot could be heard coming from the direction of the narrow road leading to the compound. Wade turned eastward and moved quickly to close the gap. He was glad to hear no footsteps behind him for the moment. Walter was making Jimmy lag behind and Wade made great haste to widen the gap.

Before he turned onto the narrow road, he looked high over his shoulder to the northeast, toward Braxton. He was amazed at the intensity of the fire as evidenced by the glowing ashes that were flying high into the sky and floating toward the town. Someone would see it and round up an army to fight it, but it would be too late.

Wade gazed down the narrow road and he could detect no movement. Carl could be anywhere now, and it would be to Wade's detriment to carry on without positively knowing Carl's whereabouts. The little road curved slightly leftward just ahead and straightened out as it topped a hill a hundred yards away. Wade crouched low to the ground and sprinted to the curve in the road. He stopped and listened. He could hear movement somewhere ahead but he couldn't judge how far away it was. He stood up and set his eyes to the middle of the road ahead. He lifted the big rifle up to his shoulder and aimed it at the top of the hill. The sky behind the trees was now bright enough to illuminate the clouds with a dim blue-gray cast and anything that stood against them would be sharply silhouetted. But there were too many tall trees peeking over the hill that would help block Carl's silhouette if he was there. Occasionally, Wade could hear a noise up ahead that sounded human enough to dispel any doubts. They were the sounds of gravel and twigs underfoot, not the sounds of the wind in the woods.

Hoping to get a better view of any silhouettes on the hilltop, Wade again crouched low to the ground. Up ahead, Wade was sure he could see a nondescript shape moving on the road. He took careful aim and began squeezing the trigger. It seemed for the moment that the figure had stopped moving. Perhaps Carl was waiting for him to get a little closer for an ambush. Then just as quickly, the figure began to move again. He could hear a voice in the distance, near the figure. Wade determined that Carl had contacted a sentry, now making his mission twice as dangerous. Possibly the sentry was hiding in the woods, taking instructions from Carl. But the woods were too noisy to be sure. The figure had moved to the edge of the road and stopped, or so it seemed. Wade had followed the figure with the sights of the rifle and when it paused Wade held his breath and fired.

The boom reverberated throughout the woods, it seemed, for a whole minute. Wade stepped back and returned to the bend in the road. Walter and Jimmy were standing at the edge halfway between the bend and the main road. He tried to listen for any noise near the figure. But everything was quickly drowned out by the sound of an approaching vehicle on the main road. The lights of the vehicle illuminated the background so brightly that Wade suddenly felt as exposed as a varmint in a freshly plowed field at midday. Expecting gunfire to shower him at any moment, he raced back to Walter and Jimmy and ordered them to drop to the ground. The car slowed, then came to a stop several yards from the narrow road. Somebody was searching for the house fire. Momentarily, the car sped up and headed for the driveway to Carl's house.

"You boys are getting too close!" Wade spat at Walter and Jimmy. "I want you both to stay back!"

Again, the sound of another vehicle was coming from the east. This one was rolling fast and it shot past the narrow road as if it were in a race. It, too, slowed down, then it could be heard moving up the driveway with its engine revving high.

Wade, Walter, and Jimmy had found a small knoll alongside the narrow road and they sat themselves upon it. Quietly, they gazed down the narrow road searching for any movement. Carl was going to get away. The thought of this likely probability made Wade feel a sense of failure and shame. He was ashamed that he had moved so impulsively. He could have waited until daybreak like he did in July and then kill Carl. The first time he shot Carl was with a smaller caliber 30-30. He was packing his 45-75 now and he could cut him in half with a single shot. But he feared now he may have lost his chance.

He listened hard for any sounds from the narrow road. If he had hit his target, he expected to hear something. The voices he thought he had heard earlier were silent. The daylight was now bright enough to enable him to see all shapes and movements clearly, all the way to the top of the hill. The movements were the trees and vines swaying in the breeze. He looked near the top of the hill where he had shot. He couldn't see anything resembling a body. He glanced at his son, then back at the hill. Walter was sitting on the other side of Jimmy. There was nothing else to say. They waited on the knoll without speaking a word, waiting for the light to increase. As it had developed to this point, improved visibility would have given Carl the advantage. It would still be too difficult to find him hiding in the woods or track him to the compound. But anyone moving along the road would be easy pickings for someone with a sharp eye. Wade would have to wait until daylight to make his move, and by then it would probably be too late.

Wade could hear a car approaching from the west. Then another one from the east. Both were heading for the fire. Wade stood up and gazed into the trees on both sides of the narrow road. He searched the woods for several minutes. Jimmy's nose had begun to run and he was working to wipe it on his coat sleeves. Walter wore a thick layer of clothes and a heavy coat. He wasn't moving a muscle. Wade made a fierce motion with his hand as if to emphasize his orders for them to stay put and not move.

It then took Wade ten minutes to return to the spot where he had fired the shot. With a scan of the woods, he looked for anything that would appear unnatural or out of place. He proceeded to the spot where he had guessed his target had been. He squatted to the ground and looked all around. He moved up several feet and tried again. He could see the dark shapes of rocks, twigs and leaves everywhere, but colors were still mottled and gray.

Suddenly, he felt something gooey as if a liquid substance was half-frozen on the ground. He shoved his finger into a broad darkened area and raised it to his nose. It had a fresh bloody scent. It was unmistakable. He had smelled it hundreds of times when he cleaned hogs or large game animals. He guessed that human blood smelled similarly enough.

He followed the large gooey spots to the edge of the tree line. His injured target had escaped to the woods and might possibly be lying dead, or still alive, somewhere out there. He had wished that things were illuminated enough for him to make a visual inspection of the blood. He had determined, though, that he had indeed wounded his enemy. He saw only one figure on the road and he hoped the sentries, if there were any, were keeping themselves hidden in the trees. He had also calculated that if he had hit a sentry he would have yelled out. Carl would not have, knowing he would have given away the fact of his injuries.

Wade aimed his rifle into the trees. He remembered that he had forgotten to rechamber a new round, so he slowly and easily cranked the lever down and forward, then back to lock-and-fire position. The action was smooth and almost noiseless, except for the ejecting of the spent casing. He raised up to a half-standing position and scanned the woods. It was full of vines and undergrowth. He looked for a pathway that Carl may have plowed through the foliage. But deer paths and breaks were everywhere. Carl could easily get himself lost in any one of them. In another thirty minutes, Wade knew that he could see well enough to track his quarry. But he was becoming more and more wary about the possibility of sentries around the compound. Perhaps, he imagined, they had evacuated the area instead of coming for him when they heard the gunshot. Or they may be moving toward him like a war platoon, or waiting in ambush over the next hill or two. He was in a bad defensive position and he had little time to waste.

Wade took a long careful step and placed himself beside a tall limbless pine along the edge. He squatted down and felt for blood. He took another step and found the opening to a deer run low in the bushes. He peered inside it, but saw blackness. As quietly as he could, he moved around a stand of blackberries and scanned again. Then he moved away from the blackberries but the bushes stuck like glue. He reached down to pull them away. His hand grasped onto a soggy string of decayed leaves that seemed to be caked with something akin to a thick layer of molasses. Again, he sniffed the substance. He could see before him a broad area of splattered darkness as if a gallon of blood had been slung amongst the foliage. Just ahead, he saw a large unmoving shape that lay prostrate alongside a fallen tree. He could see brown and gray shades with a large crimson area covering half of the body. Fearful of an ambush, he raised the rifle to his shoulder and took careful aim. He heard a snapping twig many yards away. He moved closer to the body being careful of his step. The shape of the body was a natural shape, but it was not that of a man. Or it may be a man. Another couple of yards and he would be sure.

Wade quickly scanned the woods around him again. If he had killed Carl he needed to verify the fact and get out. He thought he was looking at a heavy overcoat with a big bloodstain on it. Too many vines and branches hung between him and the body. He parted the weeds and poked the coat with his foot. It was resilient and life-like. The tree trunk blocked the light and obscured the upper half of the body. He reached down and touched it and it was wet and warm. Again, it was blood. Impatiently, he grabbed the coat near the tree trunk and pulled. He reached higher up and found a long furry neck and a tufted ear. It was a dead deer and it had lost its bowels from a strategically placed shot in the abdomen as evidenced by the deep puddles of viscera on the ground and the coagulation of blood on the weeds and on Wade's boots.

He bounced back to the road and turned southward toward the compound. He had no idea how far it was. Up ahead, the woods were thick with overgrowth; perfect for ambush cover. But Wade had come to the determination that Carl was likely more concerned with obtaining first aid for his probable burns and the frostbite from his water-soaked clothes than waiting in freezing weather for him.

Wade made it to the top of the hill and gazed all around. The narrow road kept a straight line all the way to the next ridge two hundred yards away. The sun was brightening the hollow beneath him to the point that colors were waking up and all shapes were easily deciphered. Before leaving the top of the ridge, Wade cast one last look back at Walter and Jimmy. They were standing and looking at him, but had not moved from the knoll.

***

"What's your name, son?"

Jimmy seemed to not hear the question. He was staring off at the top of the ridge where his father had disappeared over the other side. The vapor from his breathing was heavy and his sniffle was still giving him trouble.

"What's your name?" Walter asked again. His head was turned toward Jimmy, seemingly earnest for an answer to his question. Jimmy turned to him and answered. He still didn't seem to resent the fact that Walter was playing babysitter. He had pulled Jimmy back and slowed him down twice when he was following his father down the driveway. He was genuinely interested in Jimmy's well-being, even to the detriment of his own, it would seem.

Strangely, Jimmy felt safe in Walter's company. Walter had asked him for his name, then said nothing more. Jimmy had not forgotten his own impatience. He was hoping to follow his father soon. Thirty minutes had passed since Wade had fired the gun. It was nearly daylight now and two of the cars that had gone to Carl's house had returned to the main road, and it seemed that they were stopped somewhere near the entrance to the narrow road. Walter and Jimmy were out of their sight. Soon, it sounded as if another car and a wagon rig or two had joined them and someone was talking on the road.

"Is Papa going to get hurt?" Jimmy asked.

Walter looked at Jimmy and saw that his eyes appeared to be tearing up. He could hear the voices on the road and Jimmy couldn't be sure who they were. For several minutes he had listened and determined that some of them sounded belligerent, angry, or excited. Some of the migrants had probably found their way to the narrow road with the others. Perhaps the barracks had caught fire and they were looking for Wade.

"I sho' hope not, Jimmy," Walter said. "Do you know what your papa's a-doin'?"

Jimmy didn't want to talk any more. He wanted to go. He said, "Carl Kallton killed two boys up on the North Road over a year ago. And he hurt my sister." After a short pause, he added, "I hafta go now."

"Jimmy, shouldn't we waits fah some help from th' road?"

"No – I want to go now!" Jimmy said with sudden earnestness.

It was clear that he didn't want to wait for someone to come and stop him. He jerked himself away and started down the road. Walter listened for a moment to the voices on the main road, then he started following Jimmy. Jimmy looked back. He saw Walter following and seeing that he was not going to try to stop him, he slowed down to allow Walter to catch up.

***

Four cars and two wagons had found the narrow road. Tom was the first to find the burning house. He helped to douse the fire that had started on the roof of the white barracks, then he inspected the main house. Only the stone chimneys and some structural wood timbers of the exterior walls were still standing. Everything was still exhausting heavy smoke and the remaining structures were holding up streaks of glowing red, but the heat had lessened greatly. Roofing tile and wall plaster had collapsed into thick-bloated, blackened mounds in and around the foundations. The three red oak trees in the front yard were scorched and blackened on the south sides, leaving charred limbs reaching outward as if they had once begged for water before succumbing. The excited migrants had given Tom the whole story. Paul had arrived next. He had made a stop at his house and he was now fully dressed for the winter chill. He didn't say much to Tom but he was bewildered by his long-ago friend's presence. "Did you see the fire from your house? Is that why you're here?" he asked Tom curtly.

"No, Ruth came to the house. And both Esther and Kelly Jean was with her. They told us everything," Tom answered.

"How'd they get to your house?" Paul asked, genuinely surprised by Tom's words. He had not taken the time to stop by Wade's house. He assumed that the women had remained there.

"They came through the woods. That's what they told us."

Paul appeared to glare at Tom for a moment. Then he quickly decided that negative attitudes should be held in check until this was all over. "Where's Wade?" he asked. "Did he do

211

this?"

"Yeah – he did, Paul. But the men here say that he took off chasing Carl down the road south of here. After he burned Carl out of the house, he took off chasing him down the driveway. They figure Carl's trying to get to one of his operations down south of the timberlands. One man told me Carl was burned pretty bad."

Paul saw that Tom was holding a shotgun to his side. He was here to help. It made Paul feel better about things, in spite of his brother's apparent loss of reason and subsequent lawlessness. "Gene should be here soon. If Brother Silas can find him," Paul said.

"Paul, do you know that Jimmy was here, too?"

Paul shuddered with exaggeration. "What – Jimmy? Jimmy's with Wade?"

"I'm not sure how it happened, but nobody saw the boy until after the house was nearly burned down. So, I suspect, at the start of all this, that he might have followed Wade here without his knowledge."

"Where is he now?"

"I don't know. With Wade, I reckon. They tell me here that one of the Negroes went with Jimmy and followed a ways behind Wade."

Another vehicle was coming up the driveway toward the burning house. The driver stopped the truck near the wellhouse. The migrants were still throwing water onto the barracks roofs and were filling extra buckets and jugs from the well and building a reserve water supply. They were still as bewildered as they were when Wade made his initial attack, but had remained orderly and kept to themselves. The truck driver and a young male passenger stepped out. It was a church deacon with his oldest son. He saw Paul and yelled, *I seen the smoke and thought it was your house or Wade's house – is everybody okay?"*

"No, Graham – everybody's not okay," Paul answered. Then he got into his car, spun it around and drove away, leaving Tom to explain.

"This is all Wade's work," Tom said. "We all need to get together and figure out a way to stop him before he gets himself killed. I understand he's chasing Carl down through the trees south of the road here."

Graham, with his son, looked as confused as the migrants, but he was a fast study. He quickly concluded that someone had had enough. Tom had mentioned Wade's name, and putting two and two together, Graham determined that Carl Kallton's day of judgment was nigh. But he didn't need the details now; he could get those later. Wade, wherever he was, needed his help.

***

"Where's Jimmy, Paul? Where's Jimmy?" Esther was barking, bordering on hysteria again.

The fourth car belonged to Lucas. He had pulled up alongside the vehicles of Tom, Paul and Graham near the entrance to the narrow road. The main road had become blocked with vehicles parked in haphazard fashion. Esther, Ruth and Kelly Jean were with Lucas. Esther had ordered Kelly Jean to remain behind with Sandra or Annie, or to stay put at Paul's house with Mrs. Sarah and the boys. But Kelly Jean wouldn't stand for it. She had refused to get out of the car at any other place.

"He's out there with Wade. We're trying to find them right now," Paul said nervously.

"Trying to find them? *What do you mean?*"

Paul tried to push her back to the car and sit her in it. Ruth was holding her from behind. Kelly Jean, clear-eyed and calm, was in the back seat watching.

"We're going to find them right now! We don't have time for this, Esther!" Paul barked. Then he stepped away to begin preparations for his next move.

Graham had removed a large gun from the seat of his truck and was in the process of loading it. Lucas, standing near the entrance to the narrow road and gazing into the trees, had a short-barreled deer rifle that was already fully loaded. The sight of all the firearms and the preparations for war were more than Esther could manage. She spiraled back down into hysteria again almost as badly as she had done at the house hours earlier.

"Ruth, put her in the car and get her settled down!" Paul ordered. His face was flustered and angry. If he was any closer, he might have slapped her back to her senses. Ruth pulled Esther too hard toward the car. Esther tripped over and hit the gravel, almost taking Ruth with her. Kelly Jean dropped to her mother and bear-hugged her. Ruth braced herself against the car fender and held Esther's coat collar as if trying to keep her from running off into the trees searching for Jimmy. Esther managed to tear away from Ruth but she stayed put, holding her daughter and keeping her eyes to the trees southward. Graham's son, Joseph, too young for such responsibility, was instructed to stay near and watch over the women.

"Where's Gene, Paul?" Ruth yelled.

"The preacher's gone to get him."

The three men stood at the head of the narrow road and looked southward. No one had the slightest idea of exactly what was going on. They could only guess. Tom and Lucas were talking as if there had never been even the suggestion of a rift between them. Plans were made, then rejected one by one. Should they, three abreast, hike down the road together? Or should they split up and fan out in case one or two of them were stopped and the other one could continue? Should someone stay behind with the women? Should the ladies be driven to a safe place? Was there really time for all of that? And once they found their destination in the woods, whatever that might be, how were they to know who was friend or who was foe if they should encounter someone? What if they were shot at before they found Wade? Should they fire back, or retreat? Should they drive a car down the road?

Before they could decide on any answers, a horse and buggy followed by a big double-mule wagon rig raced toward them from the east. The preacher was in front in the buggy. He dismounted and ran to the men at the road. He appeared alert and sound, not exhausted and defeated like he had less than an hour earlier at the sheriff's house. The driver of the mule rig was J.C. Jourdan, the local farm and building supply merchant and a deacon at the preacher's church.

"Where's Gene, preacher?" Tom asked.

Without answering, the preacher turned back and stepped over to Esther and hugged her. She had stood herself up and now appeared reasonably in charge of her senses. The preacher didn't say anything to her. In a few moments, he turned back to the men. "He can't come right now," he answered without explanation. "I'll be taking charge here. Now what's going on?"

"Wade and Jimmy have gone after Carl down south here," Tom said, pointing down the narrow road. "They tell me that Wade burned Carl's house down and flushed him out. Carl must have got out and Wade's hunting him down right now."

"Anybody try to stop him?"

"Nobody's seen him – we don't know."

"Did I hear you right – you said Jimmy's with him?"

"Yeah, that's right. We don't know how it all happened, but I understand Jimmy is following Wade at a distance. Some black fellow is with him."

"With who?"

"The black fellow's with Jimmy."

Paul had had enough. He turned and headed down the little road. He didn't look back.

"J.C., you with us?" Graham asked.

"You can count on it."

J.C. had a long gun hanging to his side. It appeared to be an over-sized deer rifle, like Wade's. He didn't smile when he answered. He was serious and upset; like the preacher, he had kept the secret of the sheriff's suicide to himself. All the pieces to the puzzle were coming together. Yet, he had protected Carl over the months with his silence and his acquiescence to the big man's economic power. Because of the generous loads of ready cash Carl had dispensed at J.C.'s business, J.C. had kept all suspicions about Carl and his dubious enterprises safely to himself, and he now felt heavy with guilt. The money had been good and blood was on his hands. J.C. remounted his wagon and yanked the mules' reins around. In a few seconds, he had the rig aimed down the narrow road and each man loaded himself onto the rear with the preacher placing himself up on the seat beside J.C.

"Ruth!" the preacher yelled as the rig started down the road, *"If Ben and his men come this way, tell them we've gone south and to find us if he can."*

***

Wade had to slow down and use his eyes and ears to scan every square inch of woodland and to study every sound. The woods on both sides of the road had thickened like wheat, and in some places it was difficult to see farther than a few yards into the trees. Moving along quietly down the slope of a hill, he wondered what had happened to the sentry that he thought he had heard Carl talking to a hundred yards back. Perhaps there had been no sentry after all, but the noise of the winds playing with his ears. He turned and looked back from where he had come. He found a high wood-framed perch in a tree that could have been a sentry post, but he could hardly imagine such a bare outpost being used in this cold weather. From there it would have been an easy shot to make. He had no idea how much farther that he would have to go to find the compound. It couldn't be far, though. When he and Paul were captured, they had not ventured far into the woods when they were stopped.

Wade had scanned the road before him looking for tripwires. One had to be somewhere near. Again, he could hear footsteps or movements behind him. Walter and Jimmy were getting too close again. Some loud voices could be heard far back on the main road. Wade must speed up. He felt pushed.

He made it to the top of the next ridge and stopped. Down below, a long, wood-timbered bridge spanned a wide creek. It was narrow, but built to handle heavier loads than the road would suggest. He could see a broad clearing off toward the southwest where a logging operation had been constructed. That must be where Carl is employing the winter migrants he found back at the burning house, he thought. Back toward the southeast, the woods were thick as usual except that a peculiar square notch seemed to be shaped among the trees about three hundred yards away. That must be where Carl's biggest operations are taking place, he decided.

Wade searched for unusual colors and shapes along the ground and in the treetops. There were few evergreens in the area, so it was getting easier to watch for evidence of human trappings amongst the winter-bare hardwoods. Again, the sounds behind him pushed him on. A squirrel dashed across a clearing to his left and Wade swung around, ready to fire. He took the diversion to move swiftly to the bridge, and as he approached it a number of confusing attachments to the bridge were becoming evident. All the boards had been laid perpendicular to the direction of travel from one end of the bridge to the other; no long planks had been laid lengthwise that would have made vehicle traffic quieter and smoother. There was a space of an inch between each board and, the strangest of all, no nail heads were evident. Everything was attached, or hinged, from below. As Wade stepped onto the first board he watched carefully. The boards worked like piano keys, except they were hinged alternately on one side of the bridge or the other. No matter how slowly or lightly he stepped, practically every board sank an inch under his weight and created a loud popping noise underneath that he was sure could be heard for long distances through the woods. It was an ingenious project that was intended to alert sentries in the night hours.

Realizing the futility of his efforts, Wade made several long strides and jumped to the other side where he accidentally found the wire. It was maddening. Anyone else attempting to cross the bridge would have reacted similarly. Wade had crossed using the longest stride he could manage, forcing him to move quickly. Not thinking to slow down at the other end, the wire would be tripped as it had been now.

How did Carl get across so quietly? he thought. He stood beside the tripwire and looked at the bridge. A dirt path led off to the side and turned down to the creek below. A tiny, but stoutly built, footbridge crossed the creek far beneath the main bridge, then the path continued up the other side. The little bridge was nearly invisible in the shadow of the upper bridge and was further obscured by vines and foliage. Carl had gained a lot of time on Wade and now, because of the noise and the wire, he could easily determine how far Wade was behind him.

Wade saw some movement back toward the north. He looked up at the top and he saw two figures there. He could see Walter's black coat and coffee-colored face. His tall son walked next to him. Wade bent over to the wire hoping to break it. It was a very thin and taut piano-type wire. Only a wire cutter or a gun blast could cut it. With no tools, he turned and started up the next ridge.

Again, as before, a flash of sanity teased his mind and he was thinking of death. The image of Billy's dirty hands grabbing at his daughter and Carl's hitting her burned in his mind even as he thought of his own demise. In his heart he didn't want to kill Carl with a well-placed shot to the temple or heart. He wished he could maim him, then take his time about demonstrating his rage against him. Billy was gone – vanished – as everyone knew. So Wade would double his rage against Carl. But he was going to have to live long enough to get a chance to do it.

Like a hungry wolf searching the ground and underbrush for prey, Wade alternately scanned both sides of the road and deep into the woods. High up into the trees, he searched.

Sometimes he could see steps nailed to the trunks of trees or planks high up in the limbs for seats. Some of them were old and rotted; old deer stands. Small meadows were ringed with honeysuckle and laurel thickets; perfect for hideouts, or ambush points.

Then Wade got lucky. He was looking into a clearing far off to his left deep into the trees. He, for only an instant, saw a crouched figure moving quickly to his far flank, toward the bridge. Wade dropped to his knees but, realizing his vulnerability, he stepped off the road and into a deer run beneath a canopy of cedar boughs. Walter and Jimmy were crossing the bridge; it was making a racket much louder than he thought possible from this distance. He moved through the deer run at a sprint. He kept his eyes open without blinking. His eyes watered. With the rifle raised and ready, he wondered if he was really wasting his time on a decoy or an errant migrant hunting squirrels. Then he thought of Walter and Jimmy. They were moving closer and would soon be in possible danger.

Back on the road, Wade ran back to the last ridge and found Walter and Jimmy moving up toward him. When they saw him, they stopped. Within seconds, Wade was standing ten feet away. "I want you both to get back to the other side of that bridge and stay there – now!" he ordered.

Without a word, they obeyed. Wade returned to the top of the ridge. It was like starting over. But this time he moved into the trees to his right and made quick time toward the south, watching for sentries all the way, particularly the one he had spied earlier. He made it to the broad clearing where the milling operation had been, then he made a confident run all the way across to the other side where the road intersected the main logging road coming out of the mill. The bluster of the wind was still evident but it was not as bad as it had been at daybreak. Now he could hear sounds that indicated danger ahead. Back to the north he could hear a wagon crossing the bridge. It sounded like firecrackers and a mule neighed as loudly as a child's scream. He turned and continued all the way to the southern edge of the mill operation and placed himself parallel to the notched area where he figured Carl's compound to be. He stepped carefully to the edge of the road and scanned everything. Looking for an entry or path leading to the compound, he found none. He stayed within the shallow ditch alongside the road and trotted southward. Wade topped the next hill and again looked all around. It made no sense. No roads or paths intersected the road that might lead to the compound. He was wondering if he might have made a dead run, and thus lose Carl forever. Carl could have run this road all the way to the end, wherever it might lead. But Carl was in pain, soaking wet and probably frostbitten. Wade was numb in his extremities, so he couldn't imagine himself running this far, burned and soaked to the skin as Carl was, without being concerned for his physical survival. Carl had to stop somewhere.

Taking a gamble, Wade edged to the bottom of the next hollow and crossed the road. Thin evergreens were mixed with second-generation hardwoods. The tree trunks were closely planted but the undergrowth was easier to navigate. He moved into the woods, remembering from childhood that limestone rocks and fifty-foot cliffs were just ahead. He found a deer run that took him straight to the edge of the first bluff. He crouched down and gazed below the canopy of the tall timbers down into the hollow below. From here he could see the square shapes of rooftops about a hundred-fifty yards to the east. Far to the southeast he could see the yellow-gray ribbon of a road. This was an excellent vantage point. He could easily see anyone moving among the trees for a hundred yards around. The deer path continued on along the edge of the bluff to the south.

Wade looked back behind him. Again, he was lucky. He could see the top of a sapling swaying forcefully as if a man-sized moving object had brushed it aside. Wade crouched to the ground as low as he could and watched. He didn't feel safe, though, and he eased along the path toward the direction he believed the man to be moving. Southward he moved, along the edge of the cliff. Then he could hear someone walking on leaves. Out of the trees a man's shape materialized. Wade could see him from the rear. The man was holding a long gun across his chest as if ready to swing and fire. He seemed to be keeping an ear directed toward the noise of the bridge. He appeared to be a migrant worker sporting a long beard and wearing a calf-length overcoat.

Wade leaned over and hid himself behind a bush and watched. The man stepped quietly to the edge of the cliff about thirty yards south of Wade. He gazed all around, then in a moment he turned north and walked along the edge toward Wade. He kept his eyes gazing down into the hollow as if expecting to catch someone sneaking into the compound. The man paced directly past Wade. The noise of the breeze had successfully masked his efforts to hide and the guard moved on by and walked until he was nearly out of sight. Wade watched the sentry as he entered a stand of undergrowth. Then he stopped and turned his ear toward the road. The sound of the mules and wagon could be heard. The sentry turned and headed toward the road. Wade was able to use the diversion as an opportunity to make haste and run down the trail to the south.

The trail along the edge of the cliff turned down the hill and ran perpendicular into a broad road that ran from the narrow road through a long stand of trees into the compound. Wade stood on the side of the broad road and looked back toward the west. It intersected the narrow road, and the narrow road widened at the intersection and continued south, perhaps a new logging road for Carl's expanding pulpwood operations, or simply another route for moving illicit product out of the compound. A tall storage building-like structure stood at the east end of the road. Rectangular shapes stood on the other side. The water wheel of a gristmill was visible in the trees far off to the south.

It was winter. Distillery operations were down. The compound was quiet. The wide ruts of heavy truck tires creased the road and, just ahead, a wide graveled area lay stretched out near the tall building. It seemed that it had been too easy up to this point. Perhaps it was just timing. Perhaps Carl's sentry had not been a sentry at all, but a logging worker from the compound that had been alerted by the gunshots or the fire, or the noises of the bridge. Perhaps there was no one else at the compound to stop him, except Carl.

The woods seemed to have been cleared of all undergrowth for fifty feet around most of the compound. It would be tough to make that final dash to find Carl in the wide-open of this perimeter. But returning to scout the trees ahead, Wade moved forward. He looked up at the buildings and saw a plume of smoke drifting along the rooftops. Someone was warming himself at a fire inside one of the buildings.

The noise of the mules and wagon moved down the narrow road and in a few moments Wade could hear the rig stop at the intersection with the broad road. He could hear faint voices, and looking back he could see a mule's head with a plume of warm vapor boiling from its nostrils. The rest of the rig was hidden behind trees. It seemed that someone was trying to decide whether to turn or to go forward. Wade moved back to the middle of the road and began walking toward the compound. Someone from the wagon called his name.

"Wade – hold up! "

Wade turned and looked back. J.C. and the preacher were on the seat of the rig. The other men were standing up behind them as if scouting the woods as they moved along. Wade waited as they pulled up.

"Wade," the preacher said. Then he paused to study Wade's face. Something in Wade's eyes told the preacher he had better speed things up. "We know what you're doing. We don't want to stop you. We want you to let us help you apprehend Carl Kallton and bring him in." Again the preacher studied Wade closely, restraining himself from saying any more. Wade, as usual, gave no clue concerning his approval of the preacher's ideas by any change of expression.

The men had first found the torched house and the terrified migrants, and then they found the blood and the spent casing on the road and the dead deer in the trees. They had easily concluded that Wade had full intentions to take Carl with deadly force as immediately as possible. They wore somber expressions and each of them was greatly fearful concerning Wade's mental state. It was obvious that Wade was bursting with impatience to finish his mission quickly. He turned back toward the compound as if he were about to walk away. Still, there was no evidence of anyone stirring outside. The sentry was still out there, probably watching. Wade looked back at the men on the wagon. No one was moving a muscle and every eye was on him.

"Did you see that man with a gun?" Wade asked. It was evident by their expressions that they did not, so he asked, "Did you see Jimmy back at the bridge?"

"Yeah," Paul said. "He said you told him to stay there."

Wade turned again and began walking toward the compound. There was no time to organize a posse now. It was simply too inconvenient and dangerous to be standing around wasting time with fruitless discussions. So, with an angry flourish of the hand, Wade turned back and said in a fast, staccato drill, "All right, preacher; you, Tom, Lucas, Graham, and J.C. come on along with me. Paul, I want you to go back and stay with Jimmy and Walter. Tell Jimmy I said to go back home. I'll be home soon. They need to know about that man in the woods that might make trouble if he finds them, if he doesn't find us first."

Everyone seemed of a cooperative frame of mind. Wade showed no disinclination to refuse any help from Tom or Lucas. He seemed to take their presence as willingness to work as partners in the mission at hand; all past issues between them stored away in a mental safe-box until this day's battle was over. Paul dismounted and immediately started walking back to the bridge. "Paul, be careful. That man might see you alone and start trouble," Wade said.

Paul nodded and continued on. Wade turned and started again for the compound. After a few steps, he stopped. He gazed at the ground with the posture of a man burdened with a sudden leadership position he desperately wished to refuse. He spoke in a voice burdened with grave expectations. "Boys, I have no plan but to take Carl, dead or alive. I know you all want him alive. I can't promise that. He might not go so peacefully."

Tom stepped to the front of the group and offered his hand. "Tell us what you want, Wade. I can't speak for anyone else here, but I'll do anything you need me to do."

Wade, as usual, showed no change of expression. He grasped Tom's hand for only an instant, then he pointed into the trees. "We need to circle these buildings. Then we can move in and wait for Carl to come out. Tom, you and Luke get up in the trees along the north there. I thought I heard someone talking a while ago up there, so there might be more than one man watching us.

"Graham, you and J.C. get on into the trees along the south side and find a good place to watch and wait." Taking into account the preacher's age and position, Wade said, "Preacher, I wish you would just wait back here and watch our backsides. I'm going to make a run down the middle here and see what I can find."

Obediently, they moved to their stations. Wade hadn't asked, or didn't think to ask, about the sheriff's whereabouts. Everyone knew that he wouldn't wait for him anyway. No one liked what he saw in Wade's demeanor. It was clear that he had no patience for stalling tactics or trite attitudes. It was disturbing to see that Wade had every intention of carrying out this mission alone. The odds were probably no better than fifty-fifty that he would survive alone. He knew that one or two of Carl's confederates had entered the woods, and he operated as if they were only minor stumbling blocks; not serious risks to his life. At first, Wade didn't seem to notice that his compatriots had moved only a few yards away from him into the trees. They were more intent on guarding him, or perhaps working to find ways of stopping him, than concerning themselves with a single-minded mission to apprehend a criminal.

Then faint voices could be heard coming from the narrow road. They sounded angry, but Wade was deaf to them. The edge of the compound was only yards away. A narrow passage, only wide enough for a single freight truck, ran between the tall building and a barracks-like structure. A wide, flat yard of bare earth and patches of gravel spread out in a sixty-foot diameter circle beyond the buildings. More structures stood beyond the yard.

Wade glanced to both sides of the road. The four men had ignored his instructions and were staying too close. Furiously, Wade waved them away to opposite sides of the compound. Slowly, they moved north and south. Wade approached the side of the tall building and took a position alongside and raised his rifle to chest level. Again, he looked to the sides. Everyone was beginning to take his instructions to heart and surround the compound. They were doing very well at keeping their steps light and the noise level low.

Looking all around, Wade could count several buildings constructed around the yard. Some of them appeared to be attached to others with breezeways or closed-in hallways. The ones to his right, especially two long, low-built structures, matched the barracks-style buildings at the main house. The tall building where he was standing had three open ports where trucks and wagons were probably parked or repaired. A heavy freight wagon stood alone in the middle port. A second story above the ports had several small, closed-up windows spaced five feet apart. Out beyond this central complex is where it was figured that the distillery was located. A narrow driveway between two buildings on the far side probably led to it. From here he could see a low-structured building that had a very wide, low-pitched roof that seemed to spread from one end of the hollow to the other. Across the yard, Wade watched smoke drift from the chimney of a stoutly built building that he tagged as the office. Carl was probably inside repairing himself from the torments of third degree burns, exposure and frostbite.

Wade looked back behind him. All was clear for the moment between himself and the road. The mules had been tethered to a tree limb. It wasn't good that they had been left there, but there was nothing to do. The preacher, unarmed, was standing out of sight somewhere off the edge of the road. Someone, Wade knew, had seen, or heard, the men coming in. He was bothered by the danger they had placed themselves in. He jerked his head back around and dropped the thought. Regrets would come later.

CHAPTER 34

Ben had arrived at the bridge. He was alone. Walter and Jimmy were standing like wooden Indians trying to observe any activity occurring up among the trees far above the bridge. Soon, they could see Paul returning on foot down the hill.

"Where is everybody?" Ben asked. He was dressed up like an Eskimo and was carrying a double-barrel shotgun like Jimmy's.

"They done gone down to find Papa," Jimmy answered.

Ben looked at Walter and asked, "You from around here?"

"No, suh – I wuks fah Mr. Carl Kallton," Walter answered.

"You know where Carl is?"

Walter pointed up the hill and answered, "I reckon Jimmy's papa done run him up over th' hill there."

"What's your name?"

"My name's Walta, suh."

"Walter, you know what this is all about?" Ben asked.

"I reckon I do a mite, suh. I know Jimmy's papa says Carl Kallton done some bad things."

"Jimmy," Ben said, "Your mama wants you to come back to the road."

Jimmy glanced at Ben, but otherwise ignored his statement. He turned to watch Paul quickly march to finish the descent from the hill and then to begin his approach to the bridge. Paul continually glanced into the trees to his right. He was a hundred feet away when a lone figure materialized out of the trees and moved toward Paul. He glanced over at the man but continued walking as if trying to get away. Ben, Jimmy and Walter watched Paul approach the bridge at a fast clip and the man, carrying a long gun, stepped to the middle of the road and raised the gun, aiming it at Paul's back.

"Halt! I tolt yew t' stop!" the man screeched. Paul glanced back around and slowed down. He had his own gun but didn't seem willing to start flashing it around. *"Stop! Or I'll shoot yew in th' ass with a load o' buckshot!"* the man ordered.

"Oh, my God!" Ben said excitedly. "Who is that, Walter?"

"I reckon it's one of 'em logmen that wuks down yonder in th' swamps."

Paul stopped several yards short of the far end of the bridge. He turned halfway around and looked at the gunman and froze. The gunman walked down the hill several yards toward Paul and it seemed that he was aiming the gun directly at Paul's face. Ben, Walter and Jimmy were standing in clear view of the gunman. Ben was sure the man could see them.

"Walter, you and Jimmy ease on up a little. Jimmy, let him see your shotgun," Ben said. Then he walked on ahead of Jimmy and displayed his own firearm. The gunman seemed to be nervous. Unfortunately, as Ben moved to the end of the bridge, someone else was moving in the trees. Ben was showing signs of distress and began muttering under his breath. He watched Paul's captor step closer to Paul and hold the muzzle of the gun, it seemed, just inches from Paul's nose. To Ben, the man seemed a bit deranged, making him completely unpredictable. Ben looked back at Walter and Jimmy. He was having a hard time deciding what move to make next. The unbalanced man with the gun looked across the bridge and studied Ben for only a second.

"What th' hell yew a-doin' here, boy?" the man yelled at Paul. The other man Ben saw in the trees rushed out onto the road and placed himself between Paul and the bridge. The two men

were clearly outgunned, but it didn't seem to matter. They appeared to be drunk with the excitement, or the anxiety, of the confrontation. The first gunman continually turned to watch Ben and his two companions. "What're yew a-doin' here?" the man asked again.

Paul had watched Ben, and not knowing what to do, he said, "Hunting squirrels."

"Hell – is 'at what d'at wagon load o' people yew come wit' a-doin', too?"

Paul couldn't tell if these were the same two greasy migrants he and Wade had encountered back in September. They were both heavily clothed and wearing long tobacco streaked beards; probably too long to grow in that short of a time span.

"Uh – they're just passing through," Paul said sheepishly.

"What wagon yew a-talkin' 'bout?" the second man said to the first one.

"I seen a wagon load o' men come down 'ere! Didn't yew hear it?"

"Naw! Where'd d'ey go?"

"I don't know – back d'at way, I reckon," he answered, pointing southward.

"Well, w'y didn't yew say sump'm, yew dumb ass!" the second one yelled. This second man took control of the situation and ordered Paul to move back across the bridge.

"I want all four o' yew – includin' d'at nigger – to git on outta heer. Go on   git!"

The two sentries immediately turned and started back down the narrow road toward the compound. They quickly assessed that they were outgunned, and it appeared to Ben that they were making great haste to get out of gun range. Paul marched across the bridge to his friends, loudly popping boards underfoot all the way. Ben reached out and grabbed him as he stepped off the bridge and pulled him away as if he needed help to escape. Ben was still shook up and was not enjoying the events of the moment in the least. "What's going on, Paul?" he asked.

Paul was sick with worry and he stood for a moment breathing heavily as if he had sprinted all the way from the compound. He yanked the hood off his head; he was perspiring beneath his heavy attire and he gazed back across the bridge.

"I'm afraid we got some big trouble here, Ben. Wade's down there with Brother Silas, J.C., Graham, Tom and Lucas. If these two people sneak in on them, somebody's going to get hurt. We have to warn them somehow."

They stood silently for a moment struggling to decide what to do. Then Ben had an idea. "Is everybody loaded up?" he asked. They all quickly examined their own guns as if to verify the answer. "Let's just fire a few shots into the air to let our people know something's not right. I don't know what else we can do," he said. Then he cocked back the hammer on his rifle and pointed it to the ditch alongside the road. He fired, then quickly rechambered. Jimmy fired both rounds out of his shotgun and Paul followed suit with two more rounds. Ben fired one more. They gazed across the bridge and up the hill. The sentries were gone.

***

Inside, the little office cabin was nearly pitch-black. Tiny rays of sunlight managed to peek through between the barricade shutters that covered the windows from the inside. It wasn't warm in the room yet, but the fire inside the stove was growing nicely. The crackle of the fire was the only noise except for an occasional rustle of wind against the outside walls.

Carl stood totally naked before the heater stove. He was in distinct physical discomfort, which seemed to grow more intense by the minute. He had managed to undress and lay all the sodden, half-frozen clothes out on the floor to dry. He held his trousers up over the stove in an effort to dry them out. A tremor was in his movements; the pain of the burns, exposure, and frostbite were fighting mercilessly for his attention.

Jesse Bridger had stationed himself at the front window. He had opened a shutter just wide enough to peek through to the yard outside. Working sentry duty, he held a small .32 caliber revolver in his hand and seemed unruffled by his superior's worrisome appearance. For the moment, Carl didn't seem too worried about the goings-on outside. Even when distant gunshots were heard from the direction of the bridge, he said nothing. Perhaps he figured that his two sentries had found Wade and ended it all before it got started. That would be a fortunate conclusion to the day's unfortunate beginnings, he might have determined.

Jesse easily stepped to the other side of the room. Gently working the shutter a little wider, he peeked out toward the north side of the property. Just as gently, he eased the shutter closed and turned to Carl. "Boss, I see two sons-a-bitches outside here. They got guns. I know they ain't our men."

Carl looked over at Jesse and said, "Look again – see if you can recognize someone." Then he cursed the apparent incompetence of his sentries.

Jesse looked out the window again. He spied two men moving as quietly as ghosts toward a thicket along the north side of the compound about forty yards away. "If I had me a long gun I could shoot both their asses from here," he whispered to Carl.

Carl had begun to redress. He determined that he didn't have time to wait. But compared to the outside air, the clothes were warm in spite of their lingering dampness. He slipped his thick winter shirt back on, sloughing off a bloody square of scorched skin from his upper right arm in the process. He cursed in pain as he jerked on his overcoat. He moved toward a makeshift desk at the wall and yanked open a drawer. An ancient but usable .44 caliber revolver was in it. Carl, after dropping several rounds onto the floor with trembling hands, managed to load it up with six rounds of heavy-grain ammunition and then he snapped the cylinder shut. The gun was a straight shooter though, as evidenced by its long barrel and stout construction.

Carl lightly stepped over to Jesse. He looked out the window toward the thicket. Both men in the trees had positioned themselves in such a way as to make it impossible to discern their identity or status. "What do they have – long guns?" Carl asked.

"Shit, yeah," Jesse answered.

Carl moved to the opposite side of the room and checked a shutter. He had opened the shutter enough to brighten the corner of the room. Jesse looked around, apparently fretful for his boss's vulnerability in the glare of the window light. Carl edged himself away from the light but kept one eye peering through the edge of the glass. He didn't move for a long stretch of time. He was calculating the odds of his sentries losing a gun battle with the intruders from the north. The gunshots were fired in quick succession, meaning that someone was determined enough to gun down his people and move in quickly. If there were others out there, they should soon be exposing themselves if he could only wait long enough to force the intruders to act out of impatience.

Carl used his eyes to circle the central yard of the complex. He knew that several men were sleeping in the two barracks buildings on the far south side. Carl had retrieved Jesse out of the darkened black barracks and told everyone else to stay in bed after giving them a good cursing. He had easily bypassed his sentries on the narrow road. He was apparently fed up with all the ineptitude and figured that now they should all stay out of his way. He had determined that the sentries in the trees had likely fallen asleep on the job, were distracted by childish diversions to forestall boredom, or were simply not aware of the fire at the house as the wind masked too many sounds. Wade's gunshot at the deer apparently had not alerted them in time. Or they may have stationed themselves somewhere along the eastern stretches of the compound property nearly a half-mile away and likely did not know that Carl was in the area. If there had been any sentries nearby, they should have been alerted to his arrival; by the time he had crossed the footbridge, his coat and pants had frozen quite solid and were creating a muted racket akin to a stick being rubbed against tree bark.

Most areas of Carl's unburned skin had not returned to its normal color and texture. The blood veins under the skin in certain regions in the extremities and joints had ruptured and the pain of frostbite had racked him without ceasing since the fire in the stove had begun to thaw him out. His nemesis had nearly scored a direct hit with one of the fuel launches back at the house. The flames had immediately boiled off the upper layers of skin over much of his right side, arm and face. Inside the house, he had managed, throughout the battle against further attacks and the ensuing fire itself, to soak his entire body and clothing with water from a reservoir in the kitchen. In the subsequent escape, it had all frozen to sheets and chunks all over him and froze his hair stiff to his scalp. This course of events had helped greatly to staunch the pain of the burns until the thawing efforts began in front of the heater stove. Finally, all the happenings of the morning were working together to pull him into the throes of a living hell. No movement could be performed without great surges of paralyzing agony ricocheting throughout his being. He didn't want to talk much; it helped to ease the pain by keeping his teeth clinched. As things thawed out, the ice fell away, allowing little slug-like chunks of hair and skin to drop to the floor. Red patches of subsurface skin and bone were then exposed, leaving raw nerve endings to wrack his skull and jaw with the searing pain of newly-branded hide.

A migrant worker stepped out of the white barracks at the southwest corner of the compound. Carl eyed him as he stood outside the door and stretched his arms straight out and work his jaws snake-like into a big, lingering yawn. Stupidly, he scratched his crotch and started toward the tiny cookhouse next to the cabin where Carl was hiding. The worker was oblivious to the perilous happenings around him, and he shuffled halfway across the yard before he even opened his eyes wide enough to observe his surroundings.

Then the migrant glanced around. For a moment, it seemed that he found nothing unusual. But suddenly, he jerked his head in a double take toward one of the ports in the truck barn. He paused in his step and bobbed his head around as if trying to peer into the darkened port at something that was obscured by shadows. He quickened his step for the cookhouse and disappeared from Carl's view. Carl could hear the door to the cookhouse open and close. He took the migrant's reaction as a sign of trouble. Carl stepped away from the window and lightly moved to the end of the room nearest the garage, growling in pain at each step. Jesse pulled away from his post and looked at Carl. "They ain't moved a goddamn inch, boss," Jesse said, referring to Tom and Lucas hiding in the bushes.

Carl listened to the wall of the cabin that separated it from the garage, hoping to detect his attacker's movements. It was a fruitless endeavor. He turned around to Jesse and winced. The pain in his feet hardly allowed him to move. Once he jerked his foot upward as if a sledgehammer had been dropped on his toes. All these physical distractions worked aggressively to steal his efforts to stay focused. But it was time to discover what was really going on outside. It was clear that this was not a law-abiding exercise intended to apprehend a criminal, or whatever it was that Wade thought Carl was. It was personal. But he couldn't figure out who the two men hiding in the bushes could be. If the law was involved, he didn't think that it would be handled in this manner.

Carl looked over at the alarm station installed in the opposite corner of the room. He had listened and counted four strikes, signifying that the tripwire at the bridge had been tripped at least as many times. He cursed himself for retiring the second tripwire months earlier. Its maintenance had become a strain, so now he could only guess at the location of the other posse members.

A light tap on the front door was almost indecipherable apart from the crackle in the stove. Carl moved back to the window and looked out. He couldn't see who was at the front door. Looking back toward the barn he could find nothing unusual.

"Ask who it is," Carl ordered Jesse. "Don't let him in – just get his name."

Jesse eased over to the door. It was air tight; no way to see who was knocking. "Who is it?" he asked, almost too quietly.

A voice on the other side said, "It's Virgil."

Jesse looked at Carl, who had now managed to shuffle quietly to the rear window. After a short pause, Carl said, "Let him in." Then he pointed the big gun at the door. The migrant entered. Jesse quickly closed the door behind him. Carl moved to the front window and looked out. "Did you see someone out there?" he asked.

"Yeah – he had a gun!" Virgil said excitedly. The room was dark, but Virgil knew it was Carl by his voice. Then, as his eyes adjusted to the dim light, he could see Carl's damaged face and cranium. The mottled patches of crimson and hair startled him.

"What did he say?" Carl demanded.

"Nuttin'!"

"Was he one of my boys?"

"Uh – no, Mr. Kallton. I don't reckon it was. He had a rifle an' he looked real mean!"

"He look like anybody you seen around town?"

"Ah – I couldn't see much. It was dark in 'ere."

"In where?" Carl asked, still watching the barn.

"Uh – in th' truck barn."

"What kind of rifle did he have – could you see that?"

"Uh, yeah – 'e had a big one, like a deer rifle. It had a crank handle on it."

"Jesse, get back to the back window," Carl ordered. Then he raised the big pistol up to the window as if ready to fire. "All right, Virgil – this is what I want you to do. You go back out and you find out who he is and what he wants. The man's trying to kill me and I want to know why. And then you report back to me. I want you to try to get him out of the barn where I can see him – you understand me?" Virgil stood blank-faced. Then his eyebrows lifted as if he was unsure of Carl's instructions. Carl cursed the pain searing his head, then he added, "And I don't want you to answer any questions. You don't tell him I'm in here. Just get the facts and get back here to me. Understood?" Virgil nodded meekly. Then Carl said, "Get him out in the yard, so I can see him."

"Yew gonna shoot him, Mr. Kallton?"

"Hell, no – I ain't gonna shoot him, goddamn it!" Carl answered mockingly. "Now get the hell back out there – get him out of that barn!"

Virgil was fearful for his life. Carl had no concern for the possibility of Virgil's demise. He glared at Virgil because of his slowness. Carl nodded angrily toward the door. Slowly, Virgil opened the door and closed it behind him. In a painfully slow shuffle, Virgil moved back across the yard along the same route he had used minutes earlier. With fearful glances toward the barn, he inched to the middle of the yard and stopped. Then, just as slowly, he turned toward the barn.

"Get on over to the goddamn barn, you shit-ass son-of-a-bitch!" Carl hissed under his breath, pink tinted spittle flying from his lips. Then he again cursed the sentries for their apparent lack of action against these intruders trespassing into his compound.

Virgil used the head bobbing technique again trying to find movement and shapes in the shadows. Then he looked back over at Carl's window, then back at the barn. With excruciatingly slow and pensive steps, Virgil closed the gap between himself and the barn. He glanced back several times at Carl. Then it seemed that something, or someone, grabbed his attention.

***

Tom's eyes were those of an old man; failing in their sharpness compared to Lucas's. He depended on Lucas to be his eyes, as well as his ears. Lucas stood to Tom's right, and for nearly ten uncomfortable minutes they had remained silent but vigilant, neither one able to find a way to breach the still-angry wall between them. But they had thought that something should have happened by now. They had not seen Carl or anyone else inside the compound for that matter since they had arrived.

More than once, Lucas had thought that he could see some movement in the window in the little building located directly in front of them. He had scanned the woods to the far left and all he could see was the wall of a quite massive, low-roofed building many yards away behind the trees and scrub bushes. At times, he thought he could hear doors slam or other sounds, but it was hard to determine if they were human sounds or those of the breeze. He glanced at Tom and he could see that he had planted his eyes on the little window. From the start, Tom had seemed sad but determined to help somehow. They had heard the gunshots from the bridge and had determined that something had gone terribly awry.

"What do you think we should do?" Lucas finally asked.

After a long pause, Tom said, "I wish I knew where Wade is right now. I'm afraid Carl might get him first. We can't see anything from here if Wade gets into trouble."

Tom looked around the little building at both ends. Toward the left side he could see a wide passageway between the office cabin and the nearby cookhouse. It would be a good strategic spot to place themselves and to quickly bivouac from if the need arose. To their immediate left, the passage through the trees was clear except for a shallow ditch that ran perpendicular to the cookhouse. But from there it was a clear shot for anyone wishing to take potshots from the window. "You think we could get over there without anybody seeing us?" Tom asked, pointing to the passageway between the buildings. "I need to, Luke. I have to help Wade. I think I owe him that much."

Lucas had nothing to say to Tom's odd pronouncements. It seemed to him that Tom was ashamed to be so far away from his long-ago friend, Wade, whom Tom had determined to be fighting this battle on his own. But it concerned Lucas that Tom desired to be so near Wade when it was clear that Wade was itching for a duel to the finish. It would make better sense, Lucas thought, to be near Wade in order to discourage, or to stop him rather than to help him kill someone.

Lucas looked at the little window but couldn't detect any movement inside. It appeared to be covered with boards or a wooden shutter from the inside. "Let's try to ease on ever to the left, Tom," he said. "Maybe we can see a little better and get closer."

Tom turned and stepped down into the ditch. Lucas watched the window and then followed.

***

"Who are yew?" the greasy sentry asked.

The preacher had watched the man with the shotgun walk up the road toward J.C.'s mule and wagon rig and had determined that he was less than virtuous. Also, toward the north, he saw the other migrant moving toward his opposite flank. Finally, the other migrant stopped thirty yards away and stared at him while the first one gave him the third degree.

"I said – who th' hell are yew?"

The preacher introduced himself with hands outstretched to demonstrate he was unarmed. "Who are you?" he then asked of the sentry.

The sentry held up the shotgun almost as high as he did with Paul. He walked up close to the preacher and eyed him up and down like he expected the preacher to be hiding weapons. "Take yer coat off!" he spat.

Obediently, the preacher removed his coat and held it out. He looked back at the other sentry and saw that he was moving toward him. His attention was quickly drawn back to the first sentry because he began patting him down with his free hand searching for weapons. Quickly, the sentry ran his hand through the coat pockets.

"What're yew a-doin' here, ol' man?"

"Why?" the preacher asked. "Is this private property?"

"Ye' damn right it is."

"You boys doing something illegal down here somewhere?"

"Yew jist shut up, ol' man. 'at's none o' yore bid'ness!"

The other sentry stepped to the road and stopped nearby. He said nothing. The preacher put his coat back on and waited for further instructions or questions. He was standing a yard from the sentry, but he could smell the sweat and tobacco juice-drenched clothing he was wearing. He didn't have a tooth in his head and his thin hair and beard didn't seem to have known soap and water in a lifetime. The preacher determined that gentle persuasion or reasoning would be of little value to these people. As he buttoned his coat, he could hear the second sentry approaching from the rear.

"Git on out 'ere in th' middle o' th' road," the first one ordered. "Where's 'em people d'at come wit'cha?"

"I don't know," the preacher said with as much conviction as he could muster. After all, he didn't really know where the men had gone; he had no specifics. It was a white lie that he felt no negative compunction to tell.

"Al, yew stay right up b'hind 'im 'ere. If he tries anythang, yew shoot 'im in th' ass," the loud-mouthed one said. Then with a motion of the gun barrel, he ordered the preacher to follow.

"Where yew takin' 'im, Joe?" the rearward sentry asked.

The preacher could feel the prodding of the gun barrel in his back and he refused to stand for it. He turned around and glared at the guard, then eyed the end of the barrel that Al had now raised up to the preacher's face. It seemed to work as from then on he never felt the barrel thrust to his back again.

"Hell – like th' big man said – take 'im back to th' office and wait fer th' man t' come down this mornin'," Al said, referring to Carl, making it evident that he did not know that his boss was already in close proximity.

Just a few yards ahead and the preacher would see the compound and perhaps his friends. He was now hostage fodder and there seemed to be nothing he could do to change that. "Who fired them shots back there?" the preacher asked. Al didn't answer. The preacher couldn't decide how dangerous these men could actually be. He knew Jimmy had only a double-barrel shotgun, good for only two quick shots. Paul also had a double-barrel. He didn't know about Ben's arrival yet. He had counted six shots. Al was carrying a pump-action shotgun and Joe had a double-barrel. The numbers added up to a fearful scenario.

"Did you shoot somebody back there?" the preacher asked determinedly.

Again, Al simply glared at him. The preacher turned back to the other sentry and hoped for an answer. Joe gestured angrily with the gun and said nothing.

***

Graham and J.C. had circled completely around the southern perimeter of the compound and found themselves between the barracks and the short road extension leading to the expansive low-roofed building that sat thirty yards away to the east. They remained hidden, as best as they could, behind the most eastward corner of the east barracks. From this vantage point they examined the low-roofed building and determined that it was the center of Carl's biggest enterprise, whatever it might be. The sound of running, or creek water could be heard coming from near the building. The entire structure sat at an angle to the approach of the road. A large rail-mounted door, about twelve feet wide and ten feet tall, was placed centrally beneath the peak of the roof at the front. A couple of small doors with heavy hinges and locks were visible on the nearest side. It had been built using thick wooden planks with battens with the apparent intentions of making it soundproof and airtight. The roof appeared to be covered with simple roofing tin but the whole structure, including the roof, was painted flat black.

"My God, have mercy on my soul!" J.C. whispered crossly.

Graham looked at him when he spoke. J.C. seemed guilt ridden, or perhaps grieved. It was spoken as if he was at fault for something. J.C. looked at Graham and repeated the phrase with a shake of his head. "What's wrong, J.C.?" Graham asked.

"You see that rail and them wheels holding that big door up?"

"Yeah."

"Carl Kallton had me order all that from St. Louis, straight from the factory. And you see them big hinges and them locks on those little doors?" J.C. asked, pointing. Graham nodded yes. "I ordered those special made for Carl. And I gave him a discount on all that. And I sold him all that tin for the roof. One day Carl came in and said he wanted to buy some paint. And I said okay. You know I keep thirty gallons or so in the back, and I took him back there. We got back there and he said he needed a hundred-fifty gallons of flat-black paint! Can you imagine? And he told me to order it and to keep quiet about it. So I got his paint and I didn't tell nobody – just ordered it and had it shipped straight out to his house. Paid me with cash – off the books. I even discharged the shipping costs for him. And I went along and kept my mouth shut. Graham, I don't sell 150 gallons in two years!"

J.C. had scrunched up his face as if admitting to being a willing accomplice to a crime. To Graham, the guilt J.C. was placing on himself seemed excessive.

"And I can see a block-and-tackle and a few things hanging on that wall over there. I sold him everything he needed. I worked hard to get his orders expedited and shipped out here as quick as I could. I gave him discounts and gave him special treatment because of the money he flashed in my face. And all along I had suspicions about what he was doing down here."

"J.C., we all are to be held accountable in some way. But we really ain't got time right now for penance and such. We've got some serious problems here."

J.C. seemed to snap out of his sacramental trance as quickly as Graham finished speaking. He nervously worked the hammer back and forth on his rifle and looked back around toward the office building to find the migrant returning to the yard. They had watched him walk toward the cookhouse and the office, but the fronts of both buildings were out of their view. It was a poor vantage point. With a glance around the corner of the barracks, they found they had only a narrow space between the buildings to observe events. Graham quickly moved from the barracks to the end of the cookhouse. J.C. followed. The migrant had moved to the middle of the yard and appeared to be gazing into the darkened interior of the truck barn. The end of the road entering the compound was directly across from them. From this point, Wade was nowhere to be seen.

"Graham, there's a door on the back here," J.C. said.

Graham stepped to the rear of the cookhouse behind J.C. J.C. pulled the screen door open and turned the handle on the wooden door inside. Graham looked back behind the office building. He could see two men moving through the trees toward the office. It was Tom and Lucas. Graham waved and got their attention. They stopped and watched J.C. and Graham enter the cookhouse.

***

"What're yew a-doin' in there?"

Wade could see the anxiety on Virgil's face as clearly as though he stood only inches away. But he was standing about eight yards away at the edge of the reflected sunlight that pooled down from between the trees above. It was clear that the man didn't want to be here asking questions. Neither did Wade want to answer any.

"Is Carl Kallton in there?" Wade asked.

"Uh – he told me not to say nuthin' 'bout that."

"Anybody else in there with him?"

Virgil looked back toward the office, all the while working his eyes back and forth between Wade and the office. Then he jerked his head back toward Wade as if he had been slapped.

"Anybody else in there with him?" Wade asked more persistently.

Virgil took another step toward Wade and seemed full of anxiety over this strange predicament he found himself in. Wade had kept his rifle upright and considered lowering it to a firing position to speed things up. Virgil suddenly seemed transfixed in a sort of a spell. Wade wasn't sure, but he thought he could hear voices coming from the direction of the road that he had just traversed minutes earlier. It was time to make things happen.

"Are you deaf?" Wade spat at the migrant. "Who else is in there with him? Tell me right now!"

Virgil was suddenly gripped with a terror that grew stronger as the seconds ticked by. Wade began to lower the rifle at Virgil.

"G – give me yer name, an' I'll tell yew," Virgil said.

"Joseph Smith," Wade said. "Now who's in there with him?"

Virgil nodded his head as if he had accepted the answer. Then realizing that Carl would determine that he had disobeyed an order about answering questions, Virgil coughed with a start and worked gallantly to keep his wits under control. "Jesse's in there – 'at's all," he answered as quietly as he could, hoping Carl could not hear.

"Who's Jesse?"

"He's Carl's nigger. Can yew come out 'ere? I cain't hear yew."

Wade's patience broke and he dropped the rifle to fire position. Virgil danced backwards as if expecting a blast from the gun. Then he looked over at the window with the apparent hope for a signal of some sort. He looked back at Wade's rifle as if he might be staring at his own death certificate.

"Just tell me where Carl is in that shack! Is he behind that window?" Wade demanded.

The voices on the road grew louder. To speed things up, Wade clicked the hammer back and glared intently at Virgil. Virgil froze like ice.

***

"Hold up, there!" Ben yelled.

The preacher swung around to find Ben coming up the road. He was backed by several men trailing along behind him. Two men from town had found Ben and Paul. They were walking toward the preacher and the sentries. Far behind, near the intersection with the narrow road, Jimmy and Walter stood watching. Jeff Parker, a town resident who had worked for Carl for a short time, and Charles Smith, a local blacksmith, were both with Ben and Paul. All four men were armed.

"Keep moving!" Al yelled at the preacher. Joe pointed the gun at his face but the preacher rebelled.

"You wait just a minute – these are my friends!" the preacher barked.

Al chambered a round of ammo into the shotgun to reinforce his determination. He had forgotten that he already had a round in the chamber and it ejected out of the gun to the ground. He pretended he didn't notice his mistake and left it where it fell. Joe followed suit by clicking back the hammer on his gun.

"Now yew boys jist ease on outta here!" Al said to Ben and his companions. "Yer on private propity – now git!"

Ben proved his determination by stepping up his stride and closing the gap. "Ben," Paul whispered as they marched along, "Those men look pretty rough – they just might shoot at us."

Ben stopped several yards away and glared intently at the sentries. "Let my friend go and there won't be no trouble. He don't mean you any harm," he said.

Just as quickly, Jeff and Charles moved up alongside Ben and Paul and held their guns at the ready, but with the muzzles pointed to the ground. Al was showing great agitation over being challenged and outgunned. He fidgeted for something in his coat pocket as if searching for another weapon; a gesture clearly intended to be threatening.

"C'mon, now," Ben said loudly. "We've got four guns to your two. I don't think either one of you's dumb enough to try anything. Just turn him loose and we'll be on our way."

Joe looked at Al, not knowing what to do next. It was a standoff that they had already lost. Something was going on in the area of the compound that Al wasn't privy to, and the intimidation factor was rising against him. He coughed and sniffed, but he could think of nothing to say to rectify the situation to his satisfaction. He swung the barrel of the gun upwards a couple of times as if he might likely be preparing to aim it at someone, but thought better of it when the four men responded with similar actions of their own. Then he cursed aloud when he could think of nothing else to say.

"Goddamn it – yew the law?" Joe asked.

"No, but he's on his way. He'll be here in a minute."

"Gene Carter ain't a-gonna help yew!" Al retorted, not being able to think of anything to refute Ben's threat.

"Why is that?" Ben asked, looking at both sentries for an answer. He wondered if somehow they had already discovered the truth concerning the sheriff's demise. Al refused to answer.

"Go on – tarn 'im loose!" Al barked at Joe.

The preacher retreated himself into the custody of Ben and his friends. He turned and watched the sentries. With a gesture of disgust, both Al and Joe slowly turned around and started walking toward the compound. They looked back several times to see if Ben and the preacher were doing as they were told. The preacher could see, and hear, Al cursing at Joe; something about his not moving fast enough to help keep control of the situation. Joe didn't respond; he made great haste to enter the compound.

***

"Who is that?" Graham asked.

All four men, J.C., Graham, Tom, and Lucas, had entered the cookhouse and were gazing through a large square window out into the yard of the compound. They could see Virgil's backside. He was apparently staring into a darkened port of the barn.

"Must be one of Carl's men," Lucas said.

"What's he doing?"

"Seems like he's talking to somebody there in that barn."

"Reckon it's Wade?" Tom asked.

The light from the morning sky had entered the yard with enough strength to cast a glare across the window. The view into the yard would have been excellent except for the glare. Lucas stepped over to a door near the north corner of the room and looked out the little window in the top of it. "Yeah – it's Wade. And he's talking to the man, I think," he said.

J.C. scanned the yard and the buildings. He checked the windows for other signs of movement. "Where you reckon Carl's hiding out?" he asked.

"Good question," Graham said. "One of us ought to be looking out the back in case he sneaks up on us." Paul, volunteering himself for the task, quickly returned to the back door and exited.

"Look over here, Graham," Lucas said, pointing toward the office. "I think somebody's in that cabin. I thought I could see something move in that window."

"Look over here!" Graham commanded, a bit too loudly for the small room. "Two more men are coming around the barn there – see?"

Al and Joe quickly marched around the corner of the barn and found Virgil standing just yards away looking into the port.

"What're we gonna do?" Lucas asked. "They've got guns."

Without waiting for answers, Tom opened the door at the opposite end of the room from Lucas and barreled out into the yard. *"Hey!"* Graham yelled to Tom, hoping to stop him. Then he stepped out onto the narrow porch behind Tom. Virgil spun around, thinking he was being attacked from the rear. Tom was surprised by the look of fear on his face. He had no idea who Virgil was; he had never seen him before.

"Damn, who th' hell are yew?" Al yelled across the yard to Tom and Graham, clearly surprised by the presence of strangers solidly in the heart of the compound.

Al turned to look back at those still behind him. Everyone had a gun, and who was friend and who was foe, he didn't know. Virgil bent over slightly and gazed hard into the window looking for signals from Carl. The shutter appeared to narrow the gap in the window and close. Tom and Graham parted and stepped to opposite ends of the porch and held their guns at the ready position. Al and Joe stopped at the corner of the barn, standing a couple of yards apart, holding their firearms in similar fashion. Wade stood his ground inside the barn next to the wagon.

Virgil looked back at Wade and, with great apprehension, answered his question about Carl's whereabouts: "He's over in th' office there."

Al again yelled at Tom and Graham. *"I said, who th' hell are yew people?"*

He had not yet realized that Wade was hidden in the barn. Tom and Graham were nervous but intent, for the moment, on standing firm on the porch. Tom kept a vigilant eye on the window and the door to the office. He hadn't seen anything that would have drawn his attention to the little building, but he had a worrisome intuition about it.

"You get back in there and tell Carl to come out!" Wade barked at Virgil. "You tell him to come out or we're going to fill that damn shack with hot lead! You tell him he's got ten seconds. Go on – git!"

Al could hear the restrained banter inside and outside the barn. He could see that both Tom and Graham were ignoring him and were held captive by the event at the barn. Virgil had begun a slow, nerve-wracked march back to the office door. All these things both confused and angered Al. He looked back again and Ben, Paul, Jeff, and Charles were now moving up toward the compound behind him. In the distance, he could see Walter and Jimmy bringing up the rear. With great agitation, he swung his gun back around toward Ben, and Joe did the same. Then he swung back around to Tom and Graham. He moved toward the ports to see what was going on there. Joe became so flustered and confused that he swung hard back around toward the compound dropping his gun but catching it before it hit the ground. Someone yelled from the far side of the compound.

"Drop it! Drop it now!"

It was J.C., and he was standing at the rearward side of the cookhouse with his gun raised, ready to fire. Al jerked his head back and forth between Ben and J.C. Ben held his gaze on Al and kept moving slowly toward him. Al spun back around to find J.C. moving toward him with his rifle held high. In a panic, Joe tossed his gun away and raised his hands in surrender. In a cursing rage, Al did the same. J.C. sprinted across the yard yelling, *"Git down on the ground! Git down – now!"*

Ben ran up and kicked both guns away from the men, who were now lying prostrate on the ground.

***

As soon as Virgil entered the door, Carl grabbed him by the collar and savagely yanked him inside and slammed the door hard behind him. It seemed that the whole cabin shook. Virgil looked at Carl and could see tears of rage in his eyes. He ducked away but it was too late. Carl swung hard and slapped him with enough force to send him stumbling against the wall.

"Stand up, you goddamn piece o' shit!" Carl sneered. Then he shoved Virgil back against the wall. "Goddamn it – what'd I tell you to do! What the hell did I tell you!"

Virgil seemed to tremble with fear. He mumbled something but it was completely incoherent. The shutter on the rear window had been opened slightly and the room was relatively well lit. Jesse was peering out the window with his gun pointed at the glass. He was watching something toward his right in the trees. He was unconcerned with what was happening to Virgil.

Carl shuffled over to the front window and looked out. Now he could see the men at the cookhouse and in the yard. He recognized Tom, but was unsure about Graham. He heard a voice, then he saw J. C. run across the yard toward the road. Still, he couldn't see Wade.

"What'd he say, asshole!" Carl demanded while wiping away a slathering of blood and fluids that had washed down over his eye.

"'e said 'e was Joseph Smith – "

"What'd he look like?"

"Big – " Virgil said, bracing himself for another slap. "Big man – might near big as yew, Mr. Kallton."

"What'd he say? Speak up!"

"'e wouldn't say nuthin'. Jist said 'e wanted yew t' come out. H – he was a-gonna sh – shoot me if I didn't come tell yew that!"

Carl peered back out the front window. He could see Tom and Graham looking around the yard, sometimes watching J.C. near the road, sometimes gazing into the barn, sometimes looking toward Carl in the dark crack of the shutter. Carl determined that he could shoot and kill both men quite easily from his position, but figuring his real enemy was still out there, he decided to keep all his options open for the moment.

Furious, Carl slapped his hand to his temple. Blood splattered against the window and some fell down to his cheek. The burns and the frostbite had made his scalp feel as if it had been cut away by warring Indians. He reached back up to his head to find a small patch of skin and hair hanging near his ear. He grabbed it and yanked, removing a piece of left ear with it.

He turned back to Virgil and in a demonically graveled voice he said, "Get your ass back out there! If he ain't out of that barn in one minute, you are going to hell!" Then Carl shakily aimed the big .44 at Virgil's nose and pulled back the hammer. "Go on, you goddamnit shit!"

Virgil was overcome with nerves and he couldn't find the door latch. He reached for it and fumbled, then raised his hands as if surrendering. He tried for the door again and again, but failed each time. Carl worked the latch and slammed it half-open against Virgil. Virgil fell to the floor, then quickly scrambled over the threshold and, not being able to move his arms and legs quickly enough, fell to his face. He was summarily ejected from the doorway by a powerful kick to the rump. Carl slammed the door. Someone at the cookhouse yelled something at Carl, but he didn't bother to look out.

"Boss – somebody's ass is still out there," Jesse said, referring to Lucas, who had returned to stand sentry along the north.

But someone in the yard was yelling orders of some sort. Carl started back to the front window but slipped and fell on his own greasy skin parts lying on the floor. Angrily, he jerked himself back upright and looked out. The yard was a blur of activity as several men were moving back to defensive positions around the yard. Three of his workers from the barracks had stepped out, but were ordered to get back inside by someone in the yard. They promptly returned to the barracks, but continued watching from doorways and windows.

Suddenly, it was time to make a move. The enemy was building its strength. There appeared to be no options available on the south side. And the north appeared to be the enemy's weakest flank.

"You just see one man?" Carl asked Jesse.

"Yeah – just one. I don't know where the other one went."

"Can you shoot him from here?"

"I can with your gun."

Carl handed him his .44. Jesse quickly took it from Carl, but he couldn't refrain from noticing the trembling in his boss's hand and body. Was it fear or pain – or both? Jesse didn't bother to guess which it was. There was a battle brewing, and he knew where his priorities stood at the moment. He turned back to the window and worked the latch up. Then he proceeded to push the window open with the muzzle of the gun.

***

Wade had relocated himself to the north end of the barn nearest the cabin. He heard the noises of doors and movements through the wall separating the two buildings, but couldn't determine anything of value. He looked for spaces and cracks in the wall that he could peer through, but the wall was solid end to end.

The door to the office opened and he saw Virgil stumble to the ground outside. From his location, Wade was unable to see Carl kick Virgil out the door. But he heard someone in the yard yell Carl's name, then the door slammed shut. Virgil was a babbling mess and he struggled to get his footing. Wade watched him behave as if he were trying to dodge bullets or flying stones, but no one was shooting or throwing anything at him. In a moment, Virgil gathered his wits and picked himself up enough to scamper toward the barn. He fell to his hands again as he entered the barn's shadow, then he crawled inside beneath the wagon to escape the light of the yard. Wade could hear him whimpering like a whipped dog on the ground just three yards away.

Wade looked toward the back corner of the barn and found a tiny wooden staircase leading up to the second floor. He placed one foot on the first step and put his weight down. It didn't creak or make a noise; it held solid. Gingerly he stepped up, then froze. Someone began yelling.

"Carl – you in there?"

The voice was coming from the direction of the cookhouse. Wade continued to move up the staircase. Virgil had managed to get a grip on himself and stay quiet. Everyone listened.

"Carl – c'mon out! We won't shoot – c'mon out!"

It was Tom. Wade saw him standing in the little passageway beneath the porch roof connecting the two buildings. He had hidden himself from the view of the window and everyone else had found hide-a-ways around the yard with guns ready. Tom called to Carl again but no one answered from the office.

Then a gun was fired from somewhere near or inside the office. Wade grabbed the opportunity to race to the top of the stairs. In a moment, he could hear someone yelling from the north side, out in the trees. He couldn't determine who it was. Quickly, he entered the spacious, but dark, room upstairs. He tried to gaze around the room for any movement. A strange, damp odor, much like decaying flowers, filled the air. He groped in the darkness for any nearby object and then worked his way across and toward the front wall. He continued to hear someone yelling, or screaming, outside the northern perimeter. He found a window and the latch holding the shutters closed. There was no glass; just wooden shutters on hinges. He swung both little doors open. They swung outward, unlike those in the little office cabin. He used the light from the window to scan the room. No one was there as he suspected. An old chest of drawers stood in the opposite corner. A large mirror hung on the far wall and three dusty, unmade beds were spaced along the front wall. It seemed the room was used for activities other than just sleeping.

Wade looked out the window. He heard more yelling from the north side. Tom had abandoned his post. Wade couldn't see where he had gone. Graham had moved toward the corner between the cookhouse and the office. He had his shotgun raised and aimed at the window in the office. Across the yard, Wade saw that several migrants were watching events from the barracks windows and doorways. J.C. was peering from behind the south corner of the barn where he had first entered the compound.

Wade watched the office window for any movement. He carefully aimed the rifle down at the center of it. In a moment, he realized that the northern flank of the office was not properly guarded. Tom, he feared, had been moving around too much. An escape out the rear of the cabin was possible. The screaming voice probably belonged to Lucas. The fired gun likely found its intended target.

A shadow, or someone, passed before the window. Then J.C. yelled. *"Carl, just come on out! We won't shoot! Come out – put your hands up!"*

Wade set the bead of the gun barrel on the center of the window. The shadow moved again. No one responded to J.C.'s command. A decision had to be made. Was it Carl or was it Jesse at the window? He could place a half-dozen small, screaming cannonballs down through the roof and through the window and cut Carl to pieces. It should have all been over by now. Carl should have been blown to bits and splattered throughout the trees or the interior of the cabin by this time.

A commotion of some sort was going on behind the cabin. Wade could see over the top of most of the building, but his view was obscured by the corner of the barn and numerous evergreens behind the cabin. He could see a sapling move on the far north side. No one was screaming now, but everything in the yard below him seemed to have come to a stalemate.

"Anybody up there?" someone said quietly from the stairway.

The voice was shaky and fearful. Wade stepped over to look down. It was dark. He couldn't see that it was Virgil, who had moved up the stairs as quietly as Wade. "Who are you?" Wade asked as he stepped back to the windows.

"V – Virgil."

"Come here, Virgil," Wade commanded as he reestablished his firing position at the window.

Virgil's head popped above the floor at the stairway and he said, "Mr. Kallton told me to git yew out in th' yard so 'e could see yew."

"Come here," Wade commanded again.

Breathing heavily as if he had sprinted a mile, Virgil placed himself at the foot of the bed near Wade. "Where's Carl right now?" Wade asked.

Virgil was in a fog. He seemed to be in a zombie-like state with a mindset to follow Carl's orders. Even at this location, away from Carl, he was gravely fearful of disobeying his superior's orders. He seemed intent, in an attitude of dreaded resignation, on getting Wade to move to the yard.

"I said, where's Carl?"

"He's down there, sir – in 'at house."

"All right – is he at the window?"

"I don't know – 'e was a while ago."

"Where's that black man?"

"He's down there, too."

"Is he next to Carl, or in the back?"

"He was in th' back when I seen 'im."

"They got guns in there?"

"Yeah – both of 'em."

"They have a back door in that house?"

"Yes, sir."

"Why don't they use it?" Wade asked. Virgil didn't understand the question. Wade dropped the subject. Then another shot rang out toward the north. "Get down on the floor over there, Virgil – and don't move."

Virgil responded quickly, then the room fell quiet.

***

"He blowed my arm off!" Lucas yelled.

He was in great pain, but seemed actually more angry than hurt. Tom had found him in the ditch behind the office cabin. Jesse's bullet had bored a ragged hole through the muscle connecting the neck and shoulder, and had rendered his right arm useless. Against Lucas's loud objections, Tom had grabbed him by the feet and proceeded to drag him further upstream in the dried creek bed. He was too close to the cabin and Jesse was ready to try again at the first opportunity. Tom dragged him at a run causing Lucas's bad arm to bounce about. Quickly, he propped Lucas up against the ditch bank and examined the wound. Luckily, it appeared, no bone had been hit, but the bullet had entered and exited the flesh leaving a quarter-inch diameter hole and a large, sore lump that was growing on his shoulder. But judging from Lucas's reaction, it could have been estimated that he had been hit broadside by a cannonball.

Tom peeked up over the bank and looked toward the building. The window was open but all appeared dark inside. Toward the west he saw movement among the trees. He gazed for only a second, then ducked, expecting to be the recipient of the next shot. Quickly, he tried again. He could see the shape of someone moving toward the building from the west corner of the barn. Tom squinted hard and he determined that it was Charles.

"Charlie – watch out!" Tom yelled. *"Somebody's in that window with a gun!"*

Instantly, Charles ducked away and sprinted back toward the barn. Tom looked back down at Lucas. He was conscious and alert. Lucas grimaced as he worked to pull his pain-wracked arm to his lap. His shirt was growing crimson with blood, but to Tom, at least, the outflow seemed to have slowed to a trickle. "We're gonna get you out, Luke – just as soon as we can. Don't move – stay calm," Tom ordered.

Tom raised up and aimed his shotgun at the window. He couldn't remember if he had buckshot or squirrel shot in the chamber. He laid the bead on the window and waited, ducking up and down when he suspected movement in the window. Then he slowly swung the gun toward the back door and quickly pulled the trigger. The shot hit the center of the door, as evidenced by the exploding splinters and the dust that puffed out of the boards.

"That ought to keep them penned in for a while," he said. He looked back at Lucas. Tom was glad to see that he was not grimacing anymore and the blood flow seemed to have stopped.

"Thanks, Tom. I reckon you saved me that time," Lucas said with a direct, coherent gaze. The statement warmed Tom's heart but he shook his head no, as if to state that he deserved no gratitude from Lucas at all.

***

Earlier, moments before Lucas was shot, Carl had begun to slowly remove the blocker-board from the back door. He grasped the board with all his might. He could feel nothing in his hands. Everything seemed to take tremendous effort to grasp or to move, and it was almost impossible to hold on to anything for long because the blood mixed with dead, peeling flesh coated every surface with a grease-like phlegm.

Slowly, as quietly as he could, he sat the board in the corner nearby. He returned to the door and began to work the two metal latches, one high and the other low, on the doorframe. Then, just a few feet away, Jesse aimed the .44 out the rear window. Carl watched him take slow, careful aim and then he fired. Almost instantly, someone screamed out. Jesse, now excited by his good luck, stuck his face out the window. But realizing his vulnerability he yanked himself back. Carl stepped to the window and looked. The victim had fallen out of sight and Carl could see no one else in the woods, so he returned to the door to finish work on his escape.

Jesse's excited persona dropped when he saw Carl, clearly for the first time, in the light of the window. From all appearances, the man should have already been dead. The flesh of Carl's head, where it had not been burned off, had contracted where the ice had been and had pulled apart in sections, leaving scab-like creases throughout his hair where blood and body fluids were draining. His face had lost all color and the skin seemed to have already died at the bony protrusions along his jaw and cheeks. Something fell from the side of his head and left a tobacco-like brown stain on his coat. His eyes seemed to bulge unnaturally and the whites had turned yellowish-brown, as if the dying fluids of his body had drained out the tear ducts and coated them. His right arm appeared to be crippled and drawn up a bit into a perpetually bent position by burned and contracted flesh.

Jesse returned to the window as Carl stepped back to the door. It seemed that Carl had decided it was the right time to make the escape. He still suspected that someone was watching the building from the rear because he worked quietly on the latches as if the enemy stood just inches away.

Then Tom's gun blast hit the door with several pellets breaking through, leaving small round holes in the door and the adjacent wall. Long splinters exploded into the room from the boards. One pellet hit the stove flue, denting it severely enough to choke the smoke escaping out the top. Carl didn't seem to react at first. Jesse spun around quickly enough to see the bottom portion of Carl's coat snap away from his body as if an air blast from a blacksmith's furnace had blown through the door. Then Carl staggered away from the door and cursed. A cloud of dust instantly filled the room. Carl shakily looked himself over in the light of the window. Pain frontally attacked him everywhere but new ailments punished him in the eye and in the stomach. A pellet had planted itself beneath the skin of his abdomen, a minor wound; but another one had hit his left eye socket and embedded itself between the temple and the eyeball, making it impossible for his eye to pivot. Carl growled in frustration. He cursed loudly for the first time. The dust quickly entered the lungs of both Carl and Jesse, making it difficult to restrain coughing. Because of the damaged flue, smoke began pouring out of the stove vents.

Carl circled the room, trying to coerce his frostbitten feet and legs to obey his commands. He attempted to extract the pellet out of his eye with his little finger, then, when that failed, with the point of a knife. He gave up when he punctured his eye, sending a new searing pain screaming throughout his head.

Jesse pointed the gun at the window again, but he could find no target. He retreated to the back door where Carl was working and loosened the latches for him. Carl stood unsteadily behind him. Each breath was taken with great conscious effort as if it took all his strength. He inhaled slowly but exhaled with force each time. Something was seriously wrong. Carl was in great physical distress, and externally he appeared to have none of the signs of life such as the proper fleshy skin color or resilient texture. His body movements were uncoordinated and jerky. Jesse could see that his left eyeball had been forced inward, toward the bridge of the nose, and was probably sightless. His hands seemed to work only sporadically, at times exhibiting great gripping power, then seeming to go limp and useless.

But what Carl lacked in physical strength he made up for with a diabolical motivation borne out of a lifetime of inborn belligerence and practiced determination. His mental coherence and awareness was acute and he demonstrated it by ordering Jesse to reload the spent round in the gun and to give it back to him. Then he said with a voice surprisingly clear and strong but with venom directed toward Virgil, "Jesse, I want you to go out front and get everybody to move to the yard. That asshole ain't worth shit. You get out there and tell them people we want to surrender." Trying to restrain a coughing fit, he added, "I'll take care of the rest."

Then Carl took the other smaller handgun from Jesse and dropped it into his coat pocket. Carl didn't seem to take notice of Jesse's double-take reaction to his monster-like appearance, all created by the lifeless facial features and the now bulging, twisted eye. It seemed likely that the pellet had worked its way rearward in the eye socket and was now forcing the ball of the eye forward and outward, clearly exposing the little cut mark from the knife. But Jesse readily contained himself and nodded attentively at each word that Carl spoke. The gunfight wasn't festive anymore; a new plan was needed. They were greatly outnumbered and outgunned by what appeared to be a highly motivated army of well-armed compatriots who weren't going to be stopped until they took their quarry. But Jesse entertained poorly the thought of being unarmed or forced into an overwhelmingly disadvantageous position. It would be better to go out into the yard with the advantage of a hostage held in the cabin or, at a minimum, with a gun hidden in his coat. But it was clear that control of the situation had escaped their grasps and it was time to force things in such a way as to open new doors of possibilities.

Jesse returned to the front window and opened it, then he stuck his head out. He looked all around, up and down. He saw a long gun aimed at him from the far end of the barn. For the first time, he looked up. He saw Wade's rifle trained on his forehead. Wade's face, however, was obscured by the shadows. Jesse knew that he could have easily been shot and killed within the few seconds he had stood at the window. He didn't seem to feel that he was in danger as long as everyone recognized his black face as not being that of Carl's. To the left near the corner of the cookhouse he could almost see someone standing between the buildings waiting. Jesse looked back at Carl. The smoke had grown so thick that it would have been difficult to find Carl if it were not for his persistent hacking. "Go on – get the hell outta here," Carl barked.

Jesse could see a crack of light along the edge of the back door. Jesse couldn't figure out how his boss was going to pull it off. He could see that Carl had wrapped his head with a cloth or towel of some sort, whether for warmth, first aid, or for disguise, Jesse didn't know. But he turned for the door. Maybe it wasn't over yet, he seemed to think.

CHAPTER 35

"What's a-goin' on here!" Roy Kallton yelled from atop his horse and wagon rig as he rolled to a stop. Roy had his oldest son, Roy Jr., with him. He wasn't used to so many people staring at him at once. It seemed all of Braxton was stretched for a quarter-mile along the road. The crowd, now numbering well over two hundred people, was relatively subdued considering the circumstances. Most of them were standing along the edge of the road looking southward as if expecting some onerous event to happen soon. People and vehicles were also streaming down the driveway from the burned house and onto the main road, soon to be adding their numbers to the crowd. Roy couldn't figure out whether he should be curious or angry.

"What's a-goin' on here, George?" he asked a bewildered looking man who was standing near the entrance to the narrow road. Roy had initially carried an attitude of surprise, but then he gazed across the crowd like they were trespassers. George had fire in his eyes for Roy and didn't suffer him in the least. Roy dismounted.

"Where's Carl, Roy?" George asked.

"Where's Carl Kallton?" Roy answered with a question.

"Yes, Roy."

"'e's home, I reckon."

"You reckon?"

Roy looked at the people near him and determined that they were, for the most part, not friendly. George lacked a serious tone in his voice but he was dead serious with his eyes. Roy was being judged guilty for something and in the only way he knew, he defended himself.

"W'at's all these people a-doin' 'ere? Y'er all trespassin', ye know!" Roy announced as he looked back at the men milling about near the entrance to the narrow road. It still seemed that everyone was looking for some type of event to be taking place soon in the trees. Too many people were glaring at Roy and some of the men were moving in his direction.

"You know anything about Carl's operations down here?" someone asked.

Before Roy could answer, someone from the narrow road yelled, *"Are you one of Carl Kallton's men?"*

Within seconds, Roy was surrounded by a dozen angry men. Roy mumbled a few lame phrases to the questions that were coming at him.

"Where's that M.C. Colter fellow?"

"I don't know. Chicargo, I reckon," Roy answered with a wave of his arms.

"Do you know Gene Carter's dead?"

Roy looked at the questioner as if the query had been asked in an accusatory tone, which it had. Then he tried to feign a posture of surprise, then of sympathy. "Naw – when'd 'at happ'n?" he asked.

"Don't you want to know how it happened first?" George asked.

"Uh – yeah, how'd 'at happ'n?"

"He shot himself in the head."

"Why'd he do that?"

"Well, Roy, we thought you might help us answer that."

Roy danced around, looking at all the faces around him. It was as uncomfortable for him as anything could be. About a hundred feet away he saw Ruth standing and talking feverishly to someone holding a long gun. Roy pointed toward her as if he wished to talk to her. Ruth looked at Roy but showed no interest in talking to him. She continued to converse with the man on the road. Roy started to walk toward her but was stopped in his tracks. Two men moved shoulder to shoulder to stop him.

"Let's just go ahead and whoop his ass!" someone in the crowd said. Then someone shoved Roy from behind and said, "Did you hear that, boy?"

Roy looked over his shoulder at the man. He remembered him as a town resident, then he looked over the man's shoulder. With snake-like movements, Roy Jr. eased off the other side of the rig with a long gun hidden beneath his coat, the barrel hanging to his boot. Roy spun around and noticed several more vehicles rolling out of the driveway from Carl's house and coming his way.

"What're 'em people a-doin' at Carl's place?" he asked loudly, hoping to deflect attention away from himself.

"He ain't got no place, Roy – somebody burned it down."

Someone nearby shoved Roy again. A lot of anger had built up in the crowd and it needed to be unleashed. Roy glanced around. Guns were everywhere. Someone shouted from the distance again, *"Is that one of Carl's runners?"*

Roy's face had blushed and his efforts at playing ignorant fueled the rage of those nearby. Roy Jr. had worked his way from the wagon rig to the edge of the circle of men around Roy.

Then a great commotion broke out and Roy spun around to find his son being savagely trounced by two large men who had logically taken his cocking of the gun's hammer as hostile. The boy cursed with great profanity. Before Roy could react, he was hammered in the side of the head by a large, hard fist. Then all went black.

***

The front door opened slowly, then Jesse yelled, *"I'm comin' out – don't shoot me!"*

"Put your hands out the door where I can see 'em!" J.C. yelled

Jesse obeyed. Graham motioned for him to move out into the yard, away from the building. Jesse complied by walking several yards into the yard with his hands held up to shoulder level. He had a stern, serious expression and, at first appearance, showed every intention of cooperating. J.C. stepped away from the barn toward Jesse, holding his rifle at the ready. Graham kept his shotgun aimed at the darkened doorway. From the outside it appeared that something was on fire in the cabin as evidenced by the black smoke drifting out the top of the doorway and open window. Ben replaced J.C. at the corner of the barn and aimed at the window. The preacher stood nearby. He had taken Al's and Joe's guns and was guarding them, keeping them prostrate on the road.

J.C. looked up at the high window in the barn and saw that Wade had kept his rifle aimed at the cabin window as if he still had the firm intent of killing Carl. The windows in the barracks were still occupied by curious faces, and the doorway to the white barracks was open and two men were standing in it. The occupied barracks were a concern, but so far there had been no interference from any of the workers.

"Tom!" J.C. yelled. *"Can you hear me?"*

Tom, from sixty yards away, answered, *"Yeah – Luke's been hit! But he's okay!"*

J.C. had taken charge of the yard. He wanted Wade to come down and with a motion of the hand, he signaled to him. Wade retreated from the window and started down the stairway. Within his spirit he could sense Carl aiming a gun at the wall, hoping to hear his movements on the other side and make mincemeat out of him with rapid fire through the walls. He moved down the stairway as slowly as cold molasses and kept his ear to the wall.

"Charles – where are you?" J.C. yelled.

"On the north!" Charles answered, his voice faint in the breeze.

"Where's Carl?" J.C. asked Jesse.

"He's inside," Jesse answered matter-of-factly.

"Tell him to come out."

Jesse was a quick thinker on his feet. He proposed: "Tell all yer people to come here. He wants to talk to you."

"We're all here. Tell him to come out – now!"

Still with his hands up and with a calm, direct voice, Jesse said, "He wants ever'body to git in th' yard, 'cause he don't want to git shot in th' back."

"You really think we would shoot an unarmed man?" J.C. asked.

"I'm just tellin' your ass what th' man said. If all yer people don't come out front, he ain't a-comin' out."

J.C. paused a moment, then asked, "What's your name?"

"My name's Jesse Bridger, white shit."

J.C. looked at the smoke floating out of the cabin and said, "Doesn't look to me like he can stay in there much longer. Is that him I hear coughing?"

"Listen here, asshole," Jesse said with determination, already made impatient by all the questions. "He ain't gonna bring his ass out till all yer goddamn people are out here where he can see 'em."

Out of the corner of his eye, Jesse could see Wade slowly descending the stairway. Past the far corner of the truck barn, he could see Al and Joe both faces down on the ground, occasionally peeking up and looking at Jesse and J.C. To stall for time, Jesse asked, "Are you the law?"

J.C. ignored the question. The little standoff ate up a minute of daylight. Then Jesse looked around to see Wade moving toward the window of the cabin. He lowered his hands and swiveled at the waist to watch Wade.

"Who fired that shot at our man a while ago?" J.C. demanded.

Jesse looked back at J.C. and answered with the obvious lie. "It was self-defense. He was tryin' to shoot at us."

Jesse looked back toward Wade. Wade was working to get a view into the window from several feet away, and he was bobbing around as if he expected a bullet to come screaming out toward him. J.C. was unhappy with the looseness of the operation. Everyone, except Wade, was holding his position but other than finding Carl, there was no organized effort to bring this operation to a close. He felt terribly uneasy that several workers from the barracks were watching from behind and he kept casting worried glances toward them. To this point, they seemed to be only spectators and were staying put. He had not recognized any of them, and he determined that they were all out-of-towners Carl had hired to work at the steamplant and the sawmill. But his worries were worsened when one of the men in a doorway spoke up.

"You the law?" he asked. "I don't see no badge 'er nuthin."

J.C. tried to ignore the man, hoping that Paul and the preacher were watching his back. But the man was persistent.

"I said – you th' law, goddamn it?"

Angrily, J.C. answered, "Yeah, we're federals. Now you just stay put or I'll arrest you too!"

The man muttered something about his confederates, Al and Joe, being held in the dirt against their will. Then he shut up. J.C. watched Jesse to ensure that he wasn't trying to send a signal of some sort to Carl.

"Carl!" J.C. yelled, *"C'mon out here – we're not going away till you come out!"*

The cabin was silent. The door was still open but no one materialized out of the smoke. Carl had stopped coughing. Everyone stood his ground waiting for Carl to answer. The tension began building to the breaking point as the silence grew from seconds to minutes. Jesse was showing unusual patience by standing motionless and staring J.C. eye to eye, it seemed, without blinking. One of the workers from the barracks stepped out into the yard, away from the door. In reaction, J.C. moved closer to the cookhouse near Graham in order to watch the man out of his peripheral vision. So far, he could see no guns amongst the migrants. Then, with a motion of his hand, Wade told J.C. to take Jesse and to evacuate the area.

"All right, Jesse," J.C. said as softly as he could. "Walk over this way."

Jesse refused. He shook his head no and smiled. Things were getting charged up again and he was enjoying his moment in the limelight. Even though at least two guns were trained on him at any one time, it seemed to have no effect on his motivation. The standoff was a game to him and it angered J.C. that he would not take the threat seriously. One of the men at the barracks laughed out loud. Jesse looked and smiled at him; he was playing to an audience. J.C. could see that Wade was glaring at Jesse. Wade was ready for Carl to pay heavily for his crimes and he didn't need some self-serving egomaniac to stand in his way. Wade snatched his rifle down from his shoulder, then hunched down and sprinted back to the far corner of the barn where he had started. He turned and quickly motioned for J.C. to move out of the yard and out of sight toward the steamplant. J.C. eagerly complied with Graham following. "Paul, Ben – I want you both to try to stay put right here," Wade said to the two men.

It was all that Wade said. Then he aimed his rifle at Jesse's head. Jesse's silly smile dropped. Then just as quickly, Wade pulled down and aimed at a spot near his feet and fired. Dirt and dust bounced up to Jesse's face and he danced backwards. It was what was needed to bring order and discipline back into the program because the workers piled back inside the barracks and slammed the door shut. The show was over. Wade glared down at Al and Joe. They were sheepishly looking back up at Wade wondering what was expected of them now.

Jesse remained in the yard glancing down where the bullet had dug a hole in the ground just a yard away. He didn't know what to do next. If he ran back to the cabin to escape, he could be shot. It he stayed put, he could still be shot. Wade didn't stick around to see what he would do. It was clear that Carl was planning an escape out the rear. It was time to move.

"Wade – what're you going to do?" the preacher asked as Wade began walking around to the back of the barn.

Wade ignored him and moved to the clearing behind the barn. Walter and Jimmy were nearby; too close. Wade stopped before getting out of range and ordered, "Move back – now!" Then he was gone.

***

Surprisingly to Tom, Lucas was lucid and conversant. The throbbing in his shoulder seemed to have dampened itself to the point that Lucas could concern himself with things other than the pain. Soon after Tom had fired the round into the rear door of the cabin, he seemed to become overly concerned that a counterattack was imminent. He had found a recess in the bank of the creek that allowed him to view a large portion of the rear of the cabin in relative seclusion. He had quickly removed his brown and yellow-trimmed fur cap and turned it inside out with the dark gray fur exposed to the outside, hoping to be less conspicuous to those watching from the cabin.

Tom had taken the time to closely examine Lucas's wound and had determined that the bullet had entered through the back of the shoulder and made a clean exit out the front. Lucas's entire right arm felt like it had been run over by a truck, but the pain was manageable when he remained stationary. Tom continually scanned the woods all around for other sentries and was growing nervous when it seemed clear no help would be arriving soon. The stalemate had lasted only ten minutes, but it seemed to have been an hour.

Tom could see Charles crouched low in the bushes far away behind the barn, and he was easy to locate because of the design of broad red patches on his coat. Tom was afraid that such a loud outfit could alert the enemy to Charles's whereabouts but he seemed unconcerned. Charles, like everyone else, became alarmed by Lucas's screams. He had been trying to move in to investigate.

"Tom," Lucas said. His voice was surprisingly calm and contemplative. There was no trace of animosity in his tone, as Tom would expect. But he determined that he should be patient for the moment and give Lucas as much time as he could afford, given the circumstances. There was something in Lucas's eyes that locked onto Tom's and weakened his awareness of his surroundings. "I'm sorry for what I done, Tom," Lucas continued. "You was right all along. I just wish that I could have seen my way to do the right thing when you did."

Tom waited, not knowing what to say. He saw that Lucas was unaffected by the cold air blowing down through the gully with the sharpness of ice. He looked once more toward the cabin, then he moved to Lucas and said, "Your hand must be getting cold. Can you move your arm?"

Lucas looked down at his reddened hand and with Tom's help budged it enough to insert it into his coat pocket. He grimaced as he struggled but just as quickly he returned his gaze to Tom. Lucas's fur cap, identical to Tom's, needed a little adjustment around his ears, so Tom worked it down over his head and neck, then yanked his coat collar up enough to close the gap. Tom replayed Lucas's comments in his mind but was still at a loss as to how to respond. He was nervous and distracted by the war happening nearby and, suddenly and inconveniently, the opportunity to set things right with Lucas was at hand. It was too much to think about at the moment, but Lucas seemed straightforward and single-minded in his effort to engage Tom in a discussion of other things.

"Tom, I've been doing a little thinking over the last few days. I know this is not the right time for this, but I should've listened to you. You was right about making things right with the preacher and everybody. I would still be upset with you for a while, I reckon, but I should have listened."

Lucas looked off into the trees and seemed sorely racked by the thoughts of worse scenarios if the bullet had been better placed. It seemed that he was suddenly made aware of his own mortality, much like Tom after the tornado. Tom nodded, but was clearly not in the proper frame of mind to hear any confessionals just now.

Tom answered: "Luke, I hear everything you're saying, but I'm a little busy right now and – "

Suddenly, the sound of movement and snapping twigs drew Tom's attention back toward the west. Similarly to a bull trampling through the woods, the sound of someone making a last-ditch effort to make a getaway could not be mistaken. Tom quickly worked his way back up to the side of the gully and searched out the trees in the area of the noise. He turned his good ear westward. He spied someone moving quickly northward away from the building. A noise like that of a snorting deer could be heard coming from that direction. Tom gazed intently into the woods and he could only catch flashes of someone stumbling through the trees as if he were perhaps crippled or blinded. Tom looked back down at Lucas. Lucas's eyes were wide as if he was also hearing something that alarmed him. "Somebody coming at us, Tom?" Lucas asked.

Tom gazed back into the trees and strained to see all around. He looked at the back door of the cabin. It appeared to have been swung half-open. Then Tom found the runner again. It appeared to be Carl. Then he was sure of it. But Tom's eyes were inadequate for the task and the man was moving out of sight. *"Who goes there? Who is that?"* he yelled out. The man disappeared into a thicket many yards away. *"Charlie – where are you?"* Tom hollered toward the barn.

"I see him!" Charles yelled back.

Tom quickly rechambered his gun and fired a round into the air. The purpose being to alert those left behind on the other side of the buildings or to give notice for Carl to stop, he wasn't quite sure which. Someone, probably Charles, came running out of the trees on the far side and headed northward. Another noise came from the building. Tom spun around. Graham had quietly eased around to the back door of the cabin and started making efforts to open it farther. He squatted down low to the ground in order to look below the level of the smoke inside. With his gun held ready, he searched the floor, then swung the door wide. Bravely, he worked his way in and checked all the corners. The cabin was empty. He returned to the outside and gazed northward. Charles had moved ahead into a stand of trees to where Carl had escaped. Soon, Wade could be seen moving out into a clearing in clear view of the rear of the cabin. Angrily, he marched around toward the cabin with his rifle held up to fire. Graham moved away from the door. He was sure that Wade was going to fire into the cabin. "Nobody's in there!" Graham barked.

"Where the hell did he go?" Wade demanded.

"Out that way!" Graham said, pointing northward. He seemed afraid of what Wade might do, so he stepped farther away from the cabin. Wade spun around as if he expected to be shot in the back. He gazed with great intensity into the trees, and with an angry flourish he barreled away toward the north.

"What's going on up there, Tom?" Lucas asked, both of them still holed up in the creek bed.

Tom had been distracted long enough for Carl to escape. He had tried to catch up on the events by interpreting all that was going on around him. It had been his responsibility to cover the rear and he determined, with great regret, that he had failed. He turned and looked into the trees toward the north and he managed to get a last glimpse of Wade running like a deer into a thicket. A gunshot rang out deep in the trees. Then another.

"Tom?" Lucas asked.

Tom seemed to be cursing. He glanced back down at Lucas, then back at the trees. He was visibly upset. "C'mon, Luke. We gotta go – now!" Tom ordered. With care, but also with a frantic sense of urgency, he bent down and looped his arm around Lucas's back and pulled him forward, then up to his feet. Tom winced at a new pain that shot up the side of his body. The residuals of the tornado injuries were still with him. "Carl's got out and I let him get by me. Now Wade's going after him," Tom said sadly.

Lucas stood up well and didn't seem to be bothered too greatly by the wound to his shoulder. "All right, now," Tom said, as if to clear his mind and force himself to get back to business. "We're gonna walk you out of here. Can you do it?"

Lucas nodded affirmatively and proceeded to hobble up the side of the creek bank. Tom held him by his good arm to steady him, but, surprisingly, Lucas traveled well with little assistance. Soon, they were moving quickly into the clearing nearby and toward the trees.

***

The entire group of men had looped around the compound and was making its way northward toward the gunshots. The preacher returned to the wagon and turned the rig back toward the narrow road. He stopped and ordered Jimmy and Walter to mount up. The preacher, as he had done earlier on the narrow road, stared at Walter. The feeling of some distant familiarity about Walter refused to leave him. The corner of a solid red bandana or handkerchief peeked out of Walter's now-unbuttoned coat collar. It caused the preacher to recall that chanced, and unnerving, meeting with a lone black, and half-crazed, vagrant on the road to Braxton well over a year ago. This young migrant appeared to carry every characteristic the preacher could bring to mind from his remembrances of that day. The preacher turned forward to study the road then turned back for one more look. Walter never returned the gaze.

With a sure snap of the reins, the mules kicked up and yanked the wagon forward. At the intersection, the mules didn't slow down and the wagon slid across the road until both left wheels skidded into the ditch alongside, but the mules kept moving and just as quickly the wagon was back on the road and blazing northward.

***

"What's going on, Tom? Where is everybody?" someone yelled from near the north side of the building.

Tom looked around to find J.C. marching toward him. He had ordered Lucas to stay hidden in the bushes for a moment until things were better sorted out. Ben and Paul ran up behind J.C., all at the same time greatly fearful of being attacked from the building. "Nobody's in there – I checked it out," Graham said as he joined the group.

"I don't know," Tom said to J.C. "I think Carl got away and he's up in there somewhere. Wade and Charlie have gone in after him." Tom looked around and added, "Where's the preacher? And Jimmy?"

"We heard the guns go off and we figured it was getting too rough for Jimmy and the preacher, so I told them to get to the rig and get out of here," J.C. said. Then he saw Lucas materialize from behind the bushes. J.C. was aghast at the sight of Lucas's blood-soaked clothing and asked, "Luke – where're you hit? You okay?"

Lucas smiled meekly and nodded, but J.C. didn't see his response. "Tom – is he okay?"

"Yeah, I think so. I'll get Luke back. You boys better run help Wade."

Instantly, J.C. and the others marched northward into the trees.

***

Wade had moved into the trees and found Charles hunched down behind a honeysuckle thicket. Charles was searching the woods for movement. The breeze wasn't helping. Wade stood behind him for only a moment, then turned west and marched away.

Carl had escaped, but only with his life. With blind abandon he plowed through the woods like a derelict migrant on Friday drunk night with little regard for barriers such as saplings and brush. The frostbite and exposure were making a full frontal assault against his nerve centers. He could see but he couldn't discern the images of reality from visions of dancing hallucinations that bombarded him from all sides. The colors of winter trees and foliage had been replaced with the grays and blacks of single dimensioned shapes and shadows. Carl could still move fairly quickly, but his right side had begun to be taken a hold of by the impulses of a dying brain. His right leg and arm had stiffened and become numb. Soon enough, his arm had taken to swinging on its own in broad arcs near his body, uncoordinated with his stride. Finally, something punched him in the chin twice before he seemed to realize that his own fist was attacking him.

If he was aware that he could be caught with a gunshot to his back, he showed no concern by looking rearward. He traveled with comparably no protection against the little army on his trail. He had promptly dropped the .44 soon after he had entered the trees. He couldn't seem to remember in which pocket he had hidden the little .32. Or his wilting mind had forgotten about it altogether.

Carl hit a solid cottonwood and he bounced to the side. Losing little stride, he kept moving. His breathing took on a new hoarseness after hitting the tree. As before in the office cabin, he snorted harshly every time he exhaled. Now his soundings were more akin to that of an overworked plow mule on the verge of collapse. Somehow, the collision had forced his jaw to open wide and to lock tight in that position. At times, he could be heard a hundred yards away.

***

The preacher had slowed the rig down, but not by much. As he approached the bridge he saw three men on the other side coming his way. They stopped when they saw him top the hill.

"Where's Papa, Brother Silas?" Jimmy asked the preacher.

"I don't know, son. I think he's with Tom and J.C. back there," he said in hopes of comforting Jimmy, and hoping that he was right.

All along, as they traveled, Jimmy kept a searching eye on the road and woods behind them. With great trepidation he agreed to ride with the preacher. With all his soul he didn't want to be riding away while his father was in grave danger.

The mule rig crossed the bridge and stopped on the other side. The tripwire had long been snapped; its loose curls lying nearly invisible in the dust and foliage. Three migrant workers were walking southward toward the bridge. "You men better get back to the road. We need to clear everybody away from here," the preacher said to them.

"What's going on, mister?" one of the men asked. They were all workers from the barracks at Carl's burned house. They seemed genuinely bewildered and confused.

"They're trying to get Carl and take him to jail," the preacher answered. "They're all in the houses back there, trying to find him. He broke the law, men. And we don't have time right now to talk about it. You're all going to have to trust me on this and get yourselves back to the road till all this is over."

The migrants seemed open to his suggestion. None of them were armed and with no reason to continue, they turned and headed back, one of them hopping onto the rear of the wagon as it rolled past.

***

Soon, Carl hit another tree and was summarily ricocheted out onto the edge of the narrow road and he made enough noise in the process to alert everyone in the woods. He had managed to route himself away from the cliffs, and otherwise make a fairly unencumbered trip to the road through thickets and timber stands.

His right foot fell hard into the shallow ditch alongside the road and it required several halting but forceful steps before he was able to wrench himself onto the road. Crazily, he veered hard to the left and nearly tripped and fell into the ditch on the other side. He spun right and centered himself in the road. The bridge was just ahead, down at the bottom of the hill of which he was now descending. At nearly a run, he worked his dead leg like a wooden crutch. He had to rock his upper body back and forth sideways like an upturned clock pendulum in order to force his leg forward.

In no time at all, he was within yards of the bridge. The momentum of the run down the hill propelled him across the bridge, causing its rigged boards to pop. He started up the hill on the other side and never once looked back.

***

Wade tore out onto the narrow road and stopped cold. A lot of noise had begun coming from the road and Wade, like everyone else, had become greatly confused by all that was happening. From deep in the woods he had heard the preacher's mule rig. Everyone could hear it racing up the road, then across the bridge. Then another distant sound, akin to the troubled movements and the accompanying distressed noises of a newly crippled large animal, could be detected coming from an open stand of trees near the narrow road. Wade had tried to get to the area quickly, believing Carl was there. He was slowed by all the sounds of the winds, fearing that Carl was waiting in ambush behind the next tree or below each creek bank or behind each rise of the terrain. Too many men were in the trees, and with no central command or coordination between them they were left with little option but to advance forward a few feet at a time with the constant fear of being shot at at any moment. He had chased the sound hundreds of yards but Carl had kept the advantage by his nonstop march to the road, leaving Wade and the posse to fight all the competing racket in the woods.

But it became effortless enough for Carl once he found the road. The regular cadence of his stiff leg dropping to the gravel played a steady beat with his raucous breathing. Wade sprinted over the hill before the bridge. He was sure he could catch Carl there and stop him with an easy open shot without the danger of others getting in the way. But he heard who he suspected to be Carl crossing the bridge long before he could get to the top. Carl was managing to move fast, and he seemed to be staying inside the parallel perimeters of the road.

Wade ran across the bridge in time to see someone's head drop below the far side of the next hill. He moved to close the gap, then someone yelled from behind. He didn't look back. With great trepidation, he made it to below the crest of the hill and listened. The one-sided footstep had stopped. But the heavy mule-like breathing was still there. Carl had stopped and seemed to be waiting for Wade to come over. Getting ready to fire, Wade eased up a half step at a time. Then, finally, he could see the top of Carl's head. It seemed to be covered with a bloody rag or towel of some sort. Someone called from behind again. Wade looked back just long enough to wave his men off, but it was too late. They were crossing the bridge and coming up toward him far too quickly for his liking. They would try to stop him. He must act now.

Again he raised the rifle, ready to fire. He stepped up to the top. Carl was half-turned and looking, or so it would seem, directly at him. Then a bolt of great uncertainty hit Wade broadside. It wasn't Carl. But it had to be, he knew. It could be no one else. Wade could see the head and he moved up to see the rest. Carl had no gun in his hand – Wade could see that clearly. His left hand hung to his side, empty and appearing limp. His right arm seemed to be held up to his midsection, his hand gnarled and empty. Wade looked back at the face and found the apparition of a nightmare. Carl's right eye was gazing directly at him. But Wade could find nothing but a singular whitish bulge, looking from this distance similarly to a hard-boiled egg, protruding out of his left eye socket. The jaw was hanging slack, or was locked out of place, and his tongue heaved with each breath. The half-circle of teeth on the bottom fanged out like those of a rabid wolf. For another instant, Wade examined the man's skin and he could see nothing but ashen gray leather with streaks of brown and red. Where the division was marked between the burns and the frostbite damage, it was not possible to determine. Carl didn't seem to be catching his breath. He was still wheezing as badly as ever. The man was clearly dying, but he showed no inclination toward calling a halt to his escape efforts and seeking medical help for his terminal condition.

Wade stepped to the top of the hill. Carl's one-eyed gaze followed his every move. Carl was standing with his feet close together with all his weight bearing on his left leg. Then when Wade began to move closer with his rifle still ready to fire, Carl seemed to growl, or he may have been trying to speak. Wade flinched and almost yanked the trigger. He didn't know how, but he believed Carl was still capable of calculating a way to turn things around to his advantage.

Then Charles moved up behind Wade, with J.C., Ben and Paul close behind. Wade glanced back but returned his gaze to Carl. Clearly, the men were shaken by Carl's appearance. They stopped and stood speechless several steps behind Wade.

Again, Wade moved to close the gap between himself and Carl. One of the men said something, but Wade seemed deaf to their remarks. Carl's monstrous countenance didn't change, but he flinched and almost tripped over his bad leg. Wade watched him catch his balance by swinging his good arm up in the air, and Wade could not ignore how his right arm, though bent at the elbow and rigidly jointed, swung around uselessly as he moved. Wade moved closer and Carl growled bear-like. For a moment, it appeared that Wade was studying Carl to ensure that he was the quarry he was hunting for. The big man's appearance had been so devastated that no one could be absolutely sure. No one, except Jesse, had gotten a positive glimpse of Carl throughout the entire day. Wade had burned him out of his house and had chased him all the way to the compound in the morning darkness and had tried to get a potshot at him, and now he was chasing him on the road once again. Finally, he had cornered him. Finally, he had Carl's life completely in his hands. Now he could do as he wished. Carl would die – finally.

J.C. noticed that Carl glared at Wade as if all the other men were invisible to him. Not once did he make any move to recognize the presence of the others. Now about ten feet separated Carl from Wade. J.C. could see that Wade had not removed his attention from every aspect of Carl; his appearance, his gestures, his intentions as projected through his operable eye. Wade was carrying his rifle in his right hand and held it up from his waist like a pistol. For several moments, everyone remained still and listened to Carl's breathing. Wade said nothing. He was looking for some sign from Carl that would have indicated fear, resignation, or even some degree of penitence. But it was apparent that Carl's face had no pliability for expression. His jaw was still slack and he showed no more inclination to speak.

Wade moved forward and raised his rifle, still held like a pistol. Carl appeared to be fully aware and he reacted by stumbling backwards. Wade stepped forward, not willing to give Carl even the slightest advantage. Then, as slowly as the workings of a clock, Carl turned back toward the north, his back to Wade once again.

"Where's he trying to go, Wade?" J.C. asked. Wade only shook his head, then he began to follow behind Carl as he started up the road again with the rocking gait and the hoarse breathing. Then the noise of the bridge sounded. The steps of several men could be heard moving across it very quickly. Wade was keeping a distance of six feet between the muzzle of his rifle and Carl's back. Like a wind-up toy soldier with barely functional parts, Carl was keeping the march up at an even pace. Each time he rocked his body over to his right side, his foot slammed down like a sledgehammer in the dirt. Then he was forced to pull his torso around and over the dead leg, but he could pull forward quickly with his good leg, making up for lost time at each step. J.C. watched Carl twice slap at his paralyzed arm with his withered left hand as if trying to bring it under some form of submission or to discard it away from his body. It was bouncing around like a dangling sausage and it frustrated his progress each time it swung around to his chest and face. The man was drawing nearer to death with each step and seemed oblivious to the sheer hopelessness of his situation. J.C., like everyone else from the start, wondered what Carl was attempting to do, or even if he knew where he was and what was happening to him.

Shortly, behind them, the quickening steps of the men from the barracks were heard topping the hill. Everyone, except Carl, turned to look. Jesse's head topped the hill first, then he was followed by the heads of several men. J.C. quickly counted seven heads, all of them white except for Jesse's. Joe, Alex, or Virgil was not among their number. When Jesse stepped to the top of the hill, he yelled out: *"Hey, goddamnit – hold up there!"*

Everyone was armed. Ben and Paul moved leftward to cover Wade's rear flank. He still had his rifle trained on Carl. Carl didn't slow down. He seemed deaf and unaware of this newly developing event. "What's that crazy nigger trying to do?" someone asked to no one in particular.

"I don't know. Let's try to get this affair done with quick, boys," Ben said.

"One more hill," J.C. said.

Ben and Paul nodded. Everyone could hear voices ahead, and a truck engine or two. If they didn't make it over the hill soon, a gun battle would ensue. Or it could begin then escalate over the hill as other guns joined in.

"Goddamnit – stop right now, you cracker-ass sonsabitches!" Jesse shrieked.

All seven men were in full view and were coming on fast. J.C. recognized the one that had threatened him from the barracks. Ben and Paul walked backwards with their guns ready, both displaying faces drawn downward with fear. J.C. swung back and forth behind Wade, whether to cause confusion by creating a moving target or to improve his own vantage point, he wasn't sure himself.

Jesse wore only overalls, boots and a long shirt; far too little, it seemed, for the bitter cold. But he appeared unaffected by the biting breeze. All the others were heavily clothed. Bravely, or crazily, Jesse marched ahead of his men and held a long gun in one hand in similar fashion as Wade. Unlike before, he bore the expression of cold determination and meanness. Carl kept moving as if on some hidden reserve of strength. Why he kept moving instead of stopping to allow his own men to force the situation from the hands of his outnumbered captors, no one could guess. He must be deaf, J.C. thought. Or mentally demented and unaware of his surroundings. However, Carl was keeping a straight line down the middle of the road as if he knew where he was and where he was going.

A gunshot blasted from Jesse's shotgun. Everyone flinched, ducked, bobbed – one man tripped to the ground. Jesse had fired into the air over the men's heads without regard for the people that could be hit on the main road ahead. Paul and Ben jerked their guns down to fire back but mightily resisted the impulse. By now, the seven migrants had lowered their guns to fire position. J.C. placed himself behind Wade and prayed for backup from those on the road. Carl veered slightly as if he might have heard the shot but was otherwise unaffected. Wade and his compatriots showed no willingness to obey Jesse's commands. J.C., as well as Paul and Ben, wished that Wade would give it all up, but he stayed close to Carl with the rifle to Carl's back and his eyes forward, seemingly uncaring as to all that was happening behind him.

Jesse cursed again. He seemed on the verge of exploding with increasing rage. Something unfathomable had tripped inside Jesse's head and his tirade grew in pitch the longer the men played to ignore him. The dramatic shift in his personality from the daring comic at the compound to the present maniacal psychopath could not be ignored. The situation was growing exponentially desperate as the seconds ticked by. Jesse's wild eyes darted around the road searching for an opportunity to act on his last resort, whatever it might be. Then, in exact symphony with his confederates, he turned his eyes to the top of the hill ahead. His pace slowed to half-speed at the sight of something just ahead. J.C. and Paul turned to look. The heads of at least two-dozen men rose up above the crest of the hill. Their bobbing motion indicated that they were coming on fast. Then the wagon rig with the preacher on board pulled up fast behind them. Two more men, armed with long guns, rode standing in the back behind the preacher. Their eyes met Jesse's, then they cocked their guns to fire.

CHAPTER 36

Carl didn't stop. The townsmen platoon crested the hill and the men lowered their guns ready to fire like resolute soldiers in the first beginnings of battle. Jesse had stopped his advance and, with the bewildered migrants behind him, watched Carl charge ahead as if the platoon was completely invisible to him. The preacher pulled hard on the reins causing the mules to rebel by rearing up and reversing the wagon. Both men in the rear dismounted and joined the others on the ground. Carl was only thirty yards away and the gap was closing fast.

"Carl Dean!" Jesse screamed, his voice howling coyote-like. He yelled again when Carl failed to respond. He was too clever not to recognize the hopelessness of the situation. But no longer did logical reasoning seem to govern his actions. His entire livelihood was marching away in a dying body and there appeared to be nothing he could do to stop the inevitable.

Jesse abruptly halted his march and his men stumbled to a stop behind him. After several intolerable moments of helplessness and inaction, Jesse made a terminal decision. He broke from the protection of his men and began running toward the posse marching Carl Kallton to his judgment. Then things quickly began to fall apart. Jesse held up his gun to fire and made a running beeline for Carl. His confederates held back in futility and showed no willingness to join him.

At first, Paul moved laterally to block Jesse's path with his rifle held across in front of him as a barricade. Ben joined him and together they rushed Jesse and slammed the butts of their guns into Jesse's midsection. He failed to fall back and very nearly broke through. He yelled again at Carl, but Carl was imprisoned in a collapsing netherworld deep within the recesses of his increasingly nonfunctioning mind. Carl had begun to tremble and stumble and was making a zigzagged path up the road. It was clear that he was near the end of his strength and was expected to fall to the ground at any moment.

J.C. moved toward Jesse and jammed the muzzle of his rifle like a bayonet into Jesse's abdomen. Angrily, Jesse swung his gun up to fire but was instantly cut short by a blast from J.C.'s rifle. Every man flinched and danced aside to dodge return fire that never came. Wade spun around in defense, but swung back to Carl just as quickly. J.C.'s was a large caliber rifle and it blew through Jesse's upper abdomen and snapped out his spine, causing his upper body to fold forward as his lower portions fell back. A thin spray of blood and viscera splattered a couple of men far behind him. Jesse was killed instantly. The migrants recoiled and backed up, a couple of them dropping their guns and raising their hands in surrender. Far behind, on the next hill, Joe and Al were watching.

Carl continued toward the platoon of townsmen ahead and quickly enough they parted ways for him to pass. Carl stumbled toward the nearest one and, instead of allowing him to fall, he shoved Carl back toward the middle of the road. Carl closed the gap between himself and the mule rig. The mules reacted by bolting and pulling the wagon sideways off the road. The preacher, fearing he was losing control, jumped off the wagon and hopped away allowing the rig to roll with the mules into a clearing off to the side.

Everyone's attention returned to Carl. J.C. was cursing loudly. He was marching at an uneven pace as if trying to find something he had lost. He was petrified by what he had done and was fighting to regain a measure of control over himself. *"J.C. – come here!"* the preacher yelled. J.C. stepped over to him and allowed the preacher to grasp him around the shoulders and guide him alongside with the others. Everyone had surrounded Carl like a cocoon and was allowing him to continue; no man being sure of exactly what was happening now.

The final stretch of the narrow road lay just ahead. The heads of well over three hundred people materialized at the end all along the main road. A heavy truck engine could be heard idling somewhere not too far away. A long line of vehicles, stretching from east to west, became visible. Many voices rose up as the little army strode back into view. But Carl's rasping heave became more desperate and his gait began to wind down to a labored, unstable, stumbling march because, with dwindling strength, he could do no more than drag his bad leg along with each step. He no longer rocked his body forcefully as before and at times he was having difficulty keeping his head upright. His good eye gazed with intermittent openness and the big bulge in his left eye socket had protruded further, making him appear as if he might be garishly staring at everyone with great malevolent intensity; the pupil only partly visible at the inside corner of the socket. He also drew his jaw down with each breath, but he couldn't seem to consistently hold it up square and tight to the rest of his skull at any time.

The crowd on the road converged toward the entrance to the narrow road. It was clear that no one had taken charge of things and strident emotional expressions could be heard here and there. They were a hundred feet away when Carl suddenly became aware of things around him and seemed to realize that the end of his journey was at hand. He said something but it was unintelligible. He stepped several more halting steps, then spoke with frightening clarity: "Get the hell away, all you shits!" His voice was deep-throated and hoarse, seeming to flow up from his belly and out of his mouth with little movement of his jaw. He spoke again but no one could comprehend his words. He almost stopped but was prodded by a jab from Wade's rifle and he started again, seemingly unable to react willingly against Wade's control.

One of the men ahead of him could see Carl's eye searching out the road ahead. It was certain that he was aware of the situation before him. The fluids on his face seemed to have frozen to his skin and beard. From close up, it seemed that his entire facial skin structure had hardened after collapsing against the bone beneath, giving him the appearance of deathly starvation. There was no life in the skin and the only evidence of life left was that remaining in his leg movements and in the functional eye. For a short distance, he strengthened his step and straightened his path up the road. Wade looked past Carl and was searching the crowd for the sheriff.

J.C. was walking along the edge of the road with the preacher and didn't seem too concerned any more with present events. Like everyone else except Wade, he had lowered his rifle and carried it like a stick, no longer needing it for self-defense or patrol. Several times he had looked back down the road toward the compound. None of the migrants had dared follow.

Voices on the road were drawing nearer. Then the reactions of consternation increased amongst the crowd as Carl made the final approach to the end. The crowd had compacted itself into a large huddle with all eyes directed at the dying man. Word had spread quickly that the big man had been burned and had subsequently nearly frozen to death during his escape from Wade, and that his body had soon thereafter been reduced to that of a walking cadaver. Yet he was still exhibiting a diabolical strength of determination that rattled the nervous presumptions of the crowd. Now things were getting too complicated and Wade clearly resented the presence of an audience.

"Where's the sheriff?" Paul yelled. No one answered.

"Where's Luke? And Tom?" a female voice asked from the crowd. It was Sandra, Lucas's wife. The preacher looked back toward the south. Like everyone else, he had forgotten about Tom and Lucas. He searched the crowd but he knew they were not there. Pulling J.C. along, he moved quickly to Sandra.

"I said, where's Gene!" Paul yelled again. Everyone seemed deaf. They were shocked into oblivion by Carl's appearance and condition. Paul searched the crowd. He shouted, *"Somebody tell me – where's Gene!"*

Again silence. Then someone finally answered, "He's dead, Paul."

Carl entered the main road, and like everyone else, Paul turned toward Carl. If he was shocked by the response to his question, he didn't show it. Wade's face was beet red with the cold and his eyes were weary but unwavering. He still had his rifle held to Carl's spine, now just inches away. Carl didn't stop. He seemed to know where he was because he turned left in the road and began his trek westward with no one moving to stop him. It seemed that everyone was too stricken with their own trepidations concerning Carl's appearance to get within ten feet of him and everyone gave him wide berth.

Wade then searched the crowd. There was no law enforcement. He turned back to Carl and barked, "All right – far enough!"

But Carl still behaved no more considerately than a deaf man. Wade sped up and moved around to where Carl could not fail to see him. A woman's voice cried Wade's name. It sounded like Esther. But Wade kept his eyes aimed dagger-like at Carl's face. Carl's good eye danced around; first at Wade, then at others, then back at Wade, making full eye contact.

"That's far enough!" Wade again commanded. Then he poked the rifle muzzle into Carl's chest. Carl fell sideways and stumbled against the big flatbed truck a couple of his men had driven to the site. Finally, he stopped. The crowd surged forward for better vantage points. His own migrant workers from the house barracks were lost in bewilderment. They couldn't readily recognize Carl in the visage before them. Using his good arm to prop his body against the fender of the truck, Carl managed to raise himself to full erect position. He gazed at Wade again, and for a moment seemed to be studying his gun. His infamous half-smile was completely extinct and all traces of humanness were nonexistent. His hands appeared to dangle paralyzed and useless at the ends of his wrists.

Wade wasn't getting his attention in a way that he wished. Carl seemed to recognize the truck as his own and he moved toward the truck door and raised his operational arm to the handle and slapped it down on it. He managed to thereby cause his hand to grasp it hard enough to pop it open. Infuriated, Wade cocked back the hammer on the rifle, ready to fire. "This's as far as we go, you whoremongering bastard!" he spat. He punched the rifle muzzle stiffly into Carl's mid-torso forcing him to stumble back a single step. Wade leaned around as if to inspect for any innocent bystanders who might catch an exiting bullet fired through Carl's gut.

"Wade," someone nearby said. Wade turned to the voice. It was J.C. "Don't do it. The man's already near dead."

Wade neither tightened nor released the pressure on the trigger. He waited. Then to the amazement of everyone, Carl slowly hoisted himself up onto the seat of the truck. Vehicles were parked behind and in front of it. There was clearly no place to go. Wade searched the crowd. All eyes were now on him. With a flourish, he marched to the front of the truck and aimed into the radiator. He gazed up at Carl and saw the working eye staring down at him. The bottom teeth were quite visible, now in the shape of a sadistically exaggerated smile against the dark silhouette of Carl's head. Without taking his eye off of Carl's face, Wade yanked the trigger. The rifle boomed too piercingly for those nearby, causing a couple of them to curse aloud. The bullet smashed through the radiator and instantly a heavy spray of hot antifreeze arched out over the crowd, sending them running back to escape its rain. Wade rechambered and fired again. Carl didn't move, nor did he attempt to operate the truck.

Without prompting, Paul flattened both tires on the driver's side with two rounds of buckshot. The big truck heaved over to the side and Carl leaned over toward the door. He worked to slowly raise himself back aright. He turned halfway to gaze out the window at Paul. Then Paul returned to the front of the truck near Wade. The crowd had been alarmed by the gunshots. Some of them, it seemed, believed that the two men were shooting at Carl and responded with gasps and cries. Then everyone fell silent and gazed back up at Carl. The truck engine was still running and didn't seem to be immediately affected by the loss of its radiator. Carl was still making no attempt to move the truck. He stopped moving and for several moments he stared at nothing in particular out among the trees.

Paul turned and asked of those nearby, "Where's Gene? Why ain't he here?" He clearly didn't believe the earlier response.

"He's not coming – he's dead," Ben said from behind. Paul turned and looked at Ben. No one moved to contradict the answer. Paul turned back to Carl. Paul had no way of knowing the truth, but he was sure that the monster now sitting at death's door in the truck was somehow responsible. Everyone was waiting. It seemed that at any moment Carl would move or try to say something. Wade had heard Ben's answer to Paul's question but he seemed unaffected.

Sandra was near the preacher and in need of his comfort. She was crying openly but her face was hard with anger. Esther, Ruth, and Kelly Jean were still beside the car about thirty yards down the road from Wade. Jimmy was now standing near his relieved mother. Walter had retreated somewhere into the crowd. They had all watched Carl's zombie-like march to the road and stood back in fear when it became uncertain which direction he would go. It didn't seem to comfort them much that Wade had him completely under his control, along with two dozen other men. Carl was still alive, thus still, they were sure, potentially dangerous. The ladies couldn't see much over the heads of the crowd but they didn't seek a better vantage point. They could see Carl sitting high in the truck and didn't desire to move closer.

The truck's engine began to sputter and knock. The radiator had drained all its fluid and the motor was overheating. Carl, at first, didn't react to the truck's vibrations. He seemed unaware of it. Then he suddenly began to come to life as if his body had not been wounded at all. He somehow managed to grasp the steering wheel and pull himself up to the windshield. He craned his neck to gaze through the glass toward the trees along the south side of the road. The winter sky illuminated his face brightly and his ravaged facial features were clear to all. Somehow, his bottom lip and chin had drooped unnaturally and exposed the gray-white understructure of the gums, and a crimson ring of draining blood let loose streams of glistening fluid that trickled down his beard. The skin of his forehead, or the rag, or both, was hanging down to his eyebrows, giving him the presumed likeness of demonic savagery. The now-yellowed bulge of his left eye appeared to have retracted a bit, but his right eye was focused onto something far away and it was holding Carl's attention like a magnet.

The engine began to sputter more loudly and clouds of steam floated away from the radiator and drifted high up into the trees on the north side of the road. Finally, the engine quit with the echoing bang of a backfire. The smell of burning antifreeze filled the air, then, once again, all was quiet. The backfire didn't affect Carl's new vigilance to his surroundings. He was still staring into the trees along the south side.

Wade was the closest to the truck. He had the best vantage point to observe Carl's actions. However, he looked around and found a few of Carl's field workers standing with the crowd, watching. Roy was standing with his son, both still in the ditch. The look of anger had long ago left Roy's face and he was as full of curiosity and fear as many of those watching. No one, not even Wade, seemed to be looking for a way to end the episode. It seemed that everyone had nothing better to do than to watch and wait for Carl to collapse and die. Everyone seemed awed by the fact that the man was still alive. Wade slowly circled back around from the front of the truck toward the driver's side. Carl was still alert and staring into the trees.

"What're you gonna do, Wade?" Paul asked quietly.

Wade glanced back at Paul but didn't respond. He looked up at Carl. The door had been completely closed and the windows were up. Then Wade looked at one of the men who had been in the truck and asked, "There any guns in there?"

The man simply shook his head no and looked back at Carl. Whether the man intended to answer no or that he wasn't sure, it was not possible to tell. But Carl was not looking for anything nearby. The little .32 in his coat pocket may as well have not been there; he never exhibited movements or gestures to retrieve it. He was now slowly and almost unnoticeably rocking back and forth, all the while staring at the same point in the trees. Occasionally, someone would turn and try to pinpoint what was drawing Carl's attention away from the angry people around him, but could find nothing.

Carl's rocking actions gradually increased in frequency for several minutes, then his eye followed something that might be moving in the air, it seemed, several feet above the heads of the crowd. Whatever it was – guessed by some to be the hallucinations of a dying brain, or by others the long-awaited revelations of his world to come – it was invisible to everyone but Carl. His eye moved smoothly across the road from south to north and stopped in the trees along the north. Then his eye returned to the original spot and, again, seemed to follow something flying above the people's heads. Then he did it again and again. He began breathing in heaves and in a few more moments he started to lash about as if he could be fighting off dozens of tiny demons flitting about him like attacking hornets.

The murmuring among the people had stopped for several minutes but started up again when Carl began to swat at his invisible attackers and cry out loud enough to be heard through the glass. Then with a furious swing of his arm, Carl hit the door window knocking most of it out. He was going into a fit of madness, or so it seemed to some. To others, he appeared to be in great fear. He was fighting increasingly furiously to defend himself from the unseen airborne enemies as the seconds passed. The truck shook with each swing of his arm. He could be heard squealing in apparent terror and he was twisting his head back and forth as if scouting for incoming attacks.

Suddenly, as if a lever had been switched off, Carl seemed to give up to the conclusion of his inevitable demise. He gazed around once more before his arms dropped limp to his sides, then he leaned forward and fell onto the steering wheel. The horn honked once, then all was still. Wade stepped back and stood up on his toes to look at Carl's half-hidden face. He stepped to the door and reached for the handle, but he hesitated. It was as if he still expected Carl to counterattack somehow. Slowly, he turned the handle and popped open the door. He swung the rifle up and pointed it at Carl as if readying to fire a round through the door. The door creaked as he swung it wide. Then with slow, tentative jabs he prodded Carl twice.

Carl had spat, or thrown, a lot of phlegm onto the windshield and windows inside. The heater had been running in the truck and it had thawed him out, and fluids were dripping from his face and clothing. Wade could see the bulge of the damaged eye easily from his close vantage point. The skin on his face had now loosened and hung like rag pieces from the bones. The cloth on his head was loose but was held sopping to his scalp. His hands hung lifeless to his ankles. Wade watched for him to slide off the steering wheel and fall over onto the seat or to the floor. Wade, his hand gripped firm at the end of the gunstock, jabbed hard with the rifle but Carl's now-lifeless body remained upright.

Finally, Wade took a breath. The knifing pain of the cold against his ears and hands struck him suddenly as if such things had been no more than an irritating nuisance until now.

***

"I want to know what's happened to Luke! Why won't somebody talk to me?" Sandra asked furiously.

Her frustration, aggravated by a lack of a response from anyone, had been building. The preacher didn't know how to answer. He was hoping that someone, anyone, nearby would know the answer. Graham was standing nearby watching things silently like most of the crowd. He stepped over to Sandra and said, "He's okay, Sandra." His voice was subdued; clearly he had no more reason to hope for the best than anyone else. Then he looked back toward the narrow road as if hoping that Tom and Lucas would be walking down the hill at any moment. J.C. was listening, but he was still in quite a shock over what he had done to Jesse twenty minutes before.

"Then, where is he?" she insisted.

"He's been shot – but he's okay."

Sandra, with angry hardness on her face, demanded mechanically, "Then – where – is – he?"

"He's still in the woods with Tom. They should've been out here by now." Then Graham looked around, scouting the crowd. "Where's Annie, Sandra?" he asked.

"She's back home with the young'uns," she answered impatiently. "What're you all gonna do about Luke!"

The preacher was holding her, but it wasn't helping to keep her calm. Ben had rolled a cigarette and was nervously smoking it like a fast-drawing chimney. He, like everyone else, had moved out of the compound hastily, hoping to get the whole affair over with as quickly as possible. In the rush for his own safety he felt lucky to return alive and had inadvertently erased all thoughts of the possibility of leaving others behind. Graham had taken Tom's directive to evacuate and leave them behind as the final affirmative answer everyone needed to get away, and had assumed that Tom and Lucas would be close behind. He had failed to recognize that Jesse and his army had quickly closed the gap and perhaps unwittingly cut off Tom's and Lucas's escape route.

"We have to go back," Ben said to Graham quietly, hoping that Sandra wouldn't hear. He feared Jesse's confederates would exact their revenge on the two men if they found them, and it might already be too late.

"Look back yonder!" someone shouted. All heads turned. Someone was pointing eastward up the main road and said again, *"Look yonder!"*

Not everyone was able to see over the crowd, but anyone who could was not reacting with good favor. Ben moved to get a better vantage point, as did Graham. "They must have come through the woods," Ben said.

"Is that Tom? And Lucas?" the preacher asked after he was sure of the answers himself.

It was nearly at the top of the hill a hundred yards away. Two men were walking down toward the crowd at a slow, and crippled, pace. One of them was carrying a long gun with the other hand used to steady his ailing compatriot. Sandra's only response was to glare angrily up the hill at her husband. How could he so selfishly risk the well-being of his family like this? her mind screamed. First, he escaped his home before dawn this morning without a word to his wife. Then he followed his deranged cousin on some crazed mission of mercy for their old nemesis. And now this. She was fed up with the growing contempt that she had cultured against her husband for many months now because of his routine acquiescence to Tom's every vengeful escapade and imagining. But there was little she could do, she had long ago determined, to bring about effective change in things.

It took Tom and Lucas ten minutes to close the gap between themselves and the crowd. Enough time for Sandra to work on her thinking and draw up a small measure of forgiveness that was hidden deep in her heart like a candle in the night. Then tears of relief for her husband's safe return fell quite easily.

***

The show was over, and people were packing up and heading back to homes and businesses. Many of them decided to drive westward and pass by the truck in which Carl had died for a final viewing. The worst elements of his appearance were clearly visible through the broken side window and for a short while traffic backed up as the drivers crept by.

"You're next!" a man's voice barked at Roy as a horse and wagon rig rolled by with a man and a woman on the seat. Roy Jr. cursed at the man but he was ignored. No one was standing near Roy and his son. They were free to go, as far as Roy could tell. But he hesitated as another vehicle rolled by, the driver glaring at him. For the moment, he was too fearful of everything around him to move. He could see death sitting in the big truck just a few yards away and he wanted to hide his face from it, but he was too wary of his malevolent surroundings to turn his eyes away just now. Like Roy Jr., he was cold and shivering and wanting to go home.

Roy looked around the big truck and discovered that Wade and Paul were nowhere nearby. A group of people had gathered around a couple of cars about forty yards to the east. He assumed Wade and Paul had reunited themselves with their families. Other men were milling about the death scene. Some of them appeared nonchalant if not jovial, but others were serious and contemplative. It seemed to them that a good and proper thing had occurred this day and many benefits were to be had by everyone as a result. Roy became angry when he heard someone laugh. He turned to look. It appeared to come from the man whom he believed to have struck him when he had arrived on the scene.

He looked back eastward at the group. He found Wade and Paul with their wives. They were not smiling, but seemed relatively at ease nonetheless. The preacher stood with Ben and J.C., and the preacher was saying something to Tom. Tom's face was rigid and wide-eyed alert. Lucas was resting on a car fender and a couple of women were working on his shoulder.

Then the last of the heavy traffic departed and the road was opened at last. Roy turned to find Charles walking back around the truck and toward his buggy. Charles turned and looked at Roy but said nothing. He seemed to have a sneer on his face for Roy and his son and he shook his head slightly as he mounted his rig. The anger continued to well up inside Roy. But then he saw movement in the trees toward the south. He could see the small group of ragtag migrants walking slowly up the narrow road. Roy squinted his eyes and he could see that they had guns. Roy looked back to the people around him and saw that a couple of them were aware of the armed group on the little road. They didn't seem afraid. Then someone yelled, "*If you boys are coming up this way, you better drop them guns!*"

The group stopped, hesitated, and without discussion they propped their guns in an orderly fashion against a couple of trees and continued toward the main road. Roy was sickened. The migrants had come to find their fallen leader and they weren't up to a fight against superior numbers. But Roy couldn't find Jesse in the group. Reckon he's still at the steamplant, he thought.

Then, quite quickly, a small crowd developed around the preacher. By the reaction of many of the people, it seemed that he was imparting some bad, or sad, news of some sort. There was not a happy face among them. Was the sheriff really dead as the man had stated an hour ago? Was that the subject at hand? Roy didn't know; no one would speak to him. Then, to take advantage of the distraction, Roy grabbed his son by the sleeve and made a beeline for his rig parked twenty yards westward. No one made any effort to stop him. Within seconds, he had his rig turned around and rolling. Then he and his boy were gone.

CHAPTER 37

The next morning broke cold and breezy with a couple of cows mooing continuously but contentedly out on the east end. The light was just bright enough to make the herd faintly visible from the front porch. Wade gazed across the pastures and found among the grazing cattle four slightly built shapes, each with four legs like the cattle. Perhaps because of the herding instinct, it appeared that all the cattle were facing northward, as were the deer. Shortly an owl made a short, low-arcing dive into the field then quickly flew back up to the sky and disappeared behind the trees to the south.

A loose plank creaked as Wade stepped across to the edge of the porch and a chicken cackled underneath. He leaned against a post and again gazed across the pastures. He didn't feel well and he had hardly slept all night. And somewhere deep down in his belly he knew that other things were not well either. There was a crossroads or a fork in the road somewhere just ahead, and he couldn't determine why it was there or where he should turn once he got there. The problem, he seemed to know, was not out there in the pastures, in the woodlands around him, or in the offices of legal authorities in cities far away. It was somewhere nearby; so close that it was invisible to him. He had carried this feeling for a long time and it had grown like a cancer within him and yesterday's events hadn't changed a thing. But he had done his best for his family, so this restless, desperate feeling was unwarranted.

He sensed the smell of burning wood drifting in the air for only a moment. He hadn't started a fire yet, so it could only be coming from Paul's house. Or it might be that the embers had not completely burned out at what remained of Carl's house over two miles away. The bitter charcoal scent could still be moving about in the air. Then the smell was gone and no matter how hard he tried, he couldn't detect the scent again. But the wind had shifted and brought the other smells of pine rosin and manure from the southeast. Wade had started rolling a cigarette but gave up halfway through and tossed the half-made roll out into the yard. He reached down and picked up two sticks of firewood and returned to the front room and laid them on the irons in the fireplace. Then he did the same with smaller sticks for the cook stove in the kitchen. When the fires were up and crackling, he returned to the cold air on the porch.

He stood alone on the porch until daylight had brightened the pastures enough to enable him to see the swaying shapes of tree limbs and grass along the fencerows. Then he looked down into the yard for that discarded cigarette and, not finding it, he looked back up to the pastures and the barn. The cattle and the deer appeared as motionless as stone. Wade could see the whitish antlers on one of the deer but it was too far away to count the points. But he guessed that the buck was at least an eight-pointer and would probably dress out at nearly two hundred pounds. He watched the big buck rise up and swing his head back toward the south. The other three deer did the same. The buck raised his head high as if trying to find a better vantage point, then just as quickly he turned back and bolted to the trees along the north with the other deer following. Wade watched them bound gracefully over the fence and vanish into the trees. Wade didn't give it much thought and he turned back for the door, but his eye caught movement far off toward the south line of the lower pasture. At first, he thought it was the action of the wind against an evergreen shrub. But the shrub seemed to be moving like a wind-blown tumbleweed along the fence, coming toward the barn in the upper pasture. Wade worked to clear his wind-irritated, watery eyes and gaze with intensity into the distance. Then the moving shape disappeared behind the stand of trees on the near side of the upper pasture.

Wade waited. He figured a hunter had been hunting in the southern timberlands and had followed the deer to the pastures. But the deer were gone and the hunt was over. The figure was walking fast and soon he would be near the barn and Wade could identify him. But it was nearly five minutes before the man made it to the barn. Wade could see his movements here and there as he passed by a line of trees on the far side of the barn, and when he rounded the corner Wade could see that he was not carrying a long gun. Wade leaned out over the edge of the porch and tried to find the man against the background of mottled field grass and fence posts. For a moment, he thought he had lost him. He gazed into the foliage on both sides of the barn and after a couple of minutes decided that he had lost him in the trees.

Wade returned to the front room and looked at the clock. It was six o'clock sharp. Shortly, it would be time to wake Jimmy and start chores. Tomorrow he would start early again helping his uncle with the milk cows, but today he was allowed to sleep in. Wade walked back toward the kitchen and passed by Jimmy's door but he stepped back to find it open an inch. This was not unusual, but Wade gave in to the temptation to look in and with an easy shove the door swung open silently. The room was cold and quiet, and nearly pitch-black with darkness. But a faint gray light filtered through the curtain and illuminated an empty bed. In the corner, Jimmy's shotgun barrel glinted in the light. Wade felt a strong draft and looked at the window. The curtains were moving slightly at the bottoms and Wade stepped three paces across the room and parted the curtains and found that the window was up an inch.

Back in the front room, he looked out the side window toward the barn. He could see Jimmy coming through the gate and shortly he was walking quickly, almost running, toward the house. Wade watched him bound up the slope to the house and Jimmy worked his head back and forth scanning the farm for his father or anyone else who might see him.

Jimmy climbed the steps to the porch as quietly as a sparrow. Wade could hear the window slide up and Jimmy climbed through with hardly a sound.

***

An hour later, Jimmy lifted a bucket of fresh milk up to the floor of the back porch and plopped it down, splattering some of it out. He had hand-carried milk from his uncle's barn to home many times, so he should have been used to it by now. Nonetheless, he rotated his arm at the shoulder to relieve the ache of strained muscles. He gazed around the house and pastures looking for his father. He was beginning to feel desperate and alone again, in spite of recent events. The atmosphere in the house had been peculiarly awkward this morning and, as usual, everyone behaved as if something was being withheld from him. But everyone was tired from the previous day's experiences, so it may have just been his imagination – it usually was, he had long ago determined – but he had no way of knowing for sure.

The only sense of victory or accomplishment with which he could reward himself was the apparent success of this morning's before-dawn mission. He had hiked southward to explore the deep southern acreage that he suspected had been sold to save the farm. It was a necessary mission, Jimmy had determined. He couldn't seem to control his overbearing compulsion to run from the house and search for a refuge from, or perhaps the beginnings of a resolution to his life's bottomless abyss of ignored questions. Soon after the transfer of the deed over five months ago, he had heard sawmilling sounds emanating from the general direction of the southern acreage. It was his worst suspicion that his fondest childhood memories were now cut down and sawed into enough board footage to build a small town. Once his suspicions were confirmed this morning, something changed in his spirit.

He had fired the carbide beam of his lamp across the remains of his youthful heritage and found unalterable plunder and devastation. It was now a wasteland of fallen timbers, mountains of brush piles, acres of broken tree limbs and seemingly miles of deep-rutted truck tracks that crisscrossed his land like the webs of giant, demented spiders. He had waited at the edge of his new purgatory hoping without hope that the panoramic image before him was nothing more than the hallucinogenic remains of his worst remembered nightmare. He swung the lantern from due east to due west and searched for any semblance of life that could perhaps begin to prove his eyes were playing some devil's game of trickery against him. Even the sounds of the air moving through the trees were so profoundly lacking that, for only a second, he wondered if perhaps he had lost his way and ended up upon some distant farmland of newly cleared acreage that were not his at all. But he searched the remaining tree line along the northern edge in the hope of finding one of the few untouched remnants of his beloved acreage. Ironically, it was still there.

The big oak tree from which he had watched the finest bucks in the county pass beneath, then dispatched to his grandmother's Christmas dinner table, stood full-stature and unscathed by the sawmillers. Come Christmas day in winters past, Jimmy would be expected to detail, in as much youthful exuberance as was allowed in the Kallton house, every move and technique executed to take the deer from this tree. No other time of the year could produce the feeling of worth and fulfillment as the days of venison harvest in the south woods. It was the necessary pride of manly accomplishments that brings growth in a young man's standing among those around him. There were rituals to be performed, and thereby respect earned through such deeds; whether they be daring in nature or simply little more than everyday acts of mundane necessity. But it was the larger events such as these hunts that stuck in the mind, and which were drawn up from memory when the mundane seemed to dominate one's existence.

Jimmy replayed the scene in his mind. He stepped to the edge of the grave spot where Carl had killed the transient migrant. The spot could still be easily distinguished by the remaining hollow-out that sunk three feet deep a few yards from the tree trunk. As hard as he might try, Jimmy could not allow the nightmare of that night to erase the memories he had grown to cherish around this old tree. Now this part of his life was gone and there was nothing to say. If there might be anything to impart about how his life had been changed in the last year, he would have to study rigorously, and most likely futilely, as in whom he could confide. Jimmy wanted to talk, but his father had grown increasingly mute over the months, and Jimmy felt a growing desperation because of it.

But his father, if he felt any need to speak at all, continued to talk curtly about keeping things quiet and settled around the place for Kelly Jean's sake. That was all fine and well – he had long ago learned to accept this concept of family quarantine – but didn't she reveal some new revelations to the family a couple of nights ago when that old owl flew through the window? Was it still necessary to continue playing this game of family quietude against everyone outside the farm? Wasn't it time to come clean and become a member of the community of men once again?

Jimmy had clandestinely witnessed a murder over a year ago, and in spite of the dead sheriff's written confessional and numerous discussions and opinions among the locals yesterday, he was sure that no one outside the family still had any idea of what he knew. His father had kept everything so quiet and locked up that everyone was afraid to speak his or her mind. And it seemed now that this warped little family game of secrecy and quarantine was to be played out for the rest of his life.

"Jimmy – "

He spun around to the voice. It was his father standing just yards away.

"Come here," Wade ordered. Jimmy closed the gap and stood firm. After a pause, and with both their gazes locked onto one another, Wade asked, "Where did you go this morning? You was coming from the pastures at six this morning."

Jimmy's heart sank and he was sure that his father could see the change in his countenance and he tried to correct his expression by lifting his eyebrows. He had determined that it was possible that his escapade had been discovered, but he felt safe that the events of the previous day would far outweigh concerns for any lesser occurrence. He had thought that if, and when, his father ever actually did get around to questioning him, that it would be done in a much less dramatic and urgent manner. But he was cornered with no remedy.

Jimmy shrugged his shoulders as if to express indifference. He knew he couldn't lie. His father was too smart for that and he couldn't risk playing with his father's sensibilities so lightly. "I just went down to see the south end," he answered. "You know – where we used to hunt."

Immediately, he knew that his answer was amiss. It was actually a needful mission, to satisfy an overpowering urge to run a distance from his father's immediate domain. To get away a short while and seek, or hope, for answers to his growing dilemmas outside the influence of others. But he could not speak of that. Still, it wouldn't make sense that he had sneaked away to investigate the area in such a clandestine manner so soon after the tragedies of the day before. Even if his father believed that his motives were no more than to satisfy his curiosity concerning his old hunting grounds, it would appear selfish and spiteful that he would so blatantly run away for such frivolity instead of remaining with the family during this difficult time. Wade had burned a man's house down and procured his death and he was now in very probable danger of legal charges for arson and manslaughter – or murder. The sheriff had committed suicide and J.C. Jourdan was in great turmoil over his defensive shooting of Jesse Bridger; and Wade, it was supposed, was dealing with a great burden of guilt over that turn of events. Summarily, problems and burdens were great and seemingly insurmountable, and Jimmy had complicated things by adding to his parents' worries with a simple self-centered deed.

"You just wanted to take a look at the south end, huh?" Wade asked deliberately. It was dark at the time that he went south, so Jimmy knew that his simple explanation wouldn't hold water without springing a few leaks.

"Yes, sir – I took my new light with me."

Jimmy could tell that his father was not finished. Wade had turned his gaze down to the ground nearby and was uncharacteristically kicking an embedded rock loose from the ground. He should have had other things on his mind, and actually he did. But the curiosity concerning Jimmy's true motives and his veracity of abandoning his family, albeit for only a short while, bore deeply into Wade's soul. There was nothing to do in the house on this day, but it was clear that everyone was expected to stay close together as the community worked through things and come to a consensus as to how various players in recent events were to be dealt with. It would be a terrific affront to sensibilities if any member drew attention away from the immediate concerns of the family. There would be no discussions of recent events – it had always been that way – but everyone was expected to stay put until calmer constitutions prevailed.

Wade gazed away from his son and asked, "What'd you go to see down there, Jimmy?"

Feeling desperately unarmed and defenseless, Jimmy feverishly searched his mind for an answer but nothing would come up. He imagined he would feel better about getting through this inquisition if he allowed himself to cry as he did when he was just a few years younger, but the strategy would surely fail him now. He felt his father would view it as a vain attempt to appeal to his emotions, or worse – as a character flaw that needed to be exposed and disciplined.

"I wanted to see if it was all the same. That it hadn't changed none."

"Was it?"

"Uh – was it what?" Jimmy asked with a slight quiver in his voice.

"Was anything changed?"

"Uh, no. Uh – yeah! Somebody cut everything down! There wasn't nothin' left standin' down there, Papa!" Jimmy said with the emotion of someone who had suddenly lost something dear to him.

"You know I had to sell that place to pay for the dead cattle. Don't you remember?"

"Yes, sir – I do. But you and Mama wouldn't say nothin' about it so I wasn't sure," Jimmy said, exposing his own feelings of betrayal. "I just wanted to see for myself. It's all gone, Papa! They took everything! I mean everything! They cut all my trees down! Why, Papa – why?"

"Jimmy – now you listen to me," Wade said, eyeing Jimmy with eyes as hard as any his son could remember. "When you sell something to somebody, they have every right to do with it as they please. That's just the way it is. We can't change that. You understand me?"

Jimmy's eyes were aimed at his father with a pleading gaze. He was trying to understand while restraining his feelings of betrayal and loss, but he couldn't find the words that would have conveyed his ideas without causing his father to think that he was trying to question his authority. With trepidations, Jimmy pressed the issue and impulsively he answered, "Yes sir – but who'd you sell it to?"

Wade was showing a little impatience with Jimmy's persistence and said, "It was some man from Chicago. Why?"

"Chicago? Why would somebody from Chicago buy it, Papa?"

"Well, son – figure it out for yourself. You saw all the timber cut off, you said."

"You mean somebody come all the way from Chicago to buy your land just so he could sell the timber off of it?"

"Yeah."

"Oh," Jimmy said, relieved that he had managed to deflect the object of the discussion from the subject of his own clandestine behavior to the technical details of business transactions. But he determined that he should keep the momentum going. "What's his name?"

"Who – the man from Chicago?"

"Yes, sir."

Wade shook his head as if he couldn't remember. He could never admit aloud that the land had been sold to an agent for Carl Kallton, the instigator of the two hellish experiences his children will now have to suppress in their memories daily until their deaths. Jimmy would certainly see the sale to Carl Kallton as a betrayal of the worst sort. Wade had easily assumed that the details of the sale would never be the subject of any future discussions. He didn't bother considering the obvious fact that eventually the name of the owner of any land purchase would eventually be made public. He should have considered his son's curiosity.

It seemed that he had decided to discard further discussion of his son's rebellious behavior. Like everyone else, he was still tired and weary. But Jimmy had more questions.

"Papa, what happened to that old 30-30 rifle that used to be in the house? I was lookin' for it to hunt deer a couple of months ago but I couldn't find it."

If the question had been posed by anyone else in the household it would have been a strange question because they would have no reason to ask. It wasn't so strange that Jimmy asked, but Wade knew that he preferred to hunt deer with a shotgun and buckshot. But it was still odd nonetheless since many other weightier issues were at stake today – unless Jimmy suspected something that was related to the recent day's events. But Wade didn't need this. He didn't get angry when Jimmy asked the question, but he was rocked back on his heels and he was for the first time forced to consider, albeit to a small degree, his own deceit and selfishness.

Wade was coming to see that Jimmy felt betrayed by the loss of the hunting land and its subsequent destruction. But with logical reasoning and for the sake of the stability and needs of the family, he had done what was necessary and that was that. Jimmy was young, but he would learn. Now he wanted to know about the rifle.

"I don't know – don't worry about the rifle," Wade said curtly.

Jimmy gazed off into the trees somewhere toward the north. He was still thinking but he was doing it more slowly. "Papa, you remember when we went to Columbia to pick up Mama an' Kelly Jean?"

Wade nodded yes. Hesitantly, Jimmy weighed his words. He had memories of things that were too vague to describe accurately and he watched his father's gestures for permission to continue. He didn't know if his memories had merit or if his experiences were worthy of discussion with those who were wiser than he, especially when weightier matters were at hand. But his father had been greatly attentive to Kelly Jean's needs, especially yesterday. And why shouldn't he show the same concern for his son's needs, however trivial some of them may seem?

"What did you throw in that river when we went to Columbia?" Then after a long hesitation, he added, "Was it that rifle you throwed in the river, Papa?"

Wade couldn't seem to look Jimmy directly in the eye. He was sure that his son was sound asleep when he threw the rifle away on that day months ago after his first attempt to kill Carl from the early morning shadows of the trees. His son had remained asleep in the backseat of the car throughout Wade's effort to discard the rifle. Jimmy was out like a rock and Wade had gotten out of the car for only a few seconds, then they were on their way. Did his son witness a fleeting moment of his father's deed? He remembered that he had slung the rifle high into the air with both hands to ensure that it would be lost forever in the deep waters below. Jimmy could have glanced out the window just long enough to see the rifle cartwheeling high in the morning sky. But it happened too fast. It was not possible that he could have seen anything.

"You know I seen you throw it – I wasn't just dreamin' was I, Papa?" Jimmy asked uncharacteristically with a fast staccato.

Finally, Wade looked his son eye to eye. "All right – can you keep a secret, son?"

Jimmy answered instantly: "You know I can – I ain't told nobody I seen Carl kill that man down on the south end over a year ago, like you told me to."

Jimmy had answered honestly, but it sounded full of sarcasm. It was unintentional, but it solidly hit its mark. Something changed between father and son. Jimmy could sense the change even before his father spoke. With a grave tone, spiced with venom, his father spoke.

"I tried to kill Carl Dean Kallton. I shot him, but he didn't die. Now let me tell you something – "

Jimmy choked with emotion before Wade could finish. "But Papa – no! Didn't you tell me that Mr. Carter was going to get him? Didn't you say we wouldn't be bothered by him no more? I seen you down there in front of Uncle Paul's house with him layin' out water lines 'cause our wells went dry! Why was you helping him, Papa?"

"Jimmy, things don't always work out like you expect them to and you have to do things – you have to sometimes take matters into your own hands and – "

"But why didn't you tell me that? I saw him kill a man, Papa! An' you told me he was hauled away by the sheriff – but then you work on water lines with him like nothin' ever happened!"

"Didn't you ever see Carl in town last year?"

"No – uh, I don't think so. But if I did, I wouldn't know it was him! I couldn't see his face when I was up in that tree – remember? I didn't know that was him till I seen you down on the road with him! Then I learned the truth!"

Wade got a grip on himself and calmed down. He was doing poorly with his son, so he searched for words, just as Jimmy was forced to do moments earlier. Quietly, he said, "Boy, it's a hard life trying to make a living on this land. You're still young and someday you'll know how tough it really is." Then Waded turned and pointed to the pastures. "You see them cows out there?" Jimmy turned around. He could see nearly all of them peacefully grazing across both pastures. "If we lost only a couple of them, we could lose everything. You hear me? Everything! Now we lost thirteen head last year – that come to near bankrupting us. But I saved us by selling off a few acres of land and timber on the south end, and now we're okay for another year. But next year I might have to sell the timber off the north just to get us by. And then we still might not make it – but we won't know till this time next year."

Jimmy again felt that strange and overwhelming aloneness and loneliness and fragility of life that he had experienced for many days after the murder at the oak tree. His father was affirming his fears. The futility of it all was overwhelming. And then to think that his own father could so cavalierly shoot a man, albeit a malignant one like Carl, was beyond his comprehension. He had watched Carl kill a defenseless man in cold blood, and since that was the only frame of reference he had, he imagined his father trying to kill Carl in like fashion. Jimmy was shaken with this new revelation of his father as a cold-blooded killer. He could understand why his father had done what he did yesterday. At least he had captured Carl and brought him out at gunpoint. At least he had not killed him in such a cold-hearted manner. Yes, he had shot a couple of dogs and burned a house to the ground with the intent of killing its occupant – a deed in which he almost succeeded. But ultimately, it appeared that his father was trying to bring Carl Kallton back alive to face prosecutions for his crimes.

Jimmy fought hard to disbelieve what he was hearing. It was a weighty load for his young mind and he was overwhelmed with new fears. Now he wondered what had possessed his father and he wished to run away and never turn back. This urge to run was immediate and strong –

nearly as strong as this morning's when he woke up, dressed and climbed out the window with hardly a thought to consequences. But he managed to shove the urge an arm's length away and turn his thoughts back to the issue at hand. His father had won yesterday's war, but today he was finding his father to be savage and unyielding – not repentant for his actions or thankful that a year's tragedy seemed to be over. Jimmy wanted someone to care that he was lost and alone and confused out of his mind, and he feared that the more questions he asked, the more confused and fearful he would become.

"You mean that was who was in that truck we seen behind the sheriff when we was comin' home with Mama an' Kelly Jean? Was that when you shot Carl Kallton?"

"Yes – yes, son."

"But why didn't the sheriff do what he said he was goin' to do? Why did you have to do that?"

"I told you – for Kelly Jean's sake. She was losing her mind over James Buell getting killed and I wasn't going to have Gene, or anybody else for that matter, coming here all hours of the day talking to her, then making her testify in court about what she seen at the North Road. She already had more on her than she could take on, son. And all the rest of us was having to run the farm to keep from losing everything we got. If we had to run up to the courthouse and carry on with lawyers and the state police and such, we'd just lose it all – not to mention Kelly Jean losing her mind and us having to put her in an institution. You remember how she wakes up all hours of the night crying and carrying on, don't you? And how she thought that Carl Dean had come to get her the other night when that old owl come through the window?"

Jimmy nodded. He thought of the day when the sheriff had come to take Wade to jail for his refusal to cooperate in the investigations. He remembered how he was told that his father would be back home in a couple of days. He was not told that he was being hauled to jail, but he found out the truth the next day when he found his mother crying in the arms of his aunt Ruth. Then he was told. And like a good soldier, he stayed strong and never asked about it again.

Wade continued: "Well, we're just too close to the edge with this farm to be letting other folks run our lives and tell us how to run our own affairs. I couldn't let Gene get at Kelly Jean and get her so stirred up and have her to be the center of attention in this whole situation, and making a big show for everybody to see and talk about. You see, son, me and your mama couldn't have no more young'uns. We wanted more boys to help on the farm but it just wasn't going to be. So, I wasn't going to do anything that might end up with us losing one of you. And if we lost the farm, we all might have lost one another. Now would you want that to happen?"

"Un-uh."

"That's why I had to do things my way and not let the sheriff or the people from the state make us stretch it out over two or three years and break us. I just couldn't afford to take the chance of that happening."

"Papa, did you really tell the sheriff what I seen Carl Kallton do under that oak tree?"

Wade flinched but didn't answer. The question was asked as if his son had not been listening. Jimmy determined that the question was out of order and had sounded accusatory, so, as a simple diversion, he asked, "Was you afraid? Was you ever afraid?"

Wade had never entertained the luxury of feeling stable in his entire life, but at least he had conducted his affairs over the years in a steady and dependable manner, thus presenting himself as stable and unfaltering. Yes, he had been afraid. He couldn't remember a moment in his life when he hadn't been afraid to some degree. But what would be the point in discussing it, much less admitting it? – a question of which the search for its answer he had many years ago determined to be a waste of his mental energy.

"Everybody gets afraid at some time or another," Wade heard himself saying. "If you're never afraid, son, you're just not human."

Jimmy was still rocked by his father's admission of attempted murder. He had remembered the events of that week when the county was abuzz with the talk of Carl Kallton taking a bullet from some angry antagonist and then survived. He had accepted, at face value, the talk of Chicago gangsters taking a shot at him. Then he heard that it was some sort of accidental shooting. But he had assumed that it had happened either in Chicago or in a big city prison somewhere far away. He had not begun to put things together until he discovered Carl working on the water lines on the road with his father and his uncle Paul. Then he recalled back to the rumors that had sounded about soon after he had seen, or dreamed, his father throw the rifle away into the river. He had been sheltered from school, the townsfolk, and friends for months. He had overheard tidbits when the preacher visited or Paul had whispered hushed phrases to his father when it was thought that he was out of earshot. But it was always cryptic tidbits; never anything substantial that could have helped him put it all together.

"Where did you have to go to shoot Mr. Carl?" Jimmy asked. He was so weighted with rational reservations that he couldn't know how his questions would be taken. His throat had such a heavy lump in it that he was fearful of breaking and crying, but he managed to wrangle enough control over his vocal cords to continue the discourse.

"I went to his house, just like I did the other night," Wade answered. "Except I waited for him to come out at sunup."

Jimmy had wished that someone else stood nearby to listen, and to carry some of the load. Jimmy determined that he had never really known his father, even though he had lived in the same house with him all his life. Everything was confusion, secrets, deception, instability and callousness. This was not how life was meant to be. Somewhere, somehow, there had to be a better way, but this was all that he was given. He felt cheated and lied to so often in the last year, and now his father was dumping all this ugliness and treachery upon him. He wanted desperately to give his father the benefit of the doubt if he could, but he couldn't find the door to do that.

Wade continued: "Son, I just wished that things could have ended up a little more peaceful around here, but I never could see my way to do that. So, you're just going to have to stand strong and help out around here while we get through all this."

"What do you mean, Papa? Ain't it all over now?" Jimmy asked, not comprehending the full intent of his father's statement.

"I don't know. I hope the worst is over. But you have to realize that I burned a man's house down, and I went after him without the law. I don't rightly know what's going to happen now."

"But you was just trying to do right by Kelly Jean. They'll understand, won't they?"

Wade looked at his tall son. He stood equal – eye to eye to his father. Through his own deceit he had forced his son to grow up too quickly in the last year and his own fears had overruled his sense of right and wrong and brought his esteem low in the eyes of his boy. But what could he do? he reasoned. He hadn't intended for things to end up like this. All he had ever wanted was a family and a reasonably dependable livelihood like everyone else. But something had gone terribly wrong and it was not his fault. How could he get this young, immature boy to understand? The only way he knew was to hit him with the full strength of the truth when all else had failed. He had tried to protect everyone and keep each of them from harm, and hide his family from the worst that life could throw at them. But he had been backed into a corner with no remedy.

Jimmy's eyes were misty but he wasn't breaking down. Jimmy carried no resemblance to his father when Wade was his age; intellectually, physically, or in any other aspect of his being. Wade was born wise to the world and trusted no one. Jimmy could not find purpose in life if he couldn't trust, or believe in something outside of himself. There had to be a foundation, a solid footing, but it was elusive. The only ounce of consolation Jimmy could find was the feeble fact that his father had spoken more openly and at more length with him today than in any previous father-son discussion he could ever remember.

"I hope so," Wade finally answered. "But if they don't, we'll just have to get through it as best we can. We'll just have to wait and see."

***

The cold days just after Gene's funeral passed quietly and uneventfully in the Kallton homes, but soon enough a new call to order by the preacher could not be ignored.

"Brother Silas wants us all to come to church this Sunday, Wade. He wants you to come too. I know he's going to ask you today," Esther said. She had spoken in the most disarming voice she could affect, hoping Wade would not think of taking any offense against the preacher for not asking him first. "He said he wants everyone there. He didn't mention you by name, but I know he'd like to see you there."

Wade had thought that it had been enough for everyone to endure and survive all that had happened in the last fifteen months. Two weeks before, they had buried Gene Carter and it was now time to quietly recoup and get back to business. He could not muster the desire to be bothered by all this. But at the same time, he was still fighting that relentless weariness and he was growing a bit desperate to find a way out. He, as always, hated thinking or talking about his, or anyone else's, feelings, but he was being forced to react differently to the new direction his life had taken. He could go to jail now and instead of being free to protect his family from the queries and harassments of the law, he would now be the center of attention of legal authorities and public scrutiny near and far. He figured he could handle this new reality by himself if forced, but what would happen to his family if his attentions were required elsewhere for many months?

He turned to Esther and half-nodded as if he would consider the offer, though he had been forewarned of this new call to order through his brother. He should have felt better about things, though. After all, it was his idea to begin the burial fund for Gene and to give the sheriff the complete eulogy service and burial that he deserved. "Where's Jimmy?" he asked after a minute of introspective silence. He had said little to his son in the days since their little discussion after Jimmy's milk fetching at the back porch.

"I told him to go get the springhouse cleaned out. Didn't you say it ought to be running again in the spring?"

"Yeah, if the rain comes like it should."

The water supply from Carl's compound stopped the day Carl died. All of Carl's management personnel and the workers at the compound had vanished for fear of legal reprisals, thus there was no one to maintain the pumps. Wade had not regretted making the water arrangements with Carl; as usual his motivations concerned the well-being of his family. But it had not rained since, and it was probably going to remain dry until the weather warmed up. Even then, it would be weeks, perhaps months, before the water tables were up. He had felt quite humiliated when the fire wagon was commandeered by a few church folk and several hundred gallons of fresh water were brought to the farm. Then again two days later. It bothered him to know that word had somehow gotten out concerning his water problems and no one would volunteer as to who the talebearer was. But he suspected the preacher. He was sure Paul had told him.

He looked out the kitchen window down toward the springhouse. The door was open and he could see the broom swinging back and forth out the doorway with a puff of dust each time. The springhouse would not be needed until spring, over a month away, so it seemed peculiar that Esther would want it cleaned this early. Perhaps it was little more than a mother's effort to return the household to some degree of normalcy. Kelly Jean was still recuperating from lingering foot problems and had been forced to stay off her feet since the funeral. Wade could hear the crackling fire in the front room and Kelly Jean was quiet and resting there.

Wade, along with his family, had attended Gene's funeral and everyone seemed to fare well through it. But Wade was surprised by the weight of grief he felt throughout the day. The fact of Gene's suicide, and the causes of it, had torn at his heart in ways that he thought were not possible. He could not keep his mind away from the thoughts of others. He was filled with the paranoia of others' opinions concerning his actions of the past many months. Everyone was well aware of his uncooperative behavior when dealing with the sheriff, but Wade had refused to allow anyone to change his mind on the issue. He had easily convinced himself that his family's welfare was paramount and all others' opinions and needs be damned. Was this attitude selfish? Perhaps it was, but he had never allowed himself the luxury of worrying about the consequences as long as his own little kingdom remained standing.

Nearly everyone in the county had attended the funeral. Wade was arrested by the kind and conciliatory spirit displayed by both Tom and Lucas Buell after it was all over. It felt as if there had never been even the hint of discord between the families. He never knew what to expect but when Tom offered his hand, Wade was both appreciative and wary. He appreciated Tom's efforts at breaking the ice and renewing broken ties, but he was distrustful of his motives. He remembered Tom's offer to make things right by selling some land and paying for the dead cattle, so he wondered if he was beginning efforts to quietly disregard his own promise. Also, if some of Tom's land was to be sold out of the family assets then Lucas could be financially hindered if his own enterprises were stymied by Tom's impulsive actions. It was known that the two farms operated as one, much like Wade's and Paul's. Thus, Lucas had a motive to practice a double standard for reasons similar to Tom's.

"Wade, won't you come with us to church this Sunday? The preacher is going to ask, I know," Esther pushed again.

Wade, again nodding, said, "All right. We'll see."

It was enough to make Esther sing with delight, but she refrained from showing undue emotion. She returned to the stove and said, "J.C.'s going to come, he said, and help with the singing. You know his wife, Jessica, don't you? She's supposed to be related to you, isn't she?"

Wade nodded, but realizing Esther was looking away, he said, "Yeah, that's what I've been told."

The air outside was still cold all day long, morning till night every day, and it was good to be able to work fewer hours than was required during the warmer months. When the weather begins warming up he would have little time to think about things, as he was able to do now. He needed to ensure that things were running smoothly before the real work began and any legal ramifications for his deeds begin to rob him of his remaining peace of mind. Over the months he had come to feel overwhelmed with the physical concerns of the farm and family. Esther seemed only to care for the spiritual well-being of the family; she felt all other things would fall into place if things were correctly prioritized. The preacher had taught her well.

Wade, like some others, was nervous about the contents of Gene's suicide letter. He had learned that Gene had forced a confession out of Billy Wilson before killing him. And the letter was very long, meaning that many details and events must be well documented. Billy knew that Wade was aware of at least some of the circumstances surrounding the death of Earnest Jackson. And Wade, because of these recent developments, could now never be sure that Billy couldn't see him in the early morning woods when he shot Carl. Were these items included in the letter? Wade wasn't anxious to find out, but the probability that they were worked to worsen his restlessness. The thought that he could be held culpable was kept at arm's length, and, as usual, only nondescript, constructive discussions were allowed in the house.

So far, Esther had not queried him on his mentioning of the murdered migrant, Earnie Jackson, on the night of Kelly Jean's confessional. Nor had she even touched on the hard subject of the subsequent arson attack and gun war against Carl. Wade knew she had not forgotten, but he didn't worry that she would return to ask again. Her family was intact and well and she didn't want hard discussions and worrisome talk to disturb their new-found, but temporal, peace.

Finally, Esther began to hum. It was a hymn that she loved and Wade had not heard her sing it in well over a year. Then Jimmy entered the back door and stopped before his father. He was not used to seeing his father sit around and rest as much as he had in the last week. Jimmy seemed to wonder that his father may have fallen ill. Then he heard his mother's singing. Something was different in the house and he hoped it was a herald, of some measure, for good tidings to come. It was hard to tell, though. He could see his father's always-pokered face and his mother was still turned away. "Ice house is clean!" he announced in a voice meant to grab instant attention.

Then Esther turned to face him. She already had a smile on her face. Yeah, Jimmy thought, there might be reason to hope, someday, for something good in this house after all.

CHAPTER 38

The little church was filled with more smiles and greetings than the preacher could remember in all his years. Here and there, laughter pealed out so often that he felt he needed to pinch himself to ensure that all this was not just a dream.

He had just finished refilling the stove with two more sticks of firewood before sitting back down to survey all the activities before him. He saw J.C. on the front pew with the stack of hymnbooks ready to pass out at the start of the service. He was glad to see J.C. smiling like everyone else and he even laughed out loud once when someone leaned over to tell him something.

The preacher could see Tom and Annie sitting next to Lucas, Sandra, and the children about halfway back in the church to his left. They were sitting on the worst bench in the house in that it had been broken and repaired so many times that most people avoided sitting there. But Annie insisted on the family using it when the church first began to fill to capacity a half-hour earlier.

The door opened and Graham Faulk, one of the church deacons, and his family of six stepped through. The preacher watched him scan the building for a space for his family. The preacher waved and pointed to a spot near the front. Graham paused to shake the hands of those near the aisle. He didn't seem surprised to see Wade there and he waved to him; he was too far away to greet with a handshake. Kelly Jean and Jimmy were wearing clothes that appeared to have been pressed with an extra application of starch, and Jimmy's shirt looked so purely white that it glowed in the reflected sunlight of a window nearby. Kelly Jean seemed as happy to the preacher as he could ever remember. He had caught her looking and smiling at him twice and he returned the gesture with a pointing finger each time.

The preacher looked back across to the other side of the building and saw Mrs. Sarah, Paul, Ruth, and the boys sitting far behind the Buells. Gracie's head was visible between the shoulders of those in front of her. She sat between Paul's and Ruth's two boys, and the preacher could see that she was wearing the new frilly Christmas dress that Mrs. Sarah had made for her. The family had arrived late with Wade and found seats where they could. The preacher had hoped that Roy would have showed up with his boys. He had managed the audacity to visit Roy twice after the sheriff's funeral but he found no reason to hope.

He could see that everyone was aware of the sweet spirit in the building and here and there people were watching the preacher for his reactions to the scene before him. Another deacon, Ben Townsend, had moved from the front bench to sit in the deacon's chair next to the preacher. It was his job to bring the service to order for the preacher and get the song leader started. He hadn't bothered to check his watch because it seemed the service had already started because of the high spirit and gracious attitude of everyone. It seemed that the small children felt something was different and were unduly energized by the excitement.

The great tragedy was over. Carl Dean Kallton was dead. Hurt feelings had been healed and old friendships renewed. In a flash of sadistic irony, the preacher had determined that Carl Kallton may have been the best thing to have ever hit the community. He wondered if such a day as this one could ever have been possible had it not been for the deeds of that envoy from hell. The preacher's sermon was ready but its content was changing the more he thought about the excited people before him. This is how heaven must be, he thought; everyone getting along perfectly with one another, and it all would have been impossible without hardship and tragedy. It seemed to him that they had already figured that out for themselves and his sermon might become a moot issue if he preached it as planned.

He could remember the childish jealousies and hurt feelings from errant and braggadocios comments. He knew the Kalltons were brave to break with tradition and go into beef cattle farming, then, to outward appearances, make a success of it. He had heard that Tom Buell had wished to do the same for many years but didn't quite have the gumption or strength of determination to attempt such a major enterprise. And it galled him, it was told, to see Wade and Paul stay with it and succeed. Thus Tom tried purchasing modern farm equipment on credit and when some of his best machinery was stolen, the deed was traced to the Kallton clan – more specifically, to Roy Kallton. Then it was all a vertical plummet from there.

The preacher understood Wade's management style, but he could see how others would have perceived him as self-important and isolationist. It was easy for the preacher to see that Wade was basically, and deeply, insecure and frightened. The preacher was sure that Wade's desire to find a haven of security for his family could only be made possible through his own efforts and abilities. He didn't need, nor did he want, the help of others. He could do it without their prayers and support. After all, there were others who had always been dependent upon God and man and had not scratched even a pauper's existence, let alone enough to support a family, out of the ground. All of these useless ceremonies, such as church meetings, revivals and prayer sessions, only put a drag on his efforts; he needed those precious extra hours to help stay ahead of mortgage and credit payments. The preacher hoped that somehow, to some degree, Wade would see the futility of it all, as the possibility of upcoming legal retributions loomed just days away. Perhaps soon, he will realize how his actions, no matter how well intentioned, may actually end up harming those he cared for most.

The preacher glanced around the little crowd and inspected the faces of those who had taken sides, some of them aggressively, with the Buells or with the Kalltons. He remembered how foolishly many of his people had made statements that were not based entirely on fact and hadn't seemed concerned that injured sentiments or difficult situations could be worsened by their errant comments and unsubstantiated opinions. He could now see many of them engaged in animated conversations and carrying on as if no sin could be laid to their charge. Perhaps that is what he should preach about today. The people seemed rarely capable of realizing their own sins or how they sometimes appeared to other people. The preacher gave them as much benefit of the doubt as he could, realizing that many of them suffered their own problems at home and seemed to need to bring some measure of stimulating distraction into their lives, and the church was an easy place to find it. Now, he wondered too, how many people were here solely for the curiosity factor and how much they really cared for truth and the spiritual aspect of their lives.

Ben stood up and looked across the crowd. J.C. had already begun to pass out the hymnbooks and was recruiting others to help. Everyone quieted down and Ben spoke. "Brother Graham, would you open the meeting for us this morning?"

J.C. stopped passing out hymnbooks and Graham stood up and began to pray. His prayers varied little in content from one to the next and they were usually short. A child reached for a book from J.C. but he shook his head to wait. Every head was bowed and no one else moved. Graham had immediately felt the new spirit in the church, and he added a few new phrases that he felt were more attuned to the gladdened hearts.

"... And Lord, we Thank thee that You brought us through these hard times. Like Paul and Silas in the Book of Acts, You brought us to a better day. Our faith is stronger for the trials You sent us. Help us as we draw nigh to that final day. Be with Your servant, Brother Silas, as he brings The Word. We'll give You all the honor and the glory. In the name of Your son, Jesus Christ – Amen."

J.C. quickly rebounded to the front, near the pulpit, and announced the page of the first song. An old upright piano stood nearby but it had remained untuned for so long that it was no longer used. J.C. motioned for everyone to stand, then he raised his hand to start the first note. At the first stroke, the house burst forth with a chorus so voluminous and full of spirit that the preacher, still seated, felt he might jump out of his seat for the sudden elation he felt in his heart. It was a relatively new song and it was appropriate. The preacher looked around as the refrain of the third verse rang out:

> *"Not the people who are shoutin', but it's me, O Lord,*
> *Standin' in the need of prayer;*
> *Not the members I am doubtin', but it's me, O Lord,*
> *Standin' in the need of prayer!..."*

The preacher stepped down from the podium and gazed out at as many people as he could, sweeping the crowd with his eyes. Most of the people were happy and it showed on their faces. At first, it was a wonderful feeling to see so many of his people back at church and happy to be there. As he walked around, a few men reached out to grasp his hand in gratitude, to him or symbolically to the Lord, he was never sure.

Then, as the minutes passed, a new thought began to play in his mind. He began to determine that things were perhaps still not right. Some of the people were still fooling themselves, he was sure. Most of them had enjoyed the feud between the families and had probably egged it on with their false religiosity or with condemning words. Apologies were in order and redemption was needed, but the happy spirit and the fast, cheery cadence of the song seemed, he was sure, to lull the people into a false sense of Divine acceptance. They were deceiving themselves again and the preacher was going to have none of it.

As the preacher walked around, up and down the center aisle, it was supposed by most that he was greeting the happy crowd with an exercise designed to place the preacher intimately close to the people in order to stir the spirit in anticipation of the upcoming sermon. Many hands reached for his and he took each hand as it was offered and quickly let go. It was beginning to sink into the minds of the crowd that something was out of the ordinary. Something, it was soon reckoned, was seriously amiss.

There was Lucas. He had reached for the preacher's hand but was shocked to find the preacher's grip as limp as hog liver. Lucas recoiled slightly and continued singing, but in more subdued tones. Sandra, ever vigilant to body language, had stopped singing altogether and stood stone-faced looking toward the front.

When the preacher neared Wade's row, he gazed at Wade for only a moment then glanced away. He already knew that Wade was not comfortable being here, so he didn't press him for any response. But it had become evident that the preacher was not looking for physical responses from anyone; only eye contact. He had passed J.C. at the front and he still wondered how he was faring after the heavy action he was forced to take against Jesse Bridger. But J.C. was guilty for passively propping up the largest illegal enterprise that had ever been foisted upon the community. Many others, such as other local merchants, had given Carl what he desired in exchange for his money, likely suspecting all along the truth of his endeavors.

The eyes of some began to avoid the preacher's gaze. He had moved to one side of the building and was now standing near the end of the first bench at the front, not moving a muscle. One of the women, whom he knew to have engaged in excited discussions concerning the troubled families, had chosen to ignore the preacher's actions and to sing as if she had no blemish troubling her conscience.

Unhurriedly, he moved to the other side of the front and stood again before another group. J.C. was still leading the song but the energy to finish it began fading fast. Again, the preacher was as stone-faced as anyone could remember and he stood unblinkingly eye to eye with every member who would hold the gaze with him. Then he would try to catch the gaze of someone else. Someone, with an angry flourish, threw a hymnbook down to the bench and stopped singing. Several people nearby took the cue and stopped also. Then the preacher moved back toward the pulpit, but he stopped before it and turned his head toward a window and gazed out. The indirect sunlight illuminated his face and nearly everyone could see his features clearly. It wasn't right, the consensus of most seemed to be, that the preacher was spoiling the spirit of the day in this manner. The feeling seemed to spread throughout the crowd as J.C. stopped singing and the chorus quieted down. Then the building was silent.

The preacher remained staring out the window and he seemed to encourage the disturbing spirit that had infected the gathering. The silence in the building was raw to the ears and everyone remained unmoved, most hoping this strange game would be over soon; though a few were inwardly excited and were wondering what was going to happen next. The preacher spent too much time staring out the window and some people began to wonder if he had fallen ill somehow. Then a small child cried and the silence was broken.

"You know," the preacher started, still gazing out the window, "I had prayed for a good day today. I had asked the Lord for good weather and we got it. It was cold this morning but it's warmed up and the birds are singing. It's a good day for children to be playing outside."

He smiled so slightly and nodded, agreeing with himself. No one spoke an amen. After another long pause, the preacher slowly turned toward the people and gazed blankly toward the entrance doors and said, "Mrs. Annie, you reckon you and one of the ladies could take all the young'uns outside and teach them something out of the Book of Proverbs?"

Tom promptly stepped aside to allow his wife to move to the aisle. Some of the older children smiled and moved excitedly to exit the building, but parents reached to restrain them.

"I'd like to talk to the older folks here today," the preacher announced. "And it would do no good to keep the young'uns in here to listen to what I have to say."

Annie moved to the aisle and immediately began corralling all the children together as parents reluctantly relented. Another woman joined Annie and shortly the noisy, and newly excited, boys and girls bounded out the doors and into the yard in front of the building.

Tentatively, one by one, everyone sat back down. The preacher began slowly pacing back and forth in front of them. J.C. had sat down making it clear that the singing was over, and Ben moved from the podium down to a front bench. Everyone waited. After an uncomfortably long period of silence, the preacher began.

"I had a sermon ready for today and, let me tell you folks, I believe it was the best sermon the Lord's ever given me. But I'm not going to give it to you. I don't reckon I'll ever give it to you – or anybody else for that matter. Today, I'm not going to preach to you what I think the Lord wants me to preach. Nobody ever seems to listen to the sermons the Good Lord tells me to preach anyway!"

A heavy, very audible gasp spread immediately throughout the crowd. Some shook their heads in disbelief at the preacher's blasphemy and many looked away from the preacher's gaze. And others looked at spouses as if wondering if it could all be a strange prank of some sort.

"What's the Lord tell us in Proverbs?" the preacher continued in a slightly quieter voice. "What's He say in Proverbs? Well, the Lord says, 'I have called and ye refused; I have stretched out my hand and no man regarded, but ye have set at naught all my counsel, and would have none of my reproof, I also will laugh at your calamity; I will mock when your fear cometh; When your fear cometh as desolation, and your destruction cometh as a whirlwind; when distress and anguish come upon you. Then shall they call upon me, but I will not answer; they shall seek me early, but they shall not find me.'"

A resentment of sorts was being felt by some of the people for what the preacher was doing. Had they not suffered enough over the months and hadn't Gene's funeral been enough to bear? Why are we being punished now? many thought. Others were filled with a perverse curiosity and were waiting with great anticipation for the preacher's next move. And others still were haunted by a strong sense of a Divine presence that could be reminiscent of the Great Judgment Day, a feeling that was greatly malevolent. No one moved a muscle. All eyes were on the preacher.

The preacher was gazing out the window again. If he was waiting for a positive response, he should have realized that he was not going to get one. He could see Annie working to corral about two-dozen children and getting them to sit in rows on a grassy area in the warm sunlight about a hundred feet from the church. Her helper appeared to be smiling, if not laughing. The preacher seemed to smile slightly himself. He turned back toward the people and glanced around. His eyes were glazed over – it appeared that he was now trying to avoid everyone's gaze. Then he looked down at the floor before him. He crouched to the floor and it seemed that he began writing or drawing shapes on the boards with his finger.

"Jesus crouched down to the ground and drew something in the sand, and to the people and the Pharisees, He said, 'Let him that is without sin cast the first stone.' I wonder what it was that He was drawing in the sand?"

The preacher lifted his hand from the boards and looked at the floor as if he might be examining an imagined sketch he had drawn. After a long pause, he said, "I think I know what Jesus was doing. I think He was writing the names of those around him – those Pharisees that appeared righteous unto men, but within were full of hypocrisy and iniquity. That's exactly what He was doing – He was writing their names in the sand!"

Then with great flourish, the preacher began raking his index finger across the floor in furious arcs as if gashing the boards. The people could hear the preacher exhaling each time he swung his arm and the sound of his finger scraping the floor made them wonder if he was going to tear the skin off of his fingertip. Some of the men leaned forward to watch the preacher. They were fearful, wondering if the good pastor had finally lost his mind and was having a mental breakdown. A woman could be heard crying softly.

"He was blotting their names out of the Book of Life," the preacher said with more volume in his voice. He slashed the floor one more time, then said, "There – they're gone. You hypocrites – you are out of the Book of Life! I never knew you – be gone!"

The preacher stood up and searched the crowd. "What did you all come here for today? Did you come to hear what this preacher has to say about all the troubles that have befallen the good people of Braxton over the last fifteen months? Did you come to make yourselves feel better about how you had treated your fellow man when he had fallen and needed your hand? Have you sinned and your conscience is condemning you? Did you come to see a reed blowing in the wind? Why are you here!"

He turned and scanned the crowd again. He saw a few with moist eyes, and whimpering, frightened voices could be heard. Many eyes had fear in them. Others seemed hypnotized by the preacher's anguished oratory.

"For there is nothing covered, that shall not be revealed, neither hidden, that shall not be known! Whatever ye have spoken in darkness shall be heard in the light; and that which ye have spoken in the ear in closets shall be proclaimed upon the housetops! But I will forewarn you whom ye shall fear: Fear him who, after he hath killed, hath power to cast into hell; yea, I say unto you, fear him!" the preacher bellowed.

The walls vibrated with the boom of his voice. Never before had the pastor preached in the aisles before the pulpit, nor had he raised his voice to such volume. It was unnatural and otherworldly as if in a dream state. The shock on the faces of the congregation should have indicated to the preacher that he had severely breached the line of church-time etiquette and sensibilities, but he seemed wholly unaware of it. The faint voices of singing children could be heard through the closed windows, and the contrast was profane enough to cause a sense of perversity to hang in the air like a choking smoke. The preacher had stated that he wasn't going to do the Lord's bidding today and everyone seemed to take the preacher at his word. Some were probably determining that he had given up and was throwing it all away in a mad rage. But they listened. He walked back to the window to view Annie and the children. She had them all singing the same hymn the adults were singing just minutes ago.

"Not my mother, not my father, but it's me O' Lord – standin' in the need of prayer. Yes, I've always said that we should pray for one another." Then after a long pause, he added, "But I was wrong. I was dead wrong. We're all just too wicked to do that. How can a perfect and loving God answer our prayers when we are so cold and dark within? We have gossiped about the travails of our brothers and our sisters, but we haven't prayed for them with a clean heart. Some of you have taken money from one of Satan's messengers rather than consider that his deeds would consume our children. Some of you kept secrets from the rest of us. Good men, women and children have been hurt because of your selfishness. And children and a good man have died. Others have held grudges for so long that it seemed that you fully intended to carry them to your graves!"

The preacher turned around with his eyes directed toward the floor before him. He had not only stepped on many toes, it seemed that he intended on stomping them deep into the ground.

"Yes, I have been good all of my life. I have never even imagined hurting anyone in any way. Alcoholic beverage of any kind has never touched these lips, and I have prayed diligently every day before the break of dawn for each of you by name. What good has it done? Has anyone cared beyond the inconvenience of saying a good word?

"Now, you talebearers out there – don't you go accusing this old preacher of fishing for pity or acclamation of any sort! I'll have none of it! I'm just speaking my mind and that's all there is to it! If any of this offends you, then leave – do it now!"

For fear of drawing the preacher's wrath, no one moved. Someone cried, *"No!"* And other voices of disturbance echoed across the room.

"I have prayed for you folks and I have preached to you. I have preached Jesus and Him crucified and I have preached love for one another. I have preached hell and eternal damnation and I have preached on hypocrites in the church. I have warned about those among us who outwardly appear righteous unto men, but within are full of hypocrisy and iniquity. I have warned that we have become a generation of vipers and how hypocrites cannot escape the damnation of hell. I have preached: 'Woe unto you, scribes and Pharisees, hypocrites. For ye pay tithe of mint and anise and cumin, and ye have omitted the weightier matters of the law, judgment, mercy, and faith; these ought ye to have done, and not to leave the other undone. Now do ye Pharisees make clean the outside of the cup and the platter; but your inward part is full of extortion and wickedness. Beware – beware of the leaven of the Pharisees, which is hypocrisy!'

"We have just endured one of the most heart-wrenching funerals I have ever had the honor to preach. We were all grief-stricken for our beloved sheriff, Gene Carter. We have lost one who was dear to us and we will mourn his loss for the rest of our lives."

The preacher paused for a long stretch of time to allow his words to work and find their mark. He knew he had hit hard and he was sure it would be too hard for some to bear. He glanced at Wade and he found a tired face, but otherwise it held the usual deadpan expression devoid of any trace of remorse. He remembered how Wade had lingered long at Gene's coffin, no doubt guilt-ridden for his treatment of the good sheriff. But otherwise Wade had shown no outward sign of repenting for the deeds that had contributed to the sheriff's demise.

He found Paul sitting stone-faced and Ruth next to him with tears falling like rain drops. Paul had been too flippant and nonchalant about the whole affair and missed too many valuable opportunities to find an end to it all. He and Wade both had further frustrated Gene's efforts by keeping the cause of their water problems to themselves and acquiescing to Carl's water problem remedies. And Paul had too easily deferred to Wade's judgment on everything concerning the secrets of the family and the events leading up to, as well as after, the deaths of the Buell boys. Even though Gene had felt that he could approach Paul at any time to question him, it had soon become apparent that it was all a moot effort without Wade's involvement. And Paul, to outward appearances, was doing little to bring Wade around. Like Wade, he too often seemed content to let others suffer so that he could live in relative peace.

The preacher found Lucas sitting calmly with his head down. He used his right hand to brush away an errant lock of hair; the bullet injury seeming to have begun to heal up nicely. Tom was gazing straight at the preacher. He deserved everything the preacher was putting out and he accepted every word. It seemed clear to the preacher that Tom was no longer carrying a duplicitous attitude about his own shortcomings. The preacher was thankful for that.

J.C. Jourdan, like some other merchants, had profited greatly because of Carl's generosity and largesse. Surely, the preacher thought, he had reason to understand why he should feel responsible for prolonging the misery. J.C. had been hard on himself already, however, and his shooting of Jesse Bridger did much to break him and bring him to repentance. The preacher could see that he was hanging onto every word he had to say.

"What must be done?" the preacher continued. "What must be done to bring us all to true repentance? Must we all die before we can all know the real substance and results of our deeds? Must we die first? Are my forty-five years in the pulpit in vain? Must I die a spiritual pauper because the people did not hear the voice of God through me? Am I the one who is destitute? Are all of you righteous and I am the one who is destitute – without remedy?"

He seemed to wait for a response. All eyes, those he could see, were unchanged. Full of fear, anger, resignation – some of them showed a confusion of all emotions. He was used to hearing a peppering of amens throughout his sermons. He had not heard one today.

"Yes, the Lord had given me a sermon today, but I couldn't preach it. He will forgive me; he knows my heart. His grace is sufficient to cover all sins, even those that we plan and carry out to our own folly, as I have probably done today." The preacher returned to the pulpit and retrieved his Bible. He thumbed through it for a moment as if searching for a particular verse. He closed it and returned to the people.

"I remember a winters past," he continued. Then he paused for over a minute before continuing.

"I remember a winters past when we all helped one another to raise barns and feed one another and clothe one another when a house burned to the ground. And I remember a winters past when you fed me and cared for me when Mary died. Those were the best days. Those were the hardest days. They were days filled with grief and hardship, and tragedy. Those things broke us and forced us to come together. Those were days that showed us the face of God. We had nowhere to turn and we had no remedy.

"I remember when Graham's little boy was hurt and killed after he fell from the loft," he said, starting with a strong voice that tapered off. "Everybody came to ask how to help. Remember Brother Graham and Sister Mae? Remember how we all came together?"

Both Graham and his wife nodded.

"I remember a winters past when Wade's and Paul's father died. He died from a gunshot in the fall when you were boys – isn't that right?"

Paul nodded, then looked at Wade. His eyes were steady on the preacher.

"I remember how we all came together and made sure all your needs were met and that Mrs. Sarah wouldn't hurt for food and firewood – remember?

"And J.C., Sister Jessica, you remember when your house nearly caught fire and your barn burned to the ground? You remember how we all pitched in to build you a new barn? We built it in less than two weeks, right?

"And Sister Elizabeth – when Joseph died of heart failure; did you ever suffer or have any needs that were never met?" he asked. Soon, the preacher was pacing from person to person as the memories flooded back.

"Brother Tom – have you found all your needs met since your boys died? Wouldn't it be better if we all got back together instead of holding grudges against one another?"

Tom showed no offense; he nodded eagerly.

"Brother Lucas – what about that time, years ago, when you needed help fighting them weevils that got in your cotton so bad? You remember how we all pitched in to help you get rid of them?"

With vigor and energy, the preacher moved quickly back to the side where Wade sat and, without concern for Wade's sensibilities, he said, "And Wade – when your wells ran dry and you ran out of water a couple of weeks ago – what happened? We all brought you and Brother Paul all the water you needed, right? You didn't have to ask, did you?" The preacher backed away before Wade could respond and said to the crowd, "But what happened folks? What happened last winter a year ago? You all stopped. You gossiped. You took sides. You didn't care anymore – you just quit. And my sermons – my pleadings – fell on deaf ears. And I could feel within my soul the emptiness that you all had in your hearts, but nobody seemed to care. And look what happened. Our own good sheriff died of grief and heartbreak. He shot himself because nobody would lift a finger to help. I realize that the poor man had been feeling bad long before these problems came along. But we could have helped stop this tragedy by simply listening to him and helping him in any way we could when these things happened. We kept secrets from him and we made things hard for him by all the gossip and the rumor-mongering.

"Some of you were afraid of what might happen if Gene had his way and could do his job – so you kept things to yourself. Some of you were angry with him and you kept him away. You wanted him to just go away and leave you be, but nobody seemed to care for his feelings or his needs until it was just too late. But if we had just taken the time to listen and to care for one another as Christ commanded, then maybe we wouldn't have to go through such fiery trials as this.

"Don't get me wrong, folks. Don't judge me in the wrong light. I know as well as anybody the good deeds that are done. The Lord knows when we have done right. Like when some of you came together after the tornado and pitched in to help those in need around you. The Lord knows all about Sister Sarah and Sister Ruth taking care of little Gracie, who we all know comes from an unbearable and hateful home. The Lord sees all our deeds, both good and bad. But still, too many of you just gave up and drew back into yourselves."

Again, the preacher paused. He lowered his head and stared at the floor for a few moments, then he slowly stepped to the window. He looked back out at the children. The building was quiet as he watched Annie teaching the children. Soon, it became clear that the preacher really had nothing left to say. The service was over as evidenced by the prolonged silence.

Then a disturbance of sorts moved through the crowd. At first it was just the sound of subtle movements on the benches, then the sounds of muffled gasps and surprised voices. The preacher looked up and around. Someone was standing to speak. It was Wade. But the preacher remained motionless and silent, and he waited.

"Preacher," Wade said with some anxiety in his voice, "I hear what you're saying and I know a lot of those words are meant for me. I don't rightly understand everything that you've said here today. You know I don't come to church much – everybody knows that." He coughed, then continued. "I know you meant a lot of what you said for me and I reckon I'm guilty, and maybe I should repent as you always say, but you have to understand – I had no place to go. I had to protect my family. I had to put them first. If I let every lawman and the state people come in and destroy us by making us go to the courthouse every day, and then lose all we have to the lawyers and judges and such, then we would go broke and, uh, homeless. It would all be over, preacher." He stopped for a moment to look around. Then he started again.

"I only done what I had to do. You folks have to understand that. And I dare say any one of you would've done the same under the circumstances. I know I haven't always done right by not going to church, and Mama always tried to get me to go." Wade glanced down at his misty-eyed mother, then to Esther and added, "And my wife has always been good at trying to get me to come too. All I can add is I'm sorry if some of my actions might've hurt Gene – I don't know. But you know we all have to take care of our own. And if a man don't take care of his own – what is he worth? Uh, I'm sorry – uh, that's the best I can do."

Then Wade solemnly sat down, still wishing it was all over and time to go home. The preacher had listened attentively and had allowed Wade free reign to speak his mind. The preacher was still confused by some of his own actions, so he felt he had no right to stop anyone else from engaging in the morning's events in whatever way seemed right.

The preacher straightened himself up and said, "Well, Wade, I can give you one thing; no man can call you a hypocrite."

Immediately the preacher sensed he had probably sounded a bit sarcastic with that rejoinder, but he felt no necessity to turn apologetic. There was no need to make Wade feel any worse before the eyes of his neighbors, so the preacher quickly added, "Anybody else like to say anything before we close today?"

No one responded so the preacher dismissed the service with a short prayer. Then it took over an hour for everyone to ease out of the building. It seemed that everyone had to take the time to get reacquainted with others and to renew old friendships. The preacher made it a point to speak to every soul before the hour was over. He was pleased to see that for the most part he had offended no one excessively by his words, and everyone walked out of the church with many things to think about along with a new, and perhaps bewildering, respect for the preacher.

CHAPTER 39

"Where's Jimmy?" Esther asked.

Wade glanced around the churchyard. Some of the people had left the grounds and a few were already home. They had stood around with the preacher and a few others and reminisced most of that time about the past that the preacher had talked about in his sermon. Everyone stopped talking and looked around near and far for Jimmy's form. A cursory check of the outhouse and the graveyard turned up nothing.

"I seen him walking down the road there, Wade," someone said.

"Where'd he go?"

"I don't know. I thought he would come back."

Esther looked at Wade as if hoping for an explanation, but Wade was clearly as bewildered as everyone else. Quickly, everyone loaded up into Paul's car and Wade's horse and work wagon. Wade called back to the witness.

"How long ago did you see him?"

"'bout thirty, forty minutes ago."

Immediately Wade snapped the reigns and rolled down to the road and pulled away as if he knew something of a secretive nature others didn't. He took off with such aggression and speed that Paul could not get his car started and rolling before Wade and his family were out of sight.

"Why would he do this, Wade?" Esther yelled above the noise of the wheels and the wind.

Wade ignored her. His eyes were on the road before him and he seemed unconcerned that Esther and Kelly Jean were being forced to grasp the seat with death grips as he raced ahead, hardly slowing down for curves or cross-ruts. This was a work wagon, not a road carriage built for speed and distance. It could burn up a wheel hub or snap an axle if made to race for too long. Soon, Paul pulled up behind, then he sped up and raced on ahead of the horse and wagon toward home to find Jimmy. On Braxton Road a vehicle approached from the opposite direction. Wade waved for the driver to stop. "Did you see a boy in the road up ahead?" he asked.

"Yeah," the driver said. "A tall, skinny boy?"

"That's right – which way'd he go?"

"Headin' south – runnin' like a tracking dog was after him – "

Wade never said thanks. He snapped the reins hard and took off again. In fifteen minutes he rounded the southern curve in the road to his house. He saw Paul's car stopped ahead and Paul was standing at the edge of the road looking southward toward the cornfields in the distance. The rest of the family was still in the car.

"What you got, Paul?" Wade asked as he slowed the rig to a stop.

"I just seen Jimmy run across the road and he lit out across them fields there. I can't hardly see him no more!"

Wade dismounted and sprinted over to Paul and gazed out to the tree-lined horizon along the south line of the fields. It was deep into the property he had sold to Carl months before. He could find no movement on the ground. A buzzard flew high in the sky above the fields, but Jimmy was out of sight.

"Where's Jimmy?" Esther asked. She had heard Paul's statement but she wanted a better answer and her voice cracked with anxiety. Wade looked back at her with an expression that she could not recall seeing on his face before. He wasn't angry, as one would expect. Instead, he appeared as distraught as anyone might imagine. Wade gazed back out across the fields, then back at Esther, then back to the fields. The tremor in Esther's voice made it clear that she was really asking if anyone knew why – not to where – Jimmy had run.

"What'd he do this for?" Paul asked Wade.

Wade stepped across the narrow ditch alongside the road and tried again to gaze off into the distance. Almost as far as the eye could see, he could spy a white speck moving farther away toward the horizon. Jimmy's white shirt shone like a faraway lighthouse near the most distant tree line, and Wade was amazed at the short span of time his son had used to cover what was surely over a mile away.

"Somebody tell me something – tell me now!" Esther barked.

But Wade refused to respond. He seemed to hold a terrible secret that he was keeping from everyone. Paul trotted over to her and cautioned her to be patient. It was something, he said, that Wade needed to handle on his own. Esther relented but she still held her hardened eyes on Wade.

Wade bounced back to the road and ordered, "Let's get back to the house!" He ignored the sharp metallic stench of an overheated wheel hub that was smoking on the front of the wagon. The hub could possibly ignite causing the wooden spokes to catch fire and burn the wagon to the ground. But they were close to home. Wade's hands trembled as he grasped the reins, and he snapped them too hard and the wagon jerked away.

***

Jimmy entered the ragged lumberyard of his once-beloved hunting grounds. He had raced beneath the oak tree where he had hunted deer and fallen across the sunken grave beneath it. Angrily, he rebounded and stood at the edge of the tree line. He had dropped his coat and he bent over to grab it. A redwing blackbird flew directly overhead and cackled all the way to the far side of the ugly field. For a moment, he stood still to catch his breath and begin the effort to figure out exactly why he was here. All he was able to determine to this point was that he had become overwhelmed, back at the church, with an indescribable urge to run away. It was now different than before when he had experienced this compulsion. Today, if he hadn't run, he felt that his heart would have burst, he would have broken down into sobs, or he might have cursed at someone. When his father made his short statement to the church, something inside him rose up and set his emotions ablaze. He knew he would have no control over his actions this morning, so he ran. It was hard to think when running, but he had to get away as quickly as possible and find a refuge where he could discover the reason for his sudden loss of control.

He had determined that he could not confide in his father. His father was an enigma and Jimmy could trust him for nothing. So, why did he lose control now? Certainly it had something to do with his father's dealings with Carl Kallton, such as the fact that he had failed to ensure that Carl ended up in the custody of the law and pay for his crimes as he thought his father had promised – this along with his father's cooperation with Carl in the water problems. Jimmy had witnessed a horrific crime and his father was well aware of it. His father knew all along that something was wrong with Kelly Jean and that she held secrets that were devouring her spirit. Was that his plan for Jimmy? Did Wade expect his son to live the rest of his life carrying his terrible secrets to the grave? Jimmy would be alone with something that would eat away at his soul and destroy him with anger and confusion, and eventually make him a pariah even to his own family. He was not capable of thinking that far into the future, but he understood enough to know that things could not continue as they stood now. He had heard some of the discussions concerning the sheriff's suicide letter and the secrets that were exposed. Yet there were more secrets that were still being withheld from everyone. And it was now becoming apparent that, after all that has happened, his father was still intending to pretend that all was well, and that Jimmy would bear the burden of secrecy for him. Forever.

Jimmy's mind was hurting with the reality of the frightening thing he was now doing. In a sense he was relieved to know that everyone's attention would now be on him and they would be forced to ask questions. Finally, his father will understand that his son's deepest concerns matter after all. His son's stifled longings and awakening sensibilities could no longer be ignored. But Jimmy was filled with the chest-crushing anxiety that came from the knowledge that he would have a lot of explaining to do, and that he could be making things worse for his father in the district and state investigations of recent events.

Jimmy had looked back toward the road several times. He was sure he had heard Paul's car running up to the edge of the road and then stopping. He looked back and he thought he had seen Paul's light gray shirt through the trees, but he used the energy of his fear to stoke the coals and race across the fields. Too many of the corn stalks were still standing and he plowed over so many of them that his arms and legs were made raw from the collisions. The pain in his throat and chest hurt more than anything external, so he never took the time to examine the crimson streaks that ran vertically down his shoulders and sleeves.

Shortly, another blackbird passed overhead and flew southwesterly. Jimmy watched it head for a pass between two distant stands of trees. Then he followed.

**

Back at the house, everyone went inside, then watched through the windows as Wade turned back for the road to go after his son.

"Paul?" Esther said, "Would you go get Brother Silas? Tell him to come here, okay?" Paul took one look at Esther's anguished face, then made haste to fulfill her request.

Soon, Paul drove past Wade's horse and still-smoking wagon, which was again parked where Jimmy had escaped into the fields. He slowed to look across the fields. He could see Wade walking, almost running due south. So many of the corn stalks were still up that it was difficult to see Wade every moment. Then Paul drove on.

**

"Now let's just stay calm. Let's get us a little fire going and settle down," Ruth said assuredly.

As usual, she was concerned for Mrs. Sarah's heart. Mrs. Sarah watched her. She seemed calmed by Ruth's take-charge attitude. Soon, Esther became amazingly settled and lucid, and seemed happily ready to start a fire in the fireplace as if she hadn't a care in the world. She carried in two sticks of oak and stacked them carefully atop a handful of kindling that Ruth had piled on the irons. Then she went to the kitchen to start the stove. The boys and Gracie had settled themselves in the kitchen, ready to eat a meal that would be an hour yet in coming. Kelly Jean, quiet throughout the event, seemed determined to remain within inches of her mother.

Soon enough, the kitchen smelled heartily of the rich aroma of peach pie in the oven and cabbage and venison on the stove. Esther needed no encouragement to stay calm, even cheerful. Something had always been not quite right, and something deep down seemed to be telling her that what was happening down in the cornfields was necessary and everything would be all right in the end. Whether it could be faith or intuition – the impression was strong enough that she felt no motherly impulse to worry herself as to which it might be.

The excited, but nervous, small talk continued for another hour as they worked on the meal and the younger boys were put to work bringing up more firewood to the porch and fetching water from the reservoir tank in the back yard. The preacher was coming, so the meal was going to be large and filling, always with a dessert. Just as Paul and the preacher returned, the cooking was finished. Wade and Jimmy were still absent.

***

Wade gazed up into the grand oak tree but he could see from a hundred yards away that Jimmy was not up there. Why his son would be up in a tree without a gun to hunt with, Wade didn't know but he left no stone unturned. He saw the terrible grave spot as he walked up but he didn't care to dwell on it, so he moved to the center of the ravaged grounds of the woods where his son once loved to hunt. Quietly, he circled the sawdust mounds and climbed through the masses of tree limbs until he found himself in the center. He turned a full circle scanning the trees, but he saw nothing move except for a large doe that seemed unafraid of his presence and was moving unhurriedly away toward the west end of the field.

This was the first time that he had come to this area since he had sold it, and it was hard to remember how it had once looked. He looked around for the little creek that ran down the center of it but could find no trace of it. He couldn't help noticing how heavy and wasteful the destruction was. The smaller trees had been knocked over, apparently because they were in the way of getting to the heavy timber. Thousands upon thousands of cut and broken tree limbs lay everywhere. No one had bothered to pile them up and burn them or to sell it all off for firewood. Hundreds of poorly cut and warped boards lay in broken, mangled pieces everywhere. It appeared as if the timber harvesting had been performed by a band of drunks.

Alone, Wade stood in the field. His son was gone and a new fear gripped his heart. He had to find his boy and save face. He had to get him home. This would not do. He would now do whatever was required to get his son and take him home. He would fight his son and drag him home against his will, or whatever was required to bring this embarrassing episode to an end. He would find him now.

"Jimmy!" Wade yelled with all his strength. He was sure his voice would reach his son, wherever he might be. His voice would carry far in this relatively calm air. He yelled again and waited. Silence.

Jimmy had already run over six miles from the church and apparently he was still running. He had vanished without a trace.

***

Soon, Jimmy made it to the cliffs. He could see many things from the cliffs and he searched for the fabled operations that Carl had built in the woods. He determined that he should see for himself the reason for all the troubles of the last many months.

A voice passed through the trees that spoke his name. He heard it twice and it sounded far away. It sounded familiar and he wondered if a search was already underway for him. He pretended he didn't hear it and a strange peace passed over him as he moved closer to the area where he had heard that the compound should be. He was free from the constraints of home and family, and he enjoyed a new freedom that was exhilarating and energizing. Yet his body was exhausted from the journey, but he determined that he could do it again. And he would again someday, just for the fun and adventure of it.

He marched along the rocky edge of a fifty-foot bluff and all he could see from this point was a valley filled with mature woods and thickets. He picked up the pace and followed the sloping edge down into the trees and stopped at the bottom. He could hear the slow pecking of a woodpecker many yards away and its cadence was slow, so he figured it was a large, cockaded type hunting for grubs. He gazed up into the trees looking for it but soon returned his attention to the grounds around him.

Jimmy had heard of timber being cut and hauled out somewhere toward the west but he didn't know how far away it was. That compound with its distillery, he knew, had to be over a couple of hundred yards further away. He was not allowed to get close enough to the compound to see anything when he was following his father to apprehend Carl, and his curiosity had been dogging him like a chronic itch ever since. So, aiming his mental compass southwestward, he moved deeper down into the valley.

He approached a creek that he didn't remember being there before. It was a well supplied, running creek and he stood a moment to study it. He looked back toward the east and he could see the creek flowing in an almost straight line toward another bluff a hundred yards away – clearly a well-maintained water supply for some enterprise downstream. He looked westward. He could see something unusual there – a faint spark of light like the dim reflection of sunlight against a shiny surface. It caught his eye right away and he gazed at it for a minute as if trying to determine if he should move downstream to check it out or cross here and continue searching for the compound. He stepped closer to the edge and gazed again toward the western run of the creek. And that spark of light.

***

Wade returned to the farm but he didn't go to the house where everyone was waiting. There were chores to be done and he was behind in getting them done. He charged headlong toward the barn far from the house and quickly unhooked the exhausted horse at the trough. He slung a bucket of water onto the burned-up wheel hub that had locked up shortly before entering the driveway. Steam exploded upward and Wade could see the black of the scorched spokes at the hub. The wagon would now be useless until the wheel and hub are replaced. He entered the barn and began tossing out manure with a fury. It was a mess and he had put it off for too long. Jimmy should have done it days earlier but things had been allowed to go too slack lately.

He could now see Paul's car up at the house. He was sure that everyone knew he had returned and they probably also knew that Jimmy had not returned with him. Was the preacher in the house? He didn't know, but if he was there, the preacher would keep everyone calm, as well as buy a little time. Probably by now, everyone in the community knew something was wrong with the family, and that fact alone unnerved Wade badly. It would have been acceptable if Jimmy had run away from home under cover of darkness or when no one was watching. But he had done it in such a way as to make it clear to everyone that something was still terribly wrong and that Wade was not in control.

Wade jabbed the pitchfork into a large mound of manure and stepped back to the back door of the barn and heaved it as far as he could down into a depression below. He did it again and again and again until he was too winded to continue. He slung the pitchfork down and walked to the front door of the barn and looked back up toward the house. Another car was there now. It appeared to be Ben's old car, but he could also see Tom stepping tentatively around outside the house as if he were somehow reluctant to go inside. Was he here to discuss a settlement for the cattle massacre as he had promised after church this morning? Perhaps. But this was not the time for that, and Wade was unsure as to how, or whether, he should feel any measure of consternation for the man's brazen presence here at such a difficult time.

Wade began to fear that a search party for Jimmy was being organized. But that would have been a foolish idea, he thought. If his son wanted to lose himself in the woods and hide from anyone searching for him, he knew that Jimmy was well able to keep himself hidden for as long as he wished. And he would be found only when he was ready to be found.

Wade was still exhausted from the manure excavation, but he returned to grab the pitchfork and begin again. A young heifer standing outside had moved to the door of the barn and was looking in. She had a mouthful of cud and was working on it like a child with too much ice cream in her mouth. Wade stopped to watch the heifer stare back at him. Uncharacteristically, he imagined what it would be like to have no pressing obligations or worries like this little cow and to wake up every day with corn or hay waiting in the manger and blue skies and crows to watch all day. He looked out into the pasture and saw a couple of tiny shoots of bitterweed sprouting out of the ground. By late spring, there would be thousands of them to pull up in Paul's pastures in order to ensure the milk stayed tasting sweet.

He could see the side of the silo and he thought of the long days of labor that would be required to fill it with feed corn again next fall. He would need to sell enough corn to purchase some extra hay, too – it seemed that they never had quite enough to survive the winter. If no complications arose, he could expect six new calves in the spring, but there were always complications. Somehow, he would need to find the time to cut shingles for repairs to both houses and Paul's barn this spring. The wire fence was breaking loose all around the pastures; it already needed lots of attention. He would eventually need more ready cash to cover second mortgage payments on his losses and he was desperate to hang onto the remaining family holdings. The wells had dried up and he was now dependent upon the goodwill of others. It could be weeks or even months before the ground supply began to replenish. The new list of problems seemed to go on forever. Now, everything in his life added up to little more than a depressing existence heavily burdened with futility.

Wade jabbed the pitchfork into the ground and stopped his mind for a moment. Soon, the moment was past and he was thinking again. Was it all worth it? How did his father do it? He had been a dirt farmer and had worked these grounds to raise and harvest cotton and a few vegetables and performed a little sawmilling for the timber companies, some of them out of state. It wasn't the best land for crops and he had failures, but somehow, Wade remembered, they survived. His father, like him, was not outwardly happy or even content with his lot in life. But he had accumulated a proud stretch of land over the years and left it to his boys. Wade had earned the right to imagine he could also be as successful, and perhaps he already was.

But something was wrong. The feeling had stayed with him and hadn't completely vanished since it first invaded his mind weeks ago. Actually he could remember that he had felt this way off and on for months before, probably shortly after the North Road incident. Perhaps it had something to do with his own guilt over his treatment of the sheriff. But Gene was gone now and Wade had felt that he had rectified his own conscience by taking Carl out single-handedly. Carl was the reason for all of their problems and Wade had dispatched him. So why had things seemed unfinished? Going to church this morning, as he had quickly determined, seemed to only worsen his condition.

He was sure that Jimmy was too young and immature to understand many things. Wade had been so diligent and single-minded through the years that he had forgotten what it had been like to see things through a youngster's eyes and to carry the consequences through to later years. He did remember, however, that it took great effort and stamina to get to a position of independence and security. And anything that stood in the way of that goal was coaxed or pushed aside – or destroyed if it refused to budge.

Jimmy knew these things, so what was the problem? If he was upset over being corralled into playing the necessary games in order to keep the family intact, then he had some learning to do yet. The little discussion he and his son had shortly after Jimmy's early morning excursion to the south end should have made this philosophy clear and cause Jimmy to toe the line and put family and security first. Jimmy was not like his father. That was evident nearly from birth. But he showed a natural intelligence, so it was logical that he should naturally understand.

Wade looked outside and up toward the house again. He could see Tom, Lucas, Paul and the preacher out on the porch. Occasionally they would look down toward the barn at Wade. The preacher had Gracie in his arms. The little girl seemed happy enough in spite of her dire circumstances at home, so children grow up just fine if cared for properly, Wade reasoned. And Gracie, as far as Wade could see, never seemed to miss home; so children naturally adjust well to any given situation thrust in their direction. Why couldn't Jimmy?

Then a voice yelled out across the farm. It was Paul. *"Wade – is Jimmy okay?"*

Paul's voice was clear and there was no possibility of playing deaf. Jimmy should have been back by now. This game was getting out of hand and it was time to get back to a normal life. Wade could soon see several more people standing on the porch, all of them glancing down toward him.

"I'll be right up!" Wade yelled back.

***

Jimmy had followed the creek into a pine thicket. He didn't think that anyone would be around this area, so he felt free to roam. He stopped a moment to listen. It had been nearly an hour since he had heard his name called and all had been quiet since. Perhaps his father had gone home, if that's who it had been, and was waiting for him to return.

"Where is that place?" Jimmy asked aloud to himself. That compound had to be nearby. He turned to look toward the west. He found a wisp of smoke rising up among the trees many yards away. It may be a campfire or the smoke from a stove in one of the compound buildings. Perhaps he was not alone in these woods after all. But he should have been there by now, he guessed. It seemed that he had walked well over two miles since leaving the lumber field. He stopped and listened again. Would his father be heading toward him? How much worse might his punishment be because of his effort to find the compound? He could hear no footsteps or movement of any kind and the woods had been quiet enough to allow him to be alerted to anyone following.

He moved farther westward and soon the creek had turned straight and wide and was running and splashing down a long incline of battens and stones. It created the most pristine vision of water and movement that he could ever remember. He reached down to the pool and dipped his hand deep into the water. It was cold, near freezing, and his hand was numbed by it. He slung the water off and stood up. I must be close to that steamplant – just through the next tree stand, he imagined.

Jimmy had hiked another fifty yards downstream before reaching the edge of the compound. He found himself standing directly behind the distillery itself. All he could see were wide-boarded walls, all painted black. He remained here for a long while to make sure the compound was vacant. He looked for the smoke again but it was likely hidden now by all the heavy tree cover surrounding the compound. The flues atop the buildings were smoke-free – the buildings apparently vacant. So, as quietly as he could, he walked straight through the center of the yard to the far side taking time to search and examine every detail among the structures. The compound was a ghost town; not a soul stirred.

It was getting to be time to worry about going back home and meeting the interrogation, or punishment, that he knew he had earned today. Soon, it would start getting dark and the temperature was already dropping. He slipped his coat on and thought about his fate and how he was going to handle his arrival back home. Would he ask some questions of his own? What would he ask? Is it time to get bold and hit his father with the tough questions that had haunted him for all these months? Could he stand up to his strong father and stay strong himself? Never had he ever done anything as bold as defying his father as he had done today, and he was beginning to fully realize the severity of his actions. And the strong sense of imminent destruction was bearing down on him like a runaway truck. The feeling of freedom he had enjoyed for a short time seemed alien to him now. Still, he couldn't simply go back home and take his punishment in stoic manner and then live as though the demons unleashed these recent months had returned to their lairs to never haunt him again. How could he accept his life to what it has evolved and wake up each day and realize he must pretend that nothing has changed? His mind seemed incapable of organizing even the first beginnings of a single viable strategy to accomplish this end.

Jimmy's foot fell through a thin crust of ice in a puddle of water he had stepped into. He pulled his foot up, then he felt that cold flash of moisture that spread under his toes. He turned back toward drier ground and gazed up into the sky. The clouds were moving back in and he could feel his ears stiffen in the cold air. He watched the slow moving clouds close overhead to form a billowing gray cover of gloom over the land and turn the day's light down yet another shade.

Unexpectedly, a tear fell to his cheek. He slapped it off and jerked his head around to begin looking for a shortcut back to the road. All he could see was the dirt and gravel road leading from the southwestern corner of the compound. He needed to go north and find a way out there. It would take too long to retrace his steps back to the route he had come, so he paused to work out his options. He drew in a deep breath and pulled his body straight and erect. He must go home. He must do it now. Then he saw the tiny reflected sunlight he had seen earlier. He squinted his eyes and soon enough he could find the little flames of a wood fire on the ground. He aimed himself for it and stepped quietly atop the little grassy areas here and there like playing a child's game of hopscotch.

CHAPTER 40

Wade returned to the house. He was silent.

"Wade?" Esther asked, "Is Jimmy back?"

"No, he's not. But he'll be home soon," he answered quietly but forcefully.

Esther studied his face. He seemed calm enough but Esther could sense his distress. She turned back to the stove and proceeded to pay no more heed to him. She took a rag off the counter nearby and raised it to her face. No one could see whether she had begun to cry. The house was full of people. Wade did not expect to have all this attention directed toward him. It was uncomfortable and he hated it. By now, three men from the porch had entered the front room and were listening from there. Then, Ben stepped softly into the kitchen. "We just thought that Jimmy might be lost and you might need some help finding him," he said.

Then a bit of child's laughter pealed from the front room. Gracie was well practiced in amusing herself while ignoring the distress in others. Wade pretended not to hear Ben's comment as he retreated to the front room and sat down away from the others, saying nothing.

Then an hour passed, and other than short, stilted comments on weather and family health the house was quiet. In a surreal state of dusk, everyone waited for Jimmy to return home. Another lamp was found and placed in the front room. No one bothered yet to light it. Strangely, no one offered to speak aloud. Something was happening, everyone seemed to sense, that was out of everyone's control. The hush that had fallen over the house was palpable, but an answer was figured to come soon and all that could be done was to wait and hope and perhaps pray a little.

The preacher and Tom were sitting close together; clearly lost as concerning what to say, seeming as uncomfortable as Wade. Paul drew a blank knowing what to do, so he sat in the kitchen with the ladies and they all stared out the windows hoping to see someone returning home before the last of the day's light escaped. Everyone had forgotten about dinner – it was already suppertime – and the burning wood in the stove had long gone out. Only the infrequent wisp of the peach pie aroma wafted in the air. Finally, the preacher stood up and gazed down into the darkening pastures behind the barn. Ben had stationed himself at the front window and puffed on a pipe for nearly the whole time, and soon enough the sweet tobacco aroma fought with the pie for everyone's attention.

Then Wade abruptly stood up. He couldn't stand it any longer. All eyes were immediately on him. "I have to go work down at the barn," he said. Then he was gone. But Tom quickly followed him out.

"Wade?" Tom said. They had stepped out into the yard where no one could hear them. "I want you to know that I am serious about setting things right between us. But I think what's going on here at your house is a lot more important than any of that. I don't understand everything that's going on here; it's really none of my business, I reckon. But I feel I should say something." Wade's face showed no sign that he wished to hear anything Tom had to say. "I lost two good boys, Wade," Tom continued. "I just hope you don't do anything that might cause you to lose your only son. It is unbearable to lose a child through death; it might be worse to lose one while he's still alive."

Wade immediately turned away and marched briskly out into the dusky barnyard.

***

Jimmy entered the east end of the road leading from the compound. He was sure this was the same little road he had walked to when he followed his father to the compound to apprehend Carl. But he had only seen it from the western end, and looking back toward the compound he could find nothing different. But today the place was deathly quiet.

He looked for the smoke again. Moving quietly, he searched the trees north to south until his eyes landed on a thick puff of gray smoke drifting high up through the tree canopy. Following it was another identical puff. Then quickly enough, another. The combination and cadence reminded him of Indian smoke signals and he wondered if this pattern could somehow be purposeful. He moved westward along the edge of the road and gazed in the direction of the smoke source. Someone was there. But he could hear no voices, no sounds of any kind.

He walked swiftly and soon he was near the intersection. He was sure he was within a stone's throw of the smoke source. He stopped and listened. Nothing. He waited. Still nothing. He determined that it might be in his best interest to dodge the area where the fire was burning. The day was getting late and he best not get detained by any migrant riffraff in these woods. Then slowly, he turned westward toward the narrow road; soon to turn north for the main road to home.

"Jimmy?" a voice called.

Jimmy's heart dropped so fast it hurt. He spun around and nearly tripped over his own feet. His eyes darted around and quickly landed on a lone, dark figure standing about ten yards away. He was black and stockily built. The man's eyes were wide, alert, and happily surprised. He was holding his hands out to a small, twiggy campfire on the ground. The tiny fire had grown weak and was in want of more fuel to prevent it from going out. Jimmy quickly assessed that the man was a migrant worker; but why was he out here in the woods alone? It all seemed like a dream at first and Jimmy worked fast to gather his wits.

"Uh – wh – who are you?" Jimmy asked, choking down his surprise.

"Aw – you remember me, don't you? I'm Walter. Your Papa had me stay with you when he came to get Carl Kallton, remember?"

"Uh, yeah," Jimmy said nervously. He could see the earnest smile on the man's lips in the dim light, and the clear and cheerful tone in Walter's voice worked quickly to calm Jimmy's heart and nerves. Jimmy stood slack-jawed for nearly a minute as Walter fiddled with a box of matches, then lit a lantern hanging from a twig stump.

"Somethin' told me I might get to see you again. I reckon it was the Good Lord's doin's that he sent you here to keep me company while'st I cook up some vittles."

Walter tossed the match to the fire and pulled his coat up tight to his chin. He was still smiling a bit and he eyed Jimmy up and down and said, "You out huntin' some deer?"

"Uh – no, sir," Jimmy said.

"You out scoutin' for deer?"

"No, sir."

Jimmy smiled at the way the question was asked. Walter was playing with him and he smiled broadly as he asked each question. Then Walter stacked several dry sticks onto the fire and soon a fat metal pot above it was simmering with soup, all the while Walter jabbering about his praying for forgiveness for slacking on his religious duties on the Sabbath. He really wasn't slacking, though, he explained. He was alone now and the only way he could worship the Lord was in his solitude. Walter explained how that can be the best way to draw neigh to the Lord – just one on one. He knew the scriptures nearly as well as his own name and he quoted several to make his argument. It seemed that he was assuming he would have a friend to join him for supper and he was excited about the prospect. And Jimmy, with a pang in his stomach, realized he was near starving.

"Jimmy?" Walter said as they both started on the tastiest bean soup Jimmy could ever remember. "You ain't got no gun or light. You're not lost are you, son?"

"Uh, no, sir," Jimmy answered with an ounce of sadness. He watched his new friend eat the soup as delicately as a young girl and he could sense that Walter was thinking of him and his unexpected appearance deep in the woods far from home. It was a confusing paradox, though. Walter had two sets of plates, forks, and cups; it seemed that he might have been expecting a visitor. Jimmy swallowed a gulp of cold, sweet tea and studied Walter's face in the light of the fire. The initial fear he had felt when Walter first called his name had quickly evaporated and was now replaced with a similar feeling he has when in the company of the preacher. Somehow, he felt he could stay here for a long, long time and not tire of this gracious man's conversation. Walter seemed the same as on that day when Carl was taken away, but at the same time there was a contrast. He was still concerned and helpful, but now he showed no deference or subordination to his present company as he seemed to do to others on that day. Now he was strong and fatherly. Even his speech pattern sounded oddly different. He was kindly and wise and carried such contentment and humility in his voice that Jimmy wondered if he could be a preacher himself.

"Are you a preacher?" Jimmy asked.

"Oh, no, Jimmy – no – o – o!" Walter answered with a chuckle. "I ain't no preacher! But that would be nice, though. You think I would make a good preacher?"

Jimmy smiled and nodded. It was dark now and he had temporarily cast aside thoughts of going home. His spoon dug deep into the tin bowl and noisily scrapped the bottom. Walter, before Jimmy could react, dumped another heaping scoop of steaming soup into the bowl and motioned for him to continue. The tea was like his mother's and Jimmy gulped it down heartily.

"You know," Walter said, "The Lord has a list of seven sins that He hates. You reckon gluttony's one of 'em?" Then he burst out with such hearty laughter that Jimmy laughed until tears squeezed out of his eyes. Their voices carried through the woods and echoed back from the rock wall of a distant bluff, imitating the sound of a band of questionably sober migrants enjoying a good story. Walter watched Jimmy laugh in the firelight and Jimmy watched Walter throw another cup of soup into his own bowl. Never had Jimmy engaged in such silliness, nor had he ever laughed until it hurt. Like a couple of drunken transients, they laughed and dined until exhaustion, then the woods became quiet again. The fire was warm and Jimmy had removed his coat and felt free to relax against a tree trunk.

Walter poured water into the bowls and quickly flushed them out clean. He was now curiously silent and Jimmy was beginning to think of home again. The sky was black and he had determined that it would be slow going finding his way home and it would probably take nearly an hour. He could sleep here in the trees if the fire could be stoked through the night and wake up in the morning with a great adventure behind him and, to a small degree, a better hope for the future because of the stand he had made against his father. But he couldn't be sure of that. He wondered if Walter would know what to do. Then, before he could ask, Walter asked a question of his own.

"How many head of cattle do you have, Jimmy?"

"Huh? Sir?"

"I heard you got a lot of cows – you and your father."

"Uh – yeah. We got about fifty-five now, I think."

"You get to eat a lot of meat?"

"Yes, sir."

Walter smiled at the thought of it and looked back into the fire again. He slowly shook his head as if imagining the taste of a juicy beefsteak or roast. He chuckled a bit and said, "I got some turkey once. Aw – that was wonderful! But I eat some squirrel sometimes too!" He gazed back up at Jimmy and after a long pause, he asked, "You got any brothers or sisters, Jimmy?"

"I got a sister – she's older than me. An' I got two little cousins. They're like little brothers, though. They live a ways across the holler from us. I see 'em nearly every day," Jimmy said happily. He hoped that Walter had siblings and he waited for his response. But Walter only smiled and watched the fire. "You got any brothers? Or sisters?" Jimmy finally asked tentatively.

Walter tossed a handful of dry pine needles onto the fire and watched the fire flare up. Then he smiled. "Wouldn't it be nice to have lots of brothers and sisters? To be part of a big family? My, you're so blessed. You have so much to be thankful for, don't you?"

Walter gazed directly at Jimmy. There wasn't even a hint of jealousy or anger concerning his own lot in life. He was grateful that his young friend was blessed in ways that he, to outward appearances, never was. Something within Jimmy's soul felt that Walter would give all that he had to help a friend and he wondered now if he may have taken the last of his bean soup.

"Why are you here, Jimmy? You run away from home?"

The question sliced through Jimmy's heart like a dagger. Walter's face carried the expression of true curiosity and concern and he was waiting for an answer. It was clear by Jimmy's reaction that Walter had hit a nerve.

"Well, I don't know. I reckon I just had to get away a while."

Jimmy averted his eyes away from Walter's gaze and he felt ashamed. How could he explain his behavior in light of Walter's testimonial? How could he begin to explain his motives for today's actions to someone who was clearly in want of many things that Jimmy had grown to take for granted? Yet all the advantages in his life were now tainted and made valueless in light of his father's deeds. His father had done some inexcusable things, but were they unforgivable? Jimmy didn't know, but at times he had thought so. He needed answers, but he wondered if Walter would understand. Maybe he wouldn't, but he knew he would listen. And that might be just as important.

***

A little earlier, Wade could only faintly remember his trip down to the pasture and the barn. He seemed to come alert with a start and found himself standing in the cold air beside the silo. He looked out across the lower pasture but he could not see all the way to the fencerow on the far side. The light was dimming fast and the clouds were still coming in, now as low and heavy as he could ever remember.

He had to think now; things were turning against him at once. He was afraid that the fork in the road that had troubled him for weeks now had arrived. Everyone strongly suspected that the legal authorities from the state and district offices would suddenly decide to investigate the events of the last fifteen months after all. And the possibility of indictments haunted everyone, especially Wade. Obstruction of justice, endangerment, hostage taking, manslaughter; the charges were numerous enough. Even if one of them stuck, it could be enough to destroy his life. Now he knew that his knowledge of the killing of Earnest Jackson could be enough to take away all that he had worked for. In order to survive the difficulties ahead, he knew he would need the support of friends and family. But it had never been a part of his personality to depend on anyone but himself. The very idea of dependency of any kind was alien, even frightening to him. He had thought that he had been safe throughout the years. He was careful and studious and never tripped and caused problems for his family. He was right when he thought that the only real problems that had ever come into his life were caused by others. He could, with a clear conscience, state that he was innocent of wanting harm to come to others as they had done toward him.

He gazed up into the sky and he looked for God's face in the billows. Like Job in the Old Testament, he had a few issues to discuss and he wanted to do it now. No games, no intellectual bantering, or theological mind plays. And he wanted God to talk back and defend Himself against the many charges he was ready to accuse Him of. Life was simply too fragile and his family too valuable to be used as pawns in some vague game of immortal life that the Great Omnipotence wished to play at His pleasure, as well as at His leisure. Life was already too difficult and too harried to be made more complicated by thoughts of immortal gamesmanship and pretending that there is some greater plan that everyone must, sooner or later, subscribe to. Wasn't it enough to work all waking hours of every day to provide for one's loved ones, all the while fighting to keep the unwelcome intrusions of the outside world at bay?

The clouds above seemed low enough to touch and they had blackened with the sky until soon enough Wade could barely see them. Some of the cattle were returning to the barn from the pasture and, looking back westward, he found the lights up in the house were bright and constant. Everyone was still there. Why do they stay? he wondered with anger. Were they all praying now and getting themselves all stirred up with self-serving emotions? Were they planning to search for Jimmy without Wade's involvement? And most infuriating, did Tom return and self-righteously tell everyone what he had said to Wade about their sons?

It was time to go back to the house and wait for his son's return. The shame he should have felt for walking away from the house was held in check by the anger he was still holding onto with a vise grip. He looked down at the ground before him and searched the darkened features formed by grass and rocks and mulled his next move. Slowly, minute by minute, the anger lifted like layers of snow blown thin by the wind. He played with a clump of dirt with the toe of his boot and allowed his mind to relax and float free. Soon, a sense of shame began to play in his mind, then his heart. He should have felt angry again for feeling this way but he was getting too tired and depressed to care. He leaned heavily against a post and looked back across the pasture, then back up toward the house. All was black in the yards now except for the lights in the house. He was too far away to see if anyone was moving around in the house and he had not heard any vehicles starting up. He couldn't find even a trace of the clouds now. It was nothing but blackness overhead.

Like a dejected child, he slid with his back down the post and sat on the ground. It was cold but he didn't feel anything externally enough to matter. He raised his elbows and propped them atop his knees, then rested his cheeks in both palms. It was as close to a praying position as he had ever come and the thought of prayer drifted into his mind as gently as falling dew.

For a long time, Wade didn't move. The field was silent. It seemed that all the cattle had stopped moving toward the barn and the gentle breeze that had stirred off and on seemed to have ceased, and all that could be felt was an occasional zephyr that tickled the hairs on his neck. Finally, he dropped his head to his chest and took a deep breath. Then he spoke aloud.

"Well, God, the preacher says you'll listen to a sinner if he comes to you in the right way. Well, I don't know what that right way is. But I am at the end of my way and my family's in danger, and I don't know what to do anymore."

Wade then became silent, thinking he was just wasting his breath. He felt the icy chill of the air much more than he did just moments before. He tightened his cuffs and his collar to slow the escaping heat of his body. He reckoned nothing could change about his life now – there was nothing to do but wait; be patient. He must endure it all alone and take whatever is thrust upon him.

He felt silly and childish. This was no way for a man to act, he thought. Then the anger began to creep back in. For what seemed an interminable stretch of time, Wade remained motionless, falling further and further into the black void of depression; something he had never allowed himself to do before.

Suddenly, Wade was awakened from his stupor by a change of some sort around him. He opened his eyes to look at the ground between his feet. A bright light shone in a wide circle around him. It seemed someone was there with a lantern. The light was unusually intense and no one spoke. Wade could hear nothing and he glanced around to search for someone's feet or for the source of the light. But there was nothing.

The light wasn't moving and it was far too bright to be just a lantern or a flashlight, and it was instantly and inexplicably frightening. Wade yanked his head around searching for the source, then he jerked his head upward and eastward toward the clouds. He fell back onto the ground, somehow being thrust backward by the blazing white light burning down upon him. He raised his hand to shield his eyes. He was quickly seized with a paralyzing intensity of fear he had never experienced before.

He could see the moon as full, intensely bright, and as perfectly round as he could ever remember. The brilliant shaft of light from the moon bore down onto him through a perfectly cylindrical opening that passed through many thick layers of pure white clouds. The opening was as clean and flawless as a carefully crafted hole drilled through a tall stack of hay bales. He could see the curved walls of the clouds stacked atop one another, and they appeared to stretch for miles straight into the heavens toward the moon. The perfectly aimed shaft through the clouds focused the light directly at Wade like the beam of a powerful flashlight upon an insect. Nowhere else could the light penetrate other than onto the ground only a few yards around him. Everywhere else; darkness. This manifestation in the heavens was simply not possible, but Wade was a witness. His eyes were not lying.

Finally, he scrambled to one side of the pool of light, then to the other. He fell back to the middle and tried to gaze away, but he felt himself too stunned and petrified by this sudden event to move away. The light remained stationary and Wade could not doubt the reality of what was happening. His mind was numbed with the terror and the indescribable beauty of what was clearly an impossible phenomenon. He desperately wanted the clouds to move and return to their normal composition of billowing and wispy randomness. He couldn't stand to witness such terror alone.

He could see the moon's light reflecting off of the cottony billows that formed the inside of the cylindrical shaft. The moon sat perfectly in the center and its shape and clarity were sharply focused. A bright rainbow encircled the rim of its face and its colors were brilliantly hued. It was beautiful, and it was terrifying.

Wade's eyes rebelled against the intense light. His heart pounded painfully against his ribs. He would go blind if he continued in this way or he would perish from heart failure. He wanted to run, but he knew it would be a futile endeavor. The Being that controlled the heavens, the clouds, and the moon would find him if it wished. If Wade spoke, it wouldn't matter – his reasoning would be the understanding of an infant compared to such unfathomable intelligence. Suddenly, his mind no longer seemed capable of coherent thought and it lost its ability to send out commands to his body. The only part of his body that still seemed to retain any ability to perform were his eyes, and the light caused them to water to tears.

Nothing happened in the clouds. They seemed to be frozen like ice with frost dusting their pure white surfaces. And they held the cylindrical shape as steadily and perfectly as if some invisible glass barrel had been carefully inserted and the internal cloud vapors drawn out. The rainbow that encircled the moon glowed radiantly and Wade could count the colors from violet nearest the moon to blue to green, and yellow and red at the outer rings.

It seemed that a long stretch of time had passed since the miracle began but actually it had only been a minute. Then, slowly at first, his fear faded. Something, or Someone, was there within inches of him. Wade could not doubt its presence and its eternally benevolent purpose. And a new and overpowering feeling of forgiveness and grace took over control of his senses.

He was finally able to stand up as the clouds slowly began to dissipate and converge over the face of the moon. A brisk breeze picked up and the clouds were on the move again. In a few moments, they thinned out and the moon was again visible through a thin sheen of cloud vapors. A dull rainbow now encircled the moon but one had to look hard to find it. The clouds could be seen moving at a fast clip across the sky and soon enough the sky was nearly cloudless, and the pasture all around was quite visible in the light of the shining orb hanging high in the eastern sky.

Wade looked back up the hill toward the house. It was now bright and glorious in the moonlight and everyone was still there as evidenced by the vehicles outside. The inside was brightly lit now by several more lamps and Wade was glad that someone was there to comfort his wife and daughter. He tried to remember who was in the house and he had great difficulty remembering because it seemed that it had been many hours since he had left the house. Even the events of the day were vague in his memory, as if it had all been a bad dream from long ago.

Where was Jimmy? The question came into his mind like a falling leaf passing before his eyes. Jimmy could be home now for all he knew. But if he weren't, Wade would now lead a search expedition to find him. The family would be made whole again and everyone could stop worrying and go on with their lives because there was no longer any reason to doubt or to be afraid.

Wade suddenly realized what he was doing. He realized that something was different, magnificently different. He could see things in ways that he could never have seen them before, and it was as if a whole new world had been opened up to him and it made his own world seem like a tiny speck of dust compared to the endless expanse of the universe. Never before had he experienced such energy and exultation. It would be embarrassing for anyone to see him as he was now but, unlike before, he didn't care.

He gazed back up toward the moon that was now greatly obscured by moving clouds. Finally, he raised his hand to wipe his face but he inadvertently smeared a piece of cow manure across his cheek that he had fallen into. He chuckled to himself and pulled his sleeve up and tried again, then he looked back up at the house. He would go home now and find his family safe. It was long past suppertime and he was hungry.

CHAPTER 41

"What'd you do, Jimmy?"

"Uh – I got down outta that tree an' I went home. But I almost killed Papa!"

Walter paused as Jimmy played the scene through his mind and gathered his thoughts. The gravity of the event was weighing so heavily on Jimmy that it seemed he could be enduring the emotions of that frightful night all over again. He could again feel the abject terror he had experienced when Carl pulled the trigger and killed a man before his eyes. Jimmy shook his head as if to rid himself of the thought, but the memory of the moment after he almost pulled the trigger on his own father when he had mistaken him for Carl still caused him to shudder after all these months.

After talking about his sister's experiences and problems, Jimmy had told the whole story in reverse order – working his way back from today's events all the way to his first covert encounter with Carl beneath the big oak tree. Walter listened with the patience of a friend who genuinely cared. Walter asked only a few cursory questions and Jimmy embellished the story with a little family history to help bring things into perspective. He discovered he had a talent for telling a tale for which he had little opportunity to develop at home.

"Uh, Papa come lookin' for me an' he had on a hat an' a light just like Carl Kallton, an' I almost shot 'im 'cause I thought Carl was comin' back after me. I almost shot an' killed my own papa!"

Jimmy spoke as he gazed into the fire. He had never been asked to talk about the events before and he spoke of it now as if it would be the only opportunity he would ever have to do so. He looked up at Walter to check his response. Walter's eyes locked onto Jimmy's, then Walter asked, "Your papa's never asked you anything again – after that night? He never said anything about it again?"

"No, sir."

"How 'bout your mama?"

"Uh – no."

"Why you reckon they wanted to keep everything so quiet?"

Jimmy, gazing back into the fire to think, said, "'cause of Kelly Jean, I reckon."

"Is that what they said?"

"Yeah – that's what Papa said."

"Why did he want you to stay quiet and keep it all to yourself? How was that gonna help your sister?"

"I don't know. He said one time that Kelly Jean's mind was weak 'cause of James gettin' killed in front of her. He said she gets scared too easy."

"Does she?"

"Well, yeah – she got bad scared that night when I said 'Carl Dean.' She went into hysterics – that's what Mama called it. I reckon that's why."

"So your papa wanted to keep everybody away, especially the law, so that her mind would stay settled. Is that right?"

"Yeah. Uh – yes, sir."

"Is she all right now? Is your sister's mind all right now?"

Jimmy, gazing back into the fire again, thought for a long time before answering. "You know, Mr. Walter, I just about figured she's probably the strongest one of us all now. She was always scared of the dark after what happened on the North Road, but after she told everybody what really happened, I reckon she come out of herself. But she thought everybody knew as much about it as she did. But nobody did. Nobody knew nothin'!"

"What do you mean, Jimmy? You tellin' me that your mama an' papa kept her quiet, just like they did with you? Everybody just played like nothin' happened?"

"Uh-huh!"

"An' they wanted her to play along and keep things to herself, just like you was supposed to do?"

"Yeah – that's right," Jimmy answered slowly while looking into the fire with wide eyes, glancing back up at Walter only once. Jimmy was learning something about his family, and it was difficult to keep his mind on the realization that his parents were truly fallible. It was a sad realization and it hurt his heart to play it over in his mind. "That's not right, is it, Mr. Walter – what my parents done?"

Walter gazed at Jimmy but didn't respond. Jimmy was far enough along in his analysis to figure it out for himself. Jimmy's countenance sank and he leaned over to his knees and rested his elbows on them. He held a stick and played with the twigs and soil before him. He took a deep breath and let it out in a deep sigh.

"I thought parents was supposed to be strong and be right all the time. But they made us – me an' my sister – be strong for 'em," Jimmy said quietly. "Everybody's afraid of somethin', ain't they? An' my papa's afraid – that's the truth. He's scared an' he made us be quiet so we would all be safe. I even had to quit school, so I would have to stay home – "

"Jimmy, we're all afraid sometimes," Walter said in measured tones. "The Good Book says we all have to go through hard times while we're here on this earth. You know, I knew a good man who killed himself a few weeks ago. He shot himself in the head 'cause he had hard times too and he gave up. He lost hope, son. He was in the worst kind of pain you could imagine for a long time after that bullet went through his head. But the Lord gave me the privilege to be with him just before he died. I helped show him the way to the Lord. It was a real joy, young Jimmy, to see him go to be with the Lord. But first, he gave up. And he paid the price with his pain, and it made a lot of people terribly sad. You don't want to see anybody lose hope after having difficulties like my friend did."

"Yeah," Jimmy said. "Our sheriff killed hisself, too – just like your friend did!"

Walter smiled. "Yes, I know, son – he was a good man." For a few moments, he studied Jimmy's face for a reaction, which never came. "But your papa built a nice big farm and did things that nobody else was brave enough to do – like start a beef cattle farm. And didn't he go after Carl alone and bring him back to justice? I worked in Carl Kallton's vegetable fields for a while and I saw the man every day. I know Carl was too mean to let just any man do that to him. It might not have been the right thing to do, but it took a mighty brave man to do what your papa done."

Jimmy nodded but he wasn't convinced. He had held many doubts and had many questions for his father, and he had decided that he would have to accept the fact that he may never get satisfactory answers. Would things be different if he had other brothers and sisters to help carry the load? What if he had friends of his own other than his young cousins? Were other families similar to his? And had he inflated the short journal of his troubles into an enormous and exaggerated tome of personal suffering? And was he really as blessed as Walter had said? Jimmy looked up at Walter. The man was leaning back on his elbows with the worn soles of his boots warming before the fire. Jimmy had been taken aback, if not intimidated, by the unfortunate man's condition and his apparent bliss in the face of it. He had made feeble attempts to ignore Walter's threadbare clothes and obvious lack of worldly possessions, but his liabilities never seemed to stand above his spirit.

Walter caught Jimmy's eye, then smiled. "Young Jimmy, I reckon you should go on home now." After a long reflective pause, he added, "You've been blessed with a father that's a good man. He's a' honest man and he works hard to make you proud of him. I know he's lookin' for you, and they all want you home."

"Yeah – I know."

"An' don't judge your papa so hard. You know he just wants your family to be safe and healthy. He just done some things the way he done because he's a man. He's human and he's frail like everyone else. You can make things easier for everybody if you all help one another through the hard times. You know – stick together like families are s'posed to. And never give up hope. That's what the Lord made families for; to uphold one another and keep hope alive. My friend that killed himself didn't have a family like you do."

Walter's little exhortation was simple and direct, but it gave Jimmy little hope for better things in the future. He had spoken of only a vague, spiritual kind of hope; nothing concrete, nothing that in Jimmy's mind applied to the reality he must live day to day. Walter seemed to say that Jimmy was expected to return home and play the part of the conciliatory and prodigal son and, again, pretend that all was well. The idea depressed him and caused him to feel that awful sense of futility again that made it difficult to breathe deeply when he dwelt upon it for too long.

"So how do you get through hard times?" Jimmy asked. Then he quickly realized how ridiculous and laughable the question must have sounded. He could not possibly fathom the depths of the hardships and sorrows that Walter must have endured throughout his life. Surely someone of Walter's age, lowly status and race had seen some of the worst that life could shovel out and Jimmy could only try to imagine. But he had no hope of even approaching a remote understanding of Walter's world. Jimmy wasn't able to assimilate all his thoughts at once, but they came to him torturously one at a time. He lowered his head to think and to contemplate his shame.

"Well, I reckon if I didn't believe there was a God and there was no hope for Heaven then I might've given up a long time ago. But I got hope, boy! If it wasn't for that, I'd just croak!"

Jimmy smiled. Walter was playing with him again. He seemed to know exactly how to work Jimmy's sentiments in order to make him think a little more externally; not so much on himself.

"There's always gonna be somebody who has it a lot harder than you have, young Jimmy. And I'm sure you can think of a few of 'em yourself."

Jimmy wished now that he could change the subject, or go home quietly and unnoticed. He was in an awful fix and he knew there was no way to rectify it without tremendous effort. He could go home now knowing he would never see Walter again, thus his shame would be hidden forever. It could be weeks or months before things could again be normal at home, or as normal as things had once been. He wished that he could control his impulses a little better, like a man should.

He had felt much better after telling his story to Walter, but he was disappointed that his friend had little to say that could help him. There seemed to be little to hope for other than to wait patiently for death when Heaven would be his reward. Now he was so completely frustrated and depressed he wished the ground could swallow him up.

"Mr. Walter? Where'd you come from?"

"Jimmy – it's late. You should go home now."

Jimmy nodded dejectedly and began to rise up and pull on his coat. The fire was still going strong and the sparks floated upward with the smoke and he wondered how far the fire was visible through the leafless trees. The sky had cleared up; he couldn't see a cloud anywhere and the treetops appeared to be illuminated by a bright moon. It would be an easy but long walk home. He knew where he was now and when he looked westward and northward he could see the narrow road running over the top of the next hill. If he moved fast he hoped to be home in little more than half an hour.

Walter would forgive him for his presumption and attempts to engage him in mature discourse. Jimmy was sure that he had already done so. But he wished that he could stay a little longer, but Walter was making strong signals to close down camp.

"Well, I'll go home now," Jimmy said, hoping for another word of encouragement.

Walter remained on the other side of the fire. He was standing with his hands out to warm them. His coat hung wide open and Jimmy could now see a seemingly new, gleaming-red handkerchief folded squarely and protruding several inches out of his front shirt pocket. It reflected the campfire light as brightly as a signal flare. It stood out in stark contrast to the rest of his dark attire. Why it was there and how such a broken man could afford such a fine piece of finery, Jimmy would never dare to ask. He drew his eyes away and looked toward the journey ahead. He figured Walter had a long walk back to the barracks, or wherever he lived now, and Jimmy was hoping that they could walk back to the main road together and talk some more.

"Okay, son. Take care of yourself. We'll see one another again someday."

The words were spoken so clearly and kindly that Jimmy was sure that he meant every word. But Walter showed no indication that he wished to walk with Jimmy. Besides, he had a few things to do – like pack up his gear and put out the fire. Or perhaps to scrounge up more fuel and stoke up the fire if he decided to sleep in the trees tonight. Jimmy got the clue and turned for the road, feeling sure that his new friendship was meant to last forever.

In no time at all, he was moving northward toward the little hill that was visible from the campfire. The fire was still crackling and he could hear it as he descended down toward the noisy bridge that crossed the hollow. He slowly stepped across the bridge and its boards popped like firecrackers at every step. He was certain Walter could hear him.

Then he stood at the top of the hill and he looked back toward the campfire. But there was nothing. The moonlight was as bright as ever and the treetops glistened like dew-laden cobwebs in the early morning sun. But there was no fire or trace of smoke and Jimmy searched the hillside for it. He held his panting breath and listened. This wasn't right, he thought. He knew it would require a fair effort to put out a fire of that size so quickly. But there was blackness and silence everywhere around the area from whence he had come.

Out of the corner of his eye he saw a movement of sorts. He turned westward and peered deeply into the trees. Something was moving but it was too dark to see. Then he could see that it was actually a fleeting light of some kind and it was moving as swiftly and silently as a running deer through the woods. Then, just as quickly, it was gone; disappearing into the darkness far northward toward the main road.

Jimmy thought that it must be the headlights of a car sweeping the woods. Someone was out looking for him, he thought, but he could hear no motor. It had been a long day and he was beginning to realize how tired he really was. Perhaps his weary eyes were playing tricks on him. He searched the woods again for the strange light. Nothing.

Jimmy turned for home. He was alone, so he allowed the tears to fall freely knowing no one could see his sadness and ask why. Perhaps by the time he arrived home his face would be recovered and he could stand strong and take whatever was to be given him.

***

"Wade!" Esther screamed. Wade had quietly entered the house, almost before anyone knew he was there. "Wade – are you all right?"

Wade looked down at his wife and nodded affirmatively. But something was different in his countenance and it was clear to all. "I'm fine, Esther. Everything's going to be all right, now," he answered in a clear, quiet voice.

Esther tentatively approached Wade and reached out to touch him. "We've all been praying for you and Jimmy, Wade. I know it's all going to be all right."

"I know," Wade agreed. "Where's Jimmy – he never come home?"

"No," Esther answered breathlessly.

"All right – I'll go find him right now," Wade said straightforwardly.

Everyone in the room stood up, ready to help. Wade's new spirit penetrated everyone and an indiscernible yet greatly comforting sense of peace and benevolence quickly filled the room in spite of the anticipation of the difficult mission ahead.

"He's out there, but I know he's not lost – we don't have to worry about that."

"How do you want us to help, Wade?" the preacher asked.

It seemed that the preacher was studying his face for clues for the change in his spirit, but Wade dissuaded him of the effort by answering his question quickly.

"Let's all go and line up along the road and just head into the woods. Paul, you and the preacher get one of my lights and get on down toward the southeast where we first saw Jimmy go. I'm going to head back west and go in. The rest of you just spread out between us and move in, all abreast a couple hundred yards apart."

"Wade?" Lucas asked tentatively, "You don't reckon he'll run from us do you?"

It was an unlikely question to ask of Wade, and it would have brought a stern look from him only a couple of hours earlier. But Wade nodded appreciatively and said, "No, I just don't think he would do that."

He turned for the door and the men followed. With flashlights and lanterns they descended the driveway to the road and the women watched from the windows. The moonlight was bright enough that some of the lights could be turned off. Wade turned westward with Tom, Lucas, and Ben following. Then soon the three men turned off the road and entered the woods leaving Wade alone on the road where he continued westward toward the narrow road. He turned back momentarily and gazed up at the moon that hung high above the treetops. Its light fell perfectly onto the road and Wade's shadow stretched several yards westward. A faint cloud encircled the moon and gave it the appearance of a great, all-knowing, yet benevolent eye. Perhaps he would never experience this night again, but he could distinctly sense the presence of that great helpful Spirit guiding him on.

The road straightened out ahead, then it rose toward a hilltop that would be the last barrier before the final stretch to the entrance to the narrow road. Walking fast, Wade soon crested the hill and began the descent into the next hollow. He had long ago turned off his light and he gazed intently down the road ahead. Other than his own footsteps in the gravel, all was silent. He looked high toward the next hill. He debated whether he should start calling Jimmy's name in hopes of getting an answer. Perhaps he had gone too far, he thought, and he should turn back and join the others. But he had determined that his son's curiosity would likely draw him to the area of the distillery compound and he would be somewhere near there.

But suddenly his eye caught an unfamiliar shape far ahead near the edge of the road. It was quite unnatural and it glowed like foxfire in midsummer. A dim, yet distinct glow radiated from a vertical figure that stood against the backdrop of tall tree trunks that appeared at first glance to be motionless. Wade stopped and peered at the figure. The moonlight must surely be reflecting off the stump of a felled tree or some such, he thought. But he watched. Then it seemed to move. Something, or someone, was walking down the road toward the west.

"Jimmy?" Wade called. He watched the glowing figure move quickly away. At first, he was sure that it stopped and turned toward him, but now it was moving away. Wade picked up his pace but the figure seemed to grow dim, then it disappeared altogether. It was gone.

Then Wade stopped cold. It didn't make sense. He was sure he saw someone. The figure seemed to recognize Wade's presence by its movements, but it vanished before his eyes. He heard voices from the east. Someone had heard him calling for Jimmy and was trying to communicate. But Wade ignored them and he started again.

Gazing up the road, he watched for shapes and movements. In a moment, he could hear the other voices again in the distance. They, too, were now calling aloud for Jimmy. Perhaps one of them would find him first. That would be all right, but Wade was sure that he knew where his son had gone and he would be the one to find him. But now it seemed plausible that Jimmy had heard his father's voice and had run away. Further away. Surely that was Jimmy that had glowed in the moonlight. It was possible that the dew had fallen on his coat and was reflecting the ghostly light. The very thought of his son's direct and overt rejection of his father in this manner was a terribly disheartening thing to ponder.

Wade halted his incessant march again. He had to catch his breath. The distant voices had stopped and all was still. He squinted his eyes and gazed far down the road. He calmed his breath and strained to listen for any clue to the identity of the thing he was sure he saw. Then once more he called his son's name, but not loudly enough for anyone to hear more than a few yards away. His strength was spent.

"Papa?" someone said. It was a young man's voice and it was near.

Wade turned his head to find the source. He could see the entrance to the narrow road a few yards away. A figure was there. He gazed intently to study the dark shape that stood tall, like his son.

"Papa? Is that you?" Jimmy asked again, now in a strong, clear voice.

The figure didn't move, but there was no doubting who it was.

"Yeah, it's me, son," Wade said. After a moment of tenuous silence, he added, "C'mon, let's go home now – your mama's worried."

Jimmy could hear the calmness in his father's voice. As a result, his anxiety floated away in the breeze. He could see his father standing as still as a post and he made no gesture of consternation or anger as expected. Jimmy stepped across the little ditch and onto the road and walked to his father. For the first time ever, he felt his father's arm lay gently across his shoulders. Then quietly, and together, they walked home.

***

The moonlight began to fade again. The clouds returned with a gust that whipped through the trees with a frosty bite. Winter seemed to return with a vengeance, and within a few short hours the climate had changed enough to paint the landscape with a quiet beauty that brought the most complete sense of serenity and security into any home where familial love abounded. The snow covered the ground with enough depth to build snowmen and forts, and deer tracks were easy to follow. Jimmy rose from bed long before sunup to stand beneath the falling snow to listen. The breeze had stopped and he wanted to hear the snow. If he held his breath and remained perfectly still, he could hear the snow as it lit upon the ground. It was reminiscent of a hissing hickory bonfire that one might hear from a great distance. But he had to be quiet and listen.

Then he heard the sound of a door spring stretching open some distance away. His uncle Paul was getting ready to start milking and soon it would be time to begin helping him. These sounds were comforting and he realized now how fortunate he was to have good things to do, and to have good people to care for and to watch over throughout the impending tribulations as well as the joys of the months and years ahead. He felt strong now that his family was healed and whole.

He looked back at the house behind him and all the windows were black. His lantern illuminated the house and its white clapboard siding shone brightly in the light. The thick whiteness of the snow on the roof gave the house an igloo-like appearance, and when daylight comes and morning chores are done, he guessed he would build a big snowman in the yard. Then he would, with Kelly Jean's help, make a woman, then two tall children. He would stand them together and have them holding hands as if in a prayer circle; just as the family had done with the preacher last night after the visitors had left for home and before going to bed. It was to be a nightly ritual, his parents promised, and his life ahead would be forever changed because they had all discovered where true security and prosperity comes from. And it would last for all eternity.

CHAPTER 42

A smoky mist drifted across the room and the walls tingled with the faint glow of its light. Outside, the snow fell beneath a fading moonlit sky. The air was so still in the room that anything moving across the floor would reverberate throughout the thin-boarded house like the hurried footsteps of a large man. It was a night for dreams, and sleep came easily beneath several layers of thick cotton-stuffed quilts.

It had been a couple of hours since the fire in the heater stove had gone out and the only direct light in the front room came from the dimming moon through the windows. But the misty glow in the corner, a vapor of human-sized proportions, could have been a reflection of the window light and it should have moved or vanished altogether when the moon moved behind the clouds. But the strangely shimmering mist was stationary and it was not influenced in the least by the moon. There was something, or someone, awake in the room and its presence caused the sleep of those in the house to become restless and tossed. But no one awoke as the mist in the corner began to move about as if taking on a life of its own. The man of the house was deep asleep but he fidgeted frequently as if in the throes of a nightmare. The vapor seemed to be drawn to the space above the man's head. It stopped there for only a moment, then it grew a little brighter before the light vanished altogether as if it had been switched off.

The man jerked up and found himself sitting upright in the bed. Instantly, he was breathing so heavily that he was sure his heart was failing him. Not knowing why his mind was screaming, he searched the room and could find no reason for his panic. His youngest son was sleeping soundly in the makeshift cot against the far wall and the house was so quiet that it seemed that all three of his sons could be dead as evidenced by the interminable silence.

Uncharacteristically, he spoke to himself in soothing tones, but it was of little help. His heart was rebelling and he was certain to die if it didn't stop. He took long, deep breaths and managed to settle a large measure of pain that was pressing upon his chest like a bale of cotton.

Soon, the man calmed himself down enough to lie back upon the bare mattress. Then he tried to will himself back to sleep. The pain had lessened greatly but his mind was still reeling from some terrible nightmare that he could not conjure up no matter how hard he tried. He listened to the house but all was quiet. His boys were sleeping, yet they were not snoring as one or two of them usually did. His little girl, he remembered, was gone to visit the relatives she loved over a couple of miles away. If his wife was still alive he would wake her and make her fetch him some water in order to quench the awful thirst that his hellish dreams had caused, but the floor was icy cold, so he would wait until the morning light.

He exhaled so deeply that he sounded like a snorting buck. Then he realized that he did not intend to do that. What's wrong here? he asked himself. It seemed that his body was working on its own without conscious orders from his mind. He felt angry with himself for such foolishness and he ordered himself to get back to sleep. Several times he closed his eyes but to no avail. He was wide-awake and he would have to wait until sleep came to him. He allowed his eyes to close on their own but they closed only halfway, thereby giving him full awareness of the moonlight shining then fading as the cloud cover increased.

A gentle movement in the shadows was evident near the window. He could hear nothing, however, so he turned his head to watch. It seemed that a curtain was swaying slightly in a draft. It was unnatural; the air was still. He could feel no air moving across his face, though he was sure that the breeze outside should find entry through any of the cracks in the walls or floors. If one of his boys was up he would know it instantly, but there were no sounds.

He watched the curtain until it stopped moving. The last trace of light through the window faded until the room was black, then it returned only to vanish again. Soon, he felt the tug of sleep on his eyelids and he waited patiently for his mind to fade.

He was awakened again by the creak of a floorboard underfoot. His heart began to pound again and he lifted his head to search the room. The air was silent, but he was certain that someone else in the house was as awake as he was. The feeling was simply too strong to ignore.

Slowly, he reached up to search for the matches on the little table next to his bed. His shotgun was somewhere nearby but he couldn't remember where he had last put it. As quietly as he dared, he slid the box open and pulled out a single match. He felt for the little edge of sandpaper on the side and he raked the match across it. The match sparked but it didn't light. But the spark was enough. Without a doubt, there was someone standing near the window. He could, in that instantaneous flash of light, clearly see a stocky figure standing there as if it were a stone statue. None of his boys was so statured, so this was undeniably an intruder.

Savagely he raked the match again but it only sparked. Still, the prowler was there – he wasn't moving, he was only watching. The man in the bed hissed, cursing as he raked the match across the box several more times. Each time he could see a lone figure watching from near the window. Like the pulsating illumination of a poor quality picture show, he could see only flashes of the intruder's appearance, and it was maddening. He yanked open the box and grabbed a handful of matches and tried again. A flame shot up from the bunch but it was quickly extinguished by some unfathomable force that hung in the air like a breath-stealing fog.

Where's 'at damn gun? his mind screamed. There was no other sound in the house. He wanted to scream or kick his escape through the wall, but he was sure that the intruder would quickly attack if he made any such effort. His boys must already be dead, he reasoned. They weren't stirring. He could hear no breathing or any other slumbering sounds. Now the intruder will kill him and make his escape without any real effort. How did he manage to sleep so soundly through it all?

His squinted eyes darted around the room. The air was still silent. His shotgun was invisible in the blackness. Perchance that the gun was nearby, he reached around the bedpost and the walls and felt for the cold steel of the barrel, but everything held firm.

The figure near the window was black from top to bottom. The only color of note being what appeared to be a glistening patch of blood, shaped similarly to a square-folded red handkerchief, exposed near the trespasser's heart. Had he been injured and blood-splattered in a similar intrusion of some other local resident's house earlier tonight? Is this one of Carl's nigger migrants that had come to exact revenge for this man's many bigoted attacks? he wondered. The intruder's build and posture were familiar and the man in the bed taxed his mind to recall a name. All the black migrants had moved away in the few days after Carl died. But this one was one of the so-called Christians, or "choir boys." Why had he returned? The one that Carl certainly hated the most?

The man could almost feel the bed vibrate beneath him. He could feel the hairs on his neck stand up like the bristles of a wire brush and he realized that he was shaking with a terrible tremor. His nerves were on edge as bad as he could ever remember and he could not control his body as he moved from simple fear to terror.

The floor creaked again. It was time to make a move. He should, at the very least, charge this prowler and hit him and kick him as many times as possible and throw him out of the house through a window, but the man's body refused to obey his mind.

He could hear his own breathing. He was beginning to choke with rapid-fire shallow breaths and he was sure that the intruder could hear him as well. But still, he could hear nothing from the intruder. Why was he just standing there? Why wasn't he finishing up his work here in the house, whatever it could be? The man remembered the flash of light from the matches. He remembered how the entire room lit up for only a second and he could see the dark spot where the face of the intruder should have been. He couldn't remember any facial features other than the fact that the color indicated that it could be that of a black man. There were eyes but he remembered no details. A heavy coat seemed to hang nearly to his knees and there were boots, dark boots. The only color of note to stand out being the square patch of red. A pair of large, powerful, black hands hung to his sides.

The man tried to reach for the lamp that sat on the table nearby. His hands were shaking too much to attempt to light it. If he could throw the lamp at the intruder, then try to light a match again, perhaps he could frighten him enough to make him to run away. But instead, his hand only brushed the lamp causing it to tip over and fall to the floor. The crash of the breaking glass should have awakened everyone in the house, but it didn't. The house was still so deathly quiet that he was certain everyone, except himself and the intruder, was dead. How did the intruder kill his boys without his waking up? Certainly the intruder could do the same to him but, instead, he was remaining motionless, as if he could be enjoying the frustration of the terror-stricken man in the bed.

Why am I actin' like a coward? How come I cain't move? he thought. Only a couple of minutes had passed since he first knew someone was in the house. Now he was so drained of strength he could do nothing but lie flat on his back. It was time to die, he was sure, but he wished to fight back first, but his body was useless.

"What yew want?" he finally managed to ask aloud.

The quiver in his voice was so evident that the intruder could be sure that he had full control of the situation. The man lay as still as he could, waiting for a response that he wished would never come.

"Roy?"

The intruder's voice was quiet, yet strong. The man tried to move his head to see the intruder. The floor creaked as the intruder moved toward the bed a single step and stopped. The light of the moon was dim, but it was bright enough to show the partial silhouette of the intruder. Now Roy was more sure than ever that he could kill him if he only had a gun within reach, but he was in a helpless position and was sure that he could never jump quickly enough to retake control. "What yew want?" he asked again.

After a long, painful pause the intruder answered: "I want you to leave Gracie with her cousins."

Roy had managed to move in the bed as the intruder spoke, but his movements were like thunder in a cave. He sensed, from the intruder's voice, that he had better not try that again. "W'at?" he asked.

"You are to leave Gracie alone. Leave her with Paul and Ruth. Let them adopt her."

Anger welled up inside Roy but it was tempered by his fear. What business was it of anybody's to tell him what to do with his own young'uns? he thought. But he restrained himself from asking, yet he had a question that was foremost in his mind.

"Who're yew?"

The floor creaked once again, but Roy could detect no movements in the silhouette. The intruder spoke again.

"Do as I say and no punishment will come to you. If you don't, your soul will be required before your time is due."

The floor started making noises again as the intruder began walking away from the window. Roy could feel the direction of his movements by the way the hairs on his neck and face seemed to follow the intruder. There was something divine yet hideous in the manner of the intruder, and Roy was sure that he had never experienced such terror and such physical upset before in his life. Every nerve in his body burned as if they were being singed by the very fires of hell. And his skin heaved in strange places like it had been ripped loose from his body. Heavy perspiration soaked his bedclothes.

He heard the footsteps of the intruder exit into the kitchen. Then he could hear the door latch pop open, then the door opened and plopped shut. The intruder was gone.

Roy knew he could never go back to sleep. He sensed that it would not be safe to rise up and light a lamp. Somehow, he could sense the intruder still watching him. He could smell the sour scent of the coal oil that had spilled out of the lamp he had knocked over. He looked over at the window and he could see nothing in the blackness. Thirst of the most extreme sort racked his body. Then uninvited visions of hell and eternal damnation began attacking his mind. Scenes of unspeakable horror danced jigs in his head. In flashes of smoky light, he could see hordes of the damned screaming in unremitting agony and terror, but he squashed it all out of his mind quickly and he hoped to forget the horrible visions before sunup.

But he couldn't expunge the picture of someone familiar that flashed through his mind so quickly that he couldn't be sure. He imagined that it was Carl Dean Kallton. As he had seen him on his last day being marched to his death, Roy glimpsed Carl's extruded and atrophied eye, his burned hide, his withered arm, and his sorely limping gait. But this time, Carl was held firm in stout shackles and chains with heavy stone burdens dragging from the ends. A company of laughing, mocking demons prodded him with cracking whips and fiery swords along a flaming corridor of sulfuric hedge stones. He was being summarily marched through Hell for all the eternally damned to witness and behold. Somewhere a short distance behind, a black man burdened in like-fashion was being made to trail along by his own hilarious prodders. Jesse was embodied with the most recent remembrance of his past life – that being the unending agony of the gun blast to his abdomen, which still was without much of its internals. He was broken at the waist and could never right himself. Both souls were set to march for all eternity through the stony troughs and inclines of a burning Hell with no possibility of an end to their journey.

Roy found that he could easily replay the scene through his mind over and over again if he ever so desired, but he worked hard to dispel the visions and to calm himself down. For a long while, he fought to stabilize his reeling mind that seemed, on its own accord, to rush back to the visions whenever he attempted to rest. His heart was hurting again and he felt he would faint or die if he didn't get some water and rest right away. "What's happ'nin' here?" he asked aloud.

He reckoned the preacher's sermons from his childhood were returning to haunt him. He remembered that he had hated the preacher's insistence on preaching so much on hell and brimstone. And he recalled how his own liquor-sodded conscience had gotten the best of him at his wife's funeral and he felt disgraced because of it, and how he had vowed to never let that happen to him again. Now the intruder had frightened him so badly that he had soiled the bed. The humiliation he felt now was as strong as any he had ever known in his life, and his anger rose as he continued to strain to clear his head.

Roy forced himself to lie still. He needed water, but he was too tired and too afraid to move. He closed his eyes but the visions returned, forcing him to open them back up. He cursed. His boys were still asleep, or dead. His mind spun out of control and he returned to the visions of Hell once again. He screamed. He screamed aloud knowing he would wake everyone up. He began thrashing in the bed. He kicked the footboard hard enough to snap it in two. He yelled out until he felt his life begin to ebb away, and he collapsed. He fell silent until another noise woke him once again.

"Papa! What's a'matter!"

Roy flung himself up out of the bed. Then a blinding white light shone through the window with such intensity that he cowered back onto the bed and covered his eyes. He swung his fist around knocking his youngest son to the floor, causing him to curse out. His other two boys were there but stood back in fear.

Then Roy got a hold of himself. He gazed out the window into the whiteness outside. The sun was up; it was late in the morning, and the snow seemed to have its own light and the house was filled with its brightness. His eyes hurt from the light but he didn't care. He laughed. It was all just a silly dream, so he laughed out loud. The boys watched, still silent and afraid.

Reeling like a madman, Roy guffawed as if a trick had been played upon him by a mischievous friend. He looked at his boys and slapped his knee. He laughed like an inebriated juvenile for well over a minute before he began to gather his wits.

"Roy Junior!" he said with a derisive chuckle, "Look at t'at back door there in th' kitchen – is 'at door latch left open?" Roy Jr. didn't move, still stunned by his father's irrational behavior. "Well, go on, boy – look at it an' tell me if it's open 'r not!"

Roy Jr. ran to the back door and returned. "Uh – no, Papa. It's still locked like you done it last night."

Roy reared back and laughed aloud again. *"Boys, I tell ya – I gotta stop workin' so 'ard! My mind's a-gitten' twisted plumb off!"*

One by one the boys left the room as their father continued laughing, soon to hysterics. He reasoned that he had swallowed too much liquor the day before and it was twisting his mind. Yeah, he thought, that's it – too much hard work an' too much liquor. I think I'll just take the day off today an' rest. Yeah – that sawmill ain't goin' nowhere without me. So, I'll just take it easy today an' git my mind back in traction.

Roy stood up and took in a deep breath of that cold winter air and stretched his arms. Gotta build a fire, he thought to himself. He turned toward the tiny heater stove in the corner and started to walk toward it. He felt something sharp underfoot and he looked down. His heart began to pound and the laughter left him so suddenly that he felt his facial skin tug downward.

The lamp was on the floor and its globe lay broken into jagged pieces. Most of the oil had evaporated but he could, if he tried, still detect the scent in the air. Clearly, it had been there for several hours. He felt a pain in his chest; then suddenly he realized he was thirsty, very thirsty. And if he didn't get a drink of water quickly, very quickly, he felt he would die.

Epilogue

The spot near the middle of the graveyard was the highest in elevation and its point was visible from all angles if one stood looking. No one could explain why it had remained graveless until the day of Gene's burial. It could have been argued that the Lord's providence had kept it that way, waiting for the testament of the people's return to true spiritual revival to be buried there. It had taken a year to get the tall, gracefully arched and engraved headstone cut and set. And when it arrived it seemed that a new funeral was taking place because of all the parishioners who came by on the same hour of the day to see it.

Gracie, with eager, fawn-like excitement, ran up the hill first when she arrived with the Kalltons. She was not little Gracie anymore. She had grown a full three inches on Ruth's cooking in the year since she changed her residence. She squealed for Ruth to bring the baby when she looked back and found her still in the car.

There was much to celebrate on this day besides the finished gravesite. The blessedness of it all had infected everyone and was scarcely hidden from one another. The crowd had grown quite large by the time the preacher arrived and Gracie refused to conceal her glee when he walked up the hill to greet everyone. Her hair flew high like a pony's tail as she ran to him for her hug and kiss. Paul called her down but his command was met with the typical indifference of a child in the throes of heaven-sent joy.

J.C. Jourdan was a free man in spirit and in body. He had not killed a simple crazy man, as he had feared. Jesse Bridger was a consummate killer – wanted in two states on murder charges and was suspected in a number of other rogue incidences. There was no desire by state authorities to prosecute a good man for guarding and protecting his own. It was simply argued that J.C. had saved the states the trouble of continuing the hunt for a cunning and elusive felon. J.C. stood at the headstone asking, like everyone else, where the big red handkerchief had come from. It had been thoughtfully draped over the top of the stone like a decorative doily. The brisk afternoon air didn't seem to have the strength to carry it away. At first, no one ventured a guess as to who might have placed it there.

Wade approached the gravesite with Esther and Kelly Jean on either side, each with a hand grasping an elbow. Mrs. Sarah and the boys quietly following single-file. Like J.C. early last year, Wade learned just weeks ago that he was free to continue his life too; there being no one – public or private, local or state – willing to follow through with efforts to prosecute. His peace had been sorely battered for many months by the authorities that had nipped at his heels like starving dogs, but now they had gone away, leaving him free to concern himself with studying ways to rectify his past deeds and to appease his still-aching conscience. Carl Dean, along with his little malignant empire, was vanquished, leaving no reason now to harass the locals after all the hell they had been put through, though much of it self-inflicted. But the sudden sadness Wade felt upon reading the stone could not be lessened by the new freedom. He had not gotten over the truth that it was because of his doings that this good man was rested here. Wade had promised the preacher that, from now on, it would be his duty to care for the graveyard and to keep the grass down. It would be the very least he could do.

He called his tall son to stand with him at the foot of the grave. Wade drew strength from Jimmy's nearness, and he let his son know of that fact by the firm squeeze of his arm. Again, the handkerchief held their gazes and questions concerning it were now being asked about.

The baby cried out and squirmed on Ruth's shoulder. Gracie stepped over to Ruth to take the infant – her new little sister, she called her. Gracie relished the role of secondary mom and found the work of caregiver to a child to come quite naturally. Gracie, with a soft-singing voice, bounced the baby slightly in her arms, instantly quieting her. Another child squealed out and ran across the grave before Annie could stop him. Anne Marie pulled him back to where he belonged and she laughed with embarrassment at the joke of it. Tom stood cross-armed and unmoving until called by the preacher to lead the group in prayer. Lucas draped his hand over Tom's shoulder as he spoke and when it was done, it seemed no one moved or spoke for several minutes.

A work-wagon and horse rig slowly moved past the hill down on the road forty yards away. The Kalltons moved quickly to block Gracie's view to the road and force her attention to stay on the baby she was holding. The man on the wagon seat looked up the hill at the people, his eyes shielded from the afternoon sun by the wide-brimmed but scraggly hat. He spat a long yellow stream of juice to the road as if to demonstrate defiance. This unredeemable idler; still humiliated after all these months by the loss of his child-slave. He was alone – his boys elsewhere, perhaps working the woodpile at home or cleaning a winter hog. Or killing time with idle talk and braggadocio of errant deeds done or planned. He had heard of the new fancy gravestone and was angling for a view of it himself, but was too cowardiced by the gathering to push the bounds just now. A diversion was needed before Gracie grew wise.

"I hear you and your family are coming up this way to stay, Anne Marie. Is that right?" Paul asked loudly when it was determined that the wagon rider was moving away too slowly.

"Oh, we are moving to Columbia. So we'll be pretty close to Mama and Papa," she answered. "I think Papa wants to make a real farmer out of Tommy."

Everyone laughed and chuckled long enough for the wagon to move out of sight. Then a warm, boisterous breeze rolled down from the pines standing alongside the yard and snatched up the red handkerchief and carried it high. It flapped and spiraled upward like a great crimson-winged butterfly over everyone's heads – instantly too high to catch. Then it rose like a kite on an air current that seemed to shoot vertically upward until it was little more than a speck in the sky. It continued on until the clouds enveloped it and it peeked out of the cottony billows only once on its journey to Heaven.

57579978R00172

Made in the USA
Charleston, SC
19 June 2016